Praise for Porno Valley

"A consistently gripping tale . . . suffused with meticulous details and characters at the mercy of the druggy Southern California underbelly. . . . An infectious sense of humor . . . enthusiastic plot and a swift pace combine with gritty characters in a satisfying thriller." —*Kirkus Reviews*

"A blisteringly brilliant ride in the best tradition of comedic-noir crime fiction straight into the sordid twisted underbelly of Los Angeles. . . . Absolutely nails the genre; sublimely descriptive, slightly stylized and . . . told with a veneer of brutal, black humor."

—Rose Auburn, *IndieReader* (starred review)

"A crime fiction delight, with wonderful momentum, intriguing characters, and a satisfyingly solved whodunnit. . . . A complicated picture of desperation, greed, love, and the mistakes that even decent people can make."

—Gabriella Tutino, *US Review of Books* (starred review)

"Sex, drugs, and rock and roll. . . . Working toward a brutal, bloody denouement, this hard-boiled mystery hurtles from one violent episode to another [which] resolve into a single tale of betrayal, bad decisions, and greed as an aging detective cracks the last, most perplexing case of his career." —Randi Hacker, *Foreword Reviews*

"Elliott's similes are beautiful; dialogue brisk and true; and exposition lightweight and similar to screenplay action. . . . If you're looking for a fun and fast read with fully formed characters scheming in a heart-pounding plot, you can't do better than this marvel of a crime novel."

—Scott Semegran, author of *The Benevolent Lords of Sometimes Island*

"Masterfully plotted, suspenseful, and populated with uniformly complex characters . . . with a strong sense of atmosphere and a healthy dose of social commentary. A must-read."

—Mike Thorn, author of *Shelter for the Damned*

"A nonlinear mystery set in a Y2K LA so rich and character-driven that to call it noir betrays the literary aspects of the story. . . . Rather than a whodunnit, *Porno Valley* is a why- or howdunnit inside a slick page-turning noir where the sun's always at high noon."

—Tex Gresham, Humanitas Prize winner and author of *Sunflower*

"In this gripping, pulpy noir Elliott showcases his knack for crafting intricately layered stories with resonance. This hellish triptych takes us on a collision course with a cast of tragic characters who, even in their darkest moments, are relatable and sympathetic."

—Niall Howell, author of *Only Pretty Damned*

"A fast-moving and ever-changing PI novel. . . . It recalls the best of Michael Connelly as the characters and their problems are spread out on the velvet background of Los Angeles 20 years ago."

—Steve Aberle, *Great Mysteries and Thrillers*

Praise for Philip Elliott's Previous Novel, Nobody Move

Winner: Best First Novel, Arthur Ellis Awards, 2020
Winner: Indie Author Project Ontario, 2019

"Elliott has a real feel for comedic noir in the Elmore Leonard vein, and his debut novel screams cult classic." —Bill Ott, *Booklist*

"Gritty, breathless. . . . Los Angeles seems to have its own personality and Elliott's descriptions are impressively and effectively atmospheric. . . . The author also excels at bringing even minor characters to life. . . . A multifaceted series opener by a promising new voice in hard-boiled crime fiction. Fans of Elmore Leonard and Jim Thompson will find much to savor."
—*Kirkus Reviews*

"Taut and sharp. . . . A new spin on the crime thriller genre."
—Philip Zozzaro, *San Francisco Book Review*

"Sharp, stylish and well-written. It makes reading fun again."
—Joe Kilgore, *US Review of Books*

"First class neo-noir." —Rowena Hoseason, *Murder, Mayhem & More*

"Fast-paced and chock full of interesting characters and chillingly delicious evil." —James Bernstein, *IndieReader*

"Impossible to put down." —Kevin Wilson, *NYT* bestselling author

"Like Tarantino on the page . . . rushes at you from page one."
—Dietrich Kalteis, author of *Cradle of the Deep*

"Elliott has a gift for upholding momentum that never slows. The characterization is great, but it's the high-octane action and a horde of twists along with tight plotting that make the book a winner."

—*The Prairies Book Review*

"A book full of unbridled characters riding full-tilt into the abyss. . . . Any sudden action among the characters can bring everything to a brutal, bloody stop."

—June Lorraine, *Murder in Common*

"Satire at its best. . . . Be prepared not to take a breath."

—Anne-Marie Reynolds, *Readers' Favorite*

"Sensational. . . . Start to finish, *Nobody Move* reads like a crime/thriller movie, reminiscent of *Pulp Fiction*, with not a single dull moment."

—*Online Book Club*

"If you love LA crime novels that don't hold back, this one's for you."

—Wyborn Senna, author of *Porter's Fortune*

"Wonderful. . . . A precious gemstone in a genre all too frequently bereft of terrific writing. . . . Absorbing, addicting, and picturesque."

—Steve Aberle, *Great Mysteries and Thrillers*

"An awesome read. It kept surprising me at each turn. Philip Elliott is a magnificent writer."

—*Tales from NJ*

"Elliott is a skilled craftsman and killer storyteller and *Nobody Move* is a fast-paced satire with razor-sharp dialogue. It had me laughing out loud."

—John Califano, author of *Johnny Boy*

"Pulp fiction at its best. . . . Brilliant."

—*The Book Wormery*

AN ANGEL CITY NOVEL
PORNO VALLEY
PHILIP ELLIOTT
INTO THE VOID

This is a work of fiction. All names, characters, places and incidents are products of the author's imagination or are used fictitiously. Any resemblance to current events, locales, and businesses, or to persons living or dead, is entirely coincidental.

Library and Archives Canada Cataloguing in Publication

Title: Porno valley / Philip Elliott.
Names: Elliott, Philip, 1993- author.
Description: An Angel city novel.
Identifiers: Canadiana (print) 20210160462 | Canadiana (ebook) 20210160519 | ISBN 9781999086831
(hardcover) | ISBN 9781999086848 (softcover) | ISBN 9781999086862 (EPUB) | ISBN 9781999086879
(Kindle)
Classification: LCC PR6105.L53 P67 2021 | DDC 823/.92—dc23

Published in Canada by Into the Void
Printed in the United States of America
Designed by Into the Void
Typeset: Adobe Caslon Pro

Porno Valley

PART

I

Chapter One

JULY, 2000

When mickey had imagined what the pornography studio might be like, the smell hadn't factored into it. But the smell was all he could focus on now. Not the two young women, teenagers, probably, naked and writhing under and over each other on the black couch, nor the man, tan and muscular and totally hairless, erect penis pointing at the women like a torpedo. Not even the crew spread around the tiny room nor the long lamps drenching the set in blinding hot light could distract from the stench: sweat and semen and a chemical lotion smell and the warm leather of the couch and a slight burning of the lamps and intermittent drifts of perfumes and moisturizers and cheap deodorant and, mother of God, it was enough to make him sick. That couch—imagine it under a blacklight. He'd almost like to see it.

The cameraman peeking at Mickey out the side of his eye. "You having fun?" The trace of a smirk.

Mickey grimaced, the smell too much to take any longer. "Not really. I think I'll wait outside."

THE STUDIO WAS A REPURPOSED WAREHOUSE in the San Fernando Valley a few miles north of Chatsworth at the base of the rippling Santa Susana Mountains, not far from the Spahn Movie Ranch where Charles Manson and his band of weirdos holed up in 1969 before committing murder. Surrounded by parched scrubland, rolling hills, and dirt the color of rust beneath a shocking blue sky, the location could have been the site of a Wild West showdown if not for the huge porn factory shining silver under the sun like a small airport hangar and the yellow "MidnightPussy Productions" sign above the entrance, glinting now in the dazzling sunlight as Mickey gazed up at it. The sheer size of the studio made sense: According to the *Los Angeles Times*, while feature filmmaking in Hollywood had nosedived thirteen percent last year, the adult film industry was booming with production up twenty-five percent, helped along by the meteoric rise of the internet. Increasingly, Hollywood professionals looking for a side income (or any income) and wannabe stars who had never made it past auditions were coming out here in droves, leading to glossier productions and no shortage of performers. Pornography, it seemed, was the future.

Mickey walked the few steps to his '69 Pontiac Catalina convertible and sat on the hood. The Carousel Red paint job burned under the sun, heating the backs of Mickey's thighs through his suit trousers. He wiped a hand across his brow, felt a sticky film of sweat. Maybe there was something to Al Gore's recent campaign-trail talk about greenhouse gases and the warming of the planet. It sure felt hot as hell.

A scarlet-haired woman with gigantic artificial breasts had offered Mickey the opportunity to observe a shoot while he waited for his new client to show and Mickey had accepted simply to be polite. He should have waited out here.

Mickey had lost track of the time when the muscular male lead of the shoot whose erect penis had been on display minutes before exited the studio and lit a cigarette. Noticing Mickey, the man blew a cloud of smoke toward the ozone layer and swaggered over.

"What's your name, old man?" he said, sounding European. He came to a halt a couple yards away. He stood straight as an iron beam.

"Mickey. What's yours?"

"Riccardo." He sucked the cigarette and exhaled aggressively. "Mickey what?"

"O'Rourke."

Riccardo grunted a chuckle. "Your name's Mickey O'Rourke?"

"As far as anyone's told me."

"You should drop the O, tell people you're the actor. Might get more pussy."

"I'm seventy-eight."

"Exactly. You could use the advantage."

Riccardo gazed at distant mountains and sucked on the cigarette. "Then again, Mickey Rourke hasn't been in a good movie since *Johnny Handsome*."

"He's still young. I wouldn't write him off yet."

"Young? He must be fifty years old, man."

"He's young compared to me," Mickey said, gazing up at this block of a man. Despite the nonchalant conversation, there was a stiffness to Riccardo, his shoulders tense and a sharpness to his eyes, as if always on the lookout for hostility.

"What you doing all the way out in Porn Valley, old man?"

Mickey pushed off the car, suppressing a groan, and stood straight as he could. "One of your co-workers invited me."

"Oh yeah? Who?"

"Ms. Bethany Summers."

Riccardo narrowed his eyes. "Beth invited you? Here?"

"That's what I said." Mickey looked past Riccardo, growing tired of him.

"Why?"

"Ask her yourself," Mickey said, nodding at the young woman who had exited the studio and was waving to him now, wearing little denim shorts and a pink crop top. He figured, since this woman was waving to him, she must be Ms. Summers.

Riccardo glanced behind. He tossed the cigarette in the dirt, marched toward Bethany, and bent down to kiss her, making theater of it, his thick arm coiled around her body like a python.

The kiss went on for some time. Ten feet away, Mickey waited. A cool breeze ran gentle fingers across his neck.

"Mr. O'Rourke," Bethany said, breaking free at last and moving toward him. "Thank you for coming, and for taking the case." She beamed and something about her struck Mickey in the chest. Bethany looked to him like how he imagined his granddaughter might have, had he and Martha had children. Something about the way she had smiled, the way she had moved . . . it brought to mind a young Martha all those years ago when she and Mickey had first met.

"I never turn down a case, Ms. Summers. Not if I can help it. And, please, call me Mickey."

A funny look came over Riccardo. "Wait a minute. You're the guy. The fucking private eye." To Bethany: "You hired *this* guy?"

Bethany shot Riccardo a look that could paralyze. "Yes, Riccardo, I hired Mr. O'Rourke, and he very kindly accepted—"

"This man is seventy-eight-years-old, Beth."

"That's right, son," Mickey said, stepping close to Riccardo, "and I've been doing this since nineteen fifty-one, which means I've learned a thing or two."

Riccardo gazed down at Mickey, then at little Bethany next to him, a smug grin on his face. "You're the boss," he said to Bethany. "I gotta get back to the shoot. Good luck, old man. Don't hurt yourself."

He strode stiffly toward the studio.

"Sorry about that," Bethany said. "He's not rude, just Italian."

"It's quite all right. Do you have somewhere we can sit, out of this heat?"

"Sure. I was going to suggest we go to a diner nearby, but we can use the lunch room right here if you'd prefer?"

Desperate for some air conditioning, Mickey said, "Right here will do just fine."

"Okay. Let's go." Bethany spun on her heels like a ballerina and made for the studio.

Mickey started after her. Even in his youth he had never been the tallest of men, but now he was the same height as little Bethany, and it made him feel old.

BETHANY LED HIM THROUGH A HALLWAY OF CLOSED DOORS. Behind one of them, a female voice cried out an almighty moan and Mickey almost jumped. He remembered this was a house of pornography. He glanced at Bethany but her expression gave nothing away. It probably all sounded like the hum of electricity to her.

She led him into a compact kitchen area with a flimsy little table and chairs. The scarlet-haired woman with gigantic artificial breasts shut the fridge and faced them. Her lips were so blown up they could keep her afloat at sea.

"Oh, hey Beth," she said. She looked at Mickey. "And hello again to you. Did you enjoy the shoot?"

The way she was smiling at him compelled Mickey to say, "Yes, it was . . . fascinating."

The woman appeared pleased to hear this. Despite being at least twice Bethany's age, she gave off a powerful sexual energy. Or maybe the place was getting to him.

"You know, I have just the scene for you if you're interested," the woman said.

The surprise must have shown on Mickey's face because Bethany giggled. "He's just here to see me, Rach. Sorry to disappoint."

"A terrible shame," Rach said with playful tragedy. "Are you guys family?"

"No, it's . . . complicated," Bethany said.

Quickly avoiding a potentially awkward moment with the skilled practice of someone who regularly navigates such waters, Rach joked, "Lovers then." To Mickey: "You must be *wild* in bed."

"The wildest," Bethany said, swooping in before Mickey stammered himself to death.

Mickey felt his cheeks heating up. "Might have picked up a trick or two over the years," he said, thinking of Martha in her day, fierce and stunning and full of power, and how she had remained that way, right up to the very end.

"Oh I bet you have," Rach said. "Let me know if you ever want to be a star. I got just the scene for you." She touched his shoulder and breezed out of the room.

"She's serious, you know," Bethany said. "There's a scene for everyone here."

"I don't doubt it."

"Would you like some coffee?"

"I'd love some."

"Coming right up. Go ahead and sit down."

Mickey pulled out a cheap plastic chair, about as heavy as a pillow, and dropped onto it. His calf muscles throbbed, swollen from the heat.

"So tell me, Mr. O'Rourke—"

"Please, call me Mickey."

"Mickey. Nineteen fifty-one. That's a long time to be a private detective. When do you plan to stop?"

"It'll be fifty years in September. I'll stop then."

Bethany spooned ground coffee into the machine, shut the lid and pressed a button. "But that's so soon."

"Yes, I suppose it is. To tell you the truth, I'm thinking this might be my final case."

The coffee maker gurgled like a drain.

Bethany faced Mickey, back leaned against the countertop. "Have you . . ." She bit her lip. "Have you ever found someone who didn't want to be found?"

"I have, yes."

Bethany nodded. Her serious expression aged her a couple years. A roasted caramel aroma of coffee reached Mickey's nose.

Out of his breast pocket Mickey retrieved his Moleskin notebook and Fisher Space Pen (the best pen in the universe, according to the company, used by NASA astronauts in Outer Space). He wrote today's date beside Bethany's name at the top of a new page of the notebook, gifted to him by Martha on his birthday last year, a few weeks before she passed. There was a Moleskin for every year of his career stored in boxes at the house, a little bungalow in Pasadena he and Martha had bought when they had grown old enough to admit they no longer needed the extra bedrooms that had remained empty except for rare occasions when guests had stayed over. This last Moleskin was half full with recent cases—proving infidelity, finding biological parents; nothing particularly exciting. It struck Mickey now that, if Bethany indeed proved to be his final client, then the notes he took on this case would be the closing entry of his long and winding career, and that gave the case extra weight, resonance. Or did it? Perhaps not. But still—fifty years, fifty notebooks: his body of work. All he had left.

Bethany carried two cups of steaming coffee, placed them on the table, and sat on the chair opposite Mickey.

Mickey said, "Thank you so much. Okay, so, it's important that you spare no details. Even something that seems trivial might prove useful later."

Bethany held two hands around her steaming mug. "Can I ask you something before we begin?"

"Of course."

"How did you find that little girl? The one who was kidnapped a few years ago. The police couldn't find her. How'd you do it?"

"Is that why you hired me?" Knowing it was, same as every other client since.

"Yeah, I remembered you from the news. It was everywhere. You saved that little girl's life, it was amazing. When I decided to hire a private investigator, I didn't even have to think about it, I wanted you."

Bethany was looking at him with a certain admiration, the same way Jane Krieger herself had looked at him when he'd kicked in the basement door and carried her out of that godforsaken place.

Mickey gazed at the Moleskin, thinking about it. "There's no secret to how I found her. No simple answer. Every case is a matter of collecting information and following where it leads, down every dead end and back again, until, if you're lucky, after much perseverance, it might lead you to the right place. It's that easy and that hard."

"You must be real good at your job," Bethany said.

"Well, I hope so. I've been doing it a long time. Too long, probably."

"You must have seen so much."

"Much too much."

"You never wanted to be a cop?"

"Oh, I did once. I was a police officer for a little over a year almost fifty years ago now, here in LA."

"Why'd you stop?"

Memories flew at him: the flash of a muzzle in that dim apartment and the ashen, powdery taste of it on his tongue; the look of terror in the man's gaunt face, followed by resignation as the blood flowed; the stench of decay, of addiction, of a life utterly wasted; the crushing silence after the fact, then the wailing of the baby in the next room . . .

"Mr. O'Rourke?"

He looked at her. "Mickey," he said, not unkindly. "It wasn't for me. I'd just returned from the war, I was drinking all day and night, I hadn't yet met the woman I would eventually marry, and . . . well, it just didn't work out. So I rented an office downtown and became a private dick. The city back then, everything about it was different. Everything felt a little more tangible. Solid. People cared more. More passion went into things. There was a certain glamour about it all. Business was tough at first but my ex-colleagues at LAPD Hollywood helped me out from time to time. Once the cases started rolling in, I hired a receptionist and then I married her."

Bethany was watching him with interest. Self-conscious of his blabbing, Mickey said, "But, as Bob Dylan once sang, the times are a-changing. Now I work out of my bungalow, I'm sober twenty-two years, and the police don't show me one ounce of respect. And this great city has grown and grown, slowly losing what made her so special . . ."

Mickey shook his head. "Anyway, I'm just an old man, don't listen to me."

"Have you seen her since then?"

It took Mickey a second to realize who Bethany had referred to. "Yes, Jane and her family used to have my wife and I over for Christmas. But—" He hesitated, thought of Jane's parents—her wealthy father, a bank manager with Wells Fargo in downtown LA, promising him tickets to any NBA Final whenever he wanted them; her mother's howls at the funeral.

"To tell you the truth, Bethany, since you asked . . . Jane died of leukemia last year. It presented suddenly and took her quickly. Eleven years old. How's that for bad luck?"

Bethany's mouth opened but no words came out.

"Now," Mickey said, picking up the Space Pen, "when was the last time you saw Jeffrey?"

Chapter Two

JULY, 1999

HOW MANY DINERS SHOULD A MAN ROB before he turns the gun on himself? The question whispered in Richie's ear as he swallowed the last bite of pancake. He and Alabama had gotten the idea of stealing from diners when they caught *Pulp Fiction* at a four-year anniversary screening in the New Beverly Cinema in LA last year where they'd gone to shoot dope and drift among the neon haze of Hollywood glitz, thinking Shit, look how in love they are holding up that diner, that could be us. But a dozen diners later the charm had worn off and they'd returned to being just a couple junkie losers stuck in the small-time.

"You gonna finish that?" Richie said, looking at the half-eaten blueberry pie in front of Alabama. The woman never finished a meal and it drove him up the fucking wall.

"You know I can't eat when we 'bout to score, darlin'."

He held his gaze on Alabama for a moment, her looking all cute in that little yellow dress, then stared at the parking lot.

Alabama said, "You bein' all broody, baby. What's wrong?" She reached forward and brushed his long hair behind his ear.

"I'm sick of these fucking diners, that's what's wrong. We gonna be stealing pennies the rest of our lives?"

"We got almost two thousand from the last one."

"Two thousand—" Richie tossed a hand. "Two thousand is the reason we sleep in filthy motels where the mattress has bloodstains and the toilet don't flush. It's the reason we don't dress nice, or eat in half-decent restaurants. It's why we're nothing but a couple losers and everybody knows it."

The air smelled of bacon and coffee and grease, thick like lotion on Richie's skin. Truckers appeared to be the sole clientele of this shithole diner in the middle of the Nevada desert.

"So what you sayin'?" Alabama said.

"I'm sayin' it's time we moved up in the world, found a better score."

"Oh." That expressive face of hers wearing the word like a mask. "So we not doin' this diner no more?"

"No, we're doing the diner. Course we're doing it, we need to eat, don't we? But this is the last one. It's the big-time after this. We'll go back to LA. Make our mark."

Alabama smiled. "The big-time. Like Bonnie and Clyde."

"Yeah. But with a happier ending."

"Just me and you."

"Just you and me," Richie said.

"I'm ready."

"Me too."

"Kiss me, baby," Alabama said.

Richie leaned across the table and Alabama came forward to meet him. They kissed, Alabama's lips sugar-sweet with blueberry. When they released, Alabama's hand lay across Richie's, obscuring the "FUCK" tattooed into his knuckles. On the knuckles of the other hand: "LOVE." The officiator at the chapel in Vegas had found it a pretty funny combination of words to have displayed on their wedding day. Still no rings on their fingers. They'd have to fix that.

Richie slid the hand out from under his wife's and closed his fingers around the smooth wooden grip of the Model 27 Smith & Wesson revolver shoved into the back of his jeans.

He rose from the booth a man with a purpose. "All right you assholes, put your wallets on the table and your hands in the air and you might make it home to kiss your lovers."

XXX

EVEN AFTER ALL THIS TIME—a year? two? Richie couldn't remember, the whole chunk of it a smear in his mind like a light trail frozen into a photograph—anticipation of the needle filled Richie with a terrifying, ecstatic feeling of excitement mixed with dread. It made him feel alive.

He sat on the edge of the bed. The tourniquet wrapped around his arm caused his skinny bicep to throb with each beat of his heart. He watched as Alabama, sitting on the filthy motel-room carpet, held a flame beneath a spoon. Her legs were crossed and beneath her skirt pubic hair like the legs of a giant spider crept out of her underwear, but Richie barely glanced at it, too lustful for the black tar heroin dissolving on the metal. They had bought the stuff from a prostitute in Vegas on their wedding night, hoping to reach the stars with it, but it was cheap shit, hard as rock and a deep brown color, and hadn't exactly blown their minds. But it got the job done.

Alabama mixed citric acid with the water to help break the dope down and now the vinegar aroma of the mixture swirled around Richie's head. He hated that smell and he adored it.

"Eight hundred bucks," he said, irritation coming out in his voice. "Barely gets us a week. We're spending more on this shit than ever."

"It was a small diner in the middle of nowhere," Alabama said, her gaze fixed on the liquid as she placed the lighter on the floor and dropped a cotton ball onto the spoon. "I think we did pretty good."

"If you call sitting in this filthy motel room using up the last of our shitty dope with barely enough cash to make it a fortnight *pretty good*, then sure, we did fucking great."

"We're gon' back to LA tomorrow. Then things will improve." Alabama picked up the syringe and carefully sucked the heroin mixture into it through the cotton.

She looked at him then, holding the needle vertical beside her scarlet-colored bra like a horny teenager's fantasy of a nurse. "Things will improve in LA. Won't they, Richie?"

"Yeah, that's right. I'll find something for us in LA, something better, no more of this diners and motels shit."

"I'm happy long's I'm with you."

Richie let a weak smile form on his face. It took the edge off his sour mood. The woman could cheer up the pope.

"We have to sell the Harley," he said. "It's not right for the kind of scores I wanna do in LA. It's not right for small-time shit there, either. Too many people around. And cops."

"How come?"

"Remember the diner outside Portland? That fuckin' nut coming after us in the pickup truck? You were clinging onto me like a koala bear while we rode that bike a thousand miles an hour. Whole time I was thinking, fuck, one slip-up, one collision, one fuckin' pothole, and we're dead."

"I know what you mean. I had my eyes squeezed shut the entire time."

"Now imagine that in LA with a cop on our ass."

Alabama's eyes widened thinking about it.

Richie said, "I saw a used car place in that little town few miles back. We can offload the Harley there, then catch a Greyhound to LA."

"Okay."

A pause.

"We ain't gon' get chased by cops in LA, are we, Richie?"

"Nah, we'll be smart about it. I'm just sayin', the bike's gotta go."

Alabama nodded. "You best take that thing off before you lose your arm."

Richie unwrapped the tourniquet and immediately his flesh tingled as if jabbed by a thousand tiny swords. He brushed his long hair over an ear and sticky grease clung to his fingertips.

"See you on the other side," he said.

Alabama bit her lip, a hungry gleam in her jade eyes.

The needle plunged into Richie's skin like a lover.

"I'll be right behind you," he heard Alabama say, but his blood was cold now and his eyes were open but unseeing and a warmth was spreading up his bones from his toes as all tension in his body melted and seeped out his pores, all worries and fears and failures, and he knew that everything would be fine, perfectly, wonderfully fine, and that it had been silly to have ever worried at all.

I'll be right behind you. The words repeating in his mind like an echo as he zoomed far away from this dirty motel room, from this dirty life.

See you soon.

XXX

JUNE, 1998

JEMEKA SAT IN THE SILENCE of her tiny living room and listened for the sound of Ray-Ray's motorcycle. The darkness of East Compton at midnight stuck to the windows like grime. Joyriding teenagers had crashed a stolen Cadillac into the street lamp outside the house and now each time the sun went down the house became plunged into darkness and she couldn't see a damn thing beyond the living room windows, burglar bars over them like a jail cell.

Ray-Ray. Where was he? Should have been home hours ago. He'd stroll in here any minute cool as the ocean breeze feeding her some bullshit.

Ray-Ray. When they'd first met, at a house party six years ago, Jemeka had asked him why he was repeating his name like that instead of just going by Ray. He had said, "'Cause I'm so good they had to name me twice, shorty. They had to name me twice." Jemeka had laughed, thinking he was funny, probably a real character. Looking back on it now, she figured it a pretty idiotic thing to say, which made her the real fool for falling for it. She found out later that everybody called him Ray-Ray because he had a strange habit of repeating himself.

The familiar growl of Ray-Ray's Kawasaki brought the remote control into Jemeka's hand, her thumb pressing the power button and the TV blinking on. Wouldn't do any good if it looked like she'd been waiting up for him; man's head was swollen enough already.

A pretty white news anchor was speaking about politics. The screen cut to President Clinton smooth-talking his way around a journalist. Jemeka wasn't really listening but she figured the president had probably been questioned about that affair he'd had with that young woman that the media kept harping on about. Jemeka didn't understand all the fuss. So the man had an affair? Not a nice thing to do—typically, abysmally male—but wasn't it the man's own private business?

The sound of keys in the lock and the door opening, then closing. Ray-Ray stuck his head into the living room.

"What you being sneaky for?" Jemeka said.

"Oh, hey baby. I was worried 'case you was asleep."

"Yeah, and you'd tip-toe right on by me up to bed if I was."

Ray-Ray kept staring at her.

"You gonna tell me where you were?" Jemeka said.

"Me and some of the boys were playing cards after work. I nearly won too. Shit, I nearly won."

"Mmm hmm."

Ray-Ray lingered by the doorway, unsure if he was in the clear. "There any dinner left over?"

"Some pasta in the fridge."

Ray-Ray moved out of sight. Now Jemeka heard him rummaging in the fridge.

Man had no idea how good he had it. Her working hard at the salon six days a week and him coming home late after doing God knows what. Playing cards with the boys? Yeah. And she'd been playing chess with Bill Clinton.

She sighed, resolving to shake these worries from her thoughts. No point starting an argument.

She yawned and stretched and picked up the remote and made the president disappear and carried herself up the stairs to bed.

XXX

MAGIC CURLS WAS A PLACE OF SECRETS AND SISTERLY SUPPORT. Jemeka had been working at the hair salon for almost ten years now, ever since she was sixteen. She didn't earn much, but it beat twisting around a pole or hustling on the sidewalk, and the girls—co-workers and customers—were fun to be around, always full of gossip and advice. Almost ten years and they hadn't run out of ways to slap down their men.

Currently, Tania was ranting about her long-term boyfriend, who seemed to her much too happy to remain *just* her long-term boyfriend, while Jemeka ran a straightener over her hair.

"And his broke ass ain't lookin' for no job," Tania said. "Expects me to break my back putting food on the table, then when I talk about tying the knot, man has a fit."

"I hear you," Tanisha said, inserting rollers into Daniella's hair at the opposite side of the room. "Curtis don't wanna hear nothin' about nothin' except food and basketball. Goddamn men."

"Goddamn men," they all said in unison.

"Oh, that's my jam," Tania said as "The Boy Is Mine" by Brandy and Monica came on the radio. "Turn it up."

Jemeka reached over and twisted the dial. Tania sang along as Jemeka held the woman's hair in her left hand and passed the straightener over it, the stench of burning drifting up. Soon they were all chanting the chorus together.

"What about you, Jemeka?" Tania said. "Ray-Ray treating you okay?"

Jemeka remembered Ray-Ray coming home late, that dopey face of his looking guilty as hell. "I don't know . . . we could use some romance in our life, that's for sure."

"When was the last time he took you some place nice?" Tania said.

Jemeka stopped straightening Tania's hair and thought about it. "I can't even remember."

"Oh honey, you deserve better," Tanisha said across the room.

"Let me ask you something," Tania said, gazing at Jemeka in the mirror. "When was the last time *you* took *him* some place nice?"

"I guess it's been a long time since I did that too."

Tania nodded, ever the wise elder despite there only being four years between them. "Maybe that's what you should do then, girl."

"Yeah." Jemeka resumed work on Tania's hair. "Still, Ray-Ray could be treating me a whole lot better. Sometimes I feel like he forgets I'm in his life at all. Goddamn men."

"Goddamn men," they all said together.

THE LAST CUSTOMER OF THE DAY HAD EXITED THE SALON. Jemeka wiped the mirrors while Tanisha, who owned the place, swept the floor. The radio off now, peaceful silence had descended.

"You hear about young Clive Jones getting picked up by the police?" Tanisha said. "He was selling crack."

"Then he got what he deserves. That poison's destroying the community."

Tanisha stopped sweeping and leaned on the broom. "Locking up Clive won't achieve a damn thing. Kid's just a symptom of the problem. Just tryna put food on his plate, same as you or me. But they put him away because there's too much money to be made trampling over the people on the bottom and taking a cut from the top."

Jemeka resumed wiping, remembering now that Clive was the kid whose father had been shot by LAPD outside the family home a few years back following a search of the house for illegal firearms—total bullshit because the man had been a saint, beloved in the community. A sickly man, he had often spent the day in bed, and that's exactly where he'd been when the police kicked open his door. They had shot Clive's father dead in the man's own bed. The worst part: the scumbag cops had gotten away with it. No one outside of the local community had given a damn, local news stations barely mentioning the killing and when they did had loaded their language with the subtle implication that Clive's father had somehow deserved to be murdered in his own home—he had been a resident of Compton, after all.

The neighborhood had simmered with rage for months after that, and the police had stayed away for a while. It made Jemeka sick thinking about it.

She thought of her own father now, dead from a heart attack five years in December. He'd always wanted the best for her, did all he could to keep her on the straight and narrow after her mom had passed away when Jemeka was a baby. Her daddy had been a good man, and Jemeka tried every day to do right by him. But he'd been poor his entire life, and for Jemeka growing up had been a struggle, rarely enough food in the fridge or clothes in her wardrobe. When he died, he'd left her crushed by his debts—debts Jemeka was still paying off today. What use was being a good man in life only to do that to his own daughter in death?

"You're right," Jemeka said as Tanisha went into the back room.

Tanisha's head appeared in the doorway. "About what, suga?"

"Clive not having much options, being just a symptom."

Tanisha nodded. "A damn shame."

"But he did have the option of not selling drugs. He could've chose to work jobs like us. Ain't glamorous, but it's not hurting no one, neither."

Tanisha's expression said she was withholding her opinion on the matter. "Well, now Clive's the one hurting." She disappeared into the back room.

Chapter Three

JULY, 1999

GREYHOUNDS: THE VEINS OF VAGRANT AMERICA. Richie sat under the bus shelter in Nowhere, Nevada, Alabama's head on his shoulder, watching heat waves wobble above the tarmac. He'd been eager to leave the state ever since they'd arrived. If it wasn't for Vegas nobody would come to this shithole. Fucking desert in every direction. The original plan of mugging Vegas casino visitors had been, with hindsight, a ridiculous idea, and getting hitched by Elvis on a whim had been the only good thing to come from it. For the first time since leaving LA to travel up to Washington State and back down, robbing diners along the way, Richie missed home.

"Where's this fucking bus?" he said loudly to no one.

Alabama jerked awake beside him. She yawned, stretching pale arms. "What time is it?"

"Time for one of us to steal a watch."

Richie leaned forward to look past Alabama at the guy standing outside the shelter, also waiting for the bus, Richie assumed.

"Hey, buddy," Richie said.

The man offered no indication he'd heard.

"Hey, buddy," Richie said louder, "you got the time?"

The guy, a skinny skateboarder-looking kid no older than twenty-one, didn't so much as glance at Richie, gaze fixed on the street ahead. The motherfucker was ignoring him.

"Hey," Richie said, leaping up off the seat. "You hear me?"

"Richie, don't." Alabama's fingers closed around his wrist.

He yanked her hand away and marched out of the shelter.

"You ignoring me, punk?" he spat into the guy's face.

The dumb fuck just staring at him, eyes screaming.

"I asked you a question. I'm gonna give you one more chance, and you better fuckin' take it." Richie jabbed a finger into the guy's chest with each word: "What. Time. Is. It."

The kid was mouthing like a goldfish, a low moaning coming out of him. What the fuck? Was he making a joke of this?

The kid's hands came up and Richie punched him in the stomach. He gasped and doubled over.

Alabama cried out, begging Richie to stop, but what did she know—what if the guy had a gun?

Richie swung for his temple and the kid crumpled onto the dirt, blood oozing from his lip. He held his arms over his face defensively, terror in his eyes. Now he was making strange movements with his hands, mouthing again, but with fresh urgency, and there was that moaning sound again, fingers dancing before him like spiders.

"Oh no, Richie. Oh no." Alabama had her palms on her cheeks. "He can't hear what you been sayin'. That's sign language he's doin'."

Richie looked at the man drawing shapes in the breeze. She was right: he'd beaten up a deaf kid for not listening to him.

"Fuck, I didn't know. I thought he was disrespecting me. You know, too good to speak to people like us."

Alabama brushed past him.

"Let me help you," she said to the kid, who flinched. "Easy, go easy, lemme help." She placed a gentle hand on his shoulder and helped him to his feet.

"What are you doing?" Richie said.

"Helping the poor guy, what's it look like?"

Richie folded his arms, feeling a little silly about attacking a deaf guy. "Yeah, and what happens when the bus comes and this guy starts flapping his arms at the driver, pointing at us. Or worse, heads into the town right behind us, finds himself the sheriff."

"So what you sayin'?" Hands on her hips, no more patience for bullshit.

"I'm sayin' Silent Bob here's gotta go."

"What's that s'posed to mean, Richie?"

Richie glanced around. Just the warm breeze and the dusty street and the town silent behind them. His knuckles throbbed painfully where he'd punched the guy. He tugged the Smith & Wesson out of his jeans and thumbed back the hammer for the menacing click before remembering the fucking guy couldn't hear it.

"What the hell, Richie!"

"Shut up and get out the way."

"Richie, you put that away right—"

Richie grabbed Alabama with his free hand and shoved her under the shelter where she crashed into the plexiglass and fell onto her ass. He pointed the revolver at the kid's forehead. The barrel glinted in the sunlight. Richie held out the palm of his other hand, beckoning with his fingers in an attempt at communicating something along the lines of *Give me your wallet or I'll give you a bullet.*

The kid had no trouble understanding him this time. He held out his wallet.

Richie snatched it and shoved it into his back pocket.

Now the guy was taking off his watch and holding it out toward Richie. Next a Nokia left his pocket to join the offering, tears in the guy's eyes.

"Hold up hold up, I don't want this shit," Richie said. Peering closer at the watch, "On second thoughts, yeah, I'll take the watch—what is that, a Casio?" He grabbed the Casio, fake gold and tacky. Richie was about to cut the guy loose when he remembered he couldn't have him calling the cops, so he took the Nokia, too.

Richie pointed at the dry, infinite desert. He gestured with the revolver, communicating to the guy to start walking.

The kid's eyes opened wide. He brought his hands together as if to pray, shaking his head.

"I'm not gonna kill you, jackass. Walk that way."

Alabama said, "Richie—"

"Don't start," he snapped at her. To the kid: "Walk. Now." Pointing into the distance, he pressed the barrel into the guy's forehead.

The guy stiffened like a hard-on. Richie figured he was about to cry or piss himself or both but, dry-eyed and dry-groined, the kid faced the desert and started moving. He crossed the street without looking back, then broke into a run, glancing over his shoulder.

Richie watched the guy shrink as he sprinted toward the wobbling horizon.

Sitting on the ground with her back against the plexiglass, Alabama glared at him. "You're a piece of shit."

"Yeah, but least I'm not a deaf guy in the desert." He smirked, uncocked the revolver and returned it to his waist.

Alabama looked away, seething. He'd get some peace and quiet on the Greyhound, then.

He pulled the guy's wallet out of his pants and counted the take: one hundred and forty bucks and change. Not bad at all. He'd buy Alabama a pair of those fake-fancy earrings she liked, that would pick her up.

The sound of an engine and the Greyhound appeared like a mirage in the distance.

"Well, would you look at that for timing," Richie said. "Looks like it's gonna be a good day."

XXX

JUNE, 1998

RAY-RAY'S DAY OFF AND JEMEKA WATCHED HIM LIKE A HAWK. A rare event each of them having the day off, they decided to spend the afternoon lazing about on Venice Beach. The hot sand between her toes and warm breeze kissing her back relaxed Jemeka more than a bottle of wine ever could. Not that she drank often, or could afford to. Not much of a swimmer, she even waded into the Pacific up to her knees, the frothy surf splashing around her, cooling her down. She watched Ray-Ray dive into the water without hesitation to swim out far and return to her, his body glistening like a pearl. Ray-Ray was long and lanky and a little goofy but she loved him. Though it's easy to love someone on days like this when the sea is warm, the sky is blue, and life's problems are waiting at home.

Later, walking hand-in-hand with Ray-Ray along the boardwalk, watching the performers and sharing ice cream, Jemeka had almost forgotten she was mad at him.

"Shit, look at this one," Ray-Ray said, pointing at a street performer balancing a sword on his tongue. "He's crazy."

"Impressive. But can he braid cornrows?"

Ray-Ray grinned. "Not like you, baby. Not like you."

Jemeka took the cone from Ray-Ray and licked the pink ice cream, the sweet cotton-candy flavor like an explosion on her tongue. They continued through the throngs of people, in no hurry for the day to end. A group of women wearing multicolored yoga pants floated by on roller skates.

Jemeka nudged an elbow into Ray-Ray's ribs. "Stop checking out their behinds."

"I was just admiring their pants."

Jemeka steered them toward a free bench overlooking the sea where Jemeka rested her head on Ray-Ray's shoulder. The ocean sparkled beneath them like a blanket sprinkled with glitter, tiny boats inching across it. They should come out here more often, get away from all the drugs and drive-bys and thugs with badges. Sitting here like this, it was almost possible to believe they lived this life every day.

"Ray-Ray, you think our life will ever get easier?"

"What you mean, baby?"

A warm breeze tickled her neck. "You think it's always gonna be this hard? We'll always be struggling?"

Ray-Ray watched waves crawl up the shore. "Maybe. Could be we get tougher, don't find it so hard."

"This country . . . the rich get richer while the rest of us get more desperate every year. They say slavery ended but we the ones doing all the work with nothing to show for it."

"That ain't the same thing, Jemeka."

"No, I know. But it's not all that different, either."

They sat in silence and watched the miracle of the ocean.

Ray-Ray said, "I could've played pro basketball, you know."

"What? Very funny."

"I'm serious."

"I ain't ever seen you even touch a basketball."

"I played in high school. I was good. Best on the team. Coach told me I could get a scholarship, have a chance at going pro."

Jemeka observed the crease in Ray-Ray's brow, realizing there were still things she didn't know about her man, surprised at the discovery. "What happened?"

"Same thing happens most of us. I was young and stupid, didn't realize what I had, the opportunities. Cared more about getting girls and lookin' fly. Got mixed up with some fools and did some dumb shit."

Ray-Ray rubbed a hand over his chin and frowned. "After couple warnings, the school expelled my dumb ass. My mama crying, tellin' me she don't know who I was no more. But it was Coach's reaction hit the hardest. He didn't say nothin', just put his hand on my shoulder and nodded his head, like he was saying, Hard luck, you almost made it. I kept running with them fools for a while, then I cleaned my shit up and met you, Jemeka. Then I met you."

Jemeka gazed into Ray-Ray's dark eyes. She brushed her lips against the rough stubble of his cheek, squeezed his bicep.

"Well, pro basketball player or not, I'm proud of you, Ray-Ray."

She hadn't meant it, but she had wanted to.

XXX

9:45 P.M. AND RAY-RAY WAS GETTING FIDGETY, glancing at his watch. So Jemeka knew it was coming when he said, "Baby, I got to go out for a bit, see the boys. It's Jerome's birthday, I promised I would. Just one drink."

Jemeka withheld her typical responses and simply nodded. She had other ideas.

"Thanks baby." He kissed her forehead and rose off the sofa. "I'll be back in a flash, back in a flash."

Ray-Ray snatched his wallet from the old coffee table that had once belonged to Jemeka's father and bounded into the bedroom to put on his Kevlar motorcycle gear which Jemeka had gifted him for their one-year anniversary, insisting he wear it every time he sat on that death trap.

By the time the Kawasaki had growled out the driveway Jemeka was standing inside the front door, the keys of her battered '93 Ford Tempo in hand, counting down from ten. On "one" she left the house, locked the door and hopped into the car, the CD player coming alive with the engine to play N.W.A.'s *Straight Outta Compton.*

Ray-Ray had stopped at the lights at the end of the street. Jemeka slowed the Tempo to a crawl. A group of kids lingered at the corner of the intersection, a boombox on the sidewalk blasting homemade gangsta rap. Ray-Ray flipped up the visor of his helmet and talked to them. Typical: the man knew every soul in the neighborhood.

The lights went green and Ray-Ray shot across the intersection at speed, showing off for the kids. Jemeka accelerated after him, leaving the darkness of their street behind as she neared the brighter and busier East Compton Boulevard, which Ray-Ray had turned onto. Red lights stopped her at the intersection and she lost him. Thirty seconds later, Jemeka leaned hard on the pedal trying to find Ray-Ray, turning the music down, concentrating.

She had almost resigned herself to having lost him when she glimpsed the brake lights of the Kawasaki dip over the crest of the hill where East Compton Boulevard became Somerset Boulevard, the hill a precursor to the bridge over the Los Angeles River. She sped up the hill in pursuit, but upon reaching the top, Ray-Ray had vanished. A steady stream of vehicles passed by in both directions on the 710 below, but the only vehicle in sight ahead was a station wagon coming at her on the opposite side of the street.

"Where in the hell . . ." Jemeka slowed the Tempo, glancing around. She passed an opening on the left just before the river and jammed on the brakes. The opening sloped down to the bank of the LA River—merely a river of concrete during hot summer months such as this. Forty yards down the slope, Ray-Ray's motorcycle cruised slowly along the river bank approaching what looked like a Cadillac twenty yards ahead of him parallel to the wall, half-hidden in darkness.

Jemeka hesitated. She couldn't stay in the middle of the street on the bridge like this, but if she went down after Ray-Ray he might spot her. Safest thing to do: continue straight over the bridge and loop around back home, get herself some beauty sleep. She could ask Ray-Ray about this in the morning, catch him off guard. He'd unravel like a ball of twine.

Ice Cube threatened out of the speakers and Jemeka gritted her teeth. No, not this time. Tonight she would discover what her boyfriend was up to.

She killed the Tempo's headlights, a car honking for passage behind her, and spun the vehicle into the opening, letting gravity roll it down the slope. Without the lights, Jemeka could just about make out a gate at the bottom of the slope that had been pulled aside, presumably by Ray-Ray or whoever he was meeting with. Jemeka's insides coiled up like a snake. She didn't like this one bit.

She let the car roll to a stop at the riverbank and pulled the handbrake, switching the music off. In the silence, the night seemed blacker around her.

Ray-Ray had parked the motorcycle beside the Cadillac, stepping off it now, removing his helmet and placing it on the handlebars.

Jemeka squinted. The Cadillac door had opened, looked like. Yeah, a man stepping out of it now toward Ray-Ray, the look of a gangster about him: baggy T-shirt down to his knees, throwing his shoulders, blood-red bandanna around his head. Ray-Ray contrasted heavily in the Kevlar.

The gangster said something to Ray-Ray and Ray-Ray nodded, his back to Jemeka. The gangster moved toward the Cadillac and Ray-Ray followed.

They went around the rear of the vehicle, the gangster opening the trunk, obscuring both of them behind it.

Ten seconds passed.

Twenty. The trunk still open and no sign of them. Jemeka's palms slippery on the steering wheel.

Thirty seconds. What in the hell was going on down there . . .

Ray-Ray appeared, backing away from the Cadillac toward the sharp slope to the riverbed behind. He held his hands at his chest defensively.

The gangster came toward him, a pistol in his hand.

Jemeka's breath caught in her throat.

Perhaps aware of the steep slope behind, Ray-Ray switched directions, backstepping now toward the motorcycle.

The gangster raised the gun, matching each of Ray-Ray's steps with one of his own, circling around so that he became the one closest to the riverbed.

The men stopped moving, twelve feet apart. Ray-Ray, still with his hands raised, said something and the gangster replied.

Jemeka had to do something. She inhaled a deep breath, exhaled sharply, and released the handbrake, foot hovering above the accelerator. But something stopped her, paralyzing her in the seat, distorting her racing thoughts . . .

Ray-Ray darted to the left. The pop of a gunshot and Ray-Ray was thrown backwards, twisting onto the concrete near the motorcycle.

It shook the fear from Jemeka's bones. She slammed her foot on the pedal and the Tempo lurched toward the gunman like a racehorse.

The gangster snapped his gaze toward the roaring engine of the Tempo as it raced toward him. He swung his body in Jemeka's direction, bringing the gun up.

Leaning all her weight on the accelerator, Jemeka flicked the headlights on and the man lit up like a convict under a searchlight. He squinted and shielded his eyes reflexively, jerking his head back, and time slowed almost to a standstill: Jemeka saw the hairs on the man's face and the faded prison tattoos along his arms, the terror in his eyes and droplets of sweat on his brow, even the glint of the gun barrel aimed slightly above her.

Then, like a needle hopping on a record, Jemeka was staring at a cracked windshield while her foot slammed on the brakes, the tires screeching across the concrete.

The car had skidded to a stop before she could process what had happened.

Chapter Four

JULY, 2000

SHAKING BETHANY'S HAND AS HE BID HER GOODBYE, Mickey was again struck by her petiteness and how it contrasted with the aura of confidence she emitted, that confidence visible in her movements and clear comfortability in her choice of career, her seeming lack of self-doubt. "Strokes, Jeffrey Strokes," she'd said when Mickey had asked her for Jeffrey's full name, so Mickey had said, "I mean his real name," thinking it was a stage name, and Bethany had giggled, enjoying this clashing of worlds. "That is Jeff's real name," she had said. "Guy was born to do porn."

Mickey pushed through the front doors of MidnightPussy Productions into the blinding sunshine, mountains rippling on the horizon.

Born to do porn. An interesting way to describe the man who, according to a couple newspaper articles and dozens from underground zine *Sleaze*, had been *the* male star of the Los Angeles porn scene, multi-award-winning with legions of fans, until his sudden disappearance a year ago. LAPD had investigated without much success and the case had soon fizzled out. Jeffrey Strokes, it seemed, had simply vanished.

"Yo, Mickey Rourke," a voice said. Mickey glanced toward the source: Riccardo, Bethany's lover, sucking on a cigarette in the shade of the studio. "Can I've an autograph?"

Riccardo grinned at his own joke and swaggered toward Mickey. "Listen, no hard feelings about earlier. I didn't mean to suggest you couldn't do your job or nothing like that. I just never heard of an eighty-year-old fuckin' PI before, you know?"

"Seventy-eight."

Riccardo took a drag. "Sure."

"Are there any seventy-eight-year-old porn stars, Riccardo?"

"I don't know if *star* is the right word, but, sure, a few."

"Well then, if we can pull that off, I think we can manage a bit of detective work."

Riccardo tossed the cigarette into the dirt. "You got a point there."

"Finished work for today, Riccardo?"

Riccardo nodded, exhaling smoke.

"Jeffrey Strokes. You know him?" Mickey said.

"Yeah, everyone knew Jeff. He was a bit strange but we got along."

"Was?"

"What you mean?"

"You're speaking about him in the past tense."

"Figure of speech, old man. Figure of speech."

"Why do you say he was strange?"

Riccardo squinted into the distance. "You see that Coen Brothers movie came out last year?"

"*The Big Lebowski.*"

"Yeah, that's it."

"I saw it, yes."

"You know Jeff Bridges' character, The Dude? Well, imagine The Dude as a porn star who wins an AVN Award every year and you won't be far off."

"AVN?"

"Adult Video News. The Oscars of porn."

"A big deal?"

Riccardo shrugged. "To us."

"And so Jeffrey—"

Riccardo held up his palm. "This is a lot of questions."

"I have a few more."

"Yeah, well, I'm busy."

"Busy doing what? You said you're finished work."

Riccardo eyed Mickey suspiciously. He smirked. "You got me."

"Just a few more questions and I'll let you go."

"Okay Mickey, but not here."

"Not here?"

"I need a drink," Riccardo said, "and you're buying."

RICCARDO, IT TURNED OUT, OWNED A HARLEY-DAVIDSON. Mickey, in his Pontiac Catalina, followed Riccardo on the Harley for ten minutes to a dark and smoke-filled dive bar. A hand-painted, slightly lopsided sign above the door declared the establishment "Bloody Mary's." A dozen choppers sat parked in a line outside, gleaming under the sun.

Inside, Riccardo slapped hands with some of the patrons—all heavily tattooed bikers dressed in leathers—while Mickey choked on the fumes, eyes stinging. The walls were decorated with graffiti, American flags, framed photographs of motorcycles and groups of men posing around them. Aggressive rock music throbbed out of speakers. Two men who had been playing pool were staring at Mickey now, along with everyone else. Was Riccardo hoping to intimidate him, bringing him to a biker bar?

"Hey Mary, how you doin'?" Riccardo said to a skinny woman behind the bar.

"Better now that you're here." Mary's dyed-red hair and colorful tattoos appeared at odds with her weathered face and somewhat emaciated figure. "You gonna take me down the back alley today? I could use a seeing to."

"One of these days, Mary. I promise."

"You been sayin' that for two years. A woman has needs."

"I got my friend here today."

Mary appeared to notice Mickey for the first time. She looked him over. "Your friend can take me with you, if he can still get it up. I like an older man."

Mickey couldn't believe his ears.

Riccardo clapped a hand on Mickey's back. "You hear that, old man? What you think? You wanna take Mary out the back, show her a good time?"

"I think the lady ought to get to know me first."

Riccardo grinned. "You're funny. For an actor."

"You're in porn too?" Mary said, eyeballing him with interest.

"Not that kind of acting, Mary," Riccardo said. "Hollywood acting. You might know him. This here is Mickey Rourke."

"Not *that* Mickey Rourke . . ." But she sounded unsure.

"The one and only," Riccardo said.

Mary frowned, looking Mickey up and down. "You're lying."

"I wouldn't do that, Mary. Mickey here wants to get us a couple drinks."

"What can I get for you boys?"

"Bottle of Bud for me," Riccardo said.

"I'll have a cranberry juice, if you have it," Mickey said.

Mary raised an eyebrow and glanced at Riccardo.

"Actors," Riccardo said.

"YEAH, JEFF'S A UNIQUE GUY," Riccardo said, sitting opposite Mickey at a small table in a corner. "Enjoys too much of the ganja, if you know what I mean."

"He smokes marijuana?"

"Like a fuckin' Rastafarian."

"Does he use other drugs?"

"Most of 'em, probably."

"Could be he got himself into trouble with some drug dealers, had to disappear?"

"Doubt it," Riccardo said.

"Why's that?"

"Jeff's so chill he's practically horizontal. Couldn't see anyone having a problem with him."

"Bethany seems to think Jeffrey may have decided to disappear."

"Wishful thinking," Riccardo said. He drank from his beer. "Much better to think the guy's laying low than dead in a ditch somewhere."

Mickey nodded. The smoke was less concentrated in this part of the room, but still his eyes burned, throat dry, the deathly taste of it in his mouth. Bloody Mary's clearly paid no heed to the smoking ban.

"Bethany loved him?" Mickey said.

"She tell you that?" Riccardo was looking into his eyes.

"She did."

"What she tell you about me?"

"Your name didn't come up."

Riccardo's eyes narrowed. "Can't say I'm surprised. Even with the guy gone all anyone talks about is Jeff."

Mickey wrote "Jealous" beside Riccardo's name in the Moleskin.

"By all accounts, Jeffrey was something of a star in the pornography world?"

"An understatement, if anything. Jeff won three Best Male Performer of the Year AVNs in a row, probably would have kept winning 'em too. He was the highest paid guy in the business before he vanished. I'm assuming you've never been to a porno convention. You should go to one sometime, get the blood flowing. It's the women who are the stars at these things. I mean, no shit, right? But Jeff would have fans lining up to meet him. I never understood the attraction. Guy would be standing there, swaying, eyes drooping out of his head, talking like Keanu Reeves on tranquilizers. Even had a line of dildos modeled on his cock. A bestseller, apparently. But whatever."

Mickey underlined the "Jealous."

"But you think he's dead?"

"Why would a guy at the peak of his career choose to disappear? You're the PI—in your experience are missing people usually dead or in hiding?"

"Usually, no one ever finds out."

Riccardo picked up his beer. "Ain't that the truth." He downed the last of it.

"When did you and Bethany become romantically involved?"

Riccardo glanced away. "About a year ago, probably."

"Before or after Jeffrey went missing?"

Riccardo met Mickey's gaze. "After."

"You sure?"

"Yeah, old man, I'm sure."

"So a year ago at most then?"

"Must be."

Mickey scribbled "Affair?" in the notebook. Out of the speakers a man was yelling about the ace of spades to a background of snarling electric guitars and lightning-speed drums.

"One final question and I'll be off," Mickey said.

"Shoot."

"Why pornography?"

"What, like, why do it?"

Mickey nodded.

"I dunno. I couldn't much stand doing anything else. Plus I like fucking. I'm good at it."

"Does it bother you that Bethany has sex with other men?"

"No, old man, it's like that. It's a job. Just like yours."

"If Bethany had sex with another man, privately, not for her job, would it bother you then?"

"It would tear me apart."

"Funny, isn't it? The subtle distinction."

Riccardo shook his head. "It's not subtle at all. You're talking about two different things—work, and betrayal. Sex, and love."

"Poetic."

"For you maybe. For us, it's life."

Mickey stood up. "All right. Well, thanks for answering my questions, Riccardo. I'll be seeing you."

"I'm sure you will."

Mickey pulled out his chair and turned to find Mary coming toward him with a camera in her bony hands.

"Sorry to bother you, Mr. Rourke, but before you go, do you think I could take your picture to put on the wall? It's not every day we get a celebrity in here."

Mickey looked at Riccardo, who shrugged at him, smirking. "Sure. Just so long's you catch me on my good side."

XXX

JULY, 1999

THEY WALKED UP A DRIVEWAY IN WEST LA STINKING OF SWEAT, in dire need of showers and fresh clothes, each lugging a sports bag containing all their worldly possessions. The Greyhound had dropped them off near Skid Row shortly after midnight and they'd spent the night shooting up there in their own corner of that little section of Hell, keeping their heads down and waiting for morning.

Richie passed an expensive-looking Audi on one side of the drive and a tacky water fountain on the other and rang the bell of a large suburban home, big bay window on the left. It being Saturday, Richie hoped the person he was looking for was home. Alabama hadn't said a word to him since he'd sent the deaf guy into the desert, not even when he'd explained that this neighborhood was where he had grown up, believe it or not, spending more time in Stoner Park around the corner than his house, saying the park was perfectly named because all he and his friends had ever done there was get high and skateboard—friends like Scotty Browning whose very house they were outside right now. But Alabama wouldn't even look at him. He'd pushed her too far beating up the deaf kid like that. He'd have to play it safe for a while, get her back on his side.

The door opened and Scotty Browning stood looking at them with his mouth hanging open, spectacles crooked on his face.

"Scotty! My main man. How you doin'? This is my wife, Alabama. We're in town, thought we'd drop by and say hello."

Scotty just stood there, stupefied.

"Can we come in?"

THE BROWNING FAMILY HOME was exactly as Richie remembered it: comfortable and lived-in, wooden floors and wooden stairs—wood all over the place—mass-produced kitsch on the walls, such as the phrase in thick sans-serif font hanging on a frame in the kitchen: "Having Somewhere to Go Is Home. Having Someone to Love Is Family. Having Both Is a Blessing." The insincerity of it made Richie sick.

"Listen Richie," Scotty said, standing hunched by the boiling kettle, "just so you know, my mom's gonna be home soon."

Richie stared at him. "Fuck is that supposed to mean?"

Scotty glanced at the floor, adjusting his glasses. "Just thought it was worth mentioning . . . How'd you know I still live with my parents?"

Richie frowned, the wooden chair bruising his ass. How had he known that? "You know what, Scotty, it simply never occurred to me that you would ever leave here. You're not that kind of guy."

"What kind of guy is that?"

"Normal."

Scotty held his gaze on Richie for a moment, then glanced away, sinking into himself like a sack of flour.

Alabama scowled at Richie. "This is a very nice house, Scotty. You live here your whole life?"

Scotty looked at her as if trying to decipher if she was being sincere or setting him up to fall. "Yep . . . since I was a baby."

"You twenty-five like Richie?"

"Twenty-four."

"Scotty was the baby of the group," Richie said.

"What do you do for work, Scotty?" Alabama said. "If you don't mind me askin' 'bout your business, that is." She flashed one of those disarming smiles at him.

Scotty loosened like a used condom. "Computer programming. Nothing too interesting." Quiet, shy about it.

Alabama said, "Oh, I love computers. They're just like big brains that can do anything."

"Well, I guess they are pretty fascinating," Scotty said, adjusting his glass-es.

"I read somewhere it's the best industry to be in right now, and only getting bigger," Alabama said. "You got the right idea, Scotty."

"Yeah, it's really taking off. Actually, I just got offered a job down in Palo Alto with a company called Google, you probably haven't heard of them but they're growing fast, really taking over." He looked at Richie. "I'm thinking about taking the job and moving there."

"Well shit. Look at Scotty, finally growing a dick."

"We're not kids anymore, Richie. You shouldn't talk to me like that."

Richie sniggered. "Take it easy, Scotty, I'm just playing. I'm happy for you doing well for yourself. You were always the one of us who was gonna make it, we all knew that."

Scotty touched his glasses, looking a little surprised, as the kettle started screaming. He switched the gas off and poured boiling water into three cups.

"We only have green tea," he said. "You know my mom . . ."

"I'll never forget her," Richie said.

Scotty ignored him. "You want regular or lemon-infused?" he asked Alabama.

"Oooh, lemon please."

"Me too," Richie said.

Scotty rooted inside a cabinet and dropped teabags into the cups and placed the cups on the table, pale-gold liquid swirling inside them, the scent of it like citrus and honey.

Richie blew on top of his and put it to his mouth, nearly melting the lips off his face. "Fuck, that's hot. Damn, tastes good though." Sweet and very slightly sour.

"It's very healthy, you should drink it more often," Scotty said, not moving from the stove. "Or are you still set on destroying yourself?" The little fucker growing a backbone.

"Don't worry about me, Scotty. I've done things you couldn't even dream."

Silence seized the kitchen. The cuckoo clock beside the doorway counted the slow march toward death.

Scotty said, "So, are you going to tell me why you're here in my house, after, what is it, seven years?"

"Could be. I'm here because I want to ask you, as my good friend from the good old days—my *best* friend—I want to ask you if I could borrow your car for couple days. Just while we get on our feet. Three days, tops."

Scotty had a face on him as if Richie had just rolled down his jeans and shat on the floor. "You've got to be kidding me."

"Also, I was hoping we could crash here for a few days. The basement is fine if it's still got that sofa and TV down there."

Scotty shook his head. "I can't believe this."

"Hey, what's the big deal? We were friends—"

"Friends? Is that what you think? Friends?" Scotty stood up straight, gazing down at Richie with a hard look in his eyes that Richie had never witnessed in them. "You've never been a friend to anyone, Richie, least of all me. No, you can't borrow my car and you can't crash here." He pointed at the doorway. "Get out of my house."

Richie jerked his neck back. Who does he fucking think he is? The little twerp could barely make eye contact with strangers last time Richie had seen him, now he was giving orders?

Richie glanced at Alabama's knuckles turning white on the table. He could play it safe, or risk losing her.

His moment of glory behind him, Scotty didn't look so confident anymore, doubt creeping into his expression. Yeah, starting to regret it, about to shit his pants.

"For old time's sake, Scotty, I'm gonna let that slide." Richie could practically feel Alabama's ass cheeks relaxing beside him. "But you're gonna have to give me one thousand dollars along with your car."

Scotty stared at him, back to looking stupefied.

"And this time," Richie said, pulling the Smith & Wesson out of his jeans and banging it onto the table, "I'm not asking."

XXX

"DIDYA HAVE TO TAKE HIS MAMA'S JEWELRY?" Alabama said, in the passenger seat of Scotty Browning's Audi, which, she supposed, was no longer Scotty Browning's. "You got the car, a few hundred in cash. Taking the jewelry just seems mean."

Richie sped the Audi toward the end of Scotty's street and turned the corner too hard, swerving to avoid a fire hydrant.

"I told him to give me a thousand bucks or I'd shoot him," he said. "I had to get him to make it up somehow. A man's only as good as his word."

Alabama rolled her eyes. She'd remember that next time Richie promised he'd take her out to a romantic dinner if she'd suck his dick.

"And besides," Richie said, "Scotty's mom is a class A cunt. One time, when we were real young, she slapped me with a spatula. A fuckin' spatula. Bitch. She was hot, though."

Richie slowed the car as they approached a fenced grassy area. He glanced at Alabama, a coy expression on his face. "I was thinking one of those necklaces would look pretty good on you."

She shook her head. "No Richie."

The Audi slowed almost to a stop.

"You really think so?" she said.

"Yeah, to go with those gorgeous green eyes."

Her heart damn near melted every time Richie paid her a compliment, and it became impossible to be mad at him.

"Here, lemme show you." Richie brought the car to a stop along the sidewalk next to the fence, behind which was a public swimming pool with changing rooms, a small skate park where kids drifted around on skateboards and smoked, and patches of well-trimmed grass lined by benches. He grabbed the plastic bag he'd shoved under Alabama's feet and fished through it.

"Yeah," he said, grinning, "I remember this one." He withdrew his hand. A silver chain hung from his finger, a smooth jade stone dangling at the end.

Alabama's breath caught. "It's beautiful."

"It's real jade. I remember Scotty's mom saying that before. I always knew I was gonna steal this one day, I just needed to meet the right woman to steal it for."

Alabama touched the stone. Smooth, almost slippery, and firm.

"Turn your head," Richie said.

Alabama twisted her neck and felt the jade bounce against her chest as Richie placed it over her, cold on her skin, but weighty. Worth something.

"Show me," Richie said.

She faced him.

His eyes opened up. "Wow. Look's incredible on you. I was right, it goes perfectly with your eyes."

"Really?"

"Look." Richie swung open the sun visor above Alabama's head and slid open the mirror.

Alabama angled the visor, glimpsing the jade resting above her cleavage and glinting in the light like something magical. She flicked the visor and gazed into her own eyes. They were almost the same color. Richie was right: the necklace had been made for her.

"I love it," she said.

"Me too. And I love you."

The surprise of it quickened Alabama's heart. She couldn't remember the last time she'd heard it.

Richie said, "I know that sometimes you don't agree with the things I do. And I know that sometimes I can get a bit . . . frustrated." He swept his long dark hair behind an ear. "I'm just trying to do what's best for us, give us the life we deserve. 'Cause, babe, nobody's gonna give it to us, no one's ever given us a damn thing. We gotta take it. Understand?"

Alabama nodded, feeling a little heat between her legs, wanting him to stop talking and kiss her.

Richie squeezed her knee, looking past her out the window now. "This is Stoner Park I was telling you about." Onto the next thing. "What a perfectly stupid name, right?"

"Richie?"

"What?" Still staring at the park.

"Richie?"

He looked at her. "What?"

"Kiss me, you idiot."

Chapter Five

JUNE, 1998

JEMEKA'S HANDS TREMBLED ON THE STEERING WHEEL, the windshield cracked above her, streaks of blood smeared across it. She focused on breathing, tried to slow her racing breaths. The man she had pummeled with her car was a dark shape in the rear-view, unmoving on the ground. Too dark to see Ray-Ray beyond him. Jesus, Ray-Ray.

She opened the door and the light in the roof blinked on overhead as the door chime sounded, harsh in the silence. The night warm and still. The gangster lay sprawled on his back. Jemeka moved toward him carefully. His right leg had twisted unnaturally. Blood stained his T-shirt and dribbled between his lips. She nudged him with her foot. Again, harder. The man's body shook but his eyes remained shut. He didn't make a sound.

"Ray-Ray," Jemeka called. Scanning the area, she spotted him slumped behind the Kawasaki. "Oh my god, Ray-Ray!"

She rushed toward him. "Ray-Ray, you okay?" Crouching beside him.

Bewildered, he gazed up at her. "Jemeka?"

She noticed him clamping a hand beneath his ribs. "You got shot?"

He shook his head, teeth gritted. "Just nicked the skin. Hurts like a motherfucker but I'm okay. What in the hell you doing here, Jemeka?"

"Saving your dumb ass looks like. We gotta get you to a hospital."

"No, I'm fine. Besides, we can't. What we supposed to say? You just hit a man with your car." He peered behind her. "He's dead?"

"I think so. Ray-Ray, I'm shaking. I never hurt nobody before. But I had to, didn't I?"

Ray-Ray nodded gravely. "You had to. But we can't tell nobody about this, not ever."

"What you doing out here?"

"Help me up and I'll show you." He stretched out an arm and Jemeka pulled him to his feet, Ray-Ray leaning a hand on the motorcycle, groaning. Hand clamped to his side, he shuffled toward the Cadillac waiting there with its trunk open and went around the rear.

"I came here to buy that," Ray-Ray said, pointing at what looked like a brick wrapped in brown paper—the only thing in the trunk, aside from a baseball bat shoved against the side. "Lucky you came when you did. That motherfucker was gonna kill me and take my money."

Jemeka couldn't believe what she was looking at. "Ray-Ray, what is this?"

He said nothing.

"What is this shit, Ray-Ray?"

"Cocaine."

"Are you *serious*? What in the hell were you thinking? How you supposed to pay for this? How much does it cost? What were you *thinking*?" Questions were firing out between her lips and she couldn't stop them.

Ray-Ray's expression had twisted into a grimace, either from agony of the wound or the prospect of answering her questions.

"How much, Ray-Ray?"

He swallowed. "Twenty thousand."

Jemeka's eyes nearly popped out of her head. "Twenty thousand! Boy, you better be joking."

"I did it for us, baby." He reached a hand toward her.

She slapped it away. "Where'd you get twenty thousand dollars?"

Ray-Ray glanced at his feet, looking guilty now.

"Where, Ray-Ray?"

"I . . . borrowed it."

"Where from?"

There was that grimace again.

It clicked in Jemeka's mind. "Oh Ray-Ray, no. Not Marsellus."

Ray-Ray nodded.

"You damn fool."

"It's gonna be okay, Jemeka. I got the money right here, I'll give it back to him, shit, I'll give it right back."

"You'll give it back just like that, huh? Like it's nothin'."

"I only borrowed it two days ago . . ." He gazed at the gunshot wound. "Baby, this hurts."

"And what, you were gonna sell this shit?" Jemeka said.

"It's worth ten times as much on the street if we break it up. I did it for us, Jemeka. So we don't have to struggle no more."

Jemeka glanced around, becoming conscious of how long they'd been here.

"Wait a minute," she said, realizing something terrible. "Oh, you fool, Ray-Ray. You goddamn fool."

"What?"

She pointed at the brick. "Who you think this belongs to?"

"What you mean? Him right over there."

"No, Ray-Ray. He's just a thug. Only one person owns the cocaine round here."

Realization dawned on Ray-Ray's face.

Jemeka nodded. "You borrowed twenty thousand dollars from Marsellus so you could buy the man's own drugs. Must have been stolen from him."

"Oh. Shit."

"Ray-Ray, you just killed the both of us."

XXX

"WHAT WE GONNA DO, JEMEKA? What we gonna do?" Ray-Ray paced

shirtless around the living room, a bandage wrapped around his belly. Jemeka had stitched the wound with thread, relieved to see that it had indeed been a flesh wound.

"Stop running round the room like a goddamn animal, for one thing," Jemeka said, looking up at him from the sofa, a kilo of cocaine and twenty thousand dollars at her feet. "You're making me anxious."

Alarm pulled apart his eyelids. "We left a man dead beside the river. I stop moving I'll have a heart attack."

"Nobody can trace us there. First thing we gotta do is get the blood off my car. Your friend Tyrone can put on a new windshield tomorrow. Yeah?"

Ray-Ray stopped moving and looked at her. "Tyrone?" he said, face a ball of confusion.

"He's the one works at the auto shop, right?"

"Tyrone don't work much these days, not getting the business."

"Well then Tyrone be damn glad when you call him up and tell him you need some work done."

Ray-Ray nodded, forehead creased. "Yeah, I guess he would. I guess he would."

"Now, Ray-Ray," Jemeka inched forward on the seat, elbows on her knees, waiting for him to meet her gaze. "Ray-Ray . . ."

"What?" Looking at her again.

"Don't say a word to Tyrone or nobody about what happened. When he asks what happened you tell him a bunch of young thugs smashed up my car with a baseball bat while we were inside the house. By the time you got out the front they'd run off down the street. You don't say nothin' else. Less you say about it, easier it is to lie." She watched Ray-Ray intently. "You hearing me, Ray-Ray?"

"I hear you, baby, I hear you."

"What you gonna say to Tyrone?"

"Some punk kids bashed the windshield while we were watching TV. Think it was the same kids who crashed that stolen Caddy into the street lamp last week. Pretty sure those kids live in the neighborhood—"

"Damn it Ray-Ray, you're predictable as hell." Her eyes rolled in her skull.

"What you go turning this into a story for? Some kids bashed the windshield and ran off, that's all you know."

"Some kids bashed the windshield, that's all I know."

Jemeka nodded. "Call Tyrone first thing in the morning. Right now you need to get some bleach and clean my car."

"Me? What you gonna do?"

Jemeka sucked in a deep breath and blew it out. "I'm gonna straighten things out with Marsellus."

"No way Jemeka—"

"One of us has to. I got a better chance at getting outta there in one piece than you do."

"Jemeka, this ain't right. It's my mistake."

"You sure are right about that. And now I gotta fix it. Just trust me, I know what I'm doing."

Jemeka opened her backpack and shoved the brick of coke inside with the cash. She zipped the backpack shut, rose from the sofa, and swung it over her shoulder.

"I'm sorry," Ray-Ray said, looking torn up about it.

"You will be." She started toward the front door. One hand on the handle, she gazed back. "Now wash the damn blood off my car."

She turned her back to him and left the house.

XXX

EVERYONE IN THE NEIGHBORHOOD KNEW OF MARSELLUS, but few, Jemeka included, had ever met the man. Although he lived in a mansion up in the Hollywood Hills, Marsellus spent most of his time running his businesses from the back of his sleazy Compton club, Underworld. Cops steered clear of the place and Marsellus himself, probably bribed or threatened or both. Once a respected leader of the community for loudly speaking out against police violence, Marsellus had become exactly what he had railed against, tales of his brutality frequently echoing across the neighborhood. Now he was simply feared.

"You better remember this, Ray-Ray," Jemeka muttered as she approached the club. Strips of pink neon around the door frame glowed bright in the dark alleyway as the deep bass of electronic music rumbled within.

Jemeka told the fat doorman that she had something which belonged to Marsellus and he brought her through a dance floor crowded with writhing bodies to a private area in the back where a tall man with blond cornrows and gold chain around his neck stared at her coldly.

"Lady here got something for Marsellus," said the doorman.

Blond cornrows moved aside to reveal Marsellus—massive, muscular and bald—sitting on a black leather sofa between two skinny women, one pale as milk, the other dark like Java.

Something wet brushed against Jemeka's ankle. She glanced down and flinched, surprised to see a chubby little dog sniffing her legs.

"Gabriel likes to sniff strangers," Marsellus said in the deepest voice Jemeka had ever heard. "Isn't that right, Gabie? Come here." Marsellus patted his thigh and the dog waddled toward him, jumping onto Marsellus's lap with surprising grace. Jemeka wondered how the dog could tolerate the music booming in from the dance floor.

"You got something for me?" Marsellus said to Jemeka.

"That's what she told me, Boss," said the doorman.

Marsellus kept his gaze fixed on Jemeka. "Come on and sit down then." He nodded at the women beside him. They rose from the sofa and floated out of this private area toward the dance floor. The fat doorman wheezed his way out of the room after the women, shutting the door behind him. Blond Cornrows stood guard with his back to the door staring at the wall ahead, expressionless.

Jemeka sat beside Marsellus on the edge of the firm sofa, backpack between her knees. This close Jemeka glimpsed wrinkles around his eyes, a barely discernible scar at the corner of his lip. A scent of spicy cologne. She opened the backpack and took out the brick of coke.

"I think this belongs to you."

Marsellus looked at the block in her hand. He sat back into the sofa, arms wide over each side. The sheer size of the man.

"You're either very brave or very dumb coming in here with that."

"I didn't take it, I'm just returning it."

Marsellus extended his hand. Jemeka gave the brick to him. It appeared smaller in his large palm. Marsellus signaled to Blond Cornrows who drifted over and handed Marsellus a small dagger. Marsellus sliced open the paper and slipped the blade in. He raised the powdered blade to a wide nostril and sniffed. His broad shoulders shuddered.

"Yeah, that's my shit," he said. He placed the brick on the table before them. "You know how I know that? 'Cause I got the best shit. You got some explaining to do."

Jemeka told him what had happened, praying he took it well. She finished with, "My boyfriend, he's a bit slow, can't see the truth before his eyes sometimes. But I saw. There's only one man round here who this could belong to, I told him. So I came here to return what's yours so no harm comes to my boyfriend. He didn't know it had anything to do with you." She exhaled, realizing how fast she'd been speaking, aware of the slimy sweat on her palms.

Marsellus gazed at her silently.

"My boyfriend, his name is Ray-Ray—Raymond Jones. He borrowed twenty thousand dollars from you. Well, I have your money right here and I'm hoping giving it back to you will cancel the deal you had with Ray-Ray."

She retrieved the twin bundles of cash from her backpack.

Marsellus nodded at Blond Cornrows, who took the money from her.

Marsellus said, "The man selling this to your boyfriend, what happened to him?"

Jemeka fought the urge to break eye contact. "He's dead."

Marsellus watched her for a moment. He gestured at Blond Cornrows and the man came toward them, the cash still in his hands. Marsellus grabbed one of the bundles and held it toward Jemeka.

Jemeka frowned. "I don't understand."

"I reward people who solve problems for me."

Jemeka looked at the cash: ten thousand dollars waiting for her to reach out and take it. She licked her lips and unburdened the man from his money. It felt good in her hand now that it had her name on it.

"I could use a woman like you," Marsellus said. "I pay well."

She hesitated. "I can't. That just ain't who I am."

Marsellus stared into her eyes, a vague smirk at the corner of his lips, as if seeing past her words and into some truth at the heart of her. "You know where to find me when you change your mind."

Jemeka broke eye contact, shoved the cash into her backpack.

It was only later that night when she realized that, in accepting the money, she had sold murder, and Marsellus had forever bought her silence.

XXX

JULY, 1999

RICHIE PULLED UP OUTSIDE A CONVENIENCE STORE and killed the engine. The street was quiet, just a homeless man with a bottle in a brown paper bag staggering along.

"You getting something in here?" Alabama said. "Can you get me a sandwich or something? Haven't eaten nothin' in days, feels like."

"That's 'cause you haven't eaten anything in days."

Richie opened the glove compartment and took out the Smith & Wesson.

Alabama's stomach lurched. "Oh no, Richie, what you doin' with that?"

"Just giving it some fresh air."

"Ain't we got enough money already?"

"Not if we wanna stay away from shitty motels. I said we wouldn't spend another night in a motel and I meant it. We're staying in the Four Seasons tonight."

"The Four Seasons?"

"The fuckin' Four Seasons."

"Richie . . ."

"You deserve it. I want the best for you."

"That's sweet of you, baby, but that's too fancy a place for a girl like me. I don't wanna blow our money on one night. Why don't we rent a nice one-bed outside the city? Somewhere quiet where we can lie in bed together all day and listen to the birds chirping in the morning. A place we can call our own."

Richie pondered the idea, the revolver resting on his knee. "You've thought about this a lot, huh?"

"Maybe a little."

"Our own place," Richie said, as if the idea had never occurred to him. "That doesn't sound so bad."

Alabama's heart swelled. Richie blew greasy hair out of his face. The homeless man staggered past the car and Richie watched him go.

"We'll need money to rent somewhere, though. Two months' rent at least, plus the deposit. And we still need a place for now."

"I know. A motel wouldn't be so bad if it was just for a while."

Richie frowned, gazing at the gun in his hand. "No. No motels ever again. We'll find a hotel that's more affordable, stay there till we find a place."

"Sounds perfect."

"But we're staying in the Four Seasons tonight."

"We are?"

"For one night in my goddamn life I wanna see how the other side lives."

Alabama rubbed her eyes, feeling suddenly exhausted. Debating with him on this would be futile.

"Just for tonight?" she said.

"Just for tonight."

"Okay. I guess it would be pretty exciting to stay in the Four Seasons. I've never been to a fancy hotel before."

"I have, but not since I was a kid. You're gonna love it." He squeezed her thigh.

"Don't we need a credit card to stay in a place like that?"

Richie smirked. He slipped his hand inside his jeans and it came out holding a plastic card. "Swiped it when Scotty wasn't looking."

A sour feeling came over her.

"Don't worry," Richie said, seeing her expression, "Scotty and his family are fucking loaded. Call it redistribution of wealth. He probably has dozens of these things, won't even notice it's missing."

"I guess we *are* already using his car."

Richie laughed like it was the funniest thing in the world. "Yes, we are. I'm not gonna push our luck, though. I don't know his PIN for cash advances at an ATM and besides I don't wanna make it too obvious, have the bank call him up. So it's just for the hotel. Which means we gotta do this store. Okay?"

Alabama nodded, feeling a little dizzy from all this crime.

"Anyway this is a good opportunity for you to practice being the getaway driver," Richie said. "'Cause if we're gonna do a big score, it's gonna depend on you keeping your cool behind the wheel."

Butterflies took flight in her stomach.

Richie shoved the revolver into his washed-out jeans, pulling his faded Led Zeppelin T-shirt out to hide the bulge.

"Stay cool and look normal. And keep the engine running. When I come out and get back in the car, take off immediately. But slowly. Casual. Unless I'm sprinting outta there. In that case, when I dive into the car, you take off like a goddamn rocket. Got it?"

"Got it."

Richie leaned forward and kissed her. "See you soon." He grabbed his shades from the glove compartment, placed them over his eyes and exited the car.

Alabama smiled, feeling a little giddy. Look at him—like a rock star. He could do anything he wanted, wouldn't let anyone tell him otherwise.

So why did he want so little?

SHE WAITED BEHIND THE WHEEL for six minutes that felt like sixty. At last the door of the convenience store was thrown open and Richie appeared, pulling his T-shirt over his jeans, the bulge of the revolver visible. He approached the car and slipped his shades up onto his forehead and winked at her.

Alabama smirked. The audacity of him.

A man came out of the store behind Richie. Alabama pointed at the man, screaming, "Behind you!"

Richie spun, one hand tugging the pistol from his jeans.

The man—muscular with a shaved head, tan skin and tight-fitting T-shirt—raised his hands, palms open. He said something to Richie.

Alabama glanced at the street. A car was approaching from the opposite direction. They had to get out of here.

The man spoke again and Richie nodded. The man's left hand reached for his pocket slowly. Now it was clutching a wallet, which the man opened, then handed something to Richie. God—was Richie mugging the guy?

Richie pocketed the item and shoved the gun into his jeans. He tipped an invisible hat at the man, enjoying himself, and came toward the car.

He opened the passenger door. "Hey babe." Dropping into the seat. "Let's get the fuck outta here."

Alabama tore away from the curb faster than she had intended, the engine roaring. In the rear-view, she saw the man standing outside the store, staring after them.

"Good haul," Richie said. "We're staying in the Four Seasons tonight. Woo!" He slapped the dashboard. An aroma of fresh sweat drifted from him, sweet and sharp.

"What did that man want?"

"Believe it or not, he offered me a job."

"What?" Alabama turned right onto Victory Boulevard, the glare of the hot sun dazzling her for a moment.

Richie laughed. "Yeah, he came out after me, I thought he was an off-duty cop, nearly fucking shot him. Then the guy says, I got a job for you if you want it."

"A job? What job?"

"I dunno, he gave me his card, told me to call him. Hang on." Richie stuck his hand into his jeans and rummaged around, ass hovering above the seat. "Here we go." He stared at the electric-yellow business card. "What the fuck? The guy works in porn."

"Huh?" The lights turned red and Alabama slowed to a stop. "Let me see."

She grabbed the card. At the top, a logo read "MidnightPussy Productions," and, centered below, "Riccardo Milano" above a cell number and email address.

"Huh." She returned the card to him. The lights turned green. She pressed the accelerator.

"You think he wants me to fuck on camera?" Richie said.

Alabama glanced at her husband, taking in his long, grease-laden hair, skinny frame, and syringe-scarred skin. "I doubt it."

"Maybe it's the big score we've been waiting for."

"Maybe he's just a nut." She opened her window a crack and a warm breeze kissed her shoulders. The sky was huge above them, blue as a dream. Maybe they could go somewhere nice, have a picnic on the grass, enjoy the sunshine. Griffith Park wasn't far, they could—

"We need to get junk," Richie said.

Alabama's heart sank. She'd almost forgotten.

Almost.

Chapter Six

JULY, 2000

EVEN AFTER ALL THESE YEARS Mickey still got a thrill from the growl of his '69 Catalina. He still remembered the look on Martha's face when he had driven it home that first time, her standing in the driveway, hands on hips, as if to say, Don't even think about it. But it had been too late and she had known it. Not that the car had been expensive back then—$3,500 it had cost him, equivalent to about $16,500 today—he'd just brought it into their lives without consulting her. But she had grown to love the car, too. Over thirty years ago now. May as well be three hundred. Gone is gone.

Mickey turned left off Orange Grove Boulevard onto Mar Vista Avenue. He could see his little yellow bungalow from here, fifty yards ahead in the neighborhood which someone had one day named Bungalow Heaven and the name had stuck. Heaven might be a stretch too far, but he enjoyed the area. It was peaceful.

Mickey glanced at Marco's café on the corner. The place played smooth jazz all day and offered the most delicious brownies. He considered sitting in for coffee and a bite. This had become a daily struggle: cheap drip coffee from home, or pricey café espresso?

Temptation had its way with him: he pulled up alongside the coffee shop. After a day among porn stars he'd earned this small luxury.

He was sitting on a stool at the bar by the window, sipping a rich and creamy espresso while Coltrane's sax wept like God, when his ringing cell phone broke the mood.

"Am I speaking to Mr. O'Rourke?" said a man on the other end.

"You are. What can I do for you?"

"I saw you at the studio today, found your number on your website."

"The studio?"

"MidnightPussy."

"Ah." Mickey sipped the espresso, letting the rich roasted flavor rest on his tongue. "May I ask who I'm speaking to?"

"My name is Larry. I'd prefer if we met face-to-face. I have some information that might help you."

"Information . . ."

"About Jeff."

"I see. When would you like to meet?"

"Can you do tomorrow morning, early?"

"I can," Mickey said.

"How about Griffith Park? I go for a run there at six every morning."

"That'll work."

"How's seven at the observatory?"

"Seven's good."

"Okay, I'll see you then, Mr. O'Rourke."

"See you then, Larry."

Mickey hung up and took his Moleskin from his pocket, jotted the appointment down. At this age one has to write down everything. He sipped the espresso and tried to listen to Coltrane but the jazz had become chaotic in his absence.

He left a decent tip for the waitress and returned to the searing sunshine, the coffee warm in his chest.

XXX

A GIANT SUN PEEKED OVER THE MOUNTAINS as night gave way to morning. The hills either side of North Vermont Canyon Road in Griffith Park dropped away on the south side to reveal a downtown Los Angeles the size of a child's model in the distance. Sky tinted with pink and purple spread over the vast landscape like the creation of a magic wand. Mickey savored it all cruising along in his Pontiac, the empty road smooth beneath the wheels. At this early hour California may as well have frozen in time, the silence palpable.

He parked in one of the many available spaces in the lot outside Griffith observatory, then sat on the hood and watched the city far below as it awoke and the misfits of night retreated to the shadows. When was the last time he'd brought Martha up here? It bothered him that he couldn't remember. Their very last time to stand up here and look down on all of this. The final moments come quiet as the breeze, and then they're gone and it's too late. Maybe it's better that way, the final moments true as any other.

"Mr. O'Rourke?"

Mickey turned around as far as he could without getting up off the hood. A man in a parrot-yellow two-piece tracksuit approached. An equally loud headband pushed back mid-length wavy hair. The man stood in front of the car.

"I'm Larry." He stuck out his hand.

Mickey leaned on the hood and got to his feet, Larry a good deal taller than him, easily six-three. "Mickey." He shook Larry's hand.

"Nice to meet you, Mickey. You'll have to forgive me a moment, I'm absolutely parched." Larry pulled the nozzle of the pink reusable bottle in his left hand and tipped it above his lips. Bold text along the length of his sleeve read "Dolce & Gabbana." Larry looked immaculate, not like he'd been running for an hour—and was that perfume?

"Much better," Larry said. "That was a tough one today." He ran a hand over his commercial-ready hair and tossed his head elegantly. Mickey felt as if he'd just wandered into some strange advertisement for a shampoo brand.

"Mr. O'Rourke, I knew Jeff. Not very well, but we were more than merely acquainted. I would hesitate to call us friends, although, I suppose, what is a friend, really . . ."

"Call me Mickey, please. I'm going to sit on the hood of my car again because these legs aren't what they used to be. You're welcome to join me, she can take it."

"Yes, thanks, my legs could use the rest as well. She's a beauty. Catalina? Gorgeous. I love Pontiacs." Larry sat on the hood beside Mickey. "My dream car is an original seventy-one GTO Judge convertible. Only seventeen of them in the world, you know. But that's a pipe dream . . ."

Mickey stretched his legs over the hood. Larry sure could talk. "So, you knew Jeffrey . . ."

"Yes, we were co-workers."

"And you still work there, at the studio?"

Larry nodded. "I do porn, like Jeff did. Well, not quite like Jeff did, he only did male-female. And threesomes, of course, DP, gangbangs. You know, the usual. But he didn't do gay porn like *moi*. Although we did share a scene once, an interracial orgy. That was a fun shoot. Actually, it was how we became friendly. Nothing brings people together like an orgy, I can promise you that."

Mickey shook his head. If ever he'd been uncertain, now he knew: he'd grown too old for this place.

He said, "Jeffrey was quite the star, or so I'm told."

"Gosh yeah, he was pulling in five figures per shoot. That's practically unheard of. He was the first star to have a dildo modeled on his—"

"I've heard," Mickey said. He was feeling the tiredness from waking so early this morning and could use a coffee. "What is it you want me to know about him?"

"Ah, well . . ." Larry crossed one leg over the other, hands together on his thigh. "Jeff had what you might call a drug habit. By which I do just mean a habit."

Mickey took out his notepad and wrote this down. "And you think

Jeffrey might have got caught up in something? Maybe owed money to his supplier?"

"Possibly, although he earned so much and, aside from the drugs, he lived like he was as broke as anyone else."

"How do you mean?"

"Jeff was born too late, belonged in the sixties with the hippies. He had no interest in money or material possessions. He lived in a tiny rundown apartment in Long Beach for God's sake. When I first met him—see, Jeff and I were two of the first regulars at MidnightPussy, which is how we met, so I've known him for a while—"

"How long?"

"Hmm, let's see. It must have been ninety-four." Larry's eyebrows crawled up his forehead. "Wow, that long already . . . We were both turning twenty-one the following year. We could fuck and suck and do all sorts of depraved things on set, but had to ask someone to buy us beer." Larry rolled his eyes. "America."

Mickey noted the year and men's ages. "But Jeffrey had a different lifestyle," he said.

Larry pursed his lips, nodding. "Jeff didn't ever buy new clothes or even a new car. He didn't drink or go clubbing or do much of anything at all except work on set or get high at home, mostly alone. That changed a bit when he started dating Bethany, she'd drag him to parties sometimes, and they hung out at her apartment, but he didn't change *that* much. Honestly Jeff was the least LA person who ever lived here."

"When you say he got high at home . . ."

"Weed, acid, mushrooms, harmless stuff like that. The cocaine thing started much later. I can't say this with any degree of accuracy but I think the pressure of being a star got to Jeff and he began to find it difficult maintaining his performance on set. Happens all the time."

Larry leaned close as if divulging a secret. "Most men think the most difficult part of being a porn star is having sex for so long without ejaculating. They're right but for the wrong reason. It's having sex for so long and *then* ejaculating that's the problem. Porn becomes a job like any other pretty quick. Then it's all about maintaining the erection and being ready to fire on command. It's not easy, believe me."

"I don't doubt it."

"So I think Jeff got into the cocaine thing as a means to get energized before shooting. Because Jeff was *the* most laid-back guy on the planet. I mean, if he was any more chilled-out he would've had to thaw himself in the sun. And he only used the coke while on set as far as I could tell, because he was his usual self otherwise, permanently stoned."

"What was Jeffrey's and Bethany's relationship like?"

"Oh, I don't know. They seemed to get on quite well. In a strange way, they were perfectly suited to each other."

"Strange how?"

Larry tossed his hair and swapped the positions of his crossed legs. "Well, Beth couldn't be more different than the guy. Talk about polar opposites. But I think that was their strength. Sometimes we fall in love with someone from another planet, am I right? But I think it was Beth who was more into it. She adored him."

"Is there anyone who might have had a problem with their relationship?"

Larry hesitated. "I don't like that Riccardo guy she's seeing now. And I think it's a bit convenient how quickly they got together after Jeff disappeared, if you know what I'm saying. But I don't think anyone from the studio would have hurt Jeff or anything like that. He was too harmless, you know? To be honest, it wouldn't surprise me at all if Jeff is lying on a beach somewhere laughing at the idea of us all wondering what happened to him. If you knew him, you'd know what I mean."

Larry slid off the hood and stood straight, stretching his arms toward the sky with a groan. Behind him the sun had emerged fully, hovering above the city like a spaceship.

"That feels better." Larry placed his hands on his hips. "I'm telling you all this because—and this might be nothing—but one time Jeff brought me with him to pick up some coke from his dealer. We were both going to a convention for work and decided to travel together. But Jeff needed to collect some stuff along the way. So we meet this guy in a park in North Long Beach—"

"Can you describe this man?"

"Black guy, young, maybe not even twenty-one. But tough, you know? Cocky. Not a guy to hesitate. Had a real mouth on him, too. He flipped out because Jeff had brought me along. Jeff told me after that they'd had an agreement to only ever meet alone and Jeff had sort of forgotten about it, like he does. I thought the guy was just trying to intimidate Jeff at the time, but when Jeff went missing soon after, well, I remembered it is all."

"How soon was this before Jeffrey disappeared?"

"A few weeks."

"Did you tell the police?"

"Gosh yes, I walked right into the station to tell them. I even told them the car the dealer was driving, a dark blue Subaru Impreza with these horrendous gold rims. Looked like the car of a teenage street racer. The police said they'd look into it, but I don't think they did." Larry took a swig from the water bottle.

Mickey chewed his lip. This felt like something, though he couldn't say why. Detective's instinct. "I don't suppose you know the dealer's name."

Larry swallowed the gulp. "Actually, I do." He wiped his lips. "His name was Floyd."

XXX

JUNE, 1998

RUNNING HER FINGERS THROUGH LATASHA'S HAIR while a 2Pac CD played in the background, Jemeka couldn't concentrate on the task. Ten thousand dollars hidden in a shoe box in the house was burning a hole through her mind. How long would it take to earn that much at the salon? Too long.

"You okay, J?" Latasha said, looking at her in the mirror. "You ain't with us today."

"Yeah, I'm just . . ." Jemeka shrugged.

"Ray-Ray?"

Jemeka nodded.

"It'll work out, man will come around. They always do. And if they don't, then they never was right anyway."

"Yeah. Thanks, Latasha."

Marsellus's offer spun around Jemeka's head like a carousel: *I could use someone like you. I pay well.*

Poverty had lost its charm.

"Only God Can Judge Me" out of the CD player.

You and me both, 2Pac. You and me both.

CLEANING UP THAT EVENING, Tanisha sweeping the floor and Jemeka tidying the benches, just the two of them in the place, Tanisha said, "You hear what happened to Clive Jones?"

"You mean since he was arrested?"

Tanisha nodded tragically. "Poor Clive got beat up bad in the holding cell. In hospital now, barely conscious. Poor kid."

Jemeka shook her head. "Poor Clive. He's so young. Never should've been in there."

"What, you gonna say he deserved it? Shouldn't have been dealing?" Tanisha holding the broom upright, looking stern.

"No. He shouldn't have got caught."

Surprise passed over Tanisha's face. She grabbed the broom in both hands and resumed sweeping. "Ain't that the truth."

Jemeka picked up a used mug and carried it toward the back.

Ten thousand dollars. That would fix the car—hell, it could buy a new one—repair the water tank, get the filthy walls and ceilings painted, pay off a chunk of her father's debts.

What could twenty thousand do?

XXX

JEMEKA HEARD A CAR ENGINE and knew it was her Ford Tempo without leaving the kitchen. She stirred the marinara of the spaghetti-and-meatballs meal she had prepared for dinner. Usually, the fragrant tomato-and-herbs aroma of the sauce got her taste buds tingling but today other thoughts occupied her mind. She dipped a finger in the marinara and tasted it. Sweet, savory, and the right amount of salty.

The sound of the front door shutting hard.

"Ray-Ray, what have I told you about slamming that goddamn door?"

"Sorry," Ray-Ray said from the hallway. "Somethin' smells good." He entered the kitchen. "It ready to eat?"

"Yeah, pasta's over there. Make up your own plate, I'm tired." Jemeka pulled a chair out from the table and fell into it, resting her elbows on the table and head in her hands.

Ray-Ray plopped enough pasta for three men onto his plate and drenched it with marinara, then covered it with so much Parmesan Jemeka couldn't see the meal beneath, the fungal smell of the cheese wafting over, turning her stomach. Ray-Ray carried the shockingly full plate toward the table carefully, tongue peeking out his lips in concentration. He managed to get the plate onto the table without spilling a drop.

"You eat all that you might die," Jemeka said, but knew better. The man would eat every bite and be rummaging in the freezer for ice cream.

"Car's fixed," Ray-Ray said in between noisy slurps.

"What you tell Tyrone?"

Ray-Ray sucked up the spaghetti dangling from his lips. "Nothing. He did all the talking for me."

"What you mean by that?"

Ray-Ray wiped his lips, missing completely the sauce smeared across his left cheek. "Soon as Tyrone saw the car, he said, Motherfuckers got you too, huh? Told me it's the third time in the last couple weeks those punks jacked a car and crashed it. He said they oughta be rounded up and had the bullshit slapped out of 'em. I just said I agreed with him and that was that."

"Good."

"We got a problem though."

"What's that?"

"Cost a lot more than I thought. Even with the discount he gave me, we looking at a thousand. And Tyrone needs the money soon."

Jemeka thought about the cash in the shoe box upstairs. Should she tell Ray-Ray about it?

"And there's something else," Ray-Ray said, setting his fork down. "Vanessa called."

Jemeka folded her arms. "What your goddamn sister want?"

"Mama's not well, needs surgery. Vanessa's covering most of it but she needs help."

"How much help?"

Ray-Ray wouldn't look her in the eyes. "Six thousand."

"Six thousand! Where we supposed to get six thousand? Your sister think we're swimming in money down here in the slums?"

"I told her we don't have it but she said she's stretched far as she can go already."

"Oh, I'm sure she's *real* stretched all right. I'm sure she sold that Mercedes and everything."

"I'll tell her we can't help."

Jemeka sighed. She'd have to tell him about the money. But with that six thousand plus the cost of fixing her car, there would be little left. So much for paying off their debts and fixing up the house.

She said, "No. We'll help."

Ray-Ray had resumed eating, frowning at her now. He swallowed a mouthful. "How we gonna do that?"

Jemeka rose from the chair. "I got something to show you."

Chapter Seven

JULY, 1999

ALABAMA HAD NEVER SEEN ANYTHING SO FANCY. With its gold-and-cream color theme and large window with mesmerizing view of downtown LA in the distance, their room at the Four Seasons in the heart of Beverly Hills was stunning. So stunning, in fact, and such a departure from the cockroach-infested hellholes they'd been staying at until now, Alabama felt her presence here was some kind of mistake, even a crime, and the police would be kicking in the door at any moment to drag her away from it all.

The bathroom excited her most. She ran her hand along the marble tub, shuddering with pleasure at the thought of being alone in the silence of this gleaming space, bubbly water up to her neck, smelling of roses.

"What you think?" Richie's voice reverberated inside the bathroom.

Alabama spun to see him leaning in the doorway. "Oh Richie, I love it. Never seen nothin' like it before. I never been in any kind of hotel, never mind one like this."

Richie cracked a rare smile. "I'm glad you like it."

Alabama went to him, wrapped her arms around his skinny waist.

"You need a shower," she said, resting her head on his chest.

"So do you."

"I'm amazed they let us in the door."

"I wouldn't have given them a choice."

Alabama chuckled, Richie's sincerity funny sometimes. Other times it made her want to claw out his eyes.

Richie said, "We need to get—"

"I know."

"You still got the number for that guy last time we were in LA?"

Alabama hesitated.

"Do you?" Richie said.

Alabama broke from the embrace. "Richie . . . he's a Nazi."

"A Nazi with heroin."

"I don't like him, Richie. Isn't there someone else we could get it from?"

"Not at short notice, I'd have to go find some people I know in bars, ask around. We need stuff now, got none left."

"But—"

"Bama, stop fuckin' around and call him, will you?" Aggression in his voice.

Remembering the experience last time she had bought from this dealer, Alabama's guts coiled into a knot. Richie didn't know anything about that.

"Call him," Richie said and exited the bathroom.

"OKAY," ALABAMA SAID, plopping onto the shockingly comfortable bed. "Heimdall said to meet him in an hour."

"An hour," Richie said. He scratched his forearm aggressively. "Okay. Where?"

"A motel."

Richie barked a humorless laugh. "Of course."

"It's the same one as last time. The Starlight."

"We'll leave in thirty."

"I better shower," Alabama said. She couldn't stop thinking about how sleazy Heimdall had been last time, that hunger in his eyes . . .

Richie said, "Let's shower together. Maybe you can show me a little love down south while we're at it."

"Maybe you can show *me* some love down there for once."

"Get the junk and I'll hitch a tent down there, stay for the whole weekend."

Alabama laughed, knowing it was bullshit. When she gets the heroin, making love will be the very last thing on their minds.

XXX

RICHIE SILENCED THE AUDI'S ENGINE in the parking lot of the motel, cutting off Ozzy Osbourne mid-sentence on Black Sabbath's "Paranoid."

Alabama fanned her face. The sun beat on the windshield as if it had something against the vehicle.

"The Starlight Motel," Richie sneered. "Not with all the smog in this fuckin' city. Which room?"

"That one." Alabama pointed at a door near the left corner of the building. "I remember." Sleaze oozed from the Starlight Motel in the same way she feared "junkie" radiated from her and Richie.

"You gonna be okay in there?" Richie said. "Maybe I should go in with you."

"He won't sell it unless I'm alone. He's paranoid to the extreme."

"Fuckin' dealers. I'll be right here."

Alabama kissed his stubbly cheek. "See you soon."

She got out of the Audi and the sun spilled onto her shoulders like a hot shower. Crossing the parking lot, she felt eyes watching her through dirty mesh curtains. No trace of a breeze, the warm air something she had to wade through.

She took a breath outside Heimdall's door, adjusted her dress, and knocked.

"Who's there?"

"Alabama."

"Door's open."

Alabama pushed the door. A cheesy stench of feet hit her as the dim room came into view. Heimdall held a bag of chips in one hand, lying on the bed in a wine-colored dressing gown staring at the TV on the dresser opposite, the volume low. Piles of clothes littered the small space. A pistol rested on the bedside table.

He smiled broadly at her. "Alabama, it sure is delightful to see you again." His British accent was a little high-pitched. Educated. It had the aura of wealth behind it, and Alabama wondered if he had come from a rich family over there. A long way to fall selling heroin out of the Starlight Motel stinking of cheese.

"Shut the door," he said.

Alabama closed the door, banishing sunlight from the room. She saw Heimdall clearly now: albino skin, curly hair and eyebrows the same chalk-like shade, thin lips, eyes so icy-blue they were hypnotizing. He shoved his hand into the chip bag and shoveled some into his mouth. Cheese puffs. That explained the smell.

"You see this whore?" He nodded toward the TV where a young and beautiful blonde in a skimpy yellow bikini sat on golden sand and spoke to the camera, looking altogether miserable about being young and beautiful and on golden sand. "This little slut has been on this show since the first episode. *Island of Love*, you seen it?"

"Don't think I have."

"The basic concept is a bunch of whores and pretty boys live on a tropical island together and find—" he made bunny fingers—"'love.' What this inevitably leads to, of course, is everybody fucking everybody else. Plus all the drinking, partying and so forth. I've watched every episode, so I have these slutty girls figured out, and this one right here, she's playing everybody against everybody. She has these pretty boys lining up, desperate for a go on her arse. Meanwhile she's turning all the other sluts on each other. I want to marry her."

Alabama didn't know what to say to this. She waited.

Heimdall beamed at her again. It was forced, unnatural. "I have something you want, yes?" Not moving off the bed, dragging it out.

"You're selling, I'm buying," Alabama said.

He chomped the cheese puffs and wiped his hand on the dressing gown, golden crumbles of the stuff sprinkling down his ghostly chest. "How desperately do you want it?"

Alabama hesitated and Heimdall's lips came apart in a grin. "I'm just joking with you, Ms. *A-la-ba-ma.*" On her name his voice had risen a couple octaves in a mock impression of her accent. He slid long legs off the bed—slim but muscular—and rose, much taller than Alabama. "How much do you want, then?"

"Twenty caps."

He whistled. "Big spender. You'll hurt yourself with that much." The stink of cheese puffs on his breath, yellowing his teeth.

"I'll be fine."

"You're looking good, Alabama."

Alabama swept her hair behind an ear. "Can we just do this thing already?"

Heimdall picked up the pistol from the bedside table, a black swastika tattooed into his wrist. He watched her face, as if hoping to see fear. His eyes were so blue they were like something alive in his head. But they lacked any glimmer of human warmth.

"Are you armed?" he said.

"What?"

He ejected the magazine from the pistol and slid it back into the weapon with a click. "Do you own a gun?"

"Oh. No."

"That's disappointing. You should be practicing your Second Amendment right. And you a Southerner. There's a civil war coming and you should arm yourself before it does. Before the fucking feds ban guns entirely."

He watched her. "Do you understand what I'm saying?"

"I guess."

"Mixed into this civil war will be a race war. You're going to want a means to protect yourself when groups of niggers are roaming the night looking for tasty white women like you."

Alabama grimaced, this sickening display of racism hard to stomach.

"I know, it's not a nice thing to imagine," he said, mistaking the reason for Alabama's reaction. "But you can thank the liberals for that, turning the western world—*our* world—into a fucking zoo." Rage had contorted his features into a hateful mask. Or perhaps this was his true face.

Then suddenly he smiled and the hate vanished and only his ice-cold eyes hinted at what lay within.

Alabama felt herself shudder, tried to hide it.

"I have something special for you this time," Heimdall said. He went to a chest of drawers at the side of the room, placed the pistol on top, and opened the top drawer.

"I have a new supplier," he said, his back to her. "No more of that black tar crap." He withdrew a thick brown envelope and tore the elastic band free. "This, right here, this is premium, world-class heroin." He slipped a long-fingered hand into the envelope and withdrew a sandwich bag the size of a fist filled with white powder.

A rush of desire shot up Alabama's spine and her body shivered with it.

"Look how white that is," Heimdall said. "As white as, well, *me*." He laughed and it sounded like something dying. "But you have to go easy with this. It'll blow your pretty head clean off."

Alabama licked her lips, the heroin calling to her like a lover. "How much?"

"Well, that's the thing." He placed the bag inside the envelope and tossed the envelope onto the chest of drawers. "This premium stuff isn't cheap. It's not easy to come by, either. But I'll give you a good deal because I like you, Ms. Alabama." His gaze flicked down to her chest. "I'll give you this world-class heroin for the same price as the black tar I sold you last time."

"Oh, thanks."

"But there's one condition."

Alabama tensed.

"You have to show me the cute little ass you're hiding under that dress."

Alabama swallowed, her mind racing to come up with a safe response.

He stepped toward her. "You're lucky I'm offering you this deal. This stuff at full price? Believe me, you don't want to know."

Alabama stood her ground, tried her best not to look intimidated. "I can't, I got a boyfriend. I'll just take whatever six hundred bucks'll get me."

Heimdall narrowed piercing eyes and his faux friendly expression lifted enough to glimpse the hate that writhed beneath. "What's the problem? Am I not pretty enough for you?" He took another step toward her.

Alabama backed away. "No, nothin' like that, it's just I got a boyfriend and—"

"Your boyfriend won't know if you don't tell him." Heimdall opened the dressing gown to reveal his nude body beneath, a semi-erect penis swinging like a chalk-dusted hammer between his legs.

Alabama gasped. Terror rooted her to the floor.

"Relax," Heimdall said, palm raised as if she was overreacting to his sudden nudity. "You want the smack, don't you?"

"I—I—" She was shaking her head, trying to tell him to stay away from her, but her tongue had twisted into a knot and the words wouldn't come.

He licked his lips, looking her up and down. Fully erect now, his penis had become pinkish, the eye of it hungering at her. The door was on her right. She was closer to it than he was, but he was just a few feet from her. Could she make it if she ran?

"P—please, stay away."

"Stay away?" Heimdall scowled. "Am I ugly to you? Is that it? Am I ugly to you, you fucking bitch?"

"No, no. Please—"

"*Please!*" Mocking her. "Dumb cunt."

Heimdall advanced toward her. Alarms wailed in Alabama's head.

Run!

She darted for the door. A blur of white at the edge of her vision and blinding pain erupted on her scalp. Alabama screamed as her body flung backwards, legs kicking out into space. Her back slammed onto the floor.

Heimdall stood over her as she struggled for oxygen. In his fist he held a clump of her hair. "I told you to relax and you had to go and freak out. Now look where that gets you."

He bent down toward her. Strong hands gripped Alabama's hips and flipped her onto her stomach. The breath still knocked out of her, she had little strength to fend him off. His palm pressed on the back of her skull, pushing her face into the filthy carpet, rough against her skin.

"Fucking slut."

Alabama tried to scream but her lips were crushed against the carpet.

"Don't act surprised," he said into her ear, hot breath on her neck. "You're a junkie whore, you knew this was coming."

The shocking weight of him on her legs. Her dress came up, his hand tearing her panties down her thighs.

"Please don't," she said, voice muffled. A tear slid over the bridge of her nose.

The full weight of him on her now, like a ball and chain.

"Whores like you take it in the ass."

Alabama squeezed her eyes shut as Heimdall pressed himself against her and then she was floating away from her body, away from her fear—away from the world.

XXX

"(DON'T FEAR) THE REAPER" by Blue Öyster Cult had always made Richie feel nervous for a reason he couldn't put into words, so hearing it now on the radio while he sat in the suffocating heat-trap Audi outside the Starlight Motel only increased his sense of dread. Alabama shouldn't have been in there this long. Something wasn't right.

"Fuck this." He grabbed the Smith & Wesson and shoved the car door open, stepped out into the full blast of a murderous sun. The curtains of Hemidall's room were closed, no way to see inside. Richie hesitated outside the door. If he burst in he might endanger them both. Should he knock?

Inside, a male voice said something, sounding aggressive, followed by what could have been a muffled scream.

Before Richie'd even made the decision he'd swung his leg back and flung it into the door. It burst open with a splintering crunch and the sight stunned him: Alabama on the floor, dress pulled up over her bare ass, and a shockingly pale, red-robed man on top of her like Nosferatu.

Heimdall's head snapped up and he locked eyes with Richie, the surprise in them turning to rage.

"What the fuck? You broke my fucking door." Heimdall got to one knee. "You broke my fucking door!" His chest was slim but muscular. A thick vein throbbed angrily on his sinewy bicep.

Richie glanced at Alabama, staring up at him with terrified eyes, mascara like ash down her cheeks.

Heimdall got to his feet, his penis pointing at Richie like an accusation. "You broke my fucking door!" Rage turning his head purple.

Heimdall spun and snatched something from the chest of drawers behind him and when he swung around to face Richie again the barrel of a pistol glinted in his grip.

Richie remembered the revolver in his right hand and squeezed. The weapon almost lurched out of his grip as the pop of it boomed in his ears.

Heimdall cried out and staggered backwards, his left leg buckling, dropping the man onto his knees. Snarling, Heimdall raised the pistol still in his fist.

Richie fired again. Heimdall gasped. It was the sound of a life ending. He dropped the gun and collapsed. Blood oozed from his belly, neon against his white skin.

Richie stepped closer and kicked Heimdall's gun across the room. Heimdall stared up at him, one eye closed over, blood dribbling out of his mouth and dripping along his chin.

Ears ringing, Richie pointed the revolver at the man's forehead. Richie's heart thundered in his chest. The room felt tiny, all the air choked out of it. Time had lost all meaning.

Heimdall's opened eye stared into the barrel tragically. He raised a hand slowly and held it out toward Richie, as if his palm could possibly save him from the bullet that would bring his life to an end here in this filthy motel room. He gasped out a word, too quiet to make out. Maybe it had been *please.*

Richie clenched his jaw. Anticipating the recoil, he tensed his forearm and squeezed the trigger.

Heimdall's arm thumped against the floor as his body stilled. A hole in his forehead now above that startling blue eye frozen into sorrow.

Richie glanced at Heimdall's palm. There was a hole through that, too. The shock of the murder he had committed came over him and he gasped, heaving at the air, remembering to breathe again.

"Richie . . ."

Alabama on the floor, naked and assaulted.

"Bama." He shoved the revolver into his jeans and rushed to her. "Jesus Christ."

"Richie . . ." She was crying, shuddering on the filthy carpet.

"I'm so sorry," he said. "I'm so goddamn sorry." The sound of her crying like a knife in Richie's gut.

"We have to go," Richie said. "I'm gonna help you pull these back up, okay?" Gently, afraid to frighten her, he slid her underwear slowly up her legs.

Alabama finished putting them on and clambered onto her feet, Richie supporting her.

"Good, baby, good," he said. "That's it, let's go."

Alabama sniffled and wiped her eyes, swaying on her feet. She looked at Heimdall, dead as the '80s. Her gaze moved past the dead man and settled on the chest of drawers by the wall. She moved toward it.

"What are you doing?" Richie said.

Alabama didn't answer, simply grabbed a thick envelope from the top, stepped over Heimdall's corpse, and floated out of the motel room like an angel into the bright California light.

XXX

JULY, 1998

FORCING HER WAY THROUGH MARSELLUS'S CLUB felt as strange the second time. The man himself lurked in the same private area, but now four women occupied the sofa with him, all snorting thick lines of blow off a silver tray. His chubby little dog slept in a little bed in the corner and Blond Cornrows stood like a soldier by the door.

"I knew you'd come back," Marsellus said. He squeezed his big nose and sniffed. "Maybe not so soon."

"I got money problems," Jemeka said.

"What about cop problems?"

"I took care of that."

"You took care of the body?"

"I took care of the evidence. The police don't give a shit about no body. Just one more dead nigger."

Marsellus clapped his giant hands together. "You see this woman, ladies? This is a real woman."

The women collectively bitch-faced her, one of them bending down now to snort from the tray.

"You're here to accept my offer of employment," Marsellus said.

"If it still stands."

"Consider yourself employed."

He grabbed the tray from the woman and brought it close to his face and made one of the lines disappear.

"I'm gonna give you back the brick you brought me. It's been waiting right here for you since you brought it here. You know why? 'Cause you were always gonna come back. You need to get yourself some scales, split it up mathematically perfect, you hear? When people buy my product, they get what they pay for. That means you don't cut it, neither. It's been cut enough already. My shit is premium. Which means it ain't cheap. My customers pay premium prices for premium product, so the reputation of that product is everything. Understand?"

Jemeka nodded.

"I want fifty thousand back for this. You sell this at one-fifty a gram and the whole brick adds up to one hundred fifty thousand. That's a lot more than the fifty Gs you owe me now, even if you sell some of that shit at a bulk discount. Up to you how you do it. Whatever's left after my fifty Gs is yours."

Jemeka's mouth felt dry, the numbers dancing in her vision. More money than she'd ever dreamed and all she had to do was sell something.

"When you're done with this brick come back to me and I'll give you another one. The faster you sell it, the more money you'll make. It ain't quantum physics."

Marsellus rose from the sofa and stood before Jemeka, his massive frame blocking the light like a solar eclipse. She had to crane her neck to look up at him.

He stuck out his hand. "Welcome to the crew."

Jemeka took his hand and shook it. He could grind her bones into dust.

"I look after everyone in my crew long as they do right by me. But if you fuck me—" he pointed a fat finger into her face—"I'll hang you from a hook and peel off your skin." His other hand tightened around Jemeka's. "So don't fuck me."

He kept hold of her hand and gazed into her eyes. The song booming inside the club ended and in the lull that followed the dog's snoring grew loud.

"What will I do if you fuck me?" Marsellus said. Pain jolted through Jemeka's arm as he crushed her fingers.

"Hang me from a hook and peel off my skin."

Satisfied, Marsellus nodded and released her hand. Her fingers throbbed. She was scared to move them.

"Get the fuck out my club and go move some product," Marsellus said, turning his back to her.

PART II

Chapter Eight

JULY, 2000

WHEN MICKEY HAD CALLED BETHANY to give her an update, she'd asked him to grab a late dinner with her instead, claiming she found phone calls too impersonal. Surprised at such words coming from a young woman, Mickey had enthusiastically agreed, had even skipped lunch so he could savor the meal (and stick to the daily caloric limit imposed by his doctor). Now, with growling stomach, he parked outside Sunset Diner coincidentally as a bronze sun slowly descended below the horizon, the twilight sky bubblegum pink. Thoughts of the bacon, eggs, waffles and strong black coffee he'd soon wolf into made him salivate.

Customers had occupied about half the tables inside but Bethany was not among them. Mickey chose a booth by the window and marveled at how quickly the young waitress poured him coffee. He ordered the all-day breakfast and nearly drooled at the aromas of sizzling bacon and toasting bread emanating from the kitchen. He sipped the coffee: strong and dark with notes of chocolate and caramel.

He'd drifted into his thoughts totally when a hand touched his shoulder. Bethany stood beside him, big red sunglasses matching her painted lips. She wore a slim-fitting mini dress with white and baby-blue stripes.

"Heya Mr. O'Rourke."

"Nice to see you, Bethany. Please, call me Mickey. I've never been one for formalities."

The waitress was over pouring coffee before Bethany had settled into the seat. She ordered the dairy-free grilled cheese.

"Good service here," Mickey said.

"Even better food."

"Tell me, what in the world is a dairy-free grilled cheese?"

One corner of Bethany's lips raised in a smirk.

"Whatever it is, it must be the reason you look so good," Mickey said. "I could take a leaf from your book."

"Thanks, Mickey." Her smirk faded and she stared out the window.

"How was your day?" Mickey said.

"Shitty."

"Were you working?"

"No, off today. I was supposed to spend the day with Riccardo, but . . ." Staring out the window again.

The waitress brought over Mickey's all-day breakfast. He thanked her and she departed.

"You don't mind if I begin without you, do you?" Mickey said. "I skipped lunch and I'm afraid if I don't eat in the next sixty seconds, I might not make it."

"Of course not. I forgot that was even a thing. The whole waiting for everyone's food thing, I mean."

"Maybe it isn't anymore, I really have no idea." Mickey stabbed a piece of bacon into waffle and slopped some fried egg on top, raised it to his lips. The salty-smoky flavor of it heavenly.

"So how's the case?" Bethany said.

"Good. I'm only getting started, of course, and these things take time, but I have a few directions to go in." He considered how much to divulge, the line between transparency with the client and divulging information that might harm the case always a thin one. "A co-worker of yours called me, said he had information about Jeffrey that might help. So I went to see him."

Bethany looked right at him. "Who?"

"He said his name was Larry."

"Larry? There's two of those. You must mean Gay Larry."

"Do I?"

"Extremely fashionable, talks a lot."

"Ah."

"Him and Jeff were close in their own way. Jeff didn't have much friends, not really his thing. What did he say?"

"Not much, he just told me . . . he told me that Jeffrey regularly bought cocaine."

Bethany glanced away. "I always hated that."

She stared out the window again for some time until Mickey said, "Is everything all right, Bethany?"

"Not really." Her voice quiet, a little choked. Was she crying? It surprised Mickey how much the prospect of Bethany upset felt like a wound.

"What happened, dear?"

She was looking at him, considering her response. She lifted the shades off her face.

Mickey winced: an angry bruise encircled her right eye, black and purple. "Who did this to you?"

"My asshole boyfriend."

"Riccardo did this? I'll have a word with him."

"No, no—" a soft hand over Mickey's wrinkled one—"please don't."

Mickey felt a pang in his chest at the confused hurt in her gaze. This—this was why he and Martha had chosen to remain childless: the world was a tough enough place without adding to it the fears and pains of caring so deeply for daughters and sons.

"Has he done this to you before?"

"No."

"You must have been quite shocked?"

Bethany looked like a lost child. "Yes. I was."

Mickey sighed. "I hate to say it, but if you stay with him, it won't be the last."

Bethany hid her face behind the shades. "You remind me of someone, Mickey."

"I do?"

She nodded.

"Who, may I ask?"

"My grandpa."

"Oh. Well, that's nice . . . Do you see him often?"

A pause.

Bethany said, "I haven't seen my family in a long time."

She was looking out the window again, and through the gap in the side of her sunglasses Mickey saw a deep sadness in her eyes.

Cursing his lack of tact, he forked bacon into his mouth. The sun had set completely now, night black against the glass. The hour of wolves.

"Do you have grandkids, Mickey?"

"No, I don't have any children."

"Oh." Sounding surprised about it. "You just didn't want to?"

"My wife and I never really got around to it. Then by the time we flirted with the idea, it was a little too late. We thought about adopting but decided against it in the end. It was just . . . it was easier to only have to worry about one person."

"How do you . . ." Bethany hesitated. "No, never mind."

"It's okay, you can ask what you want to ask."

"How do you feel about that decision now?" She was looking at him intently.

"I think it was the right decision."

"You don't kind of wish you had kids?"

"No."

Bethany nodded. "Well, at least you and your wife have each other."

Mickey's expression must have given something away, because Bethany said, "Oh, I'm sorry, I thought—"

"It's no problem. My wife passed last year."

Sympathy oozed out of her. "Oh Mickey, I'm so sorry to hear that. You must miss her terribly."

"More than I thought possible."

At this Bethany looked about to burst into tears, so Mickey added, "But, like me, Martha was old and it was her time to go. We got to say goodbye, so I can't complain too much. I'll see her again some day."

"How long were you guys married?"

"Forty-seven wonderful years."

"That's so sweet. I hope I can say the same one day."

"Someone as lovely as you will have no problem with that, Bethany. But I don't think you'll find it with someone who would ever raise a hand to you."

Bethany sighed softly. "Yeah . . . Jeff never would have hit me. Never. I miss him."

They sat in silence as the waitress brought out Bethany's meal.

"Mmmm, looks good," Bethany said, unrolling the knife and fork from her napkin. "Hey, since you don't have kids and all, maybe we could do this again sometime?" She smiled at him.

"Yes, we definitely should." He didn't think she had meant it but it had been a nice gesture all the same.

Mickey finished his meal as Bethany began hers, thinking about the strange twists of fate that deliver us from one path onto another we share with someone else, however briefly.

HOLLYWOOD BOULEVARD AT NIGHT WAS A DREAM IN NEON. Mickey cruised along the strip, colorful lights blurring by like hallucinations. On his right, the El Capitan Theatre lured customers in like a Vegas casino, while the Walk of Fame preserved stardom on his left. Tourists bustled beneath the blinking signs like extras in the giant story of this land of stories, hoping for a real-life glimpse of that other world just behind the veneer of this place. In the '50s, Hollywood Boulevard had looked different—less buildings, less vehicles, less pedestrians—but the aura of the strip, the energy, hadn't changed at all.

Stopped by red lights at the intersection of Hollywood and Highland and inspired by the mood, Mickey inserted his cassette tape of Mile Davis's *Kind of Blue*. The walking-bass opening of "So What" soothed like a balm.

Mickey reached the parking lot outside LAPD's Hollywood Station as the song came to a close. He turned the music off, let the silence wash over him, and went inside the station.

Some young guy Mickey didn't recognize sat behind the desk.

"Can I help you, sir?" said the young cop.

"Is Officer Reggie Dixon working at the moment?"

"What do you need him for? Maybe I can help."

"Reggie's an old friend, I need to speak with him about something important. Fetch him for me, will you, son?"

The cop hesitated, then got up off the chair. "One moment, sir," he said, not looking thrilled about it, and disappeared into the station.

Alone now, Mickey examined the photographs covering every inch of the walls in this reception area, most of them annual group photos of the station's staff. He focused on one in particular dated 1946, one of the oldest on the wall. There he was, twenty-four-year-old rookie Mickey in his first and only year as a police officer. He appeared fresh-faced and eager in the photograph but Mickey saw the trauma of World War II in the eyes of his younger self. He remembered the year well. An awful year. To have experienced the horrors of that terrible war only to return and witness what he had witnessed as a police officer in his first year upon returning, it had been too much for that young man to bear.

"Well well, if it ain't the clever mick." Reggie stood by the door as the younger cop resumed his post at the desk.

"Reggie. You look older."

"I sure as shit feel it. Come on back here."

Mickey followed Reggie into the station proper. It looked exactly as he remembered it: functional, messy, saturated in testosterone.

Reggie sat behind a meticulous desk—the only one not cloaked with unorganized papers—and gestured to the chair opposite.

Mickey sat into it.

"You never came to the barbecue last summer," Reggie said. "Too busy falling in love again?"

"If only."

"Mick, you've been coming to our family barbecue for—shit, how many years is it since we met?"

"We met in seventy-five."

"Lord. So you've been coming to our family barbecue every year without fail for that long. Why'd you break the chain? Odetta was upset you didn't show."

"Oh I don't know, Reggie. I guess last year in particular I felt like an old man without a family of my own. It was just easier not to go."

"That's why it's important you came, brother. All that isolation ain't good for you. You better come this year or Odetta'll have a fit. Woman will drag you from your home and I won't be able to stop her even if I wanted to."

"You're probably right."

"So you'll be there?"

"I'll be there."

"Good. So what you want from me then?"

"I need your help looking into someone. For a case I'm working on."

"What kind of case?"

"Missing person. A porn star disappeared a year ago and the girlfriend hired me to do some digging. Hopefully not in the literal sense."

"But you're thinking the literal sense is exactly where it's going."

"It seems that way at the moment."

"Who am I looking into?"

"A drug dealer named Floyd. I haven't got a surname, but he's active in the Compton area. Or he was a year ago."

"Your porn star bought from this Floyd?"

"He bought cocaine and cannabis from him regularly."

"Your porn star's white?"

"That's right."

"And he bought drugs from a brother in Compton?"

"Nearby. North Long Beach."

"You got a description of this Floyd?"

"Young, Black, got a swagger about him."

"Oh good," Reggie said, "that sure narrows it down."

"My lack of information is why I'm here, Reggie. But I have something else. He drove a dark blue Subaru Impreza with gold rims."

Reggie scratched his silver beard. "Compton ain't in my jurisdiction, Mick. You know that."

"I'm not asking you as a police officer, Reggie. You know that."

"You think 'cause I'm Black I can just hop on down to Compton and toss some questions at the brothers?"

"You live in Compton."

"Yeah, and I get by there 'cause I don't go shittin' where I eat. Round there I'm just some old guy happens to work in LAPD Hollywood. It's a dangerous place to be a cop asking questions, don't matter what color you are."

"You've helped me out like this before, a few years back. It didn't seem to bother you then."

"I wasn't six months from retirement then."

Mickey shook his head. "All right, forget about it. I'm sorry I asked. I'll see you at the barbecue."

Reggie extended an arm. "Wait now, I'm just bustin' those low-hanging balls of yours. As it happens, I know a kid from the block who knows all the players round there. If this Floyd with the gold rims is active on those corners, this kid will know him."

Mickey stared at him. "Are you serious?"

"What?"

"You couldn't have just said that at the beginning?"

"Where's the fun in that?"

Mickey rose from the chair. "Call me when you find out something."

XXX

JULY, 1999

RICHIE'S HANDS TREMBLED as he tapped some of the heroin into a bowl.

The white stuff, he couldn't believe it. Wouldn't need the citric acid for this. Probably wouldn't even need heat. He measured out a conservative amount of the powder, allowing for the extra strength, and brought the bowl under the tap in the hotel room's mini kitchen. He paused, remembering something one of the workers at a needle exchange in Salem, Oregon, had said: *Protect your veins. Sterilize everything, even the water.*

Richie hesitated, thought about running water from the tap as it was. But, no, better to be smart about this. He filled the electric kettle a quarter of the way and set it to boil. The sound of the click as the kettle began to boil made him flinch, his mind jumping straight to the sound of the Smith & Wesson booming in his hands.

Jesus fucking Christ, he'd killed a guy. He hadn't let the fact of it settle on him yet and he was determined not to start now. The man had deserved those bullets if ever anyone had. He wouldn't go feeling guilty over killing a Nazi rapist dope dealer. Fuck that.

He was surprised by how easy it had been to take a life. It was nothing. He could do it again if he had to, and this knowledge empowered and terrified him.

Could he do it for money?

Maybe.

Would he do it for money? Not someone innocent, but an objectively bad motherfucker?

Maybe. It was easy money.

Still, that image of the guy dead on the dirty carpet lingered in Richie's periphery. Heroin would sort out that problem—it's what the stuff was made for.

Alabama hadn't moved, facedown on the bed.

"You okay?" Richie said, sitting beside her.

Nothing. Not a word since they'd left the motel.

"You're gonna feel better in a minute, I'll take care of you."

He rummaged through Alabama's stuff looking for the supplies—being the careful one, she was in charge of their drug use—and found them at last beneath layers of panties in her sports bag. Snatching a sterile syringe and needle, bag of cotton balls, and Alabama's spray bottle of disinfectant, he marched to the mini kitchen and placed the items on the sole countertop. Trying to remember Alabama's ritual which had kept them safe injecting until now, he sprayed the washboard beside the countertop with disinfectant, wiped it down, and washed his hands thoroughly. Next he poured some of the boiled water onto the heroin, his pulse quickening as the powder dissolved easily into the water, feeling that deep desire for it in his loins. Expecting the vinegary stench he had come to enjoy, Richie was momentarily surprised (maybe even a tiny bit disappointed) when no such smell came. He'd been using that black tar shit for too long. He brought his nose close to the heroin mixture and sniffed. No odor whatsoever. No—something faint, a vaguely medicinal scent. But virtually odorless, the purity probably sky-high. That familiar pang deep in his gut: a kind of lust mixed with butterflies. But the good kind. The falling in love kind.

Richie dropped a cotton ball into the mixture and watched it drink up the liquid. The pangs in his gut had swelled to his chest now, palms getting sweaty. Soon his body would be screaming for it. He tore open the packets containing the syringe and needle, attached the paraphernalia together, and slipped the needle into the cotton. The heroin was likely purer than he'd figured when he had measured it out. He would use less, see how it goes.

He pulled the plunger slowly. Liquid surged into the syringe. Richie licked his lips, Paradise within reach now, unbearably close.

But first he had to sort out Alabama.

He went over to her. "Bama." Squeezing her calf on the bed. "I got a shot made up for you. I did it right, the way you do it."

Alabama didn't respond and for a moment Richie feared the worst until she sat up and held out her arm without looking at him.

"Shit, the fuckin' tube," Richie said, and hopped off the bed to rummage again in the sports bag, one hand holding the heroin-filled syringe upright beside his head. He found the tourniquet and placed it onto Alabama's lap.

She didn't move, still staring at nothing.

"Babe, you gotta help me out here, I can't put this thing down."

Alabama shifted her gaze to the rubber tubing. Blank-faced and without a word she wrapped it around her slender bicep expertly and held out the arm toward Richie palm facing upwards, staring into space again.

A thick vein exposed itself on the underside of Alabama's elbow, dotted with needle marks. Richie scanned for a fresh entry point and, finding one, said, "Okay baby, you're gonna feel much better now." He kissed her cheek. "I'll be right behind you."

He inserted the needle into the vein and drew back the plunger a touch, wispy blood mixing with the heroin solution. Pushing the plunger until half the solution remained, Richie looked into Alabama's eyes. A sharp intake of breath as her eyes glazed over and pupils shrank to dots.

Richie withdrew the needle and Alabama fell backwards onto the bed. He watched her for a moment to make sure she was okay. Satisfied, he unwrapped the tubing from her arm and got to work getting it around his own.

XXX

A FUCKING BIKER BAR, that's where the porno guy, Riccardo, brought him. Eyeballs on Richie as he entered. Iggy Pop like a dark prophet yelling out the speakers. Smoke as if the place was on fire, the stench of it mixing with the swamp-like aroma of old beer and body odor, the latter no doubt caused by the poorly considered combination of leather and California.

Riccardo brought him to a quiet corner of the bar where they sat opposite each other at a dirty little table.

Richie came out with it: "You bring me all this way you better buy me a beer."

Riccardo showed no discernible reaction to this other than getting up from the table. He spoke with a red-head behind the bar. She looked like she could use a few good meals. Maybe a bath while she was at it.

Riccardo returned a minute later with two bottles of Bud, slid one over to Richie. Ice-cold to the touch, it went down about as smooth as Richie could have hoped.

Riccardo just sitting there, looking at him.

Richie sipped the beer again, not in a rush to get back to his catatonic wife.

"I guess you want to know what the job is, huh?" Riccardo said.

"Seems like it would be a good place to start."

Riccardo hunched broad shoulders and leaned over the table. "You ever do this kind of thing before?"

"You still haven't said what this kind of thing is."

"No, I know. I mean jobs for people. Jobs that aren't strictly legal."

Richie could have laughed at the guy. May as well humor him. "Sure, I've done this kind of thing before."

Riccardo nodded. "I thought so. Okay. Good." He wrapped a thick hand around his Bud and drained half it in a gulp. Leaning in again: "I knew you were the right man for the job the second I saw you."

"Yeah, why's that?"

Riccardo chugged the beer. "A look in your eyes. I can't really explain it, man. You walked into that store and pulled out a gun and right away I knew you were the guy. I've been waiting for you to show up, I just didn't know it."

Richie almost rolled his eyes. He had no time for this destiny-and-horoscopes bullshit.

"This thing I want you to do," Riccardo said, "it's something I've been thinking about for a long time, I just never knew what the thing was, exactly, until we met. When you walked into that store, you brought this idea with you, even if you didn't realize it."

Richie'd had enough. "You gonna tell me what the job is or hint at it all fuckin' night?"

Hunched over the table like an inmate at mealtime, Riccardo glanced over his shoulder. In a low voice he said, "I need you to get rid of someone."

Richie couldn't believe his ears.

Riccardo said, "No, no, not like that, I mean scare him away. Out of LA. For good. Is that something you could do?"

Richie sipped his beer. Was this guy for real? "That depends."

"On what?"

"How much you can pay me."

"So you think you could do it?"

"Like I said—"

"Five thousand."

Richie didn't miss a beat: "Ten."

Riccardo hesitated.

Richie said, "You really gonna haggle me on this? What the fuck you think this is, the farmer's market? Ten's the price. Take it or leave it."

Riccardo nodded. "Okay. Ten." He licked his lips anxiously. "How would you do it?"

"That's for me to figure out. How you gonna pay me?"

"Cash."

"When? How will you know the job's done?"

Riccardo frowned, clearly hadn't thought this far ahead.

Richie shook his head. "Listen—what's your name?" Pretending Riccardo wasn't significant enough to remember his name.

"Riccardo."

"Listen, Rick, I don't have patience for bullshit. I do a job, I get paid. Right then and there, no fucking around. Understand?"

Riccardo nodded curtly.

"Good. I'll bring you proof that I've completed the job. Then you'll give me the cash. Then we go our separate ways."

"What kind of proof are you thinking?"

"You let me worry about that." Richie leaned back into the seat. "Motorcycle Man" by Saxon was playing now. Probably got these bikers' dicks hard.

"So who is he you want me to make disappear?" Richie said.

"Not disappear in the literal sense. You got that, right?"

Look at the little pussy—hasn't got the balls to admit he's talking about murder. "Whatever you say, Rick. Who is he?"

"You watch porn?"

"What?"

"Do you?"

"No."

"Sure," Riccardo said, looking smug about it.

"I don't."

"Come on man, everyone watches porn."

"Not me." Too busy getting high, dickhead.

"Yeah, right. Well, if you did watch porn, you'd probably recognize him. Name's Jeffrey Strokes. He lives in Long Beach. I got his address right here."

Riccardo removed from his jacket pocket a scrap of paper with an address scrawled messily upon it. He handed it to Richie.

Richie said, "What the guy do, steal your glory hole?"

"In a way, that's exactly what he did."

"I'll be scoping the guy out before I do anything, check out his routine, so don't hold your breath." Richie stared at him. He knew he shouldn't look a gift horse in the mouth but he had to ask: "You really think the best way to do this is asking a random guy off the street?"

"You weren't a random guy off the street."

"A random guy holding up a store."

Riccardo grinned, loosening up. Maybe it was the beer. "Like I said, I had a feeling about you soon as you walked in the door. It was like . . ." He sucked his lips into his mouth in concentration. "It was like, seeing that gun in your hand, knowing you could have shot up the place with me in it, then you walking away with the money so calmly, like it was nothing—I dunno, man, something clicked in my head and a plan I hadn't even realized I'd been considering made itself known to me."

He twirled the empty Bud in his fingers. "Besides, who am I meant to ask? Not like I can look up someone in the Yellow Pages."

"One of your biker friends couldn't help you out?"

"These guys? They just look tough. Half of them work in offices. Besides, they can be linked to me. You and me, we got no connection."

Maybe the guy was sharper than he looked. But in that case, he shouldn't have brought Richie to his local haunt.

Richie downed the remainder of his beer, cool and watery and tasting slightly of sweet rice. He stood up. "I'll be in touch."

Riccardo grabbed his arm. "Don't hurt him, all right? Not more than you have to. He's not a bad guy, just in the way."

"That would make you the bad guy then, wouldn't it?"

Richie left him trying to figure it out.

Chapter Nine

JULY, 1998

"SO HOW WE DO THIS?" Ray-Ray said, sitting beside Jemeka on the living room sofa. The block of coke sat on the dressing table like Pandora's box, dangerous and intoxicating. "Well, we're gonna need help," Jemeka said. "This is a kilo. That's a thousand grams. Which means a thousand one-gram bags. We can't sell all that."

"We should do eight-balls too."

"Eight-balls?

"Three-point-five grams."

"All right. Let's see . . ." Jemeka counted on her fingers silently. "A hundred fifty eight-balls is five hundred twenty-five grams. That leaves four hundred seventy-five one-gram bags. If we do it that way, that's a total of . . . six hundred twenty-five bags."

Ray-Ray whistled. "We gonna be rich, baby. We gonna be rich."

"If we don't go to jail first. Another reason we want some help. Reduce risk. I'm thinking we don't sell any of it, leave that for the help. We reduce profits but we also reduce risk. I don't wanna be slingin' dope."

"You got somebody in mind?"

"Please. That's your job, Ray-Ray."

Ray-Ray nodded. "You know, we could be a lot richer if we turned this shit into rocks."

"No," Jemeka said quickly. "No crack. That poison's hurting too many people. *Our* people."

Ray-Ray looked about to argue it, but changed his mind. "Okay. We should at least cut it some. Double the profits."

Jemeka considered it, remembering Marsellus's warning. "No, Ray-Ray. We can make a lot as it is. Let's not get greedy."

"Okay, okay," Ray-Ray said. He stood up. "Wait here."

"Where you going?"

"To find the help."

"Right now?"

"Yeah, right now. It's time we left poverty behind." With that he slipped out the front door and vanished into the night.

Jemeka eyed the coke, doubt creeping into her thoughts.

Selling drugs.

Making money from people hurting themselves.

What are you doing, Jemeka?

But it was too late to go back now and she knew it. She swallowed her doubt and shoved the block beneath the sofa where she could no longer see it.

TWENTY MINUTES AFTER HE'D LEFT, Ray-Ray returned with a kid Jemeka recognized from the block. He wore a green Adidas tracksuit with a heavy gold chain hanging over it, fat rings on his fingers. A glint in his eyes suggested a certain unpredictability, the kind of eighteen-or-so-year-old raised on the streets of Compton forever trying to prove he belonged there. The kind of young man who would shoot you dead before he would ever admit to feeling afraid.

"This is Floyd," Ray-Ray said, entering the living room ahead of the kid. "Floyd, this is Jemeka."

"Hello Floyd."

Floyd just looked at her.

"Sit down," she said.

Floyd dropped onto the sofa as if he owned it, his back to the bay window, steel bars over the glass outside.

Ray-Ray sat on the sofa beside Jemeka. "Floyd wants to help us out."

Floyd stared at Jemeka. "You lookin' to move some powder."

"That's right."

"How much?"

"Kilo to start."

"No rocks?"

Jemeka shook her head.

"Why not?" Floyd said.

"Don't you worry about that. Can you sell it or what?"

"Yeah, but not round here. Niggas too poor for that shit here. All they want is crack. We gotta branch out."

We. Already inserting himself into it.

"How do you propose we do that?" Jemeka said, going along with it.

Floyd surprised her again by grinning at her. It looked both cheesy and dangerous. "Just so happens I got exactly the solution to your problem. In fact, I've been looking to get into this kind of business for a while, 'cause I got the perfect connections to sell a whole lot of high-end shit."

Ray-Ray said, "What connections?"

Floyd sat back into the sofa and rested his pristine Nike sneakers on Jemeka's father's coffee table. If Ray-Ray ever did that in front of her, she'd slap the cheek out of him, but she let the kid alone for now, curious to hear what he had to say.

Floyd stuck a joint into his mouth. "Y'all like movies?"

Jemeka and Ray-Ray glanced at each other.

"What?" Jemeka said.

"Me, I love movies," Floyd said. He blew smoke at them. The extreme stench of it like pineapples and pine. "Any movies. I love 'em all. Even the bad ones. I seen so many movies you wouldn't believe me if I told you." He inhaled again. "You got somewhere I can tap this shit?"

"Ray-Ray, can you go get a glass or somethin'?" Jemeka said.

Ray-Ray got up and left the room.

"What's all this about movies?" Jemeka said. "We asked you about your connections."

Floyd smoked the joint and Ray-Ray returned to the room and placed a mug onto the coffee table. Floyd leaned forward and tapped the joint into the mug.

"I saw a crazy movie this year, nearly blew my head clean off. *Dark City*. You seen it?"

Jemeka shook her head, growing impatient.

"Shit spun my head round," Floyd said. "I mean, I was high as shit in the theater, that probably had an effect. But it was one weird flick. Made me realize we're all trapped in a prison of our own making. You know? We can only escape our prison after we acknowledge the prison exists." He sucked on the joint. "It was some deep shit."

"Listen, we didn't bring you here to talk movies," Jemeka said. "So either you tell us—"

"Movies are the connection," Floyd said.

"What?"

"I got connections in a film studio in Hollywood. I been sellin' weed like hot cakes up there. Them motherfucker's crazy for it. I can sell blow up there even easier. They got *money*."

Jemeka looked at Ray-Ray, who met her gaze.

"You can, huh?" Ray-Ray said.

"I got other connections too."

"Oh yeah?" Jemeka said, warming to the kid. "Like what?"

"Y'all watch porn?"

XXX

A COUPLE DAYS AFTER SPEAKING WITH FLOYD, Jemeka and Ray-Ray sat in Floyd's car inside Universal Studios watching actors and crew members hurrying or sauntering by, depending on privilege, Jemeka supposed. Floyd had driven her and Ray-Ray here in his Subaru, midnight-blue with ugly-ass gold rims. When they had approached the studio gates, Jemeka had cringed, thinking no way the chubby white security guard in the booth would allow three Negroes off the street anywhere near this place, but to her surprise the guard in the booth had waved to Floyd, a broad grin plastered onto his face, and opened the gates, beckoning them on through. If Floyd had been trying to impress them, he had succeeded.

They sat waiting in the car in a parking lot somewhere inside the studio, Floyd bobbing his head to Randy Crawford's "Street Life" playing in the CD player.

"Here we go," Floyd said as a woman approached from one of the buildings ahead, clearly an actress: white and glamorous and thin as an ice-cream cone, wearing large red-rimmed shades over her eyes.

She leaned on Floyd's opened window. "Hey Floyd." She pulled up her shades and sparkling blue eyes surveyed the car, meeting Jemeka's gaze for a moment.

"How you doin', girl?" Floyd said.

"Pretty good."

"You making a movie in here?"

"Nah, my friend is, I'm just hanging out. I'm between projects right now but in August shooting starts for a romance flick, then next summer I'll be in New York filming this totally hilarious and beautifully strange little film by this amazing young writer-director. Guy's a real visionary, and the script is exquisite. I'm excited." She flashed a dazzling smile, teeth bleached and perfect.

"I'm glad to hear that. You know what I said before—if they're lookin' for a young Samuel L. Jackson, but cheaper, you slip my name in there."

"You know it."

"I got a little somethin' for you." Floyd reached under his seat. He rose, holding a huge vacuum-packed bag of cannabis. Must have been a hundred giant buds in there, vibrant-green with tiny purple leaves and little orange strands dangling from them.

"I love a man who brings a woman flowers," the actress said. She handed Floyd a fat roll of bills held together with a pink rubber band. "Got a little something extra for you in there."

"You're a star," Floyd said.

"Don't I know it. See you next time, Floyd." She blew him a kiss and strutted away like the superstar she was.

A moment's silence.

"Holy shit," Ray-Ray said.

"That who I think it was?" Jemeka said. "Won an Oscar this year?"

"That's her," Floyd said.

Ray-Ray leaned forward and stuck his head through the gap between the two front seats. "All right man, you cool, you cool. But what does any of this got to do with our situation?"

Poor Ray-Ray. The man would always be a step behind.

Jemeka said, "These Hollywood types gonna be our customers, Ray-Ray."

Floyd nodded, enjoying himself. "You saw how much bud she bought. Bitch probably doesn't even smoke it. These Hollywoods just got to have it, show it off to all their friends, put it in big bowls at parties next to the fruit punch and chocolate fountain. 'Cause they don't wanna be the one who *don't* got a bowl of bud at the party."

Floyd opened the glove compartment, took out a joint and set it alight. Exhaling a pungent cloud of bitter smoke, he said, "These Hollywoods get real greedy when the powder come out, you best belie' that. I've heard some stories about how much shit they snort their way through at these parties. Makes slingin' crack look like hard labor."

Floyd took another drag and offered the joint to Jemeka. She hesitated, then took it, the skinny joint firm between her fingers. She sucked on it and inhaled. The weed tasted citrusy and sour beneath the ashen flavor of burning. It had been a long time since she had smoked any and she was unprepared for the sudden heat of it in her chest. Her coughing became spluttering. She handed the joint to Ray-Ray while Floyd chuckled at her.

"Ain't no competition, neither," Floyd said as Jemeka's coughing subsided. "Nobody's turf out here. I been sellin' bud here for a while. People know me."

Jemeka had to admit it: she was impressed. "You could probably sell the whole kilo in a few sales here, huh?"

"Could be I could do it in one. I know of a big-time director with a bad habit. He'd jump at the chance to buy that much, I think. I just need to get in touch with him. And li'l miss Oscar-winner can help me do that."

Floyd reached behind and took the joint from Ray-Ray. "But if I'm sellin' that shit in bulk to these motherfuckers, they're gonna expect a good deal. That means less profit for you. But for your money, you get convenience, quick turnaround, and reduced risk from the police or some crackhead with aspirations of armed robbery. You feel me?"

Jemeka considered this, liking the sound of it. One advantage Floyd hadn't mentioned: they wouldn't have to distribute drugs in their own neighborhood, wouldn't contribute to the destruction of their community.

Floyd said, "All I'm offering here, it ain't cheap. You do it this way, I want an equal split of the profits. Partners. Otherwise you on your own."

Jemeka glanced at Ray-Ray, watching her intently.

She extended her hand toward the sharp and impressive kid in the driver's seat. "Floyd, you got yourself a deal."

FLOYD DROVE THE SUBARU WEST. They were in the San Fernando Valley now, rippling mountains on the horizon and thirsty dirt all around.

"This where the rest our customers at," Floyd said, slowing the car outside some kind of warehouse.

"What we looking at?" Jemeka said.

"You looking at Porno Valley. It ain't Hollywood but these cats snort blow like it'll save their lives." He pointed at the building ahead. "You see the sign? Above the entrance?"

Jemeka squinted. Against the dazzling sunlight she could barely make it out. "MidnightPussy Productions."

"Say what?" Ray-Ray said beside her.

"That's right. One of the bigger studios round here," Floyd said. "I got some customers in there who'd be very happy to buy some quality blow at a good price. Nobody's turf out here, neither."

"You got it all figured out, huh?" Jemeka said.

"Like I said, I been looking to expand my business for a while, got all the parts lined up just waiting to be put together."

"So what's next?" Ray-Ray said.

"Next we go eat. Then we get rich." Floyd swung the steering wheel and accelerated, heading back east. "I know this place got the best wings you'll ever taste. The third and final stop of this ride called the American Dream." He laughed.

Jemeka watched the mountains shrink in the wing mirror. Like her old life—before the gangster she had killed with her car, before Marsellus, before Floyd—it was already behind her, soon to vanish entirely.

Chapter Ten

JULY, 1999

JEFFREY STROKES LIVED IN LONG BEACH in a terrace apartment overlooking the Pacific. Richie sat in the Audi outside Jeffrey's apartment watching the surf cream and curl beneath a sky so blue it hurt. A warm sea breeze flowed through the open window, tickling Richie's skin. What a beautiful day. What a beautiful place. This was where he and Alabama should live. Right here in this little slice of Paradise. Richie had no idea if Jeffrey was even home but, eventually, the porn star proved Richie's patience fruitful by exiting his apartment and cruising off in his piece-of-shit Daewoo.

Richie ignited the engine and pursued. Day four of following Jeffrey and Richie was growing bored. The man never went anywhere but the porn studio out in the Valley and back home, maybe stopping off at a supermarket or convenience store, but never going any place he'd be alone. If today's pursuit didn't show more promise Richie would have to get inside the man's apartment somehow and do it in there. But that would be risky.

Following Jeffrey on I-170, Richie figured the man was heading toward the porn studio again and considered abandoning the pursuit when Jeffrey surprised him by taking an exit onto Artesia Boulevard. Curiosity piqued, Richie took the exit and stayed close to Jeffrey's Daewoo. Jeffrey quickly turned left off Artesia onto Butler Avenue, and shortly after left again onto Neece Street toward Coolidge Park. Jeffrey pulled in beside the park and Richie cruised past him slowly, getting a good look at the guy. Even from this distance he could see that Jeffrey was higher than Jesus, his reddened eyes visible. Long blond hair reached below his shoulders, the hint of a scruffy beard on his cheeks. Actually, he looked a lot like Jesus. A high-as-shit porn-star Jesus in a piece-of-shit Daewoo.

Richie parked fifty yards ahead and watched in the rear-view as Jeffrey exited his car and dragged himself across the street to the grass. He sat on a picnic bench beneath a massive tree, leaves like giant hands submerging the bench in shade. Content as a monk, Jeffrey pulled a fat blunt out of the pocket of his grungy, greenish, Kurt Cobain–esque shirt and set it on fire between his lips.

Richie chuckled watching him. Look at the guy—lighting up right in the middle of the park, the blunt longer than his arm. Wouldn't be too difficult to make a guy this oblivious disappear if Richie could make himself do it.

Ten minutes later, Richie getting bored now, a dark-blue Subaru Impreza with gold rims and tacky spoiler growled down the street and swung to a stop conspicuously beside the park. A Black guy emerged from the car and walked toward Jeffrey as if he owned the very park around him. Jeffrey didn't seem to notice the guy until he was right in front of him.

The guy sat beside Jeffrey, said something, and Jeffrey handed over the blunt, the guy taking a few deep drags before giving it back, thick smoke ballooning above them.

Now the guy was reaching into a pocket and handing something to Jeffrey. The porn star dug a hand into his jeans and took out a bulging wallet, counted out some notes and handed them over.

Richie shook his head. A drug deal clear as day in the middle of the fucking park. These guys were asking for trouble.

Richie smelled opportunity.

Feeling smug, he woke the engine and took off, a plan formulating in his mind.

Los Angeles, I've been away from you for too long.

XXX

ALABAMA WAS SINKING SEEMINGLY FOREVER INTO THE VOID. She had lost all sensation tethering her to the tangible world: her body, the tiles touching her skin, the fan blowing warm air across her face—all of them now just facts she could no longer perceive. Somehow, she knew that her body was still alive, waiting for her to return to it.

Sinking, sinking, sinking. Like rock to ocean floor. Dark in here. Cold.

Her mother's face, wrinkled and weathered and hardened by all the grief of Appalachia, appeared out of the gloom of this silent place, gasped Alabama's name, and faded into the ether.

The laugh of her sister—forever thirteen years old—echoed across time and space to reach Alabama here, now. Alabama wanted to cry out to her sister, to let her sister know that her sister had not been forgotten, but without a mouth in this place Alabama could not speak.

She thought of Richie, missing him, and the idea of Richie got tangled up in the knot of her memories, and she couldn't separate him from these memories nor they from him, yet she knew that Richie was different to them somehow. He was *now* and they were *then*. Wasn't he?

Richie was not *him*. Richie would never do what *he* had done to her. Richie loved her. (Had her father not loved her too in his own twisted way?)

As if in response, her father's voice boomed in this darkness like the voice of God: "Take that dress off, Alabama. Don't make me tell you again." Though she couldn't see him, she knew a belt was wrapped around his fist.

"Think you can disrespect me like that, you little bitch? Just like your mama."

"Shut yer whinin' and give me a look at you."

"Makin' me mad as all get out! Come here!"

Panic flooded this place. Alabama wanted out. She screamed but no sound occurred.

Images whizzed by like shooting stars:

Rough, weathered hands on her thighs.

The glint of the belt buckle under the light of a full moon.

Her sister's body, twisted beneath the truck.

Generations of sorrow carved into her mother's face.

The predatory look on Heimdall's face before he lunged at her.

Filthy carpet and the shocking weight of Heimdall on her back, and wasn't he her father come to finish what he'd started?

Richie pointing the gun at Heimdall.

Heimdall dropping to the floor.

She called out Richie's name. If it made a sound, she couldn't hear it.

XXX

"CALIFORNIA SUN" BY THE RAMONES chugged out of the Audi's speakers in its perfect arrangement of four rugged power chords as the song's namesake washed over the roof of the car. Richie picked up speed, excited to reach the hotel and tell Alabama about his plan. They could put down a rental deposit on an apartment like Alabama wanted. Shit, they could buy an apartment. Yeah, that sounded good. A place of their own. He could get a sweet ride, too. About time he ditched the Audi before the pigs sniffed it out. He'd always wanted a classic Chevy.

The Four Seasons approached—not very impressive from the outside, now that Richie thought about it. He brought the Audi to a stop in a parking space and walked into the lobby as an old couple came out of it, staring at him with a mixture of fear and disgust.

"Fuck you looking at, you old bag," he said to the woman as he passed, not stopping to catch her reaction. She'd probably have nightmares about him for a week.

He strode to the elevator and stepped inside.

A young mom approached holding the hand of her miserable-looking son. "Hold the elevator!" she called to Richie, while locked in what appeared to be some kind of battle of wills with the kid.

"Sorry, honey," Richie said, pressing the button to shut the doors. "No rich bitches allowed." He smirked at her stunned expression as the doors maintained the border between their worlds.

Maybe that had been harsh. She could have been a nice lady. Not *all* rich bitches were bitches. Alabama wouldn't be a bitch when she and Richie got rich. Would she? Nah. Woman didn't have a bitchy bone in her body. Well, maybe one or two.

Richie opened the door to the hotel room and stepped inside. The place was a mess: clothes strewn across the bed, dirty plates on every surface, the duvet in a heap on the floor.

"Bama?"

Dead silence. A stench of food decaying in the heat and something sour beneath it. Dread raised the hair on Richie's arms.

He made for the bathroom, the door to it half-shut. "Bama, you in here?"

Stepping into the bathroom, a stink of puke hit Richie like a bomb. Alabama lay on the floor, eyes shut, head and shoulders crumpled awkwardly against the wall. A syringe was lodged in her bicep and blood had dribbled from the point of entry down her arm to her fingertips where some of it had dripped onto the floor. Yellowish vomit had dried onto Alabama's chin and chest. One of her breasts had popped out of her yellow dress and there was vomit on that, too.

Richie's legs almost gave way beneath him.

Breaking free of paralysis, he rushed to her. "Bama! Wake up!" He grabbed her face in both hands. "Wake up, baby! Come on."

Alabama groaned and Richie almost cried. He hadn't lost her yet.

"Yes baby, wake up."

Richie dashed to the bath and twisted the cold water tap on. He picked his wife up, the lightness of her body startling him, and placed her into the bath a little rougher than he'd intended.

"Alabama, come back to me. Please come back to me." He splashed water onto her face.

Alabama spluttered, eyelids flickering.

The water had submerged her legs and most of her waist. Richie splashed her face again, not sure what to do if this failed. A tear slid down his face and this made him desperate. He slapped her cheek and the sound of it bounced off the walls. "Wake up Bama!"

She moaned.

"That's it, come to me!" He slapped her again, harder.

She mumbled something indecipherable.

"Wake up!" Richie yelled, slapping her again.

XXX

ALABAMA SHOT UPRIGHT, GASPING. It took her a moment to understand that she was lying in a bathtub. Icy water had soaked into her dress and she was shivering. The room was dim, yellow light entering through the doorway. Was it day or night?

Richie's face gazed into her own. He looked like he'd been crying.

"Are you okay?" he said, breathless.

She nodded, though she wasn't sure if she was. But she was among the living.

An acid stench stung her nostrils. She glanced down: yellow vomit smeared onto her chest, swirling in the bathwater. She wiped her chin and the stuff clung to her fingers. Her head throbbed. She felt as if her insides had been excavated.

Richie said, "Come on, we need to get you warm."

Richie helped her out of the bathtub, him doing most of the work. He peeled off her dress and dried her with a towel. But Alabama was barely present for it, haunted by how close she had come to oblivion.

She remembered injecting now, just a little heroin at first, following her plan to wean off it slowly. But it hadn't been enough to take away the pain. So she had taken more. Then she had sunk into that dark place. Now she was here again and the sickness would return soon.

"For a minute there, I thought I lost you," Richie said. He wrapped a towel around her shoulders. She couldn't stop shivering.

Richie hugged her, holding her tight. The bones jutting out of their ravaged bodies banged together.

"I really thought I lost you," he said, hugging her tight.

"I'm here," she said, though her voice had been so faint she had to question it.

IT WASN'T THE FIRST TIME ALABAMA HAD OVERDOSED, but it had been the scariest. Though she would never tell Richie this, there had been a moment during the experience—impossible to say for how long; could have been a minute, could have been an hour—when she had died. At least, that's how it had felt after she had clawed her way back from it. Death didn't scare Alabama; in fact, sometimes, part of her yearned for it. What terrified her was how lonely she had felt, lost in oblivion. No one had greeted her at the borders of another realm, because that other realm was just another lie in a world full of them. Instead, there had been nothing at all in every direction, forever. Perfect darkness. The absence of everything.

Before she had injected the second time—the time that had caused her to overdose—the phantom face of the man who had raped her had swum before her vision and she had smelled his sickening cheesy breath and had felt the heat of his groin on her back and that was when she had readied the second shot and plunged it into her arm and she saw now that, had Richie not pulled her back to consciousness, Heimdall would have succeeded in killing her after all.

Thinking about this now, lying on the bed, Alabama shuddered. "Richie," she called out weakly.

He stepped out of the bathroom clutching paper towel soggy with her puke. "Yeah?"

"I don't wanna live like this no more. I can't." A tear bubbled beneath her eyelid and slid across the bridge of her nose. Another followed, and next she was bawling into the pillow.

Richie tossed the paper towel into the trash and lay on the bed. He kissed her head and held her. "Me neither."

They lay like this for some time until Alabama's crying subsided. It felt good to cry herself out of tears, a small sense of relief washing over her now.

Nausea surged up from Alabama's belly. She leaped off the bed and darted to the bathroom where she puked into the toilet bowl.

When she got to her feet, Richie was watching her in the mirror from the doorway.

"I found our way out," he said to her reflection.

Alabama twisted the tap and splashed her face with cold water. She looked pallid and thin. Barely recognizable as the naive teenager who had fled her backwater town to the City of Angels in search of a better life. What a joke that had turned out to be.

"The score," Richie said behind her. "The big one. The one that's gonna pay enough to get a place of our own and start a new life."

She faced Richie, her back against the sink. "Will this new life have heroin in it? Because I don't want it if it does."

"We'll get clean."

"Is it dangerous?"

"No more dangerous than robbing diners. Well, maybe a little."

"When do we do it?"

"You're sitting this one out, babe."

"What?"

"I don't want you anywhere near this one."

"How you supposed to do it by yourself?"

"Who said I was doing it by myself?" Richie smirked.

"Richie, what are you talking about? What's the score?"

Richie disappeared into the bedroom.

Alabama exited the bathroom. Richie was sitting on the bed. She crawled onto the mattress and lay on her belly. Her heart thumped weakly beneath her ribs.

Richie said, "Remember the guy outside the convenience store?"

"The porno guy?"

"Yeah. Riccardo. I met with him a few days ago."

"A few *days* ago? Why didn't you tell me?"

"Bama, you've been totally out of it ever since—" He paused. "You weren't here is what I'm saying. For a while there, I thought I might lose you for good."

Alabama closed her eyes. Her head throbbed. The unceasing agony of it, like a hammer pummeling her brain.

"What was the job?" she said.

"Get this—dude wants me to *make someone disappear*. His words."

"I don't like the sound of that."

"Yeah, me neither. Guy's a porn star—the guy he wants me to get rid of. Name's Jeffrey Strokes. And that's actually the guy's real name. Riccardo offered me ten grand to do it."

"What did he say when you said no?"

Richie shot her a coy look.

"Richie . . . no."

He appeared amused.

Despite the immense effort it required, Alabama sat up on her knees. "You can't kill somebody! Jesus, Richie."

"Hey, I don't wanna kill anybody. What do you think I am?"

"But then why—"

"I have a plan."

Alabama rubbed her eyes. They felt like they were coming loose. "Ten thousand's a lot but it's not gonna get us our own place, Richie. Not for long, at least."

Richie raised his legs onto the mattress and lay flat, hands behind his head. "Oh, that's not the big score." He was staring at the ceiling.

"Richie, I'm tired. Where you goin' with this, what's the big score?"

A devious glint in Richie's eyes now. "Well, it's kind of a funny story. It has to do with that porn star, Jeffrey Strokes . . ."

Chapter Eleven

JULY, 2000

AT HOME, EXHAUSTED FROM THE LONG DAY, Mickey sat in his armchair in front of the TV as a rerun of an old *Starsky and Hutch* episode unfolded onscreen. He'd stopped watching it almost as soon as he'd begun and it was simply happening now on the screen. Something about this Jeffrey Strokes case had stirred up memories of Martha. Well, not quite the case. It was the client. Bethany. He couldn't explain it, but it almost felt like there was a blood connection between her and him. She was so like Martha had once been. Perhaps it was merely loneliness. Or perhaps it was simply that Martha had not been gone from his life for very long and he missed her.

A couple lines from a poem by Irish poet William Butler Yeats came to him: *But one man loved the pilgrim soul in you; And loved the sorrows of your changing face.* How did that poem go? He had known it all by heart once; in fact, he had recited it to Martha once, before they married, and though she had laughed and he had felt a little silly, he had glimpsed a glimmer in her eyes. Not long after, he realized what that glimmer had been: she had fallen in love with him. Simple as that. Thank you, Yeats.

He leaned on the armchair as he rose, shuffled to the large bookshelves by the rear wall, and pulled from the top shelf a dusty hardcover of Yeats's *Collected Poems*. Rifling through the pages like an eager child, he at last found what he sought: the poem "When You Are Old." He recited it to the empty room, but in his mind he saw Martha sitting in her chair, not looking at him but *there*, face half-turned to listen.

A tear threatened to spill from Mickey's eye and he let it. The sad day would be the day tears stopped coming.

With a sigh, Mickey returned the book to the dust-smeared shelf, switched the TV off, and retired to his bedroom to wait for morning.

AT 6 A.M., DRENCHED IN SWEAT, Mickey woke to the chirping of birds and the soft light of sunrise. The summer so far had been outrageously hot and this morning signaled another scorcher ahead. Global warming is easy to believe when it's happening to you.

He sat up and tried to plan the day. Not much he could do with this case until he heard from Reggie. He could have another crack at that Italian, Riccardo—intuition told him the man was hiding something—but it would be smarter to hold off until he had more to go on, catch the big guy off-guard.

It seemed Mickey had the day to himself, to do with whatever he pleased. He scoffed at the thought. A day to kill, more like. Retirement would not be kind to him—why he'd avoided it so long.

He swung his legs out of the bed and planted them on the floor. Not retired yet, old man. Not retired yet.

MICKEY WAS SIPPING COFFEE AT THE KITCHEN TABLE when the doorbell rang. He frowned. Who on Earth could be out there looking for him at 6:30 in the morning?

Self-consciously, in blue-and-white striped pajamas and fluffy slippers, he shuffled through the hallway, photographs of Martha and him and various dogs long gone on the walls. He peered through the peephole he'd had installed when Martha and he had begun to feel old.

"Of course," Mickey muttered upon seeing who stood on the other side of the wood. He opened the door.

"Top of the mornin' to ye," Reggie said in some sort of leprechaun impression, holding a tray containing two disposable coffee cups. He wore his police uniform, obviously on duty or about to be. "Hold these, will you? I got some donuts in the car."

Accepting the tray, Mickey watched Reggie take his big strides to his car and had to smile. Whatever he was here for, Reggie could have said it all over the phone. He came here because he didn't like the thought of Mickey alone.

THEY SAT AT THE LITTLE PATIO TABLE IN THE BACK YARD and listened to the birds wake up. Already, Mickey's back felt sticky with sweat.

"You've let this yard go to all hell, Mick."

Mickey glanced around. Where once the yard had been neat and well-maintained, decorated with an assortment of beautiful plants and the grass perfectly trimmed, it had grown messy and a little, well, *grown*.

"It was Martha who looked after all that. She loved it out here. Sometimes she'd sit right here with a book and not move for hours."

"What do you think she'd say if she could see it now?"

Mickey knew where this was going.

"Woman would be spinning in her grave," Reggie said.

"You're not wrong."

Reggie sipped his coffee and observed Mickey. "Your life didn't end with hers, Mick."

"If you say so, Reggie. If you say so."

Reggie picked up a chocolate-covered donut and bit it in half. "How's the missing person's case?"

"In progress. I've got a suspicious player involved, boyfriend of the ex-lover of our missing porn star. I know Jeffrey was buying hard drugs regularly and may have been feeling the pressure of whatever kind of stardom porn stars can attain, but aside from all that—" Mickey shrugged.

He said, "The frustrating thing about this case is that this Jeffrey fellow didn't seem to have anyone in his life beyond a girlfriend and work colleagues. No parents to speak of—mother's dead, father's senile in a nursing home—no siblings. The man was like a ghost, and he vanished like one."

"Well you can cheer up, buttercup, 'cause I might have something for you. I spoke with my nephew about your Floyd."

"Your nephew? What about your contact?"

"My nephew is the contact."

"Which one?"

"Roland."

"Isn't he a bit young?"

"The last time you seen him, sure. Kid's nineteen now."

"Nineteen?" Mickey shook his head, trying to imagine Roland now, unable to.

"That's what I been sayin', Mick. You don't come round no more."

"All right, I get it. What did Roland find out?"

"He knows Floyd. So does everybody else, apparently. Floyd's still around, dealing."

"Where can I find him?"

"Easy there, sharpshooter," Reggie said. "We can't have you doing that. You think an old ex-cop cracker like you can just stroll into that neighborhood lookin' to nail a brother?"

"I just want to speak with him."

"Yeah, I bet that's just how he'll see it." Reggie took a swig of the coffee. A colorful bird fluttered across the yard behind him, probably some kind of parrot.

Reggie said, "There's more, but Roland wants to tell you himself."

"More about Floyd?"

"I suppose so, he wouldn't tell me. Something about not snitching to the police."

"But he'll tell me?"

"You gonna have to dig around some, but maybe." He stared at Mickey. "All right, look, when I said he wants to tell you himself, what I really mean is he don't wanna tell nobody nothin'. Roland's a smart kid, knows it's dangerous to have loose lips on those streets. He knows something about something and you got to extract it from him."

"He's your nephew, Reggie."

"It's your case, brother. And you ain't a cop. Far as Reggie needs to know, you never were. You're just a concerned freelancer trying to locate a missing white boy. Besides, I ain't getting on bad terms with my nephew for no missing porn star."

"All right. When do I meet him?"

"Well Mick, we're having the family barbecue at our place this weekend, and guess what, you're invited. I made Roland promise he was gonna show up. Do I gotta make you promise too?"

"I'll be there." Mickey looked into Reggie's eyes, his friend youthful and alert behind that aged face. "A barbecue with your family sounds like just what the doctor ordered, to tell you the truth."

Reggie clapped a hand on Mickey's back. "I'm glad to hear that. Sorry in advance about Odetta."

"What do you mean?"

"You think I've been giving you a hard time about not showing your face? You just wait till that woman sees you."

Mickey chuckled. "I'll come prepared."

"So long as you come, brother."

Reggie appeared to be chewing on a sentence.

"What?" Mickey said.

"Roland's boyfriend will be there too. At the barbecue."

"His boyfriend?"

"That's right." Reggie didn't break eye contact.

"Oh. Okay. I look forward to meeting him."

Reggie's expression lightened a touch. "He's a good kid. The boyfriend. Name's Carlos. Studying to be a veterinarian."

"A vet in the family. Impressive."

"Well, he ain't in the family yet, but it wouldn't surprise me. He's all Roland talks about."

"Carlos, is he—"

"Mexican, yeah. He's from the neighborhood. Well, pretty much. Next one over. Compton's more Hispanic than Black, did you know that?"

Mickey had been about to ask if Carlos was the same age as Roland, not about his heritage, but he let that go. "No, I don't think I did."

Reggie nodded. "Most people don't. Mexicans are good people. Hard workers. They stick to themselves, but they're all right."

Mickey drained the end of his coffee and sat with Reggie listening to the birds. They sounded like a new beginning.

XXX

JULY, 1999

RICHIE DROVE TO LONG BEACH with, in a rare turn for him, a pop music station on the radio, currently playing the obnoxiously popular "Californication" single by Red Hot Chili Peppers which had only recently been released but seemed already to be part of the very fabric of this place, and which Richie tapped along to now himself—it was a great song. Frequently he would lock eyes with himself in the rear-view and try to think up something clever that he could say to this porn star Jeffrey Strokes when the man opened his front door. Richie felt pretty sure Jeffrey would indeed be home because, after following the guy for four days, it had become clear that Jeffrey did nothing but work, smoke and sleep on a reliable schedule.

So Richie was surprised when he pulled up outside Jeffrey's as a cute little blonde entered his apartment, Jeffrey holding the door open for her. As she passed Jeffrey, the blonde placed a hand on his chest in a way only a lover would and Jeffrey shut the door.

Shit. What if the blonde stayed in there all day and night? A little pink car sat parked outside the building. The blonde's, no doubt. Richie was not a patient man, but, since telling Alabama about his idea, he'd been pumped to approach Jeffrey today. Alabama's reaction hadn't been quite what he'd been hoping for: "I don't know about this, Richie . . . sounds a little like Vegas all over again, and you know how *that* ended . . ." But she hadn't discounted it entirely, and he had asked her to trust him—he knew what he was doing.

The street ended in a cul-de-sac and beyond it the Pacific sparkled for miles and miles. Richie exited the Audi onto glistening tarmac sticky with heat. He walked toward the end of the cul-de-sac where steps took him down to the waterfront. He sat on a bench and listened to the surf break, hypnotic and eternal.

He should bring Alabama down here, let her hear this soothing sound. Couldn't remember the last time they'd been to the beach together, couldn't be sure they'd ever been to the beach together, in fact, and this bothered him. What had he let their life become? Spending all their time and money on dope. Jesus. Why had he ever started shooting that shit? Whatever the reason then, it was a different one now: addiction, pure and simple. A few hours without dope now and his body trembled with ache, like a throbbing, furious itch in every nerve ending while his brain pushed up into his skull. They had to get clean or it would kill them, and the habit was unsustainable besides. They were shooting hundreds of bucks' worth per week, never enough to feel right, just enough to hang on by their fingernails for a little longer. Their time was running out. Especially Alabama's. What that animal had done to her in that motel room had burned a hole right through her and she was using heroin to plug it. She wouldn't survive another overdose.

A group of kids dressed up like '70s punks sauntered by, one of them with a Mohawk so tall it could stab the sun.

Richie stared at the ocean, already dreaming of the junk in the hotel as the most recent shot tapered off, hating himself for it.

This world was no place for a junkie.

SITTING IN THE AUDI AGAIN, getting scratchy, needing a shot, Richie had almost called off the whole thing when the blonde stepped out of Jeffrey's apartment, shared a kiss with Jeffrey, and got into her little pink car. Jeffrey stood watching her leave, smoking a joint in such a natural fashion he could have slipped out his mother's pussy with it. Richie wondered if the man was even capable of what Richie had in mind for him.

Jeffrey waited until the blonde had driven out of sight, then returned inside the building and shut the door.

Richie got out of the Audi and approached Jeffrey's building. Glancing over his shoulder (no one appeared to have seen him), Richie tucked his long hair behind his ears and pressed the buzzer labeled "J. Strokes"—the ground-floor unit. Richie expected Jeffrey's voice to interrogate him through the intercom, in response to which Richie would improvise some bullshit, but instead the door to the building opened and there stood Jeffrey, naked head to toe save for extremely tight boxer shorts which, despite Richie's best attempts, drew his gaze like a searchlight toward Jeffrey's crotch where a frankly shocking bulge hung from the man's groin.

Tearing his eyes from the bulge, Richie said, "What the fuck? You had clothes on not twenty seconds ago."

Jeffrey glanced at his body, as if surprised to see it exposed. Remarkably, the joint remained between his fingers.

"I was about to have a bath," he said calmly, as if this was perfectly obvious. He sucked on the joint and exhaled slowly, blowing smoke into Richie's face and watching him with a kind of detached interest. "So what do you want?"

Richie laughed, couldn't help it. If the guy was any more relaxed he'd be in a coma.

"I want it all, Jeff, and you're gonna help me get it."

Chapter Twelve

"YOU A FAN OR SOMETHING?" Jeff said, puffing on the joint. Richie found the man's almost full nudity extremely distracting.

"You're gonna be a fan of *me* when we're done. Can we go inside? Confidential stuff, you know?"

Jeff scratched his chin and yawned. "I guess." He turned around in a heavy, lethargic manner and moved through the hallway.

Richie glanced behind and followed, shutting the door.

Jeff opened a second door and went through it. Going after him, a pungent, skunk-like stench of weed hit Richie, and beneath it vague scents of masculinity—sweat, sports deodorant, pizza—and something more vague again: the very smell of time, so much of it spent in this place. Richie found himself inside a small living room, messy and largely undecorated; or rather, decorated with the mess: a large throw lay haphazardly across a sickly-green couch, Hindu elephant-god Ganesha holding a human palm up on the throw's design; only one frame had been hung on the walls, inside it a poster of the film *Boogie Nights*; in the far corner a glass display case held an assortment of what appeared to be awards, the ones on the top shelf like knock-off Oscars; opposite the couch, on a cabinet, sat the biggest TV Richie had ever laid eyes upon—the only thing in the apartment of value, it seemed.

"That TV," Richie said. "What is that, seventy inches?"

Jeff shut the door to the apartment. "Eighty."

"Holy shit. Must be the biggest TV in America."

"Actually—" Jeff sucked on the joint, exhaled—"it's the biggest TV in the world."

"You serious?"

"Yeah dude. Mitsubishi VS-eight-O-eight-O-three."

"How much you pay for it?"

"Ten thousand."

Richie gazed at the TV, the price of a small car. "That's a lot of cinema tickets."

Jeff sat on the couch and squashed the tiny remainder of the joint into an ashtray filled with dozens of roaches. Immediately he set about rolling another. Richie watched in stupefied fascination as this man who had let a random junkie off the street into his home sat there rolling a joint now, calm as the Caribbean, not even looking at Richie, without having yet asked what, exactly, Richie wanted from him. In fact, sitting hunched over the coffee table, quietly packing cannabis into rolling papers with the focus of a samurai, the impressive bulge of his underwear the only indication of the man's choice of career, it seemed Jeff might have forgotten about Richie entirely. Not one to question his own decisions, Richie questioned this one. Time still to change his mind, walk out that door.

Walk out that door and remain a junkie burning through cash like the flame burning dope-cradling spoon.

Walk out that door and remain too poor to acquire a half-decent home, doomed to watch his wife OD on the filthy floor of a bug-infested dump they'd had to shoot up in just to tolerate.

No. That life had ended, one way or the other.

Richie committed to the plan: "Jeff, who's the guy you buy your drugs from?"

Licking the lip of the paper and sticking it around the cone, Jeff looked up at him. "Are you a narc, man? Is that what this is?"

Richie laughed. "Do I look like a fucking narc to you?"

"No, but that's how a narc would look—not like a narc."

"What? I need to be smoking that shit just to understand that. No, I'm not a narc. I'm a fucking junkie, you want to know the truth." Richie flipped his right arm and held it toward Jeff, a dozen or so painful little holes dotted along it.

Moving only pink eyeballs, Jeff looked at them.

Richie said, "I want to rob your dealer and I need your help to do it."

Unfazed by this remark, Jeff rummaged around the stained couch for at least thirty seconds. At last he found a Zippo with a green cannabis leaf embossed on the side—the kind of crappy souvenir tourists buy from stalls by the beach outside—flicked it open with the air of a man who had done it ten thousand times before, and set fire to the joint clamped between his lips.

"You should sit," he said. "You're making me paranoid." He smoked and watched as Richie lifted what appeared to be some kind of musical instrument off the other, smaller, couch and sat in its place.

"What the fuck is this, an accordion?" Richie said.

"Yeah."

"You play?"

"No."

"Right." Richie set the accordion on the floor. "So like I was saying—"

"You want to rob Floyd."

"If that's the name of the Black kid you bought some shit from yesterday, sure."

Jeff screwed up his face—the first change in the man's expression Richie had yet glimpsed. "You saw that? You *are* a narc."

"Shut up with this narc shit. What you think this is, a movie? Some copaganda flick with a pig so deep undercover he's injecting dope into his fuckin' dick? I was watching you for a very different reason completely unrelated to your substance-abusing habits. But I gotta be fucking frank with you, man, I've got maybe thirty minutes left until I start clawing the skin off my face and puking on my hands and knees. I need to get the fuck out of here and get my medicine, so we need to hurry this shit along."

Jeff watched Richie, unreadable and vacant.

Richie leaned forward. "I want to rob this Floyd, yes, but he can't be carrying that much shit at any one time. We're gonna find out where he keeps it, all of it, and—" Richie frowned, thinking of something. "What was it you bought from him? I assumed it was something more valuable than grass. Don't tell me it was just grass."

Jeff smoked, blinking at Richie as if deep in thought, but probably not thinking at all. "Yeah, I bought weed from him." He paused, inhaled, exhaled. "But I bought coke, too."

"Coke, huh? Doesn't really seem your style."

"I don't like the stuff, I just take it for work."

Richie searched for a sign of sarcasm on the man's face but he was unreadable.

"You want some of this?" Jeff said.

"No, but I'd love some blow."

"You're not shy, are you?"

"Well, I'd prefer a couple Oxys but I don't suppose you got any of those."

"Just bud and blow, man. Actually, I have some acid too now that I think about it. I've got a little DMT as well, left over from—"

"Just the blow man, Jesus."

"You're lucky I believe in *xenia*, dude," Jeff said as he rose from the couch.

"What? You mean that TV show with the black-haired chick in the skimpy armor?"

"No, but I do like that show. I'm talking about Ancient Greek hospitality."

Jeff approached a bookcase and lifted a couple hardbacks off the shelf. Behind where the books had stood sat a small wooden box. Jeffrey carried it over to the coffee table as if it was sacred treasure dug up from the Amazon.

"The Ancient Greeks believed that no stranger should be turned away from their door, and that all visitors should be bestowed upon with a gift. Let this be my gift to you. Help yourself."

He opened the box and sat back onto the couch, right foot balanced sideways on his left knee, the shocking bulge of his groin so visible he could have been nude. It occurred to Richie now how strange it was that Jeff had not put some clothes on.

Richie leaned over the table. A small mound of white powder lay inside the box and behind it, almost the length of the box, a steel straw.

"Gotta tell you, Jeff, this ain't the possession of a man who doesn't like blow." He plucked out a sizable amount of the stuff and shaped it into a line on the table.

"It was a gift," Jeff said, but Richie was barely listening, bending down now with the straw in hand. He hoovered up the coke in a single snort. For a moment: nothing, just an itchy nostril and the globular, chemical sensation of it in the back of his throat. Then: like switching the light on in a room long black. He could see again, clearer than ever, the waters of his mind transformed from murky swamp into crystal lake. The edges of every surface in the room appeared sharp and defined.

"Not bad. Not bad at all," Richie said. "You not having any?"

Jeff shook his head, but slowly, so slowly. "Like I said, it's just for work."

"Fuck you mean it's for work?"

"To help me maintain my stamina."

"You talking about your dick?"

"In a way."

"What? Don't tell me you can't get it up fucking beautiful women for a living."

Jeff smoked and gazed at the wall, possibly considering a response but who knows with this guy? Richie noticed his own hand tap-dancing on his thigh. He commanded his brain to still the rogue hand but some kind of disconnect was going on between brain and limb and his fingers danced like a tarantula.

After what felt like a generation but was likely no more than thirty seconds, Jeff said, "Beautiful women, sure. But they're friends, colleagues—familiar faces, generally. You know what I mean? I have a girlfriend. I don't know if I love her, but I definitely like her. This fucking-for-a-living thing, it's not what you think it is. It's work, plain and simple, and I need a little pick-me-up to perform, that's all."

Richie laughed and it felt great. "Man, if you think I'm gonna feel sorry for you 'cause you get to bang bitches and make bank, ain't gonna happen." Now his leg was jittering along with the hand. He must look like a goddamn chimpanzee on, well . . . cocaine! He chuckled at this thought and suddenly he was on his feet, head bobbing to a song he couldn't hear.

"That's a nice art piece you got there," Richie said, wandering over to the *Boogie Nights* poster.

"Yeah, dude. The director gave it to me as a gift. Not just me, a few of us over at MidnightPussy. He signed it too. Nice guy. He can snort that stuff like you wouldn't believe. Had enough to kill a mule one night but you wouldn't have known it. And only a little guy. He's the one who gave me that box."

Richie saw the signature now—a hard-to-make-out black squiggle over the dark background above the title.

"He was researching for the film, hanging out with porn stars," Jeff said.

"That's fuckin' cool."

"By now, seeing as how I've given you blow and conversed at length, you're probably aware I'm not entirely disinterested in your plan."

"I knew you'd be interested before I even met you."

"How's that?"

"Greed is the most dependable of human weaknesses."

Jeff inhaled a final pull on the joint and squashed it into an ash tray shaped like a penis. He noticed Richie's gaze. "Another gift." Was that a smirk at the corner of his lips?

Jeff sat back into the couch, arms stretched across either side. "Greed? I don't know about that. I have money, but not enough to stop working forever. I'm not a working man, it's just not in my blood. All I can do is porn and I can barely do that anymore. And I'm not naive, I know I can't do porn forever. It's a short-lived career even for the best of us. You make as much cash as you can while you can. Most porn stars have back-up plans or at the very least can see themselves in another job of some kind. Not me, man. I'm just not a man for hard labor. So if there's a way I can make enough money to quit the business forever and disappear into some quiet, forgotten corner of the world, then you've got my attention."

Richie almost fist-pumped. Standing up in this strange, smoke-filled living room, he felt a crazed need to dance and settled instead for bobbing about.

"That's fuckin' fantastic," he said.

"But you better have a solid plan, 'cause from where I'm sitting a stoner and a junkie are a little outmatched by virtually anyone."

Richie nodded, his leg jittering beneath him like Elvis. "We'll do it right, don't worry about that." He ran a hand over his head, feeling hot now, much too hot. Christ, he was going to burn up if his heart didn't explode first.

"You all right, dude?" came Jeff's voice, but garbled, as if underwater.

"I think I'm about to have a heart attack." He glanced at Jeff. Through the blurry haze his vision had become he saw the porn star watching him from deep within the clutches of the couch.

Jeff said, "Yeah, that line you did was pretty big. Huge, actually. This blow is super pure, man."

"You could have fucking told me." Richie was panicking now, daggers of pain shooting up his left arm.

"I thought I did."

"You did not."

"Maybe you're right. I definitely thought about it. Hey, you never told me your name."

I'll tell you my fucking name, Richie wanted to yell, but he was on the floor.

XXX

JULY, 2000

WHEN ODETTA SAW MICKEY come through the doorway into the back yard, she did a double-take of the exaggerated, comedy-film kind, hands on her hips, mouth hanging open. Then she came at him like he owed her money.

"Michael O'Rourke! Just where in the hell you been hiding from me all this time?"

Every person attending the barbecue swiveled their heads his way as Odetta pressed an artificial fingernail into his chest.

Mickey smiled. "Hello Odetta."

"Too good for the Dixon family barbecues, that it?"

Mickey knew the protocol for an Odetta attack: say as little as possible and don't be smug. "I could never be too good for you, Odetta."

"So where you been all this time then?"

Mickey glanced at Reggie by Odetta's side, the man smirking but offering no indication of an intention to interfere. "I've been with me, myself and I, and that's about it. I've missed the Dixon family barbecues, if it means anything."

Something like sympathy glimmered in Odetta's eyes and her expression softened. "Mickey, you silly old fool. You men are all the same. You're here now, that's what matters. I'm glad to see you. Come on, let's get you fed."

She spun on her heels and made for the barbecue where Reggie's brother, Curtis, was flipping burgers. On the grass at the rear wall a squealing group of children splashed in a blow-up paddling pool while family and friends of the family sat chatting at the table on the patio or stood in small groups with beers in hand—mostly men in this latter category, discussing basketball and work, probably.

The scent of charred, marinated meat on the grill had Mickey salivating.

Curtis said, "What's happening, Mickey? Good to see you."

"Nice to see you too, Curtis. How are the girls?"

Curtis flipped the final pink burger, his rotund belly almost being grilled along with the meat. "Moody, man. Moody. Even my youngest is a teenager now, so it's drama drama all day every day. But they good kids."

Odetta grabbed a paper plate from the stack next to the barbecue. "Burger or chicken, Mickey?"

"That's a tough one."

"Have both," Curtis said. He clamped a large chicken wing between tongs and plopped it onto the plate in Odetta's hand. He placed a burger next to it and Odetta handed the plate to Mickey.

"Thank you. Both of you," Mickey said.

"No problem, brother," Curtis said. "Grab yourself a drink from the cooler. I'll be over soon to catch up with you."

"I'll get that drink for you, sugar," Odetta said. "You take a seat beside Reggie over there. Buns and condiments on the table."

"Thank you, Odetta, I really appreciate—"

"Yeah yeah, I know. Go on over there now and I'll bring your drink. What you want? Soda?"

"I shouldn't, but I suppose one won't kill me."

"It won't be soda that kills you, I can promise you that. Go on over to Reggie, I'll be over in a minute."

"Thanks, Odetta."

"Yeah, yeah." She waved him away.

MARINATED IN THE DIXONS' SECRET RECIPE, the chicken tasted truly divine. Mickey tore into it like a starved mutt.

"Damn, Mick. You not been eating lately?" Reggie said.

"I've been eating, but nothing this delicious."

Reggie took a swig from his beer and belched.

"Goddamn it, Reggie, I'm eating here," said Odetta's sister, Tori, sitting opposite.

"Better out than in." Reggie winked at Mickey. "You know, Mick, I think I'm starting to feel old."

"Only now? I felt old when I was still young."

"War will do that to you."

"Yes sir."

"Do you ever think about it? The war?"

"I make it a point not to."

Reggie nodded, expression serious now. "Creeps in sometimes, though. Don't it?"

"Yes, it does."

"I would have preferred your war," Reggie said. "At least you were the good guys."

"You'd think differently if you were there that day at Dachau."

"I witnessed my share of horrors in Vietnam," Reggie said.

"I know you did." Mickey sighed. "But I'm not so sure we were the good guys, exactly. Hiroshima? Seventy thousand civilians vaporized in an instant. Nagasaki? Innocent people trying to live their lives, all murdered simply because they were Japanese. Is that really so different from the Nazis?"

"Maybe it ain't. Maybe it ain't." Reggie sipped his beer, a wounded look about him. "It's the children that haunt me. I see them in my dreams some nights. They looked at us the way you must've looked at the Nazis."

Tori leaned across the table. In a hushed voice, she said, "Boys, I don't mean to interrupt this little nostalgia session you got goin' on, but this ain't appropriate table talk."

Reggie frowned, averting his gaze. "Sorry. You're right, it ain't."

Tori smiled sympathetically and squeezed his hand before returning to her previous conversation.

Mickey glanced around the yard, watching the kids and their parents go about their lives on this sunny summer's day, not one among them knowing the evils of war and Mickey so very glad of it.

ROLAND AND HIS BOYFRIEND SHOWED UP LATER as night approached and much of the heat had been sucked from the day. Mickey almost didn't recognize Roland. The quiet boy he remembered had become a six-foot-four man walking with a swagger and draining beers like they were orange juice. It amused Mickey to see Roland wearing a golden Lakers jersey, just as he had virtually every time Mickey had ever seen him, clearly still as fanatical about the team as Uncle Reggie. This one had on the back above the number eight the name of promising youngster Kobe Bryant who last season had signed a $70 million contract with the team. The Lakers had won the title, beating Indiana Pacers in the finals last month to avenge their disappointing performance in last year's strangely shortened fifty-game season (due to a labor-dispute lockout). San Antonio Spurs had won that year—the team's first time in the NBA Finals. Celebrations upon the Lakers's win last month had been so seismic one would have been forgiven for assuming an earthquake. LA never misses an opportunity to party.

Roland's Latino boyfriend (Mickey couldn't remember his name) was a head shorter than Roland and couldn't have looked more different; he wore a lilac pullover with a floral shirt collar folded up out of it at the neck over extremely tight-fitting jeans, while his jet-black hair was shaved tight at each side but medium-length and combed back on top. A gold earring hung from his right earlobe. He seemed the life of the party, standing beside Roland with a beer in hand and chatting with the other men relentlessly, making them laugh. Roland couldn't take his eyes off him.

After an hour or so of chatting with Roland's uncles and downing beers, Roland's boyfriend kissed Roland goodbye, bid goodbye to the family, and left the party, probably busy from all those veterinary studies. Soon after, Roland disappeared inside the house with Reggie who flashed Mickey a wink as they walked toward the house, one arm around his nephew's shoulder.

It was time.

Mickey disengaged from the conversation he'd been having with Tori—about Martha, who had adored Tori and been adored by her—and entered Reggie's house in pursuit. No one in the kitchen, but Mickey knew where they'd be. He shuffled into the hallway, nodding hello at one of the family friends—if Mickey had met her before, he couldn't remember it—and opened the door to the basement.

Sounds of sports commentators and squeaks of trainers on polished maple made their way up the staircase, followed by Reggie's howl of celebration and Roland's laughter. A replay of some legendary game, no doubt. Reggie had seen them all a hundred times each and still the man yelled with glee when the Lakers scored.

Mickey descended the staircase and entered into what could only be described as Reggie's giant shrine to his beloved basketball franchise. Framed jerseys from various eras signed by their wearers hung on the walls, Reggie's most prized being the Magic Johnson jersey the man himself had won the 1980 Finals in as the first rookie to ever win MVP in such a game, worth a small fortune now, probably, though Reggie would never sell it. A full-size Lakers-branded Pop-A-Shot arcade game sat in one corner and in the other a small collection of basketballs used by the team at various points in time rested inside a glass display case. In the center of the room Reggie and Roland sat on a plain sofa, cans of PBR in hand, watching the game on a large TV.

"Who's winning?" Mickey joked as he approached. The game unfolding onscreen was the closing game of the recent NBA Final.

"Mick," Reggie said. "You know Roland."

"I sure do, although he looked a little smaller last time I saw him. How are you doing, Roland?"

"Not bad, sir."

"Sit down, Mick," Reggie said. "Don't got no soda down here but all that sugar ain't doin' you no favors anyhow."

"No, it's not, is it?" Mickey sat between the two men and watched as young Kobe Bryant intercepted a toss at the net by the Pacers's Jalen Rose, the home crowd at the Staples Center erupting in cheers.

The three of them watched the game for a while, chatting a little, until Reggie stood up to fetch more beer. With a hand on Mickey's shoulder, he said he needed to make a pit stop at the bathroom first and it wouldn't be quick.

When Mickey heard the door to the basement shut, he said to Roland, "Great game, wasn't it? You must have been celebrating with the rest of the city."

"I was celebrating all right. Maybe a little too hard. My head *still* hurts." He grinned.

Mickey chuckled. "I remember how that goes. You'd love to be at the Finals next year, I'm sure."

Roland's eyes went wide. "I'd do *anything* to be at one of those. Won't ever happen, though. I got a better chance learning to breathe underwater."

"Lakers could make the Finals again. They could be right here in LA."

"They're gonna win, sir. And the year after that too."

"I like your optimism. I didn't get an opportunity to meet that nice fellow you brought along with you today. What's his name?"

"Carlos," Roland said, his face lighting up.

"He seems like a nice fellow."

"He is, he's the best."

Mickey gave it a minute.

"Listen, Roland, do you happen to know of a drug dealer in the neighborhood named Floyd? He drives a blue Subaru with gold rims." Just like that. He watched Roland's face for any change.

"Yeah, I know him," Roland said, friendly enough, gazing at the TV.

"Do you know where I could find him?"

"I'm not gonna tell you that." Less friendly now. "With respect, sir, he'll pop you. And me. Even if I didn't go with you, he'd find out it was me who told you where to find him. It's not hard to connect you to my uncle and him to me."

"I'm not police, I don't want to arrest him. I'm not even interested in him, exactly. I'm investigating the disappearance of a young man and Floyd might know something about him. I just want to speak with him."

Roland looked at Mickey—really looked. "You *were* a cop, though. Right?"

"Why do you think that?"

"You still got the aura about you. We're trained to spot cops round here. Survival. Plus, you know my uncle. Floyd, he'll take one look at you and toss you in the trash. I don't mean to be rude, just being real with you. Sir."

Mickey nodded. He'd expected this. "Would tickets to the NBA Finals change your mind?"

Roland's head swung so fast on his shoulders it almost came loose. "What?"

"I had a client a while back, a banker with a contact in the NBA. In return for the job I did for him, he promised me a pair of tickets to any Finals game I wished. I don't have much interest myself, so I didn't ask for any. Truthfully, I was planning on surprising your uncle with them as a retirement gift when he leaves the force next year. I still can give him one, of course, but I can make sure the other ticket goes to you. Otherwise, I think Reggie might bring one of his sons. Don't you? Mike, probably. I know Reggie wishes he saw him more, and Mike would certainly fly over from Tampa for that."

Roland was looking at him like a hungry pup. "All right. You win."

The door to the basement swung open with a bang and down boomed Reggie's voice: "What I miss?"

Chapter Thirteen

DECEMBER, 1998

FIVE MONTHS OF SELLING COCAINE—or, rather, of Floyd selling cocaine—and the stacks of cash were beginning to outgrow their hiding places in Jemeka's home. A nice problem to have, she supposed, but not as nice as she had imagined it would be. Something about the ease of it all, the nature of it, didn't settle so fine at the back of her mind. Whenever she opened the wardrobe (or the closet or the cabinet) where she had stashed the bills, a creeping anxiety rose in her chest. There's a steep price to this money, the anxiety told her, and you know you're going to have to pay it one day. Sometimes another, quieter, voice whispered to her in the dead of night: What would your daddy think?

But today the voices didn't worry Jemeka. Today she was leaving her job at Magic Curls as the proud owner of her own salon fifteen minutes away in Lakewood, a result of her winning a "scratch card contest" (she was vague with the details whenever anyone pressed). By running her own business she could launder the money through it (a lot of it, anyway) and would no longer have to work for someone else, which had become old fast in the wake of her new career. It was a giant leap toward the life she had craved for so long, a life not dominated by counting quarters and filling up her weeks with as many hours of work she could get. A life not decayed by exhaustion and stress. A life which would allow her and Ray-Ray to start a family one day without fear of how they could ever afford to take care of their children—children who could go to college and thrive rather than stumble through the societal cracks poverty leaves behind, submitting to the same cycles of substance abuse and crime and imprisonment and death-by-cop which Jemeka had witnessed too many kids from the neighborhood fall prey to.

Now, finishing up her final shift in Magic Curls, Jemeka was almost breathless with excitement.

Tanisha, who had been somewhat cold to Jemeka since the announcement, approached her now as Jemeka held the mirror for old Louise in the chair, who nodded and smiled with approval: "Perfect, dear. Just perfect."

Tanisha touched Jemeka's shoulder gently and when Jemeka faced her Tanisha had tears swelling beneath her eyes. In her hands Tanisha held a long swivel scissors. "I can't believe I'm losing my longest-serving employee. But I'm happy for you, Jemeka. This . . ." She looked at the scissors and held it toward Jemeka. "It was the first scissors I ever bought when I decided to open the salon. I kept it all this time because, to me, it was proof that, at one time in my life, I did something brave. Lemme tell you, opening a salon all by myself in this neighborhood back in eighty-five, that wasn't easy. I'd like you to have it."

"Tanisha, I can't do that."

"Yes you can and yes you will. Take it."

Jemeka accepted the scissors. Now she felt like tearing up herself. "Thanks Tanisha. This really means a lot."

Tanisha wiped her eyes and beamed. "The apprentice becomes the master. Well, ain't this bittersweet. You better not take any of my customers."

"They'd never leave you. Isn't that right, Louise?"

Louise, tactless as the old often are, appeared to consider this gravely. "Well, I sure do like the way you have with my hair . . ."

"All right hush now," Jemeka said, tapping the woman's shoulder. She glanced out the window and her heart nearly stopped: Floyd stood on the sidewalk outside wearing a blue Adidas tracksuit that matched his ugly car, which he was leaning against staring right at Jemeka. He smirked and wiggled the fingertips of his right hand in a greeting, a thick gold chain swinging over his chest.

Jemeka swung her back to him and surveyed the women in the salon. None appeared to have noticed Floyd.

What if he came inside?

Jemeka grabbed her handbag and hurried through brief goodbyes to the women, thanking Tanisha again for the gift and promising to come by again soon, and to invite Tanisha to the new salon, of course, just as soon as it's ready.

She pushed open the door and stepped onto the street, ignoring Floyd as if he was a raving crackhead.

She'd gone twenty steps before he caught up with her. "Yo, what the fuck you playin' at, Jemeka?"

She spun on him, finger in his face. "What are *you* playing at? Damn fool. I'm not supposed to even know you. Don't ever come by my place of work again."

"All right, I get it. Chill, woman. Damn. We got a problem."

"What problem?"

"I'll show you."

"No Floyd. I'm going home."

"You're gonna want to see this."

"Why can't you just tell me what it is?"

"Better if I show you."

Jemeka sighed. "Pull up around the block."

She continued on ahead, the knot of nerves in her belly tightening.

THE MAN—kneeling on the ground, gagged, hands tied behind his back—stared at her with screaming eyes.

"What the hell is this?" Jemeka said.

Floyd, standing before the man, pistol by his side, said, "Crackhead jumped me in Wilson Park while I was selling some blow. Nigga almost stabbed me but I heard him behind me just in time."

Jemeka glanced at Ray-Ray standing silent and withdrawn in the corner of this small storage unit half-filled with cocaine and cannabis. The storage unit was one of many stacked on top of one another over four floors of an industrial park near LAX. Floyd had driven her here from Compton. When they'd approached, she had thought for a moment it was a gigantic shipping container he was bringing her to, as from the outside that's exactly what the building looked like: a gigantic, luminous-orange shipping container. But after Floyd had punched in the code on the gate outside, parked the car, and they'd entered the building, it had turned out to be subdivided into hundreds of smaller containers locked from the outside with heavy-duty padlocks. "This is where I keep the merchandise," Floyd had said. "Under a fake name. You don't ever wanna keep that shit in your own turf. You do that, pretty quick you find out which homies ain't homies, you feel me? Smart, huh?" Grinning at her like a mako shark.

"Was bound to happen eventually," Floyd said now. "Question is what we do with him."

Jemeka gazed at the man on the floor, pleading with his eyes. Above him a single bulb dangling from the low ceiling of this storage unit bathed him in dirty yellow light. She exhaled, trying to adapt to the situation. "Why were you selling in Wilson Park? You said you wouldn't have to do that if we sold to your Hollywood contacts."

"I got a few bags left over sometimes. Don't wanna waste it."

"No, Floyd. That wasn't the deal. You're earning more than enough already."

"If I want to sell the extra blow ain't a damn thing you can do about it."

"You sure about that, Floyd? What would Marsellus think when I tell him your carelessness is risking his money?" Jemeka stared at Floyd, giving nothing away but hoping he wouldn't call her bluff. If Jemeka said such a thing to Marsellus she would appear weak. She could imagine the man's response, something along the lines of *Deal with Floyd or I'll deal with you.*

Floyd held his gaze, eyes narrowed, then dropped his head. "All right. No more street sales."

"Good. Greed will be the end of you, Floyd."

"Funny thing to hear from a drug dealer."

Jemeka's face must have twitched because Floyd followed this up with, "What? You think your hands are clean 'cause you ain't out there putting this shit in people's hands? Your hands are dirty as mine. Difference between us? I got no problem with dirty hands."

Before Jemeka could say anything, Ray-Ray piped up from the corner: "I think we should let him go."

Jemeka and Floyd looked at Ray-Ray; Jemeka had forgotten he was here. Floyd too, probably. No one said a word for a moment; even the man, who had been moaning unintelligibly behind the duct tape, had fallen silent.

Floyd said, "We let this motherfucker go he tells every crackhead from here to Miami 'bout a bitch-ass dealer named Floyd. They gonna be jumpin' my ass every ten minutes. And now he seen where I keep this shit."

"What are you saying?" Jemeka said. But she knew.

"You need me to spell it out?"

"We can't kill him," Ray-Ray said, stepping out of the corner. Indignation rippled across his face.

Floyd looked calmly at Jemeka, knowing that unlike Ray-Ray she saw the terrible logic of it: Letting this man go would only mean they would have to kill another later. Or many others. Or be killed themselves. But still—to actually kill this man? In cold blood? Like this? The sheer wrongness of it surpassed pragmatism.

"Jemeka." Ray-Ray stared at her, wounded. "How could you even consider—"

"We're not gonna kill him," she said. "So you can all get that out your minds right now."

Relief beamed from the gagged man's eyes as tears spilled down his gaunt cheeks.

Floyd shook his head. "This the wrong move, Jemeka. I'll do it, don't bother me." He racked the slide of the pistol and pointed it at the man's temple.

The man screamed behind the duct tape, eyes almost popping out of his face, pleading with her.

"I said *no*!" Jemeka stepped forward. She gazed at the crackhead. "I'm gonna take this tape off. You start screaming and he'll shoot you. You hear me?"

The man nodded rigorously.

Jemeka tugged at the tape. It tore free of the man's lips with a sickening rip. Must have taken half his mouth with it.

Jemeka said, "In exchange for your life, you won't say a word about this to anyone. Yes?"

"Yes ma'am, not a word, on my life, you got it." The man nodding like a bobblehead.

She reached into his jeans and found his wallet. Empty of cash, it held what she was looking for: a California driver's license.

"Wesley Patrick Brown," she said. "Ain't that a mouthful. You still live at this address, Wesley?"

Wesley nodded.

Jemeka tossed the wallet at Floyd. "Take him home. Ray-Ray, go with Floyd, make sure he doesn't do something stupid. And you, Wesley Patrick Brown, you say a word about this to anyone, I'll send these boys to burn down your house with everyone in it. You got that?"

"I sure do, ma'am, I won't say nothin' to no one, I swear." Half of Wesley's teeth were missing and the rest were the color of mustard. She couldn't help but pity him.

Satisfied as she could be under the circumstances, Jemeka said, "I'll make my own way home." She spun on her heels and walked out the storage unit into the ghostly hallways of this lonely building, passing locked storage units on either side.

She feared this decision would come back to haunt her. Like a prophecy, she knew, deep down, that it would.

XXX

JEMEKA WAS HOME WITH RAY-RAY watching *The Jerry Springer Show* when Floyd called.

"Jemeka, I been thinking . . . I think we could do more."

"What you mean?"

On the TV a dwarf sprinted around a ring of chairs on the stage, evading the giant security guard attempting to catch him while Jerry oversaw it all like some dark sorcerer as the audience feverishly chanted his name.

"I mean we could take over this whole damn city. Ain't nothin' to say we couldn't. Word on the street? People are pissed with Marsellus, not just Gs but the whole community. He been pushing his weight round for too long, treating everybody in the neighborhood like dirt. He's no better than the police. Maybe worse. If someone were to take his place, treat people right, stand up for the neighborhood against the police and not the other way around, I don't think nobody would have a problem with it."

"Floyd, you could get us all killed for even *thinking* something like that. I don't wanna hear this."

"Ask yourself something, Jemeka. Are you really content with this being the peak of all we achieve? Selling blow to a few actors and porn stars? Or do you wanna make something of yourself? Make your mark on this earth before you die and fade away?"

On the TV the security guard had successfully grappled the dwarf into a chokehold, the audience of this modern coliseum erupting with bloodlust.

"I want to pay my bills and keep my damn head down, not get my ass killed. So stop telling me this shit. Okay?"

"A'ight, a'ight," Floyd said. "I'll talk to you later." He hung up.

The dwarf was being dragged off the stage now, the audience howling hysterically as this little man's life was being systematically destroyed before their eyes on national television.

Floyd's words rattled around Jemeka's head. She imagined herself rising up in the world, making her mark, doing things *her* way, nobody standing above her. She hated that the thought excited her and she knew that this thought had been lingering in her subconscious ever since she held that first brick in her hand after ramming that gangster with her car. Killing a man—something she had always figured as the most difficult of actions—had turned out to be one of the easiest things she'd ever done. What else could she accomplish if she set her mind to it and let nothing get in her way?

"What did he want?" Ray-Ray said.

"Floyd thinks we could take over from Marsellus."

Ray-Ray shook his head, disbelief written across him. "No way, Jemeka. That's crazy talk."

"Yeah," Jemeka said, agreeing with him, but something in the way she had said it must have failed to convince Ray-Ray because he was looking at her like a man on a mission.

"You shouldn't listen to much of what Floyd says. He's a bad dude, Jemeka. A bad dude."

"We ain't exactly angels, Ray-Ray."

"We're no angels, but Floyd . . . he's something else. Just don't pay him too much attention is all."

Jemeka returned her focus to *Jerry Springer*. Onscreen a young white girl dressed up like a goth—black hair, black nails, black lips, black clothes, everything black except her ultra-white skin—pouted miserably above a caption that read "My daughter thinks she's a witch and tried to kill me with a hex."

America.

Chapter Fourteen

JULY, 1999

JOHNNY CASH'S "MAN IN BLACK" PLAYED FROM THE RADIO—Alabama had changed channels until she'd found a country station. She listened to the dark troubadour tell it straight, his voice like blood slow-flowing from an unhealable wound. She had searched for this music because she had wanted to remember from where she had come, not because she missed that toxic little town or her violent, perverted father, but because she missed the young woman she had been. The young woman with hope in her heart and dreams nestled alongside. Rage flared inside that heart now. Mr. Cash knew how she felt.

The sound of the lock on the door beeping open and Richie crashed into the room like a thunderstorm. Beads of sweat dripped from his forehead, the cheeks below it pale and skinny.

"Help me," he pleaded, breathless, and collapsed onto the bed.

"What's wrong?"

"Shot. I need a shot."

Alabama's heart sank. Of course.

She gathered the equipment and went through the process mindlessly, knowing it better than she knew herself, careful to use only a small amount of this highly pure powder.

After she had finished, Richie lay flat on the bed.

"Better?" Alabama said, sitting on the edge of the bed beside him.

Richie nodded slowly, face a vision of trauma. "Even a few hours without it is too much now. It'll kill us if we let it." He appeared resigned to this fact, that Richie fire gone from his eyes.

"No, we'll get clean. It'll take some time but we'll do it, and then—"

"And then what?"

Alabama flinched at the aggression in his voice.

"Sorry, I didn't mean to snap. It's just—" He gazed at the duvet, then looked at her in a hard but not unkind way. "Say we do get clean, and I'm not sure we can, we're in real fuckin' deep, but say we do . . . it's gonna take two things we don't have—time, and money. We don't have much time because we don't have money, and if we keep robbing diners for money, we're gonna run out of time."

Richie sat up with a groan and shimmied his back against the headboard. It appeared to take tremendous effort. "Way I see it, this plan I told you about? We need to put it into action ASAP."

"I know," Alabama said. "You were gone for a long time. How'd it go with the porn star? What's his name again?"

"Jeff. I was gone so long because he had some chick in there with him and I had to wait outside. It went okay with Jeff until the fuckin' withdrawals got so bad I had to rush here."

"Feeling better?" She rubbed his thigh.

"A little."

"That's good, baby." She rubbed his cheek, felt the bone beneath. "So you gon' tell me how it went with Jeff or what?"

Richie nodded, a little excitedly, coming back to life now. "Yeah. So, I go introduce myself to Jeff. We're sitting in his apartment. Guy's got money I think but he lives almost as bad as we do. Place is a dump. Except he's got this gigantic fuckin' TV. I mean *huge*, I wanna get one for whatever apartment we move into after this score. He's an oddball, Jeff. He's like . . ." Richie concentrated for a moment. "You remember that Coen Brothers movie we saw last year? After the diner we did in—shit, I don't remember where. But, after, we got those amazing lobster rolls and shot up in the theater."

Alabama smiled. That had been a good day. "*The Big Lebowski*."

"Yeah, that's it. Well, Jeff's like the guy from that movie. The Dude abides, man. High as a kite and cool as the breeze. I told Jeff what I planned on doing. Turns out he's got his own reasons for wanting some quick cash, so he's in."

Alabama bit her lip. "I don't know about this, Richie. Those diners . . . they were just regular people grabbin' a bite, not wanting any trouble. It's not the same for drug dealers."

"It is the same when you get right down to it. You point the gun, you take their shit, you leave. Come on, we talked about this already."

"And you want me to just wait here while you do it? I'll be worried sick."

"Well, about that . . ." Richie rubbed his chin. "Originally I was thinking just me and Jeff would do it. Get in and get out with the car waiting outside. Get Jeff to drive so I can keep my hands free if it all goes south. But . . . I dunno, there's something about the guy, he's not all there. I don't feel good enough about it being just the two of us and no one in the car. I want you to wait in the car like we always said. Me and Jeff go do it, then you drive us the hell outta there."

"Oh."

"You'll just be in the car, all you gotta do is sit there. It'll be easy. Like I said, in and out."

"Okay." Panic like a bat in her belly. For the first time since the overdose she heard heroin whispering to her, promising to take her fear away.

"You okay?" Richie said.

Alabama swallowed her rising anxiety. "Is there a record store near here?"

Richie blinked at her. "What? Why?"

"I want to get a Johnny Cash CD."

"Yeah?" He looked confused.

"Uh huh. A Johnny Cash song came on the radio before you came in and it made me feel . . . well, I don't know really, but I liked it and I'd like to listen to some more."

"Okay? Well, we could drive to my favorite record store in all of LA in five minutes. Tower Records on Sunset Boulevard. Once, when I was a kid, I saw Jimmy Page in there."

"Who's Jimmy Page?"

"Who's Jimmy Page, are you serious?"

She shrugged and Richie laughed.

Alabama touched his thigh. "How about you take me there right now and show me around?"

"Right now? Yeah, all right, I'm feeling a little better. Let's do it."

He leaped out of bed, that Richie fire back in his eyes.

"You gotta explain this whole Johnny Cash thing on the way," he said.

Alabama squeezed her husband's hand. "Deal."

XXX

IT LOOKED EXACTLY AS HE REMEMBERED IT. Vivid red paint covered the four walls of the flat, single-story building, a thick yellow border above it reading "TOWER RECORDS" in the same red. Giant posters of new-release albums hung on the walls next to one another all the way around the store; in Richie's line of sight now: Red Hot Chili Peppers's *Californication*; Britney Spears's *...Baby One More Time*; TLC's *FanMail*; Backstreet Boys's *Millennium*; Blink-182's *Enema of the State*; and *Significant Other* by the nu-metal abomination known as Limp Bizkit. The way Richie saw it, something had happened to mainstream music during the post-grunge phase of the '90s and so far this year's releases had been the most vapid of the lot, save for a few that maybe had some artistic expression if you listened hard enough (and excluding the Chili Peppers record, which ruled). Corporate major labels and *MTV* had joined forces in a union of evil to destroy all semblance of art from the world and churn the charred remains—not art anymore but *products*—through a dollar factory of unfettered capitalism, squeezing out the big bucks as quickly as possible before the whole crazy ride comes to a screaming, bloody end. Which it would. All of this would come to a tragic end; the whole western world had gone mad, taking mindless consumerism to dizzying new heights as most of the East scrambled to get in on the action. Meanwhile, people like him and Alabama slip through the cracks and no one in this apathetic hellhole gives a shit, too busy patching over the vacancies of their lives in desperate attempts to forget the dreams they abandoned when they sold out to the machine. Of course he and Alabama were junkies. Of course they were thieves. What choice did they have when you got right—*right*—down to it? Their fates had been sealed when society had set itself upon this dark path, and there would be many more Richies and Alabamas to come so long as it stayed the course.

"We goin' in or what?" Alabama said, dragging Richie from these cynical thoughts. She stared at him impatiently from the passenger seat.

"Well, since you're pulling my arm." He winked at her and opened the door.

Inside the store, Slayer's "Angel of Death" played from speakers dotted about the place. Ken Wong—the very same Ken Wong who had been manager when Richie had frequented the store—stood behind the counter wearing a yellow Tower Records T-shirt, bobbing his head to the song, his trademark super-long jet-black hair almost reaching his bellybutton and a traditional Chinese dragon tattooed up his entire left arm. Ken might have to put up posters of the latest pop crap on the walls outside but he'd never play that shit in here. Richie was glad to see him.

He wandered to the punk rock section, Alabama in tow. Born in 1974, Richie had been too young to experience the birth of punk in LA, but by the time he had turned thirteen he'd begun devouring the music like his life had depended on it (and maybe it had). From punk rock Richie had discovered metal, and from metal his vinyl collection, already towering above him by this point, had grown to include classic rock records, which held a special place in his heart now. Something about that music and its paradoxical qualities of timelessness and nostalgia had intoxicated young Richie, sending him into a dreamland he had never let go of, and this intoxication with fantasy, now that he thought about it, had perhaps been a sign that later he would seek bigger, better dreams inside the needle. But before the needle there had been music and it had given him life rather than take it away.

"Hey, you okay?" Alabama said, nudging an elbow into Richie's ribs. "You're not even looking at the CDs."

Richie glanced down. The albums sat in their positions as before, nothing in Richie's hands. Jesus, had he been standing here gaping like an imbecile?

"Yeah, just deep in thought. This place brings back a lot of memories. Now that I'm here, I think I was avoiding it for a long time. Let's go get you some Johnny Cash."

He brought her to the country section and, sure enough, there was the Man in Black front and center, at least a dozen of his albums.

"Hmmm, I don't know which one to get," Alabama said.

"Can't go wrong with a greatest hits collection." Richie picked one up: *The Man in Black: His Greatest Hits*. On the cover, Cash's face, emerging out of a pitch-black background like a spirit, stared knowingly, even smugly, into Richie's eyes. It was a look that could end your life or save it, depending on the man's mood. Richie checked the back cover. It more or less had the songs a Cash fan would want it to have.

"This one looks good," he said.

Alabama took it. "Okay."

"How are you gonna listen to it?"

"I was thinking it could be for the car."

"The car? Well yeah, but that's not enough. You're gonna want to listen to it by yourself too. Let's get you a Discman."

"Oh, we don't need to spend that much on me. The car will be just fine."

"Nah, we do. It doesn't matter, we'll be rich soon."

He retrieved a Discman from the equipment section of the store. "All right, let's pay for these and get out of here."

He brought the items to the counter where Ken Wong scanned them absentmindedly, nodding his head to Slayer, long hair rippling like midnight waves.

"I'm glad to see you're still working here, Mr. Wong," Richie said.

The gold ring dangling from Ken's ear glinted under the fluorescent light in the ceiling. If he recognized Richie, he didn't show it. Instead he nodded, as if in simple agreement that, yes, it *is* good that he still works here.

"That'll be forty-five dollars and eighty," Ken said. He put the album and Discman into a small carrier bag.

Richie almost laughed. Ken was probably high as the blue sky.

"You don't remember me? Richie Leonard. I used to hang out here all the time when I was a kid. I was one of those punk kids used to skate out in the parking lot. One time, a cop beat on Scotty, the weird kid who followed us around, so we smashed up the cop's cruiser. Pigs chased us around the neighborhood for weeks, even putting the heat on you if I remember correctly."

Ken's mouth came open, a funny look on a guy who usually appeared oblivious to the world. "Richie . . ." He ran his eyes over Richie. A look formed on Ken then, a little too close to pity for Richie's liking, morphing now into . . . repulsion?

"It's nice to see you again, Richie." Ken's eyes said different.

A hot poker of anger prickled Richie's spine. What the hell kind of response was that? He forced a smile. "Funny how time flies, isn't it?"

"Sure is," Ken said, no joy in it.

Silence.

"That's forty-five eighty," Ken said.

Richie looked at the plastic Tower Records bag on the table. Back up at Ken. Definitely repulsion in the man's eyes. It said: *Pay for your shit and get out.* Years of business, of youth, of history, and this was what Richie got for it: made to feel like a piece of shit on the man's shoe.

Ken reached out a hand and placed it on top of the bag. A tattoo foo dog snarled up at Richie as if daring him to try to take the bag.

Sensing the vibe, Alabama stepped close. "Richie, pay the man."

Richie stared at Ken. "Say it."

"Say what?" Ken said.

"What you're thinking."

"I don't know what—"

"Say it."

"What are you—"

"Say it, Wong. Say it. You think I'm a fuckin' loser. Say it. Say it!" The red haze had descended now and there was nothing to do but see it through.

"Richie!" Alabama yelled. "Stop it! Stop!" Her hand on his bicep, pulling him toward her.

He looked at her. Terror on her face.

A gasping sound.

Richie turned his head: Ken lay on the floor behind the counter. Blood dribbled out of his mouth onto the yellow Tower Records T-shirt where it merged eerily with the crimson text, indicating the transformation of this record store into a house of blood and Richie responsible for it. The Slayer bellowing out of the speakers—"Alter of Sacrifice" currently—seemed rather sick now, as if this moment preordained.

"What have I done . . ." Richie said. But it was done, and he had done it.

He swallowed the shame and the regret and accepted the fact of it. He was a dirtbag and he was tired of pretending otherwise.

Beside him, Alabama's hands clutched her cheeks, gazing at Ken in horror.

Richie grabbed the Tower Records bag from the counter and shoved it into her chest. "Take it."

She took it.

He stepped over Ken still gasping on the floor, opened the cash register, and grabbed the bills it contained, shoving them into his pockets.

"Let's go," he said. He marched past Alabama out the door.

He was a dirtbag, and he was tired of pretending otherwise.

RICHIE SPED THE AUDI ALONG THE STREETS OF LOS ANGELES like a madman. He was furious. At Ken Wong. At America. At God if there was a God to be furious at. But, really, he was furious at himself. Alabama sat quivering in the passenger seat. He'd gone and broken her heart again and that hurt most of all.

He gritted his teeth and flung the car around a corner to a chorus of honking horns. The sun in his face now, half blind, Richie pressed harder on the pedal, daring the universe to kill them and put an end to this desperate cycle of mistakes.

Less than five minutes later, the hands of fate delivered them safely to the Four Seasons.

Alabama got out of the car without a word and marched into the hotel. The Tower Records bag remained on the seat. Richie looked at the blood on the knuckles of his right hand, some of it his. The FUCK tattooed into his skin seemed, like it had many times before, a declaration of regret screamed into the void of this twisted heart of America. There would be no fixing this with her, and he wouldn't try. There was nothing left now but to move forward. It was time to do the score.

He grabbed the Tower Records bag and exited the car.

ALABAMA HAD LOCKED HERSELF IN THE BATHROOM by the time he got up to the room. He heard a tap come on, water splashing loudly into the bath. She'd be in there for hours. He checked the stash: no dope missing. Just a couple Oxys. Relief swept through him. But so did the itch, that whispering voice in his head growing steadily but surely into screams.

If she could leave it, why couldn't he?

Could he?

He twisted the lid off the OxyContin bottle and palmed a couple of the little pink twenties. Wouldn't do much but they'd take the edge off. He plucked a sheet of tissue out of the box on the bedside table and dropped the pills into the center of it, their pink skin bright against the white tissue. He wrapped the pills in the tissue and dropped it on the floor and stamped on it, rotating the heel of his boot to crush the Oxys. Satisfied, he retrieved the tissue from the floor and poured the pills, now crushed into a coarse powder, onto the bedside table.

A straw lay on the bedside table and Richie picked it up. He shaped the powder into a rough line, pressed the straw into his right nostril, and snorted. The chemical burn of it like an old friend. Felt like sand at the back of his throat. He swallowed lumpy saliva and next came the sour chemical flavor, like the most burnt and bitter day-old coffee you could ever drink, a taste he would never get used to. But, already, his muscles were relaxing, heart rate slowing in anticipation of the release it would provide, however brief.

Richie sat against the headboard and swung his legs onto the mattress. Not even the Oxys could dull the rage that throbbed through him like a wound. He was tired of waiting. He'd go see Jeff again, finish the conversation they'd started and set a date for the score.

Making this decision softened Richie's rage a touch (or maybe it was the Oxys kicking in) and he felt a warm tingling in his groin.

Was he . . . horny?

He listened for any sound of Alabama finishing up in the bathroom. Nothing.

He switched the TV on, turned the volume down to two, and navigated to the pay-per-view pornos. He chose one titled *Hard Evidence* because of the big-titted brunette on the cover and a woefully scripted police interrogation scene in black and white like film noir began to play out on the screen, the brunette from the cover handcuffed to a chair while a greasy-haired detective in a suit threatened his prisoner that if she didn't start cooperating he'd be forced to bring his partner in here and she wouldn't want that. The woman's dark eyes seemed to disagree, flicking down flirtatiously to her cleavage bursting up out of her little leather jacket. After some moments of this, the detective left and another man entered. Richie's jaw almost hit his balls: the man was Jeffrey Strokes. A little younger, hair a little shorter, standing a little straighter, but unmistakably Jeff.

Smirking, Richie tugged his pants below his thighs and wrapped a sweaty palm around his dick.

Chapter Fifteen

JULY, 2000

COMPTON AT NIGHT WAS NOT FOR THE FAINT OF HEART.

Cruising down Compton Boulevard in the Catalina, Mickey sensed the charged atmosphere of the place, an energy that said anything could happen. Young men loitered in groups on the sidewalks in baggy T-shirts and bandannas while young women strolled up and down, smirking at the men hollering after them and whistling. When traffic lights turned red, blank-faced children appeared out of the darkness under overpasses like wraiths to sell drugs to drivers. Prostitutes wobbled along the streets on high heels, many of them with the vacant gaze of the addicted, while men with hard hearts and a lust for blood watched their every move. All the while well-intentioned families who called Compton home got ground up in the giant machine of this nation, slipping further toward poverty and the tragic moment when pressing need overtakes good intentions.

Even still, Compton was no longer what it once was. Ten years ago, Mickey might not have driven through it, and certainly wouldn't have stopped and wandered around. But the homicide rate had decreased steadily since

'94, down to forty-eight murders in '98 from a peak of eighty-seven in '91, and small businesses were slowly but surely returning to the city. It bothered Mickey deeply that the state of California, with an economy greater than that of most countries, wouldn't help these people, or that the federal government of the United States, the richest country in the history of the world, wouldn't help them either, instead spending hundreds of billions of dollars per year on warfare and destruction. The people of Compton could be lifted from poverty with the signing of a bill, and it was no wonder, when you got right down to it, why so many had resorted to crime.

Mickey spotted an olive sign for Locust Avenue on the corner ahead and turned onto it. According to Roland, Floyd spent much of his time at a place known as the "pink house," a once-residential home now occupied by a faction of the Bloods street gang. Mickey had asked why they called it the pink house. "Because it's pink," Roland had said, as if the question had been a dumb one, and, sure enough, Mickey saw now in the distance ahead a two-story house softly pink in the glow of a streetlight.

He slowed the Pontiac. Lookouts would have flagged him already, alerting fellow gang members about an unknown vehicle cruising toward them. Mickey swallowed, his throat suddenly dry. He could hear Roland's many warnings in his mind, the kid practically begging Mickey not to drive down here and especially not alone, but Mickey needed to drive down here and alone was the best way to do it—they'd kill Roland for bringing Mickey down here, and they'd kill Reggie if they discovered (or already knew) he was a cop. Alone, Mickey wasn't a cop, and he was old, and he was white, which was to say he wasn't part of the Bloods's world, and, with a bit of luck, Floyd wouldn't mind him asking a few questions about an old customer he might not even remember.

Well, that had been the idea. Now that Mickey was ruminating on it, it did sound a little thin. But it was too late to turn back now. He met his own gaze in the rear-view and chuckled. Getting shot by a street gang in Compton at seventy-eight years old during his final case as a private investigator would be, all things considered, not the worst way to go.

The pink house was just a few buildings over now. A line of bushes ran around the perimeter, about the height of a tall man. Mickey killed the engine and exited the car. Though almost always dry, the warm Los Angeles air felt humid now, suffocating. The dull *whummp whummp whummp* of bass boomed from the house. Mickey couldn't see the eyes staring at him, but he sensed them.

He moved toward the sound of music, passing a tiny bungalow with bars over the windows, no lights on and no car in the drive. He passed another bungalow, this one spilling bright light onto the street. Young people moved about inside, and smoke with the resinous, sour smell of cannabis curled out of the opened windows.

The pink house sat just one house over now. As Mickey closed the gap between himself and the house, the recklessness of his actions became clear—Roland's concern for Mickey perhaps less misplaced than Mickey had given him credit for—and he wondered what Martha would think, if she saw him now, and maybe she could, and yet feeling all of this in no way made Mickey want to turn around, and he wondered what that said about him.

He stepped beyond the bushes, bringing the front of the house into his line of sight. A young man in baggy jeans and a red T-shirt stood right there smoking a cigarette. Mickey almost bumped into him.

"The fuck? You lost?" The man was a foot taller than Mickey.

Mickey forced his shoulders straight and looked up into the man's hard eyes. "I hope not. I'm here to speak with a fellow named Floyd. Is Mr. Floyd here?"

"What are you, a cop?"

"I'm not a police officer, no."

"We kill cops round here, bitch. We kill white boys too."

"Well, it's a long time since I was a boy."

The threatening expression on the man's face remained and the situation could have gone either way until he said, "What you doin' here then?"

Mickey exhaled quietly as a tremor passed through his hand. He'd have to play this right. "I'm a private investigator—" a look of menace swept over the man's face—"*not* a police officer," Mickey hastily added, "a *private* investigator. I've been employed to find a man who went missing some time ago.

Mr. Floyd did business with this man from time to time, so, maybe, if we're very lucky, Mr. Floyd might remember something significant this man may have said to him. It's a longshot, I know, but, to be frank with you, I'm out of options."

The man shook his head. "You must be crazy comin' here like this. You might not be a cop, but you was a cop. Am I right? All you *private investigators*—" mimicking Mickey's voice sarcastically—"was cops before. And you got that way about you."

Mickey nodded. "You're right, I was a cop. But just for one year, a long, long time ago. I quit as a rookie."

"Why?"

Mickey considered the question, remembering that dark night which had led to his current career path—to this very moment.

"Brutality. The police didn't treat the people on the street right. At first I thought the cruelty was an unfortunate side effect of the job. Pretty quickly I realized the cruelty was the point. I tried to change it, and when I couldn't, I quit. Couldn't be part of it."

The man observed him. Hostility had left his expression, and Mickey thought he saw a trace of respect.

"Go home," the man said. "Turn around, get back in your car, and go home. Floyd, he ain't as nice as me."

"I'll take my chances."

"Whatever. Wait here."

He turned and made for the house, a pistol visible above his jeans. He opened the door of the house and hip-hop blasted out of it until the door shut, dulling it back to the thump of bass.

A blue Subaru Impreza with gold rims sat parked in the drive. Curtains covering each window made it impossible to gauge how many people were inside. The paint on the exterior of the building was flaky up close, painted on a long time ago. Perhaps the building was once a small nursing home, or a community center. Something useful, rather than the waste of space it had become.

Music poured out of the house, clearer and louder. The man had come out of it. He waved for Mickey to follow. Mickey crunched across the gravel toward the house. An aroma of cannabis grew stronger with each step, citrusy and bright.

The man entered the house. Mickey followed.

The man shut the door behind them. The awful music thudded like a headache. Despite the overpowering stench of pot, Mickey had not yet seen anyone inside. Laughter sounded somewhere within.

"In here," the man said.

Mickey followed him through a narrow hallway into a dirty kitchen empty of human beings but littered with bundles of cash and beer bottles and ashtrays and dirty plates. They continued into a dimly lit living room. Smoke hung in the room like the web of a giant arachnid. Mickey's eyes watered, head feeling light immediately. Three men sat on a sofa, each with a fat joint between their fingers. A young woman lay sprawled across another, staring at Mickey with detached curiosity.

The man who had brought Mickey into the room nodded at the men on the sofa and left. The man on the left of the sofa gestured to the woman. She stood up, and, moving with the fluid grace of a dancer, she approached a gigantic home stereo system and rotated a knob, bringing the volume of the music down, before returning to the sofa and sprawling onto it.

The man on the left—shorter than the other two and younger, with alive eyes, the only of the three not wearing red—gazed at Mickey with amusement. "Marcus, tell me something," the man said. "Do you see an old-ass cracker-lookin' motherfucker standing right there or am I high outta my goddamn mind?"

"I see an old-ass cracker standing there," said the fat man in the center of the sofa.

"What about you, Shawn? You see an old-ass cracker too?"

"I see him," said the man on the right of the sofa. Marcus and Shawn. That made Floyd the one on the left who liked to talk.

Floyd said, "What the fuck you want, cracker? I ain't sellin' you no rocks so don't even ask."

Mickey spluttered on the fumes. "I'm not here to buy or sell anything. May I sit?" He gestured to the couch behind him.

"Go ahead." Floyd turned to Marcus. "This motherfucker."

The three men laughed.

Mickey said, "Well, Mr. Floyd—"

"Mr. Floyd, you hear this nigga?" Shawn said.

"I like it," Floyd said. "Man showing some respect."

"Mr. Floyd, I'm a private investigator. I was hired to trace the whereabouts of a man who went missing a year ago. I believe that you may have been acquainted with this man—" Mickey coughed, head beginning to float—"and therefore it's possible, if unlikely, that perhaps this man once said something to you that might help me locate him."

Floyd sucked on the joint. "You using too many fancy words, cracker. You tryna make me feel like a dumbass nigga?"

Mickey shook his head, eyeballs burning. His thoughts seemed to be simultaneously merging and coming apart. "Of course not, I'm just talking how I talk."

Floyd grinned. "I'm just playin' with you, man. You got some balls coming in here saying that shit. If a brother from the block came in here and said that, he might not make it out. You know what I'm saying?"

Floyd leveled a curious gaze at Mickey. "You ever consider I might admit to poppin' whoever you're looking for? Then what?"

Mickey hesitated, not sure how to respond. He had not considered this outcome.

"Relax, cracker. I know you ain't dumb enough to come in here and say this shit if you thought I had anything to do with it. Who you looking for?"

"His name is Jeffrey Strokes. He was in the pornography business before he disappeared." Mickey could have sworn that, for a second there, at the mention of Jeffrey's name, a shadow had passed over Floyd's face—almost a look of fright—so quick he almost hadn't seen it. Or maybe the smoke was getting to him.

"Jeffrey Strokes? Hell kind of white boy name is that. Nah, I never heard of him. Porn? The fuck you think I have to do with that nasty shit?" He had passed off this denial as natural, but there had been a slight delay, as if he'd been considering his response. Or had there?

"Are you sure about that?" Mickey said.

"Am I sure? Fuck kind of question is that? You disrespecting me in my own house?"

"No, I—"

"Who told you I knew this dude?"

"A colleague of Jeffrey's. He saw you with him once, heard your name. It wasn't hard to track you down from there."

"Track me down how? Who you been talking to?"

Mickey bit his lip. The last he wanted to do was implicate Roland. "I asked people on the street, I don't know their names."

Floyd didn't look so entertained by it all now. "What you mean someone saw me with this dude? You're telling me you already knew I knew this guy but you come in here and try catch me out?"

"I'm not trying to catch anyone out, Mr. Floyd. I'm just trying to do my job."

Floyd didn't look happy. "I used to sell weed by some of the porno studios in the Valley. Dude must have been one of my customers. I can't remember everybody, shit. You really come here 'cause I sold weed to this cat? You gonna track down his hairdresser too?"

"I'll speak with anyone I can."

"They don't make 'em like you no more. You look like you from an old movie." He glanced at the men beside him and said, "Philip motherfuckin' Marlowe here."

Shawn and Marcus laughed.

Floyd scowled. "Y'all don't even know who Philip Marlowe is." That shut them up pretty quick.

Mickey said, "Well, it was worth a try. Thank you for your time, Mr. Floyd." He struggled up off the couch, the room spinning around him, hoping Floyd wouldn't prevent him from leaving.

Floyd raised a palm.

Mickey stopped in his tracks, heartbeat in his ears.

Floyd seemed to change his mind. He shook his head and sat back into the sofa. "Get him the hell outta here," he said to the woman.

Mickey glanced at her, staring back at him with a mischievous grin on her lips.

She stood up gracefully and took him by the hand and led him out of the room.

"Yo Marlowe!" Floyd called after them. "You ever come back here, I'll kill you."

His words followed Mickey out of the building. The young woman blew him a kiss and shut the door.

Mickey gulped at the fresh air like a drowning man. It was only now, away from the smoke, that he realized the extent of its effects on him. He felt like a head hovering above its body, filled with thoughts that knotted and pulled apart in a repetitive, oceanic rhythm. For some reason he could not fathom, he imagined the sensation not dissimilar to how an octopus traversing the lonely ocean floor might feel.

He trudged through slimy air toward his car, then drove down Locust Avenue and turned onto Compton Boulevard, where he parked by the sidewalk and waited, playing a hunch. He had never expected Floyd to admit to anything. He had intended simply to rattle Floyd's cage and see how the man reacted.

Twenty minutes later, the pot wearing off, Floyd's blue Subaru drove up Locust Avenue toward the intersection.

Mickey ducked as the Subaru passed by headed west on Compton Boulevard. He got a clear view of Floyd in the driver's seat, alone. Two traits most career criminals had in common: impatience, and a paranoid fear of talking business over the phone. Learning how to effectively exploit these reliable traits had done wonders for Mickey's career over the years.

He counted to ten, ignited the engine, and swung the Catalina around onto Compton Boulevard in pursuit.

XXX

DECEMBER, 1998

CHRISTMAS HAD BEEN TOUGH WHEN JEMEKA WAS GROWING UP, her father never with money to spare and the empty spaces in their home that her mother might have occupied had she hung around all the more visible. But this year, sharing a cheese platter with the man she loved in a fancy restaurant in Beverly Hills on Christmas Eve, glass of fine red wine at her fingertips, Jemeka felt whole.

"This sure is a nice place, huh?" she said, glancing around the oval-shaped dining area of the restaurant. Mirrors running along the walls made the space seem infinite, and a huge aquarium built into one of the walls added to this sense of grandeur. In the center of the room a dainty pianist fluttered long fingers over the keys of a cream grand piano, creating blissful melodies. Named The Long Goodbye, the restaurant had only recently opened, almost immediately gaining a Michelin star, and, following a glowing write-up in the *Los Angeles Times*, had become the new place-to-be for LA's elite. Jemeka could see why. She and Ray-Ray shouldn't be here, of course, being seen in a place like this the very opposite of laying low, but it was Christmas Eve and she allowed the exception.

"Sure is," Ray-Ray said. "Feel like I don't belong in a place like this." Dressed in a tailored suit and tie which Jemeka had picked out for him, Ray-Ray looked handsome and a little uncomfortable, which made her love him more. She knew she looked pretty in her Prada dress and Tiffany earrings.

"These people are no better than us, Ray-Ray. Maybe they were born into this life, but they're just people. We had to struggle our way up from the bottom. If anything, that makes us better than them."

She picked up her wine glass and swilled it beneath her nose: strawberry and sweet and very slightly smoky. "All that ever made them different was money. In this country you're rich or you're nobody." She tasted the wine: sour and smooth, then fruity with a dry finish.

Ray-Ray appeared about to say something, then glanced away.

"What?" Jemeka said.

"Nothing, nothing."

"Ray-Ray."

"Just leave it, Jemeka. It's nothing."

"I can do this all night, Ray-Ray."

"Goddamn it, woman."

She raised an eyebrow.

Ray-Ray sighed in resignation. "Do you think it's right to be doing this?"

"Doing what?"

"Living this life knowing where that money came from. What we might be doing to our brothers and sisters on the streets."

Jemeka gritted her teeth. "Are you serious? Right now? Christmas Eve and you wanna do this shit right now?" It had come out more aggressive than she'd intended.

"Forget it."

"Yeah. Yeah, I am gonna forget it. Can't I enjoy one night? Christmas Eve of all nights. Life hasn't been easy, Ray-Ray."

Ray-Ray nodded and watched the pianist.

Jemeka followed his gaze. The woman leaning over the keys as she played, eyes closed, pouring herself into the music. Jemeka envied the woman then, envied her passion, her ability to lose herself in something so pure, so harmless, so true. Jemeka envied her wholeness.

"And besides," Jemeka said, feeling rage bubbling up, "you're the one who started selling this shit in the first place. I had to save *your* ass. So don't lecture me on morals, Ray-Ray. I'm doing what I have to to survive."

Ray-Ray looked at her with an expression that said he wasn't buying her bullshit, that dining in this silly restaurant was a longshot from survival. But Jemeka wasn't buying her own bullshit, either. The truth of it was she despised being poor and could never return to that life. She'd rather be dragged to Hell by her fingernails if that was what it came to—and it might. She wasn't hiding from this truth, she'd accepted it. Christmas Eve simply wasn't the right night to discuss it, that was all.

"I'm sorry," she said. "I just want to enjoy the night, you know?"

Ray-Ray nodded. "I'm sorry too." He closed his big, warm hand around hers.

"I love you, Ray-Ray."

"Love you too." But something in his voice hadn't sounded quite right.

"Let's go home."

ONE OF THOSE SILLY MAGAZINES in the salon claimed that snow hadn't fallen in Los Angeles since 1962. Although there was no chance of snow tonight, an icy breeze snaked around Jemeka's bare legs and rattled her teeth. She pulled her coat tight around her waist and linked arms with Ray-Ray. Dozens of similar couples wandered up and down the streets taking in the festive displays in store windows of Santa Claus and snowmen and giant boxes meticulously wrapped with pretty bows on top. A feeling of hope hung in the air, the kind of hope specific to this particular holiday period, hope that said you've survived another year and the next one will be easier.

A young family of Asian heritage stood on the sidewalk ahead, two little girls with beanie hats pulled tight over their little faces pointing wide-eyed at a giant reindeer in a window display. Looking at those little girls Jemeka felt a powerful yearning to create a family of her own with Ray-Ray and watch them grow bit by bit, guiding them toward good lives. This urge took her by surprise. Since when had she wanted kids?

"Ray-Ray—" Jemeka began, but a black limousine with tinted windows had rolled up beside them.

The rear door flung open and Marsellus gazed at her coolly from the back seat. "Get in."

JEMEKA SAT NEXT TO RAY-RAY IN THE SPACIOUS LIMOUSINE. Marsellus faced them on the horizontal side of the long L-shaped seat. On the seat next to him his fat dog snored contentedly. An overwhelming aroma of

Marsellus's cologne filled the narrow space, smelling of cinnamon and cedarwood and spicy cloves.

The vehicle rolled forward and Marsellus lifted the top off a glass whiskey decanter and poured the amber liquid into three glasses arranged in a ring around the decanter. He handed a glass each to Jemeka and Ray-Ray and picked up the third.

Ray-Ray sipped at his but Jemeka felt no such desire; the woody, syrupy scent of it mingling with the cologne was making her light-headed.

"Where we going?" she said.

Marsellus watched buildings pass by. "It's a surprise." Not looking at them.

The knot in Jemeka's belly tightened.

"I ain't ever been in a limo before," Ray-Ray said. "Sure is nice."

Marsellus ignored him. "You look like you've been having a good night," he said to Jemeka. "Beverly Hills. Not quite Compton, is it?"

Nobody said anything.

"But you know what they say," Marsellus said. "You can take a nigga outta Compton . . ." looking at Jemeka, malicious amusement behind his eyes, ". . . but that nigga still a gangsta."

Marsellus resumed gazing out the window and Jemeka did the same, anxiety swelling inside her like the tide.

Chapter Sixteen

JULY, 1999

10 P.M. AND LOS ANGELES HAD SETTLED INTO ITS NIGHTTIME GROOVE. Richie parked the Audi outside Jeff's apartment. Fifty yards away the ocean sparkled silver in the moonlight, the sound of it like the planet breathing. Faint music reverberated from an apartment across the street. A woman laughed. A man yelled something jovially. It was a good night to be young in LA.

Richie took the steps to the door of Jeff's building two at a time and rang Jeff's buzzer. He waited, then hit the buzzer again.

"Who is it?" came Jeff's voice.

"Your new best friend. I got something to tell you."

A pause.

"Think you have the wrong address, dude," Jeff said, drawling it out, clearly stoned.

"What? It's Richie, man."

"I don't know any Richie."

"Fuck you talking about? I was in your apartment last night."

No response.

Richie shook his head. "For fuck sake, just open the door."

The door buzzed and Richie pushed it open. At the end of the hall, the door to Jeff's apartment opened and Jeff's head poked out, angled in such a way that his long blond hair fell over one side, luscious and shiny. The man had beautiful hair, no doubt about it. An aroma of cannabis wafted out the door with him. Probably through the rice-paper walls of this dump, too.

"Jeff! Great to see you, my man. You remember me, right?"

Jeff hesitated. He nodded, but it didn't look convincing.

"Can I come in? Got something important to tell you. Our conversation got cut short last time."

Jeff rubbed his face. "I guess." Didn't seem thrilled about it. He stepped to the side and Richie entered the apartment.

Inside, the sheer intensity of weed-stink was astonishing. Smoke hung in the air like Jeff's very own sky, difficult to see through. Richie's eyes stung in the attempt.

"I was just watching a movie," Jeff said. He fell onto the couch and sank back into it, the couch sucking this human morsel into itself greedily. On Jeff's giant TV, frozen like a photograph, was the face of a young Cuba Gooding Jr.

"What movie?"

"*Boyz n the Hood*."

"The guy from N.W.A.'s in that, right?"

Jeff's pink eyes squinted up at him. "I thought he looked familiar. You wanna watch it?"

Richie thought about it. "Shit, yeah, I wouldn't mind. You far into it?"

"I can start it again. Kinda forgot what the hell's going on, tell you the truth."

Richie didn't doubt it. "I better tell you why I'm here before we start watching a movie, though."

"Oh. Yeah. Why are you here?"

"I got something to tell you." Richie glanced in the corner where something caught his eye. He went over. Inside a glass cabinet stood dozens of awards. The top shelf held three of the same award. Tall and gold, they looked a little like Oscars.

"These all awards?" he said.

Jeff, rolling a joint now, looked up. "What? Oh, yeah. Awards." Back to rolling.

"They mean much to you?"

Jeff shrugged. "Not really." But he had displayed them inside a glass cabinet.

"What are these on the top shelf?" Richie peered closer; written on each: "AVN Awards" and below it "Male Performer of the Year" above Jeff's name. The awards covered three consecutive years, the most recent being 1999.

"AVN Awards. Those're the best ones, so I keep them on top."

"These all for pornos?"

"Yeah."

"They give out porno awards? For real?"

"We take our jobs seriously, even if nobody else does."

Richie frowned. "So, what, they're awarding your fucking skills, is that it? Or is it for the acting? Like, how well you played a schoolgirl's teacher before you fucked her in the ass."

"Those are more for the Best Actor award. I got a few of those on the shelf below. Male Performer of the Year is more about popularity, I guess."

Richie chuckled. Fucking LA. Always finds a way to surprise you.

Jeff licked the rolling paper and rubbed his finger along the finished joint. He grabbed a Zippo from the coffee table and set the joint alight.

"You want some?" he said, in between tokes.

"Yeah, all right." Richie took the joint and inhaled. "Damn, tastes good. Sort of tastes like—"

"Bubblegum?" Jeff said. He grinned. "Yeah dude. That's 'cause the dominant terpenes in this strain are humulene, caryophyllene and myrcene."

Richie blinked at him, no idea what the fuck he just said. The smoke Richie had inhaled had added to the second-hand smoke in the atmosphere of this little apartment and already his head felt light, thoughts crashing into cacophony.

Jeff said, "It's the perfect strain for chilling with a movie. A little euphoric, but relaxing, without making you sleepy. You know what it's called?"

Richie shrugged. "I dunno man, what's it called?"

"Bubblegum." Jeff laughed. It lit up his face, made him handsome. Richie could see women falling over themselves for him. Trust talk of weed to bring a smile to the man's face.

"So you want to know why I'm here or what?" Richie said.

"Oh, yeah. Why are you here?"

Richie navigated his way around the coffee table and sat on the couch beside Jeff. "You work with a guy called Riccardo? Big guy. European, I think."

"Italian."

"Well, Riccardo had an interesting proposition for me. A job he wanted me to do. A job involving you."

Jeff exhaled smoke, adding to the mass of it in the room. "Oh yeah? What job?"

"Riccardo wants me to get rid of you."

Jeff sucked on the joint and looked at him. "How do you mean?"

"Just what I said. He wants you gone."

Jeff frowned. "Why would he want that?"

"I didn't ask."

"How much is he paying you?"

"Five grand," Richie lied.

"Huh." Jeff smoked some more. "Well, are you gonna?"

"What?"

"Get rid of me?"

"No."

Jeff nodded. "Well, good." Smoking again. "When you say *get rid*—"

"He wants me to kill you, he just didn't want to say it like that. He even pretended to ask me not to hurt you. Fuckin' asshole."

Jeff shook his head—a man dumbfounded by the world around him but not particularly caring about it. A good way to be, Richie was beginning to think.

Richie said, "But I told him I'd do it. If the man has five Gs to spend on a goddamn assassination, I'll take it from him."

"But you're not gonna do it?"

"Don't worry, Jeff. You're not gonna die just yet."

"Glad to hear it." Jeff sucked on the joint.

Richie had to marvel at the guy: informed that a co-worker wants him dead and he responds as if Richie had told him the weather.

"But I still want that five large," Richie said. "So I got a plan. We take a couple photos of you, dead as can be, lying in a hole in the dirt. Put some mascara on your forehead with some fake blood around it, dripping down your head, like a bullet hole. Make your face white. Then I meet with Riccardo, show him the evidence and collect the cash. We split it fifty-fifty, twenty-five hundred each. What d'ya say?"

"I can do that."

"Course you can. You're an award-winning actor. Pass me that shit."

Jeff handed him the joint and Richie puffed from it. "Shit, that's good," Richie said. "Let's watch this fuckin' movie. You know, I should bring my girl around here sometime, I think you'd really like her. You'll meet her soon anyway. For that other job we talked about."

He gazed at Jeff. "You remember the job we talked about, right?"

Jeff looked blankly at him.

"Rippin' off your dealer, man! Please tell me you remember."

"Oh. Yeah. Yeah. I remember. I'm just pretty blazed right now. I wouldn't forget the job that's gonna make me rich enough to start a new life."

Richie clapped him on the back. "My man. I say we do it the day after tomorrow."

"Do what?"

"The fuckin' job man, Jesus."

"Oh. Day after tomorrow?"

"Yeah."

"That's pretty soon."

"No time like the present. Can you do it?"

Jeff stared blankly at the TV. Thirty seconds later he was gazing blearily at Richie again. "Yeah, I can do it."

Richie clapped his hands. "Fuckin' A, man. Fuckin' A. I feel like celebrating. You think I could get a bump of that coke?"

"Go ahead. On the shelf over there."

Richie stood up and moved toward the box, knowing exactly where it was.

When Richie sat back down, the box in his hands, Jeff gazed at him with an earnest expression and said, "Dude, be honest with me. Are you an assassin?"

Richie sniggered. What the fuck kind of assassin would be riddled with needlemarks, skinny as a motherfucker, and eager to knock off a drug dealer for some quick cash?

"No, man. I'm not. That's what's so funny about this whole thing."

Jeff shook his head, baffled, and sucked away at the joint, and something about the whole thing became suddenly hysterical to Richie. He couldn't stop laughing.

Watching Richie, that baffled look on his face, Jeff began giggling himself and soon the two of them were in knots on the couch together, cannabis smoke swirling around their heads like the afterglow of magic.

Returning to LA was proving to be the best decision Richie had made in a very long time.

XXX

DECEMBER, 1998

THE LIMOUSINE DROVE INTO A MARINA AND PARKED. The driver of the vehicle, who Jemeka recognized as the blank-faced man with blond cornrows, exited the car and opened the rear door.

"Get out," Marsellus said.

Jemeka clambered past Marsellus and his dog out of the limousine, Ray-Ray close behind. After they had exited, Marsellus got out and shut the door, leaving the dog inside.

"I won't be long," Marsellus said to Blond Cornrows. "Leave the AC on for Gabriel."

Blond Cornrows nodded, standing by the driver's door.

An umami fragrance of seaweed mingled with the diesel smell of machines. Boats, hundreds of them, floated on water black and slick like oil. A sickle moon reflected off the lapping waves, its light like silver paint illuminating the rippling surface.

"This way," Marsellus said. He walked casually but quickly in the direction of a small boat bobbing by the jetty. Inside the vessel, the silhouettes of two men stood watching them approach.

Jemeka followed until she noticed Ray-Ray's absence. She looked behind. Ray-Ray remained by the limousine.

"Ray-Ray," she said.

"I ain't gettin' on no boat," he said. "This some bullshit."

"You'll do what I tell you, Raymond," came Marsellus's deep voice.

Ray-Ray shook his head.

Fear coiled around Jemeka's bones. "Ray-Ray, do what he says." She had tried to keep the anxiety from her voice but it had crept through. "Please." She tried to make her eyes say what her lips could not: *These men will shoot you if you walk away.*

Ray-Ray held his gaze on her and for a few heart-stopping seconds she thought he would remain standing there, refusing Marsellus's order, until he came toward her. "Whatever you say, baby. Whatever you say."

Jemeka exhaled. Ray-Ray reached her and they walked side by side toward Marsellus and the boat waiting ahead.

"Get in," Marsellus said when they arrived at the boat.

The men in the boat watched them with hostile faces. Black-oil water lapped at the jetty by Jemeka's feet as if reaching up to drag her in. How quickly a body would disappear beneath the slick surface.

"Don't make me say it again," Marsellus said.

"Marsellus—"

Shhlick: the sound of a pistol being cocked choked the words out of her throat—one of the men on the boat. Moonlight glinted off the silver metal in the man's hand.

Jemeka swallowed a lump and extended her leg across the narrow gap between the jetty and boat, the water waiting below like a hole in the universe.

Ray-Ray went across after her, followed by Marsellus.

"Sit," Marsellus said, pointing to a bench at the rear.

They did as commanded.

Marsellus sat opposite.

The man with the pistol sat beside Marsellus, never taking his gaze off them for a moment, as the other man stood at the wheel and brought the boat to life. With a low rumble the boat glided away from the jetty out onto the Pacific.

A cold, salty breeze whipped Jemeka's skin and stung her eyes. She shivered. Beside her, Ray-Ray reached out and held her hand in his, Marsellus observing this without expression.

A few minutes passed with only the sounds of the growling engine and splashing waves. Jemeka couldn't take it any longer. "Where are you taking us?"

"My yacht," Marsellus said. "If you look closely, you can see it."

Jemeka squinted into the distance, seeing only shades of black and gray where the sky met the sea and the ghostly glow of the moonlight in a vertical line across the water. No—there was something ahead, shining in the moonlight. It looked like a radio tower, and she saw now something below it, bobbing on the horizon.

"Where we going after that?" Ray-Ray said.

"The yacht is the end of the line."

Nausea bubbled inside Jemeka's belly. What if Marsellus dumped them into the ocean and left them there?

A stupid question: Jemeka couldn't swim.

IN TYPICAL MARSELLUS FASHION, his yacht was gigantic, composed of four concentric levels, each shorter than the one below like layers of a wedding cake. On the lowest level where they had embarked moments ago, a hot tub overlooked the ocean from a perch and beyond it a bar display held dozens of liquor bottles. Jemeka could imagine the parties Marsellus no doubt hosted on this vessel.

Marsellus led them through the interior of this lower level of the yacht—as elegant and luxurious as a five-star hotel—and out the other side. On a helicopter pad at the very nose of the ship, three men with assault rifles surrounded a man on his knees. The man's head bowed. Blood dripping from his forehead onto the deck.

Something rigid pressed into Jemeka's spine. She glanced behind: one of Marsellus's men shoving a gun into her back. He gestured with his stony-eyed head, directing her to follow Marsellus.

Heart rate climbing, Jemeka started moving. Panicked thoughts flooded her mind. She glanced at Ray-Ray behind her, the fear in his eyes palpable.

"I believe you three already know each other," Marsellus said, gesturing to the bloodied man who had not raised his head.

Closer now, Jemeka saw that the man was kneeling exactly on the center of the "H" inside a white painted circle denoting the boundary of the helicopter pad. Men holding assault rifles stood at the perimeter of the ring as if it was a boundary they couldn't cross, like this whole thing was a ritual to the Devil. Then Marsellus strode into the ring and grabbed the man by the man's short curls and jerked his head up. Though bloodied and swollen, Jemeka recognized the man's face: Wesley Patrick Brown. The man who had tried to rob Floyd, and, by extension, Marsellus. The man Jemeka had let go.

"Look familiar?" Marsellus said.

Wesley gazed hopelessly at Jemeka through his open eye, the other swollen shut.

"Oh man," said Ray-Ray behind her. "Oh man oh man oh man. I don't wanna die. Please, man. I don't wanna die."

"Shut him up," Marsellus said.

One of the men thumped Ray-Ray with the butt of a pistol and Ray-Ray staggered onto his knees with a moan.

"I don't wanna die," he sobbed, quieter now.

"It's gonna be okay, Ray-Ray," Jemeka said, surprised by the calmness of her voice. To Marsellus: "How did you know?"

"I know everything that happens on my streets. Every goddamn thing. I know this fool tried to steal *my* product, and I know *you* let him go."

"We scared him. Man was petrified. He swore never to do it again."

Marsellus grinned, something evil in it. Still looking at Jemeka, he extended his hand toward one of his men, who reached behind his own back and handed a long dagger to Marsellus.

"Did I or did I not tell you that no one steals from me and lives to tell the tale?" Marsellus said.

He waited.

"Did I?"

"Yes."

Marsellus nodded, that awful grin replaced now by the cold certainty of violence. He clamped a bulging bicep beneath Wesley's chin, raising the man's head to expose his throat.

"Please . . . don't," Wesley choked out.

Staring into Jemeka's eyes, Marsellus brought the sharp blade to Wesley's throat and slashed it across his neck as if the neck was a violin and the knife a bow with which to play it. Then came the sick music: Wesley spluttered as blood spurted out of the gash below his larynx. In his eyes swirled confusion and tragedy. Marsellus held Wesley's head in place, letting the blood flow unhindered onto the H and spill out over the circle. Wesley's blood rushed along the deck toward Jemeka and encircled her Gucci heels. She watched, nauseous, as the confusion in Wesley's eyes became replaced by a hopeless acceptance, the blood still coming—so much blood, how could one body contain so much of it? We're all nothing more than walking hot water bottles, waiting to be slashed open. Jemeka didn't want to look but she couldn't tear her eyes away until life had left Wesley entirely.

At last Marsellus released Wesley but the man's soul had already departed and what flopped onto the deck was merely a sack of decaying flesh and bone. Marsellus stepped over the corpse like it was nothing and strolled toward Jemeka.

Behind him, the three men picked up Wesley's corpse and tossed it overboard. Three long seconds later a quiet splash sounded in the silent night, as if they'd chucked nothing bigger than a rock overboard.

One of the men handed Marsellus a towel, which he used to wipe his bloody hands. "Next time someone tries to steal from me, you deal with it the right way. Or next time that will be you going overboard. You understand." It wasn't a question.

"I understand," Jemeka said.

"Now get the fuck off my yacht." He turned his back to her.

Jemeka nodded and helped Ray-Ray onto his feet. "Come on, Ray-Ray, let's go." He looked traumatized, tears streaming out his eyes.

As they followed Marsellus's men toward the rear of the yacht, Marsellus called out, "I almost forgot. It's after midnight. Merry Christmas!" Deep laughter bellowed after them.

Jemeka gritted her teeth and continued on. Rage simmered within her, one thought reverberating in her mind: Marsellus had been at the top for too long. About time someone took him down.

XXX

JULY, 2000

IN HIS BLUE SUBARU, Floyd led Mickey from the pink house to a strip mall in Lakewood where he parked outside a hair salon. Almost 11 p.m., the strip was empty, all the stores closed except possibly this salon: the lights were on but he couldn't see anyone inside. Approaching the salon in his Pontiac, Mickey watched as Floyd exited the Subaru and entered the salon. A young woman appeared out of some back area of the place as Floyd entered.

Mickey cruised the Pontiac by the salon slowly, catching a glimpse of Floyd speaking to the woman. He drove out of the strip and came back up the street parallel to it, where he pulled in and parked directly opposite the salon, fifty yards away. With his Minolta Maxxum 7000—an excellent camera bought for him in 1986 by Martha which he'd never felt any need to replace—with telephoto lens attached, Mickey zoomed into the scene and snapped some photographs, capturing detailed close-ups of Floyd and the woman. They looked worried, speaking quickly to each other. Now Floyd had a hand on his head, brow furrowed. The conversation culminated in Floyd throwing open the door of the salon angrily and speeding out of the strip in his car.

Mickey debated whether or not to follow. His gut told him he needed to learn more about this woman in the salon, so he let Floyd go.

This—getting wise to something secret—was the best part of the job and he was enjoying it. He felt like singing along to something. The glove compartment held a rotating selection from his tape collection. He dug out Tom Petty's *Full Moon Fever*, inserted the tape into the player, side A facing up, and hit play. The music began a few bars into track two, "I Won't Back Down." It had never sounded better.

MICKEY WAITED OUTSIDE THE SALON under a pitch-black sky. A new moon tonight meant that the moon was on the same side of Earth as the sun, invisible to the naked eye, the dark and light sides of the moon switching positions. Conjuntion, a *Discovery Channel* documentary had called it.

He wasn't waiting long before the woman in the salon switched off the lights and locked the doors. She walked a few steps to a brand-new Lexus—a nice car for the owner of a small salon in a quiet part of town—and drove out of the strip mall. Mickey followed her onto the Artesia Freeway, then back off it at Atlantic Avenue where she crossed the dry concrete of the Los Angeles River into East Compton. After a total trip time of fifteen minutes, she parked inside the driveway of a small residential home in a poor neighborhood in East Compton, burglar bars over all the windows, and went inside the bungalow.

Mickey took note of the house number and continued on by. Time to sink into a hot bath. He'd earned it.

Chapter Seventeen

JULY, 1999

ALABAMA WOKE SCREAMING to the hallucinogenic twilight of sunrise. She had dreamed of a faceless man injecting heroin into each of her veins, one after the other, laughing as the drug killed her.

She sat up on the bed, shuddering. Richie lay still on his side beside her, knocked out by the dope he'd shot up last night. Outside, sounds of the city coming alive drifted up from the street.

Alabama slid the duvet off and slipped out of bed. She entered the bathroom and switched on the light. Her nude body appeared in the mirror like a phantom. Her once slim-but-curvy figure was now sunken like an empty glove, skin clinging to her bones everywhere except her breasts, which had never been tiny but now, in contrast with her skinny torso, jutted out of her chest grotesquely even despite shrinking a little themselves. How long had it been since she had looked in a mirror and felt good? How long had it been since she had felt anything at all?

The heroin called to her from the bedroom. She'd shot just a little last night, the only way to get any respite from the cravings so she could sleep, and her body hungered for more.

One shot would melt away this pain.

One shot and the sense of failure gnawing on her would recede.

She licked her lips, imagining the rush, how it would make her whole.

No. Heroin wouldn't make her whole. Heroin *was* the hole. You can't compromise with the hole, can't wean yourself off the hole. The hole will suck you in, every time. She wouldn't give in to the hole. Not anymore. Not even if it killed her.

A shiver vibrated through her. She let it pass. OxyContin would take the edge off. They were running out, though. They'd need to get more soon. Without the Oxys she had little hope of holding off the cravings. Even with Oxys it would be an uphill battle.

Alabama closed her eyes and asked for help from a god she didn't believe in.

XXX

RICHIE DIDN'T WAKE UP SO MUCH AS RETURN FROM OBLIVION. The nameless void of a heroin high had the effect of vanishing from memory almost as soon as it faded. Back to cruel reality.

He raised his head and felt a sticky film of saliva pooled on the pillow. He wiped his cheek and a coating of the stuff slid across his hand, slime-like. Bright morning light beamed into the room through a crack in the curtains. The bathroom door hung open, the light on inside.

"Bama?"

Alabama appeared out of the bathroom. Richie did a double-take. She'd put makeup on, skin smooth and no longer pale, lips big and red, mascara making her eyelashes longer, black eye shadow giving her a sexy, smoky look. Hair washed and blow-dried, she wore a white summer dress dotted all over with little red cherries.

Richie said, "You look . . . amazing."

Alabama smiled shyly. "I used a few dollars to buy a little bit of makeup, hope you don't mind. I just needed to feel pretty for once. The dress I already had. Dug it out from the suitcase."

"I remember the dress. You were wearing it on one of our early dates. I told you it looked good on you."

"You said I looked sweet as a cherry."

"Did I?"

"Uh huh." She giggled.

"Lame . . . well babe, you look sweet as a cherry."

She smiled, less shyly this time.

"Today's the big day," Richie said. "You ready?"

"I think so."

"Jeff's meeting Floyd at twelve. But I gotta meet with that dipshit Italian first, take his money. What time's it?"

He glanced at the clock on the bedside table: 08:57. "Okay. Plenty of time. I'm starving. There's a diner nearby. I'd kill for some blueberry pie. How about we go soon as I get back? We can pick up Jeff on the way."

"Sounds good to me."

Richie stretched. His hip throbbed where he'd dug a needle into it last night, the wound scabby now, bruised. Finding new or sufficiently healed areas in which to inject was becoming difficult. And he'd need to find another soon; it wouldn't be long before the shivers were at him.

He said, "We should shoot first. Won't be back here till after the job's done."

"Not me."

"What?"

"I don't want to."

"Can't have you getting sick during this."

"I'm not doing that shit anymore."

"But—"

"Richie, no. If I don't quit now, I never will. I can't be this person anymore. I'd rather it kill me than be that person again. I won't do it."

Richie sighed. "You better at least take some Oxys."

"Those are okay. For now."

"I'm not taking any chances, I need a clear head today. Can you help me?"

Alabama nodded, not looking too happy about it. But she retrieved the dope and the equipment and set about fixing him up and right now that was all that mattered.

RICHIE RACED THE AUDI ON I-5 THROUGH BURBANK, listening to The Replacements loud on the radio. This particular tune happened to be his favorite song, "Bastards of Young," and he took this as a sign that things were finally on the correct track. On his right, the rippling Verdugo Mountains watched over the city of Burbank like lazy gods, a yellow blur of a sun burning above them huge and hot. The junk felt good in his blood, his body light as the warm breeze flowing through the opened window, and his spirits were lifted up and up and up as the car zoomed toward the horizon. Bar a few recent fuck-ups, he'd made the right decision coming home. Nobody knows Los Angeles until they've been entranced by it, corrupted by it, cast out from it, and returned to it on their knees begging it to save them, and Richie knew Los Angeles. He knew it better than anyone. This time he would tame the beast and make it his own—this time he would win.

On Laurel Canyon Boulevard, just a few minutes from Richie's destination, a police cruiser flashed its lights behind him.

Fuck, had the cop seen him speeding?

Richie slowed the Audi, hoping the lights were for someone else.

The cruiser remained up Richie's ass. Its siren screamed, then silenced.

Fuck.

Richie pulled onto the verge and slowed to a stop. He turned off the radio. Silence fell like an anchor.

Oh fuck—Scotty's Audi. Richie didn't have papers for it, and little prick Scotty definitely would have reported it stolen by now. On the passenger seat lay an envelope containing photographs of a murdered man . . . at least, that's how it would look to this cop. All in all a pretty disastrous aligning of circumstance.

The police cruiser parked twenty yards behind the Audi. The driver—a big slab of white meat, no partner with him—exited the vehicle and surveyed the area while adjusting the belt on his hips. Look at him—pig thinks he owns the place.

Richie opened the glove compartment and shoved the envelope inside, then withdrew the revolver and placed it into the compartment at the bottom of the driver-side door where the cop wouldn't see it but Richie could grab it quickly if he needed to. He shut the glove compartment and watched the cop approach.

Two sharp raps on the window.

Richie rolled it down. He shot the pig his Sunday smile. "How's it going, Officer?"

The cop, a broad-shouldered neckless thug with a head like a tin of paint, stared at him. "In a hurry?"

"No, not at all. Was I going too fast? My mind gets away from me out here. I think it's the mountains." Richie beamed.

The cop's eyes narrowed. He looked Richie over. "You been drinking?"

"Drinking? This early? No way, Officer."

"On any drugs at the moment?"

"Drugs? Me? No, no, never."

The cop's gaze burned into Richie's head. "Where are you headed?"

"A film studio."

"Where?"

"Here in the Valley."

"You an actor?"

"Sort of."

The cop wasn't giving him an inch: "Sort of? What's sort of supposed to mean?"

"Uhh . . . I do porn."

The cop grimaced. "Arms full of holes like that, I hope you wear a rubber."

Richie held in what he wanted to say.

The cop reached behind his back. A moment later he was pulling blue nylon gloves over sausage-like fingers. "I'm gonna need you to step out of the vehicle."

Panic like an alarm clock in Richie's skull. Thoughts raced through his mind, all of them variations of the same mantra: *No matter what, stay in the fucking car.* He glanced at the Smith & Wesson. "Listen, Officer, I just want to get to work. I've had a rough week, my mom passed away. Lung cancer. It's been a—" he sighed dramatically, dragging it out—"terrible year. I just want to get to where I need to be. You know?"

Phluuup: the cop had stretched the glove at the wrist and released it like a spring. "Listen to me, you lowlife junkie piece of shit. You step out of the vehicle or I'll drag you out through this window. Your call."

Richie narrowed his eyes, rage starting a fire in his gut. Couldn't fucking believe it—this fucking pig talking to *him* like that? This asshole worked for *him*, his wage paid for by Richie's taxes (well, if Richie had ever paid taxes, that was, which he hadn't since they'd been automatically deducted from his miserable paychecks as a teenager, but, still, the point stood).

"Okay, Officer," glancing at the Smith & Wesson, "I'm coming."

He'd never killed a cop before, never killed anyone aside from that rapist Heimdall, but how different could it be? He'd killed one fascist thug and he could kill another. The world would be better off. More importantly: If Richie went to prison now, what would happen to Alabama? All alone, no reasons left to lay off the dope. She'd be dead within a week.

He opened the door a couple inches and leaned toward it as he did, hiding his hand now as it closed around the smooth wooden grip of the Model 27. Looking up at the officer staring down at him with contempt, Richie imagined the man's life, the little house in the suburbs and the wife and kids waiting for him there.

Jesus Christ, he was really going to do this.

The cop watching him closely, Richie continued his exit from the vehicle, one foot on the asphalt now. He lifted the revolver a few inches, ready to lunge—

The radio on the cop's shoulder crackled like aluminum foil as a demonic voice said, "All units—eleven ninety nine at Branford Park. Code three."

Without a microsecond's hesitation the cop spun on his heels, sprinted to the cruiser, and sped the vehicle by Richie, siren wailing.

Richie stared in disbelief as the cruiser shrank on the horizon, the siren fading from a piercing shriek to a distant moan. He heaved oxygen into his lungs, realizing now he'd been holding his breath for the past minute.

He stepped out of the car and sat on the hood with his head in his hands, marveling at how close he had come to murdering a police officer. He viewed this close call as another sign that the universe was finally in his corner. The score would go smoothly today and he and Alabama would begin the first day of the rest of their lives, smooth sailing from here on out.

Richie got into the Audi and drove deeper into the Valley. "Don't Fear the Reaper" was playing again, and although he had felt that the song seemed to be following him around, as if the universe was trying to communicate something to him through the radio, he ignored those silly superstitions now and sang along.

WHAT A FUCKING NAME, Richie thought when he reached the porn studio Riccardo had chosen as the meeting place. MidnightPussy Productions. He wouldn't mind him some midnight pussy, whatever the fuck that was.

He parked the Audi a bit away from the building. Nothing and nobody around, just heat and dirt and the mountains watching over their vast and empty domain. Where was this guy? Richie glanced around and Riccardo appeared out of the shade of the building like something evil that lived there, smoking a cigarette. He tossed the cigarette onto the dirt as he approached the Audi.

Richie leaned across the passenger seat and opened the door.

Riccardo threw a glance over each shoulder, sat into the passenger seat, and shut the door.

"You did it?" he said, fixing a hostile gaze on Richie. The man's shaved head sat like a bowling ball on his muscled neck.

"All business, aren't you, Rick? Don't you wanna know how my morning's going?"

Riccardo stared angrily at him.

"Tell me something, Rick. How many hours does a porn star put in per week?"

"Varies."

"Do you do the fucking or do you record others doing the fucking?"

"I do a lot of things. Did you do it or what?"

"Be honest with me, because I really am dying to know. Do you get tired of all the pussy?"

Riccardo appeared to debate whether or not to answer the question. "No, man. I never get tired of the pussy, and the pussy never gets tired of me. Now did you—"

"Yeah yeah, course I fucking did it. Wouldn't be here otherwise, would I?"

Richie popped open the glove compartment—to which he had returned the Smith & Wesson, pointed intentionally at the passenger seat—and made a show of casually picking up the revolver and rummaging around for the envelope. He retrieved the envelope, placed the gun onto his lap, and shut the glove compartment. ("Glove compartment"—the only thing Richie had never seen inside one was a pair of gloves.)

"Here's the proof," he said. He tossed the envelope at Riccardo.

Riccardo slipped fat fingers into the envelope and pulled out the photographs. Richie watched the man's face as he realized what he was looking at: shock, then horror, now rage.

"What the fuck!" Riccardo threw the photographs at Richie, desperate to be rid of them. "What did you do?"

"Only what you asked me to, Rick."

Riccardo looked about to combust. "I told you to—"

"Get rid of Jeffrey Strokes. Make him go away so he won't bother you anymore. He certainly won't bother you now."

Eyes stretched wide, Riccardo shook his head, attempting to process his responsibility for this killing. "What have you done . . ." He shot Richie a look of pure hatred. "You fucking animal."

Richie laughed at this juicehead getting all riled up over a murder that never happened. "I was merely the triggerman, Rick. I was doing a job. *You* were my employer."

"No, that's not what—"

"It doesn't matter now. Jeff is dead. Witnesses can put me and you in that bar, outside that convenience store, and maybe here too if we wait long enough. We're in this together."

"I'll tell the cops what you did. I never asked you to kill him."

"We both know what you were asking me, you just didn't have the balls to come out and say it. You go to the police and believe me I will take you down with me. If you want this to be over, pay me my money and I'll be out of your life forever."

Riccardo hesitated.

Tired of this game, Richie picked up the revolver and thumbed the hammer. "Give me my fucking money, Rick."

"If I give you the money, I don't ever want to see you again."

"Feeling's mutual. You won't see me ever again. But if you talk about this to anybody, I'll put you in the ground beside Jeff."

Looking weak now, pale, Riccardo nodded in submission. He slid a hand into his jacket. Richie tensed, out of instinct, but the man's hand returned holding a wad of cash wrapped in an elastic band.

Richie's heart fluttered at the sight of all that green. Keeping the gun pointed at Riccardo's chest, he said, "Count it."

Riccardo counted the bills one by one on his lap, reaching ten thousand dollars.

Richie was so thrilled he could have jerked the guy off. "Perfect. Toss it inside the glove compartment."

Riccardo opened the glove compartment and placed the bills inside.

"Pleasure doing business with you, Rick. Now get the fuck out of my car."

Like a neutered mutt Riccardo did as he was told. Rather than return inside the studio, he stood watching as Richie drove out of the parking lot.

As he drove away from MidnightPussy Productions, Richie gazed in the rear-view. In the empty, dusty parking lot, Riccardo stared after the Audi with his shoulders slumped—a lonely figure whose world had just collapsed around him.

Richie grinned. Conning that idiot had been a hell of a lot easier than robbing diners. Provided a bigger payout, too. But look at that sorry bastard staring after the car. Richie almost felt sorry for him. Fuck him—he had it coming.

Richie couldn't keep the grin off his face. He turned the radio up loud and enjoyed the warm breeze on his neck as he sped the Audi toward Beverly Hills.

Only when he reached the Four Seasons did Richie consider that he might have it coming, too.

Chapter Eighteen

ALABAMA PLAYED DISC ONE OF THE JOHNNY CASH CD in the car while Richie drove. Now the Man in Black crooned about a girl who had left her hometown for Hollywood stardom only to give it all up and return, the City of Angels for her more a City of Assholes. Of broken dreams and shiny things. It was exhausting, this place, Alabama saw that now. She'd rather be just about anywhere else. Except Pine Ridge, Alabama.

Richie parked the car on a residential cul-de-sac. Beyond a low wall ahead, the Pacific Ocean glittered like a dream.

"Jeff lives in there." Richie pointed to a small apartment building across the street. "I'll go get him. Wait here." He left the car.

Alabama stared at the ocean while she waited, listening to the melancholy of Mr. Cash. A queasy sensation was brewing up in her belly and she knew why. She hoped she could hold off the worst of it until this whole thing was finished. Richie would kill her if she messed it up.

THE SOUND OF THE CAR DOOR OPENING WOKE HER. The CD must have reached its end, silent now.

"This is my wife," Richie said, standing by the opened driver-side door. "She's hot, right?"

A man with hair as long as Richie's but blond like a surfer's bent down to stare at Alabama through the window next to her. "Definitely hot," he said, his voice dulled by the glass between them. Bright blue eyes like jewels in his head.

Richie and Jeff were both dressed in black tracksuits—"to be anonymous," Richie had explained to her while he was putting the tracksuit on in the hotel, "specially for Jeff 'cause he knows the fuckin' guy." They had probably also figured the outfit would make them look professional and therefore intimidating. Looking at them now, Alabama disagreed. They looked ridiculous.

Richie stuck his face into the car. "Bama, this is Jeff."

She brought her window down. "Nice to meet you, Jeff."

Jeff extended feminine fingers toward her and they shook hands through the opened window. The whites of his eyes bloodshot, he looked like he could fall asleep on command, but he was handsome, taller than Richie with broader shoulders and cleaner, even beautiful, hair. He smiled at her, showing off a perfect Hollywood smile.

Richie got into the driver's seat and Jeff into the rear. "All right all right all right, let's get some fuckin' pie." Richie's foot hopped erratically on the floor of the car.

"You want some music?" he said to Jeff. Without waiting for a response he ejected the Johnny Cash CD. "This mopey shit won't do. We need some fuckin' *music*." He tossed the disc into the glove compartment.

"Hey, don't damage it!" Alabama said.

Richie ignored her. "Shit, why don't we have any CDs?"

"Because *you* never got any from the record store, just stood there staring into space."

"Fuck it." Richie switched the radio on and a swooning, joyous rock song unfolded, a British guy singing about girls and planets.

"Fuck yeah, The Only Ones," Richie said. "Haven't heard this tune in years. It's not really about girls, it's about *heroin.*" He spat this last word and laughed. Leg still jittering, Richie pinched his nostrils and sniffed. He was wide-eyed and alert, not at all like the doped-up junkie who'd disappeared inside Jeff's apartment. Jeff, on the other hand, nodded along lethargically in the back seat, looking dazed but quite content. They made quite a pair.

Richie shoved the gearstick into drive and spun the Audi around the cul-de-sac.

Alabama stuck her head out the window to touch the salty ocean breeze. If she didn't feel so ill, it almost might have smelled like freedom.

IN THE DINER, ALABAMA FELT TOO NERVOUS TO EAT. Although the Oxys had taken the edge off her cravings, they weren't doing enough, and the shivers were returning. Richie and Jeff experienced no such problem, attacking the pie as if it had once betrayed them. Deep in conversation, anyone would think them lost brothers. Two of the biggest misfits Alabama had ever seen. But it was sweet. Maybe Richie needed a friend. Maybe Jeff did, too.

She said, "I hope you don't mind me askin', Jeff, but I'm real curious about how you got to doin' porn."

"It's kind of a funny story," Jeff said, chewing a chunk of pie. He swallowed and washed the food down with coffee. "I had this girlfriend—well, she's still my girlfriend, technically—she works in porn too. Been in the industry ever since she was seventeen. She's twenty-five now. In our world, that makes her something of an old pro. Me too, I guess."

"How long you been doing it?" Richie said.

"Six years."

"Must've had a lot of pussy."

"I've done a lot of shoots, yeah."

"How many?" Richie said.

"I dunno, dude. A lot." Jeff gazed into the distance, thinking about it. "A *lot.*"

Richie said, "Some of those pornos have the funniest names. I saw one once, fuckin' cracks me up, it was called *Titty Titty Gang Bang.*" Richie laughed, eyes squeezed shut. "Oh man. What's the funniest title of all the pornos you've done?"

Jeff gazed at the table thinking about it. Ten seconds later he said, "*The Sexorcist.*"

Richie exploded into laughter, smacking his fist onto the table. "Holy shit, that's incredible." He shook his head, grinning. "Wait, don't tell me you fucked some chick dressed up like she's possessed?"

Jeff nodded.

"Wow," Richie said. "Unbelievable. Was her face all messed up too?"

"No, but she did fuck herself with a crucifix."

"Okay boys," Alabama said, anticipating where this was heading. "You said your girlfriend works in the industry too, Jeff?"

"Yeah, but she didn't tell me that at first. Just said she was an actress. I figured, in this city, who isn't? But then one day—"

"Wait, don't tell me," Richie said. "You walked in on her fucking some guy, thinking she was cheating on you, but it was for a porno."

"Not exactly."

Alabama said, "You saw one of her movies."

Jeff made a gun with his thumb and forefinger and shot Alabama with it. "Bingo."

"Must've been tough," Alabama said.

"Actually, it turned me on. I don't know why. Something about seeing this cute girl I really liked secretly getting boned on camera when I wasn't around, I dunno, it exposed a side to her I hadn't known existed, I guess."

"Yeah . . . don't think I'd have the same reaction," Richie said. "She wasn't wild in the sack with you? Being a porn star and all?"

"We had good sex, sure. But here's the thing about sex workers: sex is our *job.* When work's over, sex is the furthest thing from our minds. And when we do have sex, we like it to be intimate and pretty far removed from all that shit at the studio. Sometimes it gets wild at home, sure, but mostly it's just nice, you know? We're regular people."

"I get what you mean," Alabama said. A wave of sickness swept over her.

She shuddered but otherwise ignored it. She glanced at Richie, knowing she shouldn't say what she wanted to. Screw him, she was curious. She leaned over the table and in a low voice said to Jeff, "You must be pretty well endowed down there."

"Hey, what the fuck?" Richie said.

Jeff didn't seem embarrassed or shy or even proud by the remark; more like he was used to it. "That's the other part to the story. When I told Beth about seeing her in the porno, she said she'd been planning on telling me about it. She told me that since our first night in bed together she'd wanted to float the idea of me taking up her choice of career. Because of my . . . genes."

Richie didn't look so amused by this turn in conversation. "Enough about your fuckin' genes already man." He tossed a hostile glance at Alabama.

Jeff swept his luscious hair out of his face, eyes less blazed now but still a little pink. "I was unemployed back then, and overall just not really the kind of guy to do hard labor. Then this hot chick was telling me I could make a shit-ton of money just by screwing other hot chicks? I said, Beth, tell me where to sign."

"And now you wanna get out of it," Richie said.

"Like I said, I'm not the kind of guy does hard labor. It's been six years. I must've done five hundred shoots by now. When you've been doing the job this long, it takes a *toll*, dude, you don't wanna know."

Richie's face said he very much did want to know, practically salivating at the thought.

Jeff said, "And, believe me, porn's not easy. It's not just screwing hot chicks. Especially when you've made a name for yourself. A lot's expected of you, man. A *lot*. Sometimes for hours. You got all those crew members standing around expecting you to perform, waiting on you, wanting to get home to their wives or their kids or whatever but they can't till you do what you gotta do. And it's repetitive. There's only so many ways to fuck somebody. And most of your co-workers become friends and you get to know them too well, to the point they irritate you, and there's just no sexual chemistry most times—like I said, it's a job—and you gotta psyche yourself up, like training for a marathon. I'm tired of it, dude. I just wanna make some fast cash and blow this town. Live out the rest of my days on a beach somewhere in the Caribbean."

"What about your girlfriend?" Alabama said. "Is she coming with you?"

Jeff bit his lip, glanced away. "Beth . . . she wouldn't understand. She likes her life here. Likes doing porn. Loves it, in fact. Lives for the glamour of it all out here. You know that Doors song, 'LA Woman'? Well, that's Beth, the most LA woman who ever lived. I'm not even sure why we're together, to be honest. We couldn't be more different. She's better off without me, even if she doesn't know it yet. She'll be okay." He emitted the aura of a man trying to convince himself.

"Have you told her you're leaving?" Alabama said.

Jeff shook his head. "She'll be okay."

Alabama felt strangely disappointed by this response.

Richie exhaled loudly, like he was bored. "Well, nice hearing your fuckin' life story and all there Jeff, but we gotta talk about this job. Make a plan in case shit goes south."

Jeff nodded. "We'll need masks of some kind, I assume?"

"You assume correctly, Jeff. I got us a couple balaclavas. Unfortunately, fuckin' things are pink. All I could get at the time."

A cold shiver seized Alabama's body as nausea swelled up. At once the lights were too bright, the scent of greasy food heavy in the stifling air. Richie and Jeff were two black shapes.

"Pink?" Jeff was saying, but Alabama could barely hear him, the sickness seizing all her attention.

She leaned on the chair and stood up, half-blind under the dazzling lights. Her hands trembled. "I need the . . . bathroom," she said breathlessly and staggered toward the sign. Richie said something behind her but she didn't catch it, all the sounds of the diner combining into white noise inside her throbbing skull.

She made it to the bathroom where she sprayed hot puke onto cracked tiles.

XXX

"YOU OKAY?" Richie asked Alabama when she returned to the table. Something about her didn't look right, all the color drained from her face.

"Fine," she said. But she shuddered.

He let it go. They didn't have time for this bullshit now, already 11:30.

Jeff said, "We're meeting Floyd at Coolidge Park. It's in North Long Beach, right before Compton. Next to the freeway."

Richie figured as much. "Your usual meeting spot then."

Jeff appeared surprised. "Oh, I forgot you saw us there. Yeah, I usually meet Floyd there, or sometimes at the studio if I'm working."

Richie nodded. "Let's get the fuck outta here." He threw down some bills for the meal. Didn't leave a tip.

AT COOLIDGE PARK, Richie parked the car in almost the exact spot he'd parked it in back when he'd been following Jeff. He watched as Jeff, now his partner in crime (funny how life goes), sauntered over to the same picnic table he'd sat on before, took a fat joint out of his breast pocket, and set it on fire. A group of teens threw a frisbee at one another on the grass nearby and Jeff watched them, smoke turning the sky gray above him.

"This fuckin' guy," Richie said, chuckling. "Lives on another planet."

"Could say the same 'bout you and me, darlin'," Alabama said.

Richie glanced at her. She offered him a weak smile, avoiding his gaze. Beads of sweat clung to her pallid forehead.

"You're sick," he said.

"I'll be fine."

"You sure about that?"

She nodded, still not looking at him.

"Because if you won't be—"

"I'll be fine." Her tone left no room for debate.

Richie put it out of his mind and watched Jeff sitting at the picnic table, sucking on the joint.

A blue Subaru with gold rims passed on the street. Richie got a glimpse of Floyd in the driver's seat.

"There he is," Richie said. "In that blue piece of shit with the gold rims."

The Subaru parked abruptly by the sidewalk on the other side of the street and Floyd leaped out it. The drug dealer swaggered over to Jeff and the two men clapped hands together. Floyd sat on the bench and Jeff offered him the joint, which Floyd accepted.

"Look at them two," Richie said. "Unbelievable."

The whole thing was so much a reenactment of the previous meeting in that same spot, Richie was getting déjà vu.

The deal completed, Jeff waited until Floyd got into the Subaru and drove almost out of sight before hurrying toward the Audi and hopping in. He brought a musty stench of weed into the car with him. Smelled like someone had put out a fire by pissing on it.

Richie's nostrils stung with it. "Fuck man, you stink."

Alabama rolled down her window and stuck her head out of the car. "I'm gon' be sick."

"It's not that bad," Jeff said.

"No, I mean I'm gon' be sick."

Richie groaned. "Fuck sake, I knew this shit was gonna happen. I can't stop or we'll lose him. Do it out the window."

She did, much to Richie's disgust.

After a few minutes of them following Floyd at a distance, Jeff drawled, "Dude, what if he doesn't go to his stash?"

As if Richie hadn't thought of this. "Doesn't matter. First chance we get we grab him when he's alone, make him bring us to it."

"Ohhh . . ." Jeff's eyes red as balloons. He'd smoked an entire joint sitting on that goddamn bench. "Right on."

Alabama groaned in the passenger seat, palm on her drenched forehead.

Richie gritted his teeth. Between the stupefied stoner and dopesick junkie, he'd have to carry this score by himself. He was worried. This time, they weren't risking prison. They were risking their lives.

THEY FOLLOWED FLOYD OVER THE LOS ANGELES RIVER into suburbia, family homes and strip malls far as the eye could see.

"Where the fuck are we?" Richie said. "This still Long Beach?"

"Lakewood," Jeff said. "My mom lived here before she died."

They passed a line of well-kept bungalows painted hues of pink and orange. Across the street was a park with grass trimmed like the green on a golf course beside a small softball field named after a Lisa Fernandez. A pavilion next to it declared itself Mayfair Park.

"Shit, it's not so bad around here," Richie said. "We should check out apartments here, Bama."

No response. He glanced at her. Her head leaned on the window, eyes shut. Sweat collected on her forehead and slid along the bridge of her nose.

"Fuck," he said.

"What?" Jeff said.

"She's really sick." To Alabama: "We'll fix you up soon as we get this done. Okay, baby? Hang in there."

Alabama nodded weakly.

Jeff said, "She got the flu or something?"

Richie glanced at Jeff in the rear-view, not sure if the guy was joking.

"No, not the fucking flu. She's dopesick, man."

"Ohhh." Saying it like this news came as a revelation.

Richie shook his head. This was not going well.

Finally, Floyd turned into a strip mall and parked outside a hardware store. Richie followed him into the strip but turned in the opposite direction, parking outside a fast food joint at the other end. He killed the engine and a mist of silence descended. It was quiet out here, nobody around.

Floyd exited the car. He walked past a few stores and disappeared into one halfway between the Audi and the Subaru.

"What is that, a salon?" Richie said. "He came all the way out here to get a fuckin' haircut?"

"Must really like the service," Jeff said.

Silence, interspersed with Alabama's groans.

"We do it here," Richie said.

"Here?" Jeff sat up and looked around.

"Yeah." Richie opened the glove compartment. The balaclavas lay inside, pink as cotton candy. He picked them up, exposing the Smith & Wesson beneath, and tossed one to Jeff, then grabbed the revolver and shoved it into his jeans.

"Bama, you able to drive?"

She squinted through her illness at him. "Can I *drive*?"

Richie dug into his pocket. "Chew these." He handed her a couple twenties he'd pocketed before they left the motel. She accepted them like a beggar accepting change.

A few minutes passed in silence.

"You feeling better?" Richie asked his wife.

"A little."

"Can you drive?"

"Maybe."

"You're gonna have to. When Floyd comes out of that salon, me and Jeff will intercept him and make him drive us in his car. So you gotta follow us. Okay?"

She nodded, looking so crestfallen for a moment that he pitied her deeply. He ignored this pity. They needed some fucking money and they needed it now.

Richie watched the salon. A kid drifted by the Audi on a skateboard.

Alabama said, "Richie, are you sure this is a good idea? I got a bad feeling about this."

Not feeling particularly great about it himself, Richie did not want to hear it. "You'll feel a lot worse when we run out of cash. For all our troubles, we've never had to experience withdrawals while living on the street. You want to find out what that's like?"

That shut her up.

In an attempt to distract himself from these morbid thoughts, Richie changed the subject: "Tell me somethin', Jeff. You can't be paying too much for that little place of yours, right? And you don't do much, aside from work? You must have a lot of money saved up by now."

"I got some money, sure."

"So why are you along for the ride on this? Don't you have enough money saved up to get away like you want?" Richie turned in the seat and gazed at Jeff in the back. His shocking blue eyes and long blond hair contrasted heavily with the black tracksuit. Fuck—that hair; he should have tucked it into the hoodie. Floyd would have to be an imbecile not to recognize it.

Jeff said, "You don't understand. I don't want to get away. I want to *disappear*, man. Off the face of the earth. Some little beach hut somewhere by the ocean, trees all around, grow my own food. Some place where the sun shines all day and the sky is so blue it hurts and there's so much flower you couldn't smoke it all even if you had eternity to do it."

Richie shook his head, grinning. "Shit, we all want that. You're one funny motherfucker, Jeff. But listen, man, that hair of yours is supposed to be *inside* the hoodie—"

Floyd appeared out of the salon. "Shit, he's coming out," Richie said. "We gotta do this now." He opened the door, hesitated, and faced Alabama. "Follow us, okay?" He kissed her cheek, moist with sweat. "Love you, Bama."

He was relieved to see that she looked a little less sickly. "I love you too, Richie. I'll be right behind you."

"See you soon."

Richie pulled the balaclava over his head and exited the car.

Chapter Nineteen

AUGUST, 2000

MICKEY RANG THE DOORBELL. In his other hand he held a box of donuts and a tray containing two coffees from Marco's café balanced precariously on top.

The door opened, Odetta standing there. She beamed. "Mickey."

"Morning, Odetta."

"Morning yourself. You looking for Reggie?"

"I sure am. He's got Tuesdays off, right?"

"Uh huh. Good luck getting the man outta bed though." She stepped to the side. "You know where to go."

"Thank you. Would you like a donut?"

"Oh Lord you know I would, but I'd be over my Weight Watchers points till supper."

"I admire your dedication." He offered Odetta a smile and walked through the living room.

The Dixons' home felt cozy and lived in, photographs of the family over the years on every wall. The kind of home a man could enjoy growing old in, warm memories of his life in each corner.

Mickey reached Reggie's bedroom and rapped on the door. He waited five seconds and pushed it open and went inside. Reggie lay on his side with his back to the door.

Mickey sat on the edge of the bed and said Reggie's name.

The man didn't stir.

He said it again a little louder.

Still nothing.

He placed the donuts onto the bedside table and held Reggie's shoulder and shook. "Reggie."

Reggie's eyes fluttered open. "What you want, woman? I'm tryna sleep damn it."

Mickey chuckled.

Reggie's squinting eyes made sense of what was happening to him. "Mickey . . . what in the hell you doin' in here?" His voice was gruff, cloaked by sleep.

"Trying to wake you up."

"I can see that."

"This ought to do the trick." Mickey held one of the coffees in front of Reggie's nose. "I have donuts too." He tapped the box. "Returning the favor."

"It ain't a favor when you got to wake a man up to do it. What time is it?"

"Just after seven. It was even earlier when you called around to my place, so I figured this was fair game."

"Yeah, but I was working then. This is my day off." He sat up with a groan, accepted the coffee and sipped it. "That's good."

"It's from the café by my place, the one I'm always telling you about. The Italian place."

"Uh huh, I sure can taste Italy. What you want?"

Mickey slipped a hand inside his jacket and withdrew a large brown envelope folded in half. "I was hoping you might recognize someone. She lives just a few streets over." He flattened the envelope and pulled out a few black-and-white photographs he'd developed in his little darkroom in the bungalow.

Reggie took the photographs, flicked through them.

"What are you up to, Mick?" An edge to his voice.

"Do you know her?"

A pause. Reggie seemed to be thinking about what to say. "Yeah. I know her."

"How?"

"She was Odetta's hairdresser. I don't know her beyond that. What you taking photos of her for?"

"See that man with her? That's Floyd, the drug dealer Roland pointed me toward. The one who might know something about my missing porn star."

A serious expression on Reggie's face now. "You mean your missing porn star has something to do with Jemeka?"

"Well, no, I'm not saying anything so clear-cut just yet. But it is curious, because I spoke with Floyd right before these photos were taken, asking him about Jeffrey, and almost as soon as I left, he drove straight to that woman. As you can see, it looks like they were worried about something."

"You spoke with this guy alone?"

"Me, myself and I."

"That was foolish, Mick. You should know better."

"Maybe, but I survived. It's curious though, don't you think?"

Reggie seemed to be considering his words carefully, anxiety written all over him. "Listen, Mick . . . maybe you should cool off this whole thing."

Mickey frowned, confused about Reggie's strange response. Maybe he was a man one simply shouldn't wake up. "Why would I do that? I'm onto something here."

"That's exactly the problem, Mick. This isn't some cheating husband you're dealing with here. This could get serious."

Mickey blinked at him. Of all the responses he'd anticipated . . . "Reggie, I fought Nazis."

"You're getting reckless without Martha around. And you know it."

Mickey bristled, getting irritated. "What's it to you?"

"I care about you is what it is."

A tense silence took hold.

Mickey said, "Well, do you have any idea why Odetta's hairdresser is meeting with a drug dealer?"

Reggie shook his head. "Ex-hairdresser. Odetta ain't bothered going out to Lakewood just to get her hair done. I don't know anything about this, Mick. Jemeka worked at a salon round the corner for years until she started her own salon. About a year ago probably. That's all I know about her."

Mickey had the sense Reggie was holding something back. "You think she could be involved in the drug business?"

Reggie sighed. "Round here anybody could be. Not much opportunity otherwise." He rubbed wrinkled fingers over his eyes.

"What did you say this woman's name is?" Mickey said.

"Jemeka." Reggie placed the cup onto the bedside table with a smack. "Jemeka Johnson." He sighed. "I'm getting too old for this, Mick. We both are."

"Yeah, but what the hell else are we supposed to do?"

"Ain't that the truth."

"You sure you don't know anything else about Jemeka?"

"I'm sure, Mick, but Odetta might. Go bug her about it and get the hell outta my bedroom."

"All right. See you later, Reggie."

"Uh huh."

Mickey groaned as he stood up, pain like needles in his knees.

"See, you're too old for this shit," Reggie said.

"I agreed with you. I just don't care."

"You will."

XXX

JULY, 1999

FLOYD HAD HIS BACK TO THEM, walking toward his car. Richie fixed his gaze on Floyd and marched toward him. In his sweaty hand he clutched the

Smith & Wesson, confident in the damage it could wreak having witnessed it with his own eyes in the Starlight Motel. The weapon was no longer the threat of future violence—it was violence itself, ready to do its work with the tiniest movement of Richie's index finger.

Richie glanced at Jeff, two steps behind. The man's long blond hair spilled out over his shoulders beneath the balaclava—a dead giveaway. Idiot. Jeff did not have a gun and Richie hadn't figured him the knife-wielding type, his added presence more the point. But now that they were doing this, one gun between the two of them seemed a bit of a fucking oversight.

Richie was just a few steps behind Floyd now. The sound of a vehicle passing by on the street outside the strip mall faded and Floyd's steps grew loud in the ensuing silence.

Floyd had reached the hood of his Subaru, Richie close enough to touch him, when Richie's shoe crunched on an empty bag of potato chips. Richie hesitated and at the same moment saw Floyd glance at the hood of the Subaru which reflected like a mirror the pink balaclava hovering over the man's shoulder.

Richie went to raise the revolver but Floyd spun faster than the King of Pop and punched Richie in the gut. Richie gasped, the wind knocked out of him, as his finger tightened around the trigger reflexively, firing a bullet somewhere into the surrounding area. His body bent over, lungs desperate for oxygen. Gasping for breath, he watched as Floyd's shoes came toward him, the man about to finish him off. Then Jeff rushed past Richie and the sound of a struggle ensued.

Richie forced his body straight, gulping air into his lungs, and saw Floyd slap—literally *slap*—Jeff's face, knocking the porn star onto his ass.

Richie raised the revolver and thumbed the hammer: *klickk*.

Floyd froze as Jeff picked himself up off the ground.

Richie glanced behind. He couldn't see anyone but that gunshot wouldn't have gone unnoticed. They had to get the fuck out of here.

"The driver's seat," he commanded Floyd. "Move."

Floyd narrowed his eyes, not moving an inch.

"I'm not messing around. Get in the fucking driver's seat now." Richie heard the desperation in his own voice.

Floyd hesitated, weighing Richie up. "Key's in my back pocket. I gotta reach behind to take 'em out."

"Take his keys," Richie ordered Jeff.

Warily, Jeff circled around Floyd like a hiker who'd stumbled across a spitting cobra. Floyd watched him with an amused expression until Jeff was behind him, reaching now into Floyd's pants, looking like he was fingering the man's ass until he held the keys up like buried treasure finally uncovered.

"Open the car," Richie said. He kept his gaze firmly on Floyd as Jeff opened the driver-side door. "Check for weapons. Glove compartment, under the seats, all that shit."

Richie and Floyd stared at each other as Jeff searched the car, Richie not lowering the revolver for a second.

Jeff exited the car and nodded to Richie.

"Cat got this man's tongue?" Floyd said.

"Get in the driver's seat," Richie replied.

The hint of a smirk on his lips, Floyd moved toward the car and got into the driver's seat. Richie kept the gun trained on him.

"Get in the back," Richie said to Jeff, then moved around to the passenger side, keeping the gun aimed at Floyd. Richie opened the door and entered. Facing his body toward Floyd, Richie pointed the gun at the man's throat.

"Drive too fast, I pull the trigger. Drive too slow, I pull the trigger. Try any bullshit, your brain shoots out the back your head onto the fucking street. You hear me?"

"I hear you, man, I hear you. But I need to know where you want me to go."

"You're gonna take us to where you keep all that blow."

Looking right at Richie, Floyd grinned. "Okay Boss, but I'mma need those keys."

XXX

THE POP OF THE GUNSHOT STOPPED HER HEART. Then it fluttered back to life, pounding against her ribcage.

Paralyzed in the silence of the Audi, she watched as Jeff tackled Floyd and Floyd swung a hand at Jeff, knocking him over. Now Richie was pointing the gun at Floyd, making him do something.

Alabama glanced around. She couldn't see anyone. But police mobilized quickly in nice neighborhoods. They had to move.

Jeff appeared to be rifling through the inside of Floyd's car. He got out and Floyd entered on the driver's side, Richie coming around to the passenger side now, the gun pointed at Floyd.

Alabama's hands shook. She remembered the sickness. A cold shiver equal parts fear and withdrawals seized her body as nausea swelled up her esophagus from her belly and for a moment she considered giving up and letting America happen to her. ("'Merica ain't nothin' 'bout freedom, that's a lie," her ex-army cousin had told her once. "'Merica's something that happens to you. Something you gotta survive.")

Alabama forced the nausea down her neck. She didn't have time to be sick. Richie needed her.

She ignited the engine.

XXX

SILENCE IN THE SUBARU HUNG THICK LIKE FOG. Floyd drove them by Mayfair Park, heading north. The balaclava itched Richie's face, made him hot.

He glanced behind and spotted the Audi a few car lengths away. He noticed Floyd watching him.

"Eyes on the road," Richie said, the revolver never wavering from its position on Richie's lap aimed at Floyd's windpipe.

Leaned back into the seat with one hand on the wheel, Floyd gazed ahead, looking much too comfortable for Richie's liking.

"Y'all got nice hair," Floyd said, still staring ahead. "Y'all in a rock band or something?"

"Shut up," Richie said.

"Long hair like that, don't see it too much these days. Specially you in the back. That's some *distinctive* hair you got."

"Shut up and drive," Richie said. "Where are we going?"

"Now you givin' me mixed messages. You want me to shut up, or you want me to tell you where we're going?"

Richie glared at him. The bastard was enjoying this. "Where are you taking us?" Richie said.

"Not far. I keep my shit in the only place the fuckin' pigs would never look. Bompton, baby—" emphasizing the B—"Hub City."

"Compton?" Richie said, surprised that this surprised him.

"Where you think I keep it, Beverly Hills?"

"If you're fucking around I will blow your head clean off, man. I don't give a shit."

"Yeah yeah, you told me already."

Richie glanced in the rear-view, checking for Alabama, and again Floyd's hawkish eyes took note.

Floyd drove the Subaru onto the Artesia Freeway, heading west, and picked up speed.

"Not so fast," Richie said.

"Mind if I open a window?" Floyd said, fingers creeping toward the door. "One of y'all been smokin' the ganja big time. Shit stinks."

"Keep your hands away from that fuckin' door."

"A'ight. Chill." Floyd glanced in the rear-view. "Bet it was you in the back. Pink as pussy round those blue eyes. Shit, must be floating on a cloud back there."

Jeff said nothing.

Floyd laughed. "Yeah, you high. I think I know what strain you been smoking. I got a real good nose for this kinda shit."

"Shut the fuck up," Richie said.

Floyd took the exit onto Atlantic Avenue, watching the rear-view as he did. Alabama followed in the Audi, not keeping enough distance between them.

"That your woman?" Floyd said.

"What?"

"That bitch following us since we left Lakewood. She your woman? Or your sister or some shit? Shit, she's probably your woman *and* your sister—"

"I said shut the fuck up!" Richie jammed the revolver into Floyd's side.

"Chill, man. I don't blame you. She's pretty. The kind of face a man won't ever forget."

Richie gritted his teeth. Motherfucker was begging for a bullet. He pushed the barrel as deep into Floyd's flesh as it would go. "One more word and I pull the trigger."

Floyd kept quiet but his eyes were laughing and it was driving Richie up the fucking wall.

They had arrived in Compton.

PART III

Chapter Twenty

THE OXYS WEREN'T WORKING. After the initial rush had subsided, Alabama had felt as if she'd never chewed them at all and the shivers had aggressively returned. Her legs were always the first part of her to ache when the dope left her body, welcoming back pain like an abusive lover, and her calfs throbbed now, as if the muscles had lumped into knots down there. Moving her feet on the pedals of the Audi was becoming difficult and a fever was coming on, her forehead clammy, temperature soaring. Over sixteen hours without heroin. Put another way: *only* sixteen hours without heroin. The withdrawals would get a lot worse. She was more addicted than she had realized.

Alabama ignored the sickness as best she could and focused on the blue Subaru. She'd driven the Audi too close to the Subaru a couple times and, the second time, Floyd had locked eyes with her in the rear-view and she had known right away that he knew she was following him. So now she didn't bother to keep her distance. She didn't know Los Angeles like Richie did, didn't know where Floyd was taking them.

A red light stopped the Subaru at a three-pronged intersection where a McDonald's sat opposite a KFC which sat across from a Taco Bell and waiting behind the Subaru on her way to a robbery Alabama watched as a monstrously fat woman marched out of the McDonald's while guzzling from a box of fries and continued right on into the KFC and Alabama noticed now a billboard high above the KFC upon which a skinny blonde with perky tits wrapped in the Stars and Stripes stood on top of an aggressively masculine pickup truck like a white-trash Wonder Woman beside giant text which read "PICKUP A HOT CHICK IN THE NEW DODGE RAM" and for one revelatory moment that passed just as quick Alabama had never in her life felt so American.

The lights turned green and Floyd took the Subaru left onto a busy four-lane blacktop, the sign beneath the traffic lights declaring it Compton Boulevard. A yellow school bus empty of children drove by heading the opposite direction. Mexican fan palms lined the street like giant birds' nests balanced on stilts. A man with a blank face and hyper-alert eyes stood beneath a palm tree with a sign hanging from his neck declaring in large red letters "REPENT: TURN TOWARD JESUS OR BURN." There was a certain simplicity in laying out the stakes like that, making it black and white: Jesus, or flames. Her own family had viewed the world in the same rigid dichotomy back in Pine Ridge. Yet, despite this man and his sign, nothing was black and white here. The closer you looked at Los Angeles, the less sense the place made. Living here was like living inside a confusing dream that threatened to plunge into a nightmare at any moment. Richie viewed LA as their salvation, but Alabama saw the truth: It wanted to consume them.

After a couple minutes on the Boulevard, the Subaru turned onto a narrow residential street. Iron bars over the windows shielded the little bungalows on each side from late-night intruders. The street was empty of people but Alabama sensed the eyes watching her from inside the homes. A gut feeling gnawed at her. Something wasn't right about this. She caught a glimpse of Floyd in the Subaru's rear-view. He looked calm. Entertained, even. Beside and behind him, pink balaclavas advertised with terrible clarity the reason for their wearers' presence in this neighborhood. What had they been thinking? This was the worst idea in the world. Why hadn't she told Richie that it was a crazy, stupid idea and she wanted nothing to do with it?

Alabama slowed the Audi, letting the Subaru gain some distance until it stopped outside a detached two-story house painted vibrant pink. She stopped the Audi twenty yards behind. Look at that: a big pink house among all these drab little bungalows. There was that sense of unreality again, dreams and nightmares in the City of Angels.

Thirty seconds passed with the men still inside the car. Then Richie got out, followed by Floyd, Richie pointing the gun at him in broad daylight, the balaclava over his head even pinker than the house.

Jeff exited the Subaru and followed behind as Floyd led them toward the house, Richie right behind him, the gun almost jammed into Floyd's back.

Alabama felt she might puke, and not because of withdrawals.

XXX

"YOU KEEP THE BLOW IN THERE?" Richie said. The house was, strangely, pink like the balaclava heating his face. Floyd had stopped the car outside the building and the three of them sat in tense silence. Richie stared at the place. Covered by curtains behind iron bars, the windows offered no view of the inside. What would they be walking into?

"You're lying," Richie said. He jammed the gun into Floyd's face.

"No I ain't. Where you think I keep that shit, the bank?"

Richie looked at the house again. "All of it's in there?"

Floyd nodded.

"How much?"

"More than you two could carry."

Richie licked his lips, dollar signs floating before his eyes. "It's really in there?"

"Shit, what you want me to say?"

"How many people are inside?"

"I dunno, man. Probably not more than two. You want, I can give 'em a call, find out. You know, discreetly."

"Yeah, nice try." Richie glanced behind. Alabama had stopped the Audi a few car lengths away, staring back at him. He saw the fear in her eyes from here.

"What do you think?" Richie asked Jeff.

Jeff shook his head rigorously and jerked a thumb back the way they'd come.

Richie sighed. Fuck that, they'd come this far.

To Floyd he said, "Get out of the car."

"Okay Boss," Floyd said. Again it bothered Richie that Floyd appeared to be enjoying himself, or at the very least he didn't seem worried. Maybe he was simply a good actor.

"Bring the bags," Richie commanded Jeff.

They got out of the car.

"Lead the way. Slowly," Richie told Floyd, who began moving toward the pink house. Richie followed close, pushing the revolver into Floyd's spine. A car door shut. Richie glanced behind to see Jeff following with two empty black sports bags, one over each shoulder.

The street eerily silent. Richie felt eyes watching them.

They reached the door of the house. Could be anything on the other side. Richie glanced at Jeff, the man's pinkish eyes wide with worry. At least something had finally woken the guy up.

Richie pressed the barrel into Floyd's back. "Open the door."

XXX

ALABAMA WATCHED THE PINK HOUSE SWALLOW RICHIE. An overwhelming feeling stirred in her gut telling her she would never again see her husband, and the realization that without Richie she was utterly alone in this world crashed onto her shoulders like freezing water. But it snapped her out of paralysis. She needed Richie, and right now he needed her to keep her cool and be ready to speed them out of here the second he rushed out of that house.

She took a deep breath, exhaled slowly, and let the Audi roll closer to the Subaru. She stopped a few yards from the vehicle and kept the engine running. Her head ached almost beyond belief and her legs throbbed as if they'd succumbed to frostbite and been rapidly thawed and even under these dire circumstances with her husband in mortal danger concealed inside some drug dealer's den she could not stop thinking about heroin. She had been a fool to quit, she saw that now. You can't quit the hole. The hole quits you. Another few hours of this and she would do anything—*anything*—for a shot.

Alabama glanced in the rear-view and her heart stopped: Three men in baggy clothing were approaching the Audi. One of them, the shortest one, had a bandanna around his head, while the tallest of them had long locs dangling almost at his waist.

She locked the doors, then remembered the passenger-side window was open. She pulled the button to suck the window up as the men reached the Audi, two on the driver's side and the other staring at her through the passenger window.

The man with locs tapped on the window next to Alabama's face. "What's up?" he said in a voice made distant by the glass.

"You lost?" said the man on the passenger side.

Locs rapped on the glass again. "What you doin' here?"

Alabama pushed the button beneath the window until the glass came down two inches. "Can I help you?" she said to Locs towering above her on the other side of the window, trying to sound as if she was barely bothered by these guys.

"What you doing here? You know where you are?"

"Yeah, I'm . . . waiting for somebody."

The other two men had come around this side to stand beside Locs and gawk at her.

"She from the South or some shit," said the one with the bandanna, looking amused about it. "Probably thinks this is Hollywood." He laughed and the short one laughed along with him. But Locs appeared irritated by them.

"Hey, that's not a very nice thing to say to someone you don't even know," Alabama said. "I said I'm waiting on somebody, so can y'all leave me alone please?"

"That's no way to treat a lady," Locs said, scowling at his friends. "I'm sorry about that."

"That's fine. But like I said, I'd like to be left alone."

Locs nodded. "Okay. No problem. But tell me one thing. The person you're waiting for, are they inside that house right there?" He nodded at the pink house opposite.

Should she lie? What was the use, he probably already knew the answer. "Yeah, my man's in there. He'll be out here any minute."

"Oh yeah?"

"He's got a gun."

At the mention of a gun the three men glanced at one another.

Locs said, "It's that kind of vibe, huh?" Glancing at the house now, looking wary.

A sharp pain in her palm and Alabama realized she was digging her nails into it, drawing blood.

Locs backed away from the car. "We the peace-loving type, lady. Don't want nothin' to do with whatever you got goin' on. But I gotta tell you, whoever you're waiting for in there, they ain't worth it. That house right there, that house got some bad people inside. You had any sense you'd drive away from here right now."

Alabama said nothing but his words had stirred something inside her. She had never wanted anything to do with something like this. She'd come to LA to get *away* from trouble. What the hell kind of situation had she found herself in?

"Peace," Locs said, throwing up the two-fingered symbol of the word like Bob Marley. He moved away from the Audi, the other two following suit.

Sudden pain shot through Alabama's gut like a dagger, twisting it into knots. The presence of heroin in her blood had put her digestive system to sleep but it was waking up now as her body got wise to the absence of the drug. She cried out and crumpled in the seat as the pain intensified.

"Shit, you okay?" she heard Locs say.

The pain had a chokehold over her, so intense she was almost blacking out. She heard someone try to open the locked door.

"She might need a hospital or some shit," Locs said.

Alabama squeezed her eyes shut, praying the pain away.

"I don't know, man," said one of the other men. "I don't want nothin' to do with this."

"She's hurt," Locs said. "She needs help. Look how skinny she is. What would your mama say if she saw you leave a woman hurting like this?"

Alabama squinted through the pain, the three men staring at her through the window like she was an endangered animal in the zoo.

I'll be okay, she wanted to say, but the pain roared inside her and she cried out and Locs jumped into action, telling her to unlock the door. She did and he opened the door and helped her out of the car and almost immediately she puked on the pavement but not much came out of her, barely anything in there to begin with, and she sat on the pavement with her back leaned against the Audi while Locs asked if she was okay and the other two stared at her in silent bewilderment and despite the pain it was almost funny seeing these guys standing there unsure how to deal with this strange Southern girl who'd rolled into their neighborhood in an expensive Audi, told them her lover had a gun, and collapsed in agony.

Then a gun went off and nothing was funny ever again.

XXX

SHIT HIT THE FAN ALMOST THE MOMENT THEY WENT INSIDE.

A stench of weed. Not fresh—old, noxious, ingrained into the walls.

The sound of something sizzling in the kitchen area ahead. Richie thought he could smell bacon. From here, he could see into half the kitchen. A man's bald head appeared suddenly exactly where Richie was looking. He had no neck to speak of, clearly fat. When the man saw who had entered the house, his eyes went wide and the head vanished behind the wall.

Fuck.

Richie pointed the pistol at the kitchen and pushed Floyd forward, Richie shielding his body with Floyd's.

In there, the man stood by the wall with his hands raised, one of them gripping a greasy spatula. Beside him strips of bacon hissed in a filthy pan on the stove, the kitchen filled with the scent of cooking flesh.

"Don't fucking move," Richie said quietly, pointing the Model 27 at the guy's nose.

Floyd said, "What did I tell y'all 'bout keeping a lookout? Dumb motherfuckers."

"Keep your voice down," Richie said, strengthening his hold over Floyd.

"Man, you in way over your head. This really your plan? That other fool don't even have a gun."

"Shut up."

"Look, I get it," Floyd said, striking a sympathetic tone. "You saw an opportunity and you took it. But you didn't plan for it right. You should get out while you can."

Richie swallowed, throat like sandpaper.

"We can work this out," Floyd said, sounding so convincing Richie almost believed him.

"I said shut the fuck up." Richie pulled Floyd close, reminding him who had the power here. To the fat chef Richie said, "How many others are in here?"

The man glanced at Floyd.

"Don't look at him," Richie said. "How many others?"

"Three."

"Where?"

"I dunno, the living room? Shit, I'm just tryna eat. Can I turn off the stove? Gonna burn the house down."

The bacon was beginning to smoke in the pan. Richie didn't want him anywhere near that sizzling oil.

"Don't even fucking think about it," Richie said. "Drop the spatula."

The spatula clanged onto the dirty floor.

Richie glanced around the tiny kitchen. There was a door opposite him, a little to the right, and at the rear of the room a wooden table, on top of which was a gigantic bag of weed, some half-smoked joints, couple ashtrays, empty beer bottles, and a bulging backpack.

"Go over beside the table and get on your knees," Richie told the fat chef. "Slowly."

The man glanced at Floyd and started moving. Floyd was quiet, too quiet. Richie didn't like it.

The man was halfway to the table now, hands raised. Richie kept the gun on him, Richie's chest pinned to Floyd's back.

Floyd lurched suddenly and Richie gasped for breath, bending forward reflexively—Floyd had elbowed him in the gut. The revolver almost went off in Richie's hand as he struggled to hold onto it. At the corner of his vision, Richie saw the fat chef dart through the door ahead, the door swinging shut now. Now Floyd was struggling for the gun in Richie's hand while Richie tried to get air into his lungs.

Then Jeff was there. He grappled Floyd into a headlock from behind.

Breath returning, Richie gripped the Smith & Wesson by the barrel and swung it hard in a long arc, smashing the hardwood grip against Floyd's skull. A sickening crunch and Floyd collapsed onto his back, unconscious.

Richie and Jeff looked at each other.

The sound of scurrying footsteps on the other side of the wall. It sounded like an advancing army. This had all gone to shit fast.

"Grab that bag!" Richie pointed at the backpack on the kitchen table. Bulging with contents, he hoped there was something worthwhile inside because they had to get the fuck out of here right now.

Jeff scurried over and took hold of the backpack. At almost the same moment Richie noticed the door ahead open a crack. He fired the revolver, blowing a hole through the white-painted wood. A man screamed on the other side.

The hallway behind them—there were other doors back there. Richie whirled, sure that someone would be standing back there holding an AK-47, about to blow them away. But the hallway was empty—for now.

"We have to go," Jeff said, clutching the backpack with both hands. His eyes alert for once.

Richie knew he was right but they hadn't got what they had come for. He'd wanted to fill the sports bags with drugs or cash or both. He hoped to Christ it was blocks of coke inside that backpack.

Movement on the other side of the door.

"Go!" Richie yelled at Jeff, pointing to the hallway, exactly as an explosion of sound erupted. The wall behind them was coming apart as a torrent of bullets riddled the kitchen, splinters of wood and chunks of drywall flying into space around them.

"Get down!" Richie yelled, diving onto the floor.

Jeff dropped prone beside him and began crawling out of the kitchen as the house came down around them.

Richie dragged himself after him.

The shooting ceased. Richie's ears squealed like balloons releasing air. "Run!" he yelled at Jeff, who scrambled onto his feet, the backpack across his arm, and sprinted toward the front door of the house.

Richie was right behind him. As he exited the kitchen, he glimpsed a doorway on the right of the hallway opening slowly, the barrel of a pistol pointing out of it, aimed at Jeff. Richie kicked the door with all his strength and a man on the other side groaned and began to fall backwards but Richie wasn't hanging around to watch the guy hit the floor. He lunged toward the front door of the house, which was wide open now, Jeff halfway up the driveway.

The pop of a pistol behind and a hole appeared in the wall beside the opened door, almost exactly in front of Richie's face. Without stopping Richie fired the revolver at the shape of a man in the kitchen. He saw the shape take cover behind the kitchen wall, then Richie darted out of the house into the driveway, slamming the door behind.

Outside, sunlight dazzled Richie. He had almost reached the street when he heard the door of the house crash open. Ducking as a gunshot sounded, he made it onto the street, joining Jeff taking cover behind the hedges that formed a perimeter around the front of the house.

Then he saw Alabama.

She sat slumped against the Audi surrounded by three gangster-looking men staring back at him.

"Richie," she said. She sounded weak, as if Richie's sudden presence had just interrupted these bastards from beating the crap out of her.

One of the men—the tallest one with long locs—stretched out a hand

and said "Hey man—" while simultaneously the hand of the shortest man moved toward his waist. Richie didn't hesitate: The pistol in his right hand rose like a fifth limb and his finger curled around the trigger. The gun went off like a small explosive and the bullet tore through the short man's cheek. Without pause Richie aimed at the third man and fired. As that man dropped, Richie pointed the gun at the tall man, the man's hands clasped prayer-like now, stunned terror on his face. The man went to speak again and Richie squeezed. The bullet punctured the man's heart. Maybe took a finger with it. The man hit the ground like a stone along with the others.

An expression of horror had taken over Alabama's face as she gazed at the dead men, mouth frozen open. Suddenly she pointed at Richie and yelled his name.

Richie felt the bullet before he heard it: like a punch to the lower back from Mike Tyson. He collapsed onto his knees. A second bullet whizzed by his ear and ricocheted off the street.

He had dropped the revolver. It lay on the street a few yards ahead. Richie lunged toward it as another pop sounded, closed his fingers around the grip, and rolled onto his wounded back. The shooter stood half-hidden inside the doorway of the house. Richie fired at the pink wall next to the doorway. A scream of pain told him he'd hit his mark, Richie stunned by his aim, this natural affinity he had for murdering people. Then the gun clicked uselessly in his hand.

Richie struggled to his feet. A burning heat raged in his lower back. Felt like a hot poker had gone through it and out his side.

A flash of movement inside the house.

Richie sprinted for the car, leaping over corpses. Jeff lay prone and useless in the back seat, the door hanging open. In his hands he clutched the backpack as if it could shield him from death.

In the driver's seat Alabama shut the door and ignited the engine as Richie wrenched open the passenger door and flung himself inside. "Drive! Fucking drive!"

The car screeched forward. Its opened rear door smashed into Floyd's

Subaru as the Audi raced away from the house. Richie watched through the rear window as two men rushed out of the driveway onto the street.

"Get down!"

The window exploded into shards. A second bullet pierced the windshield, inches from Alabama's head.

She veered the Audi around a corner, the car almost leaving the ground, and the shooters disappeared.

It was then, as Richie was exhaling with relief, he noticed the blood leaving his body by the gallon.

Next came pain.

Chapter Twenty-One

JEMEKA RAN HER FINGERS THROUGH JENNY'S LONG HAIR, checking the layers were equal on both sides of the woman's head. Jenny tipped better than most of Jemeka's largely white clientele, so Jemeka was extra thorough with her. Not that Jemeka needed the money; a year of reaping the profits from the sale of cocaine to the wealthy and crack to the poor had made her rich beyond her wildest dreams. Branching into crack had been Floyd's idea. She had been hesitant at first, the idea of hurting her brothers and sisters an unwelcome one, but, as Floyd had pointed out, crackheads would find what they needed one way or the other, she may as well be the one getting rich from it, and she could make sure her crack was pure, not cut with poison like the crap crackheads would buy off someone else. Looked at that way, selling crack wasn't so bad. It could even be said she was doing something good for the community. He had a mind for business, Floyd, and she kept him close because of it. Not like Ray-Ray; man had a heart of gold but the business-mind of a four-year-old. Between the blow and rocks, profits had doubled, and Jemeka danced her way through the days, putting hours into the salon every week to keep up appearances—and launder the money. But that money had quickly grown beyond anything a single salon could wash. Jemeka smelled a franchise. Truthfully, it wasn't the money that made her feel so good. It was the freedom. She was (pretty much) her own boss, using her God-given skills to make something of herself, something far beyond anything most girls from the block could aspire to. No longer spending every hour worrying about where the money for groceries would come from this week, Jemeka at last knew what it felt like to thrive as an American citizen deserving of a life of dignity and finally acquiring it.

"Oh honey, you are looking good," she said to Jenny. Christina Aguilera crooned her little heart out on the radio.

"You think?" Jenny said.

"If you looked any better you'd be on a magazine cover."

Jenny almost blushed. "I don't know about that, but thank you."

Jemeka smiled. Did the woman a world of good hearing something nice about herself since her husband left her for another woman—a woman he'd secretly been raising a family with for years. Crazy. If Ray-Ray pulled that shit on her, she'd kill him.

Jemeka's cell phone buzzed on the ledge beside the mirror. She glanced at the pink Nokia 3210: "Fl." calling.

"Sorry suga, I gotta take this. I'll be back in a minute, okay? You want some more coffee?"

"No thank you, I'm fine."

Jemeka picked up the phone and accepted the call. She brought it into the back area of the salon.

"What?"

"You busy?" returned Floyd's voice.

"I'm always busy. What you want?"

"Something . . . happened."

"Well I would assume so, Floyd. We got a problem?"

A pause before Floyd said, "We got three of 'em."

XXX

"OH MY GOD RICHIE, ARE YOU OKAY?" Alabama glanced at her husband writhing in the passenger seat. He looked anything but okay. She'd managed to force down the pain in her own gut but she could sense it would rear its head again any minute.

She faced the road as a pedestrian stepped onto the street a few yards ahead. She jerked the wheel and slammed on the brake, swerving around the pedestrian in a near miss.

"Keep your eyes . . . on the road," Richie wheezed.

Alabama chewed her lip like it was gum. "We have to get you to a hospital."

He shook his head. "Cops . . . questions. And Floyd might . . . look for us."

"You'll bleed to death!"

"I can suture him," Jeff said from the back seat. "Got a first aid kit at my place." Saying it like it was nothing.

Alabama glanced at him in the rear-view, his startling blue eyes glowing out of that pink balaclava. "You sure you can do that? He's bleeding bad."

"Pretty sure. He's right, we can't go to the hospital." Jeff's voice calm as a summer lake.

Alabama exhaled, her leg trembling so severely it was difficult keeping it on the pedal. "Can you take that damn thing off your face? It's creepy."

"Oh. Yeah. Totally." Jeff pulled the balaclava off his head and tossed it onto the seat. His handsome face smiled at her.

Alabama frowned. There was something . . . not quite *there* about this man who appeared to be over the whole experience already, chilling in the back seat while her husband bled to death beside her. Or maybe Jeff just didn't give a damn.

"You gon' have to direct me to your place, Jeff. I don't know this city."

"No problem. Stay on this street for a little bit, then take the Gardenia Freeway east."

Alabama's palms slipped on the steering wheel. The nervous tremor in her leg alternately made the engine growl and silence.

"You okay, Richie?" she said, glancing at him.

He nodded subtly but his eyes were shut, hand clamped over his side. Dark blood soaked through the tracksuit and coated his hand.

Hot tears burned Alabama's eyes. "Don't die, Richie. Please don't die. Please don't leave me." She wiped her eyes and tried to keep the Audi moving without killing them all in the process.

Richie's wheezing breaths were his only response.

Traffic lights turned red at an intersection and Alabama stopped the Audi. Tears were flowing fast now and she shuddered with them, unsure where her grief ended and dopesickness began.

Something touched her shoulder. She glanced back to see Jeff's hand there.

"Richie's going to be all right," he said calmly, staring into her eyes like Christ. He sounded so utterly certain of these words that Alabama instantly believed them to be true. She felt lifted up by them. Her tears ceased.

"How do you know?" she said, wiping her eyes. Cold discharge dribbled from her nostrils and she wiped that away, too.

"I just do. Trust me." Jeff smiled, squeezed her shoulder, and sat back into the seat.

The lights turned green. Alabama accelerated. She felt calmer.

"What in the hell happened in there?" she said.

Jeff took a while to respond. "Sometimes, the plans we make go smooth as a dream. Other times, they fall apart completely."

What the hell kind of answer was that?

"It could be worse," Jeff said. "We got away with our lives. Richie will be okay soon as I suture that wound, and everything will return to normal. It'll be like none of this ever happened." He gazed out the window at the city passing by, looking like a man in a cab on his way home from work. Looking like a man who believed what he was saying.

His words stapled themselves to Alabama's insides. A return to normal was about the worst thing she could imagine, save for the thought of losing Richie.

A sign for the Gardenia Freeway approached. She accelerated the Audi and took the turn.

"In about a minute, take the exit toward Long Beach," Jeff said.

Alabama nodded. She glanced at Richie, still wheezing with his eyes shut. "Richie, are you okay? Can you hear me?"

Nothing.

The Audi picked up speed as the freeway opened up.

A shudder passed through Alabama then and nausea swelled up from her belly and sudden pain like a blade twisted in her gut. She cried out, bent over the steering wheel, as her weight pushed the accelerator to the floor.

"What's wrong?" she heard Jeff say but the world had gone black around the edges again and Jeff's voice sounded far away.

The Audi roared as it lurched forward and Alabama moaned, pain ripping through her, eyes shut now like her husband's beside her, both of them dying, both of them hurtling toward oblivion, together.

XXX

AUGUST, 2000

PARKED OUTSIDE THE SALON IN LAKEWOOD, Mickey gazed in the rear-view mirror and adjusted the tie he'd put on for this occasion along with an expensive gray suit (his *only* expensive suit). Martha's funeral had been the last time he'd worn the suit—he'd refused to wear black (Martha had hated black but she had loved this gray suit). He picked up the gray fedora from the passenger seat and placed it onto his head. Now he really did look like Hollywood's idea of a private investigator. Most people had the wrong idea about what PIs do, the day-to-day workings of the job, but today Mickey would come a little closer to those expectations. Gazing into his own eyes, he smirked: it had been a while since he'd had some fun.

At the Dixons', Odetta had told him about a man known as Ray-Ray who Jemeka Johnson had been dating for a long time, they had even lived together, until one day, coincidentally the same week Jeffrey had disappeared, Ray-Ray had vanished from the neighborhood without a trace nor a goodbye. Rumors had abounded about a terrible break-up but Odetta had never learned the truth of the man's departure.

Mickey entered the salon. Jemeka was blow-drying an elderly woman's perm, while an employee—a young white woman—swept the floor. Pop music, vapid and mindless, played from a radio by the door.

"Hey there," said the young employee as the door swung shut behind. "Can I help you?" She beamed, looking like a model in an advertisement.

Jemeka glanced his way before returning her attention to the perm.

Mickey replied loudly enough for Jemeka to hear: "I'm hoping I could speak with Ms. Johnson. Is she in today?"

Jemeka looked his way. The hairdryer silenced. "Hello. This ain't about hair, huh?"

"Not quite."

"I'll be with you in a moment, okay? Take a seat. We got some car magazines for the men who arrive early to pick up their wives. Know y'all like cars."

"Great, thank you." Mickey turned toward the cushioned chairs on one side of the door.

"Unless it's urgent?" Jemeka said.

"No, no," he faced her, "it can wait."

"Would you like some coffee? Just made a fresh brew."

Mickey went to decline reflexively but it came out, "I would love some."

"Bailey, can you fetch this man a coffee?" To Mickey: "Cream and sugar?"

"A pinch of both would be perfect."

Bailey nodded her understanding and glided out of sight.

Mickey sat in the chair closest to the window and scanned through the stacks of publications on the coffee table: about a hundred women's magazines, the covers of which all seemed to promise the same three things: diet tips, advice for spicing up your sex life, and celebrity gossip. He spotted a greasy old copy of *Car and Driver*. He had no intention of reading it. Though he loved his Pontiac, Mickey had about as much interest in automobiles as he had in molecular chemistry. He would rather read the dreary contents of one of the women's magazines than stare at pictures of machines whose sole function was to transport people from point A to B. He settled instead for observing the world outside the salon.

Bailey arrived soon with a steaming cup of coffee and set it onto the coffee table. The hazelnut aroma of it mixed with the bitter chemical smell of hairspray and the fruity scent of Bailey's perfume—a head-spinning concoction.

"Thank you so much," Mickey said.

"If you'd like it any sweeter, just let me know."

"That's quite all right. I was treating myself by having any sugar at all."

Bailey graced him with a youthful smile and returned to sweeping the floor.

Mickey sipped the coffee: watery, bitter and exceptionally sweet. But he appreciated the gesture and resolved to finish it.

Mickey was thinking about how Martha, determined always to look pampered and proper, had gone to the salon once per week without fail right up to the very end despite even the illness that had robbed her of almost everything else, when a nearby voice jolted him back to the present.

Jemeka was looking at him.

"Oh, I'm sorry, I was away in the clouds and my hearing's not what it used to be. What did you say?"

"I said we can go talk in my office now."

"Ah, excellent."

"This way." Jemeka made for the rear of the salon. Mickey leaned on the chair and straightened creaking knees.

BORING AND FUNCTIONAL, Jemeka's office offered no clues about her potential connection to the drug trade.

"Have a seat," she said, gesturing to the chair in front of her as she sat behind her desk. "How can I help you then, Mr. . . ." She smiled, sitting relaxed and cross-legged in the leather office chair. "I didn't catch your name."

"My name is Michael Hannity, but you can call me Mickey. I work for the IRS."

Jemeka went taut as a drum skin. "Aren't y'all supposed to send me a letter before coming out here asking about my finances?"

"Certainly, Ms. Johnson, certainly, but I'm not here to ask about your finances."

"Not about hair, neither."

"No."

"Then what are you here for, Mr. Hannity?"

"I'm here to ask you about Raymond Jones."

Jemeka's eyes subtly narrowed. "What?"

"Raymond Jones, Ms. Johnson. The most recent tax return we have for Raymond indicates he lives at your place of residence. Is that correct—does Raymond live with you?" Mickey glimpsed Jemeka's hand clutching a pen on her desk, the knuckles turning white.

"No. Ray-Ray—Raymond—and me, we split up. I don't know where he lives now."

"Oh. I see. I see. When did you split up, if I may ask?"

She stared at him.

"It's important for the record I know when Raymond changed his place of residence," Mickey said, doing his best to sound apologetic, as if he hated the process as much as she did.

"Man left about a year ago." She held her gaze on him, trying to make it friendly, but Mickey's eye, honed by fifty years of detection, noticed the tension in her jaw, the eye contact a little forced.

"And you have no idea where he might be now?"

"Not a clue. He left with barely a word. Said he was leaving California. Where to I don't know."

Mickey made a show of frowning in disappointment. "That's a shame, a real shame. Did he say anything that might offer a clue as to where he might be going? A job prospect, maybe?"

The friendliness had vanished totally from Jemeka's features now. "I'm sorry, Mr. Hannity, but do you have some identification?"

"Yes, of course. Well, in a manner of speaking, we're not exactly the FBI—" he smiled, making sure it reached his eyes—"but here's my card." He reached into his pocket, withdrew his wallet and pulled out of it a paper business card with "Michael Hannity" centered on it above an email address, phone number, and mailing address at the IRS. It was a fake card he had used with success many times over the years. He did not enjoy deceiving people, but he was not opposed to it if it got the job done.

Jemeka glanced at the card. "Ray-Ray told me nothing, just up and left. It was hard on me. I don't like thinking about it. I don't like talking about it, neither."

"Of course, Ms. Johnson. I completely understand. I'll be out of your way. Thank you for your time. If Raymond ever happens to get in touch, please give me a call, my number's right there on that card." Mickey stood up, groaning intentionally. "These knees aren't what they used to be."

"Have a nice day, Mr. Hannity."

"You as well, Ms. Johnson," Mickey said, shuffling toward the door. "Beautiful salon you have here. If my Martha was still around I'd be sending her straight here."

At the door, Mickey turned around. "Oh, Ms. Johnson, one last question before I go. Do you happen to know which bank Raymond was with?"

"Wells Fargo. Same as me."

A stroke of luck: he'd been hoping that would be her answer. With Wells Fargo having the most branches of any bank in California, it had not been an unlikely one.

"Thank you for your time, Ms. Johnson."

"Tell me one thing, Mr. Hannity."

"What's that?"

"Why are you looking for Ray-Ray?"

"Well, I can't say too much about it—procedure, you understand—but a large inheritance came Raymond's way recently and it's my job to make sure it's taxed accordingly. Thank you again for your time. And the coffee."

Jemeka looked puzzled.

Mickey tipped his fedora to her, returned it to his head, and hurried out of the salon before she could ask him anything else.

Chapter Twenty-Two

JULY, 1999

RICHIE OPENED HIS EYES and the world came at him like a fist. The popcorn ceiling above him meant he was on his back. A golden-haired man came into view, hovering above Richie like an angel.

"You okay, dude?" said the angel, and Richie realized the angel was Jeff.

"Alabama," Richie said. "Where is she?"

"Over there, dude."

Richie raised his head and followed Jeff's gaze. Alabama lay writhing on a sickly-green couch.

So they were in Jeff's apartment. Richie noticed the aroma of cannabis now, part of the very atoms of this space.

"Bama, you okay?"

She couldn't seem to hear him, twisting herself into knots.

A chemical taste lingered at the back of Richie's throat. A dull throb in his side. He remembered the wound and looked down to find himself shirtless. Stitches where the bullet had tore a chunk out of his side.

Jeff said, "Sutured you up, man. You were passed out. Lucky for you 'cause it would've hurt like hell. The bullet went right through you, which is good 'cause I probably couldn't have done much for you otherwise. I was worried you might be dead so I rubbed some coke into your gums. Then you woke up." Incredibly, Jeff was holding a lit joint between his fingers.

Richie went to sit up and Jeff held his shoulders. "Take it easy, man. You'll rip those stitches."

"I need to go to my wife."

"Won't do any good. She's been like that for a while."

Jeff stood up and took a pull on the joint. He brushed his long hair out of his face and curled it over an ear. "Happened to her in the car. Nearly crashed. I had to drive us here while you were passed out and she was like that. But it's all good. What friends are for, right?" The pleasant expression on the guy's face bothered Richie, like this was all a big joke.

"It won't be long before I'm like that too. We need heroin, Jeff. You're gonna have to get it for us."

"Look, I like you guys, I do, but I've done enough already."

Richie sat up slowly and dragged himself to the couch. He leaned his back against it, one hand over the wound. "Would you rather two dead junkies in your apartment? One with a gunshot wound. Try explaining that to the cops. Because if she dies, I'll kill myself right here on your fucking floor."

A glimmer of surprise in Jeff's stoned eyes. "That's pretty weird, dude. Romantic too, I guess."

Richie faced Alabama, touched her leg. Cold as death. She paid no heed, clearly in immense pain, and not just physically. Something bigger than withdrawals was happening to her, compounded by dopesickness but not solely caused by it. She was lost.

Desperation flooded Richie. He softened his voice: "Please help us out, Jeff. Just this one last time. I can't drive like this, I can barely move. All you have to do is go to our room in the Four Seasons hotel. There's a sports bag in there with everything we need."

Jeff appeared to consider it.

"Look at her," Richie said. "It's the right thing to do."

Jeff sighed. "All right, all right. Tugging on my damn heart strings." He sucked on the joint and exhaled wispy smoke. "I'll go get your dope, but you guys gotta get clean before that shit kills you."

"I know." Defeat like battery acid on Richie's tongue. Carefully, he slipped his hand inside a pocket of the tracksuit, wincing at the sharp pain in his side. He pulled out the hotel keycard and held it out toward Jeff.

Jeff took the card. "Plan really went to shit, huh?"

Richie didn't say anything. He felt so utterly beaten he could just die right here, and maybe he would if it wasn't for Alabama.

Jeff said, "It was a dumb plan anyway. No offense."

"The backpack," Richie said, remembering it suddenly, feeling a jolt of hope. "Do you still have it?"

"Yeah." Jeff gestured to the single-seater couch at the side of the room, upon which sat the backpack. It looked a little less bulging than Richie remembered. Maybe he'd only seen what he'd wanted to see then.

"What was in it?"

Jeff went over to the couch and picked up the backpack and tossed it at Richie, who zipped it open eagerly.

"What's this shit?" he said, pulling up a large bag of cannabis.

"It was just weed in there, dude. Not worth much. Sucks." Jeff shrugged.

Richie felt his body deflate like a tire as the last remnants of hope faded. He released the bag of cannabis and it dropped inside the backpack. He tossed the backpack onto the carpet beside the couch.

Jeff moved toward the door. There, he stopped and gazed at Richie. "This probably won't mean much to you right now, but the way things went might have saved your life. If you guys came into a load of cash right now, you'd shoot it all into your veins. If you wanna get rich, you gotta get clean first."

Richie shot Jeff a hateful stare, feeling irrationally furious at this remark but not wanting to piss Jeff off before he'd retrieved the dope.

Perhaps sensing Richie's rage, Jeff simply nodded, a kind of sadness in his eyes. Maybe pity. He opened the door and slipped out of the apartment and when the door shut it was as if Jeff had never been here at all. That final image of Jeff's pitying gaze lingered in Richie's vision. The tragedy in Jeff's eyes—like he was apologizing for something.

A car engine sounded outside the apartment and faded into the distance.

Silence.

Richie watched Alabama writhing on the couch. Sweat coated her skin, teeth gritted, eyes closed. He touched her forehead: icy cold, as if she was already dead.

"Hang in there a little longer, baby. You're gonna feel better soon." Ignoring the pain in his wound, he leaned over her and kissed her clammy cheek.

Alabama's eyes fluttered open. Unfocused. Glassy. "Richie?" She couldn't see him.

"I'm here."

Her jade eyes focused on him, seeing him. "I don't feel so good, Richie."

"I know. You just have to hold on a little longer. Jeff's getting the dope."

"It's too late."

"Too late? What do you mean? Just hold on a little longer, Jeff will be here soon."

"No." She shook her head. It appeared to require tremendous effort. "They were helping me." Her voice little more than a whisper. "And you killed them." Her eyes shut again. "It's too late for us . . ."

Richie frowned. She was delirious with dopesickness, that was all. It would pass when Jeff returned with the heroin.

"Just hang in there, Bama. Just hang in there and everything will be better soon." But the knot in his gut said otherwise.

He chewed his lip and waited, trying to ignore what Alabama had said, and thoughts of what might happen to her if Jeff didn't return.

XXX

AUGUST, 2000

MICKEY PARKED THE CATALINA in the underground lot beneath Pershing Square in downtown Los Angeles and walked for five minutes on sun-drenched streets amid sounds of traffic and hustle-and-bustle toward his destination, the Wells Fargo at 707 Wilshire Boulevard, across the street from Los Angeles Central Library, the latter a beautiful building in the style of modernist Art Deco where Mickey had spent much time over the years researching for cases like Philip Marlowe or merely browsing good fiction. The bank, on the other hand, was located on various floors of the twin skyscrapers at the Wells Fargo Center, to Mickey's mind two of the ugliest buildings ever constructed. Towers one and two stood at seven hundred and twenty-three feet and five hundred and sixty feet, respectively—gigantic, trapezoidal, black shapes jutting out of the earth like Darth Vader's watchtowers, described by cultural critic Frederic Jameson as an example of the depthlessness of postmodernism, who had likened it to the recurring monolith in Kubrick's *2001: A Space Odyssey*—that mysterious alien structure which cannot be understood yet seems to symbolize, even trigger, movement into the future—transformation—from which humanity can never return. But in the case of the Wells Fargo Center, this movement away from romantic LA was a violent replacement of the past with nothing to offer in its place other than a thin veneer of progress and submission to the almighty dollar. LA now: colored families priced out of their neighborhoods, young people working two jobs to barely pay the rent on tiny apartments, creative types leaving in spades for greener pastures, politicians' faux progressivism masking a soul-selling worship of corporations. This city had been changing since the beginning but now these transformations were occurring more rapidly than ever and soon there would be nothing left of the Los Angeles which had once put a spell on the world, and on Mickey himself. But what did he care, really? His life was nearing its end, and the future of this city did not include him in it.

Mickey reached tower one and stood at the base of the monolith. He craned his neck to gaze up. This close, the top of the building was too high to see. It blotted out the sun. Mickey thought now of *Blade Runner*, struck by the realization that the film's dystopia was not some far-away possibility but was sprouting up around him here and now. Did no one else see it, or was he going mad? Maybe this was simply what it felt like to grow old.

Mickey was four steps inside the bank when a pretty young woman in a slim-fitting suit asked how she could help him today.

"That depends, how long have you got?"

Her confusion betrayed her.

Mickey chuckled. "Just kidding. I need to speak with Mr. Krieger."

The woman beamed at him. "Do you have an appointment?"

"I'm afraid I don't, but it's important."

The woman frowned with insincere sympathy. It looked like a grimace of pain. "I understand, sir, but Mr. Krieger is very busy, and without an appointment—"

"Tell him Mickey O'Rourke is here to see him. He'll want to see me, you can bet your bottom dollar on that. I'll wait over there." Mickey pointed at some seats by the elevator and shuffled toward them without pause, the heels of his shoes loud on the marble floor. At the edge of his vision he saw the woman hesitate, then move off somewhere, heels clicking, hopefully to contact the bank manager, Harvey Krieger.

Mickey listened to the music playing quietly from hidden speakers: smooth jazz, but the artless kind, the commodified "easy listening" background noise used exclusively to foster a human aura in a place that had none. Sitting down now, Mickey's legs ached terribly. He was getting too old for all this investigating. It was a good thing this case would be his last because he wasn't sure he had another in him. Though he wasn't sure he could face the slow death of retirement, either. When a man devotes his entire adult life to investigation, the excavation of truth, what does that man become when he retires? A sack of bones, without even a woman to make the quiet nights go by a little easier.

"Mr. O'Rourke!"

Dragged out of his reverie, Mickey located the speaker: Harvey Krieger stood smiling at him outside the elevator, from which he must have emerged.

"To what do I owe the pleasure?" Harvey said.

Mickey shot back a grin of his own. "Harvey, it's great to see you. And please, you know to call me Mickey by now. I'm afraid I have something important to request of you."

"Okay, Mickey. We best go on up to my office then." Harvey thumbed the elevator call button. "It's great to see you, though, really. Hard to believe it's been almost a year since . . ." Harvey gazed at the floor and grimaced, looking like his employee had moments ago but this time the pain was real.

The elevator doors opened. Harvey and Mickey stepped inside after some people exited. Harvey pressed the button for floor seven. The scent of a woman's perfume, spicy and expensive, lingered in the small space.

"Yes, it is hard to believe," Mickey said. "The funeral was beautiful. The most beautiful funeral I've ever been to, in fact."

Harvey nodded, his eyes far away. "I couldn't give her a beautiful wedding, so the funeral had to do."

He glanced at Mickey and smiled, eyes vibrant again. "Anyway, how have you been? You're still working?"

The elevator doors opened on floor three. Plain-faced people in drab suits entered into the steel box.

"I am, although not for long," Mickey said as the doors shut. "After fifty years, this one is my final case. This case is why I'm here, in fact."

"I figured as much."

HARVEY'S OFFICE WAS LIKE EVERY BANK MANAGER'S OFFICE except for one element: Jane's smiling little face watched you from framed photographs on every wall and surface, dozens of them, and in this way the room became a shrine both to Jane herself and to Harvey's pain. To go through the agony of losing a child to kidnapping only to recover her and lose her again a few years later to leukemia, forever this time, that kind of pain is beyond the realm of the imagination, and Mickey could not have sympathized more deeply with Harvey, especially because he had grown fond of Jane himself since getting her out of that godforsaken place. No—he'd fallen for little Jane even before then, during the investigation when each day he would look at a particular photograph of her—smiling at the beach, always smiling—which he had kept framed on his desk as motivation to find her.

But after the case had been completed, Mickey had put that photograph away. Harvey had taken an opposite road.

Harvey sat behind his broad desk made of old hardwood, polished like a bowling ball. It must have weighed a ton. He gestured to the chair in front of the desk and Mickey sat on it gratefully. Ninety percent of the job: taking photos of people or sitting in someone's office. So far this case had demanded both.

"I'm assuming this isn't about more NBA tickets?" Harvey said.

"No, although it is the same case those are for. Thank you again for that."

Harvey waved this gratitude away. "What can I do you for?"

"Well, Harvey, one of Wells Fargo's customers changed their place of residence about a year ago. I have no idea where to but it's vital I find this person. If he's still a customer of this bank, I'm hoping you may have his new address on file."

Harvey observed him, giving nothing away.

Mickey said, "I understand the gravity of what I'm asking. Totally against policy, I know. But—" Mickey sighed. "Without this information I fear I've reached a bit of an impasse."

"What is the case, if I may ask?"

"A man disappeared a year ago. His girlfriend has tasked me with finding him . . . or what happened to him."

Empathy seized hold of Harvey's features. "A missing persons case, I knew it. If that isn't fate, I don't know what is. Of course I'll help you, Mickey. You saved my daughter's life. I'm forever in your debt. Even though Jane is gone, those two years you gave us together were . . ." Harvey's eyes grew moist. "They were everything is what they were. Do you have the name and social security number of this person you're looking for?"

"I have the name and previous address."

"That'll work. Write it down for me and I'll get my assistant to look it up. She's better at these computers than I am. If she can't find him, no one will." He slid a cube of yellow Post-It notes toward Mickey followed by a ballpoint pen.

Mickey scribbled the information and handed the notes to Harvey who took them and got up from the desk and went toward the door.

One hand on the door, Harvey faced Mickey. "You know, Mickey, whether you find this person you're looking for or not, you've done more by rescuing Jane from that awful place than most people achieve in their entire lives. I mean, look at me. All I've ever been is a banker. I've added nothing positive to the world. Perhaps I've even made it worse."

"You brought Jane into the world, Harvey. That's more important than anything I've ever done."

"We both did that, Mickey." He smiled. It was both joyous and sad. "I'll be back in a jiffy. Make yourself comfortable. I'd offer you some of my whiskey but I know you wouldn't drink it." With that, he left the room.

Mickey let the silence settle and gazed around the office. Wherever he looked, Jane Krieger was smiling at him.

Chapter Twenty-Three

JULY, 1999

A SENSATION LIKE A SWORD TWISTING IN HER BELLY brought Alabama back to reality. She opened her eyes to find herself lying on a couch in somebody's living room. Richie sat on the floor beside her, watching her.

"You're awake," he said, sounding hopeful.

"Bathroom," she said, holding her belly, and clambered off the couch.

Richie helped support her through this messy apartment stinking of marijuana to a tiny bathroom with cracked tiles and rust stains around the toilet bowl. She tore down her jeans and flung herself onto the toilet bowl right before a violent expulsion of her insides occurred. It went on for some time. When it had ended, she felt relieved, lighter. But the sickness was far from gone.

Alabama returned to the living room and collapsed onto the couch beside Richie. "Water."

Richie went into the kitchen and fetched her a glass.

She sipped the water. It tasted somehow revolting, like how she imagined bleach might taste, though she suspected the problem lay with her taste buds, or rather the part of her brain that translated the water on her taste receptors into flavor. Never had her body felt so fragile, her bones so heavy under pale, punctured skin.

Richie watched her sipping the water, relief on his features. "You're through the worst of it. I was really worried there for a minute. I didn't know if you were gonna make it. Jesus." He wiped a hand over his face.

"Ain't over yet," Alabama said. "Don't know if I can take much more of this."

"I'm scared 'cause I'm starting to feel it too. Jeff better come back with the dope real fuckin' soon."

"What happened? Everything went wrong, there was shooting—" A flash in her mind of Richie aiming the revolver. Three bangs as it went off, those men dropping to the ground. "Oh no, Richie . . ."

"What?"

"You killed them . . ."

"Who?"

"You came out of that house and you shot them dead."

"I saved our asses, you mean."

Alabama shook her head. "No."

Richie screwed up his face. "No?"

"They were helping me, Richie. They were nice to me. And you killed them."

"What?"

"I was in pain and they helped me out of the car, sat me down. They wanted to call an ambulance but I said no. They told me to get far away from that house, that bad things would happen. Then you came out and bad things did happen. But they happened to them."

What little color Richie's cheeks had held drained from them now. "They were helping you?"

Alabama nodded weakly, too tired to say anything more about it.

Richie sat in silence, processing it. After a while he said, "I'm sorry that I did that to those guys. I thought you were in danger. I thought I was saving your life."

"I know."

"Anyone would have made the same mistake."

You mean anyone *white* would have made the same mistake, Alabama wanted to say—that mistake being seeing three Black guys near your wife and thinking they meant her harm. The mistake being racism pure and simple.

Apparently Richie needed to justify it some more: "We were in those guys' turf doin' a robbery. I come out, you're on the ground, bullets are flying. I saw those guys and I pulled the trigger. And I don't regret it, either. I was protecting you."

"I know you were, Richie. But I also know that we'll have to pay for it. Don't you see?" She looked at him and she saw that he did see, probably saw it clearer than her. And despite everything—despite one disaster after another he had put her through since the beginning of their relationship with its continuous downhill trajectory toward addiction, poverty, desperation, crime, and murder—she saw in his face that, somehow, even though at times it was damn near impossible to believe, Richie had only ever meant well. That was the crazy part about the whole thing.

Richie crawled onto the couch and she leaned her head into his chest and they sat embracing each other for some time, just the sounds of their breaths and occasional evidence of a world still spinning outside.

"What if Jeff doesn't come back?" Richie said finally. His leg had begun to jitter.

Alabama did not respond, exhausted from hopping problem to problem.

"We're gonna have to go over there if he doesn't come back soon," Richie said. "Dumbass probably went to the wrong hotel."

Alabama sat up straight and looked into her husband's eyes. "What if we don't use again?"

Richie opened his mouth but before he could disagree, Alabama said, "Hear me out. We could leave LA right now, hole up in some motel until we're through withdrawals. Then we could leave California, go somewhere quiet where nobody'll bother us. Like, I don't know, Alaska."

Richie screwed up his face. "Alaska? You serious? You wanna freeze your tits off up there all year?"

"Somewhere else then. Richie, I don't like it here. And this shit we keep putting into our body . . . if we don't quit now, when will we?"

"I thought you said you couldn't take withdrawals any longer."

"I'm having a breakthrough moment and I need you to do this with me, it's the only way I can do it."

"I can't. I just can't."

"You can. *We* can."

Richie shook his head. "I can't."

Alabama took Richie's hands into her own and waited for him to look at her.

"You can," she said.

He was considering it. Maybe she had a chance of convincing him.

"I dunno, Bama. I'm scared." She had never known him to admit to feeling afraid. He buried his head into her chest and Alabama stroked his greasy hair.

"I know, baby. So am I."

He pulled his head back and looked at her. "We gave it our best shot, didn't we?"

"Yeah, but maybe we tried the wrong thing. Maybe now it's time to try the right thing."

Richie's forehead wrinkled and she saw in his eyes the realization her words had provided. "Maybe you're right. I'm sorry I brought us back to LA. I'm sorry I made us leave here in the first place. I'm sorry for everything."

"I forgive you."

The sound of a car engine outside. The sound grew louder, then silenced. A car door shut. Then another. It struck Alabama now that this awful little living room was windowless.

"Must be Jeff," Richie said, eagerness in his voice. He stood up and moved toward the door.

Alabama frowned. The engine hadn't sounded like that of Jeff's little car.

"Wait," she said, but Richie had already opened the door.

"What?" He gazed back at her, the door wide open.

"I don't think it's—"

A loud thud boomed through the hallway, followed by another. Wood splintered and crunched.

"Oh shit." Richie backed away from the doorway, alarm on his face.

Alabama's stomach dropped. It was too late. In her heart she had known they were doomed the moment Richie had shot those men and now the universe was proving it. She felt the will to survive seeping from her body, replaced by cold acceptance of this, their reckoning.

"Don't move!" snarled a voice in the hallway. Richie raised his palms and froze.

Weary beyond exhaustion, Alabama remained on the couch and awaited her fate.

XXX

"WHERE IS HE, MOTHERFUCKER? Don't make me ask twice," Floyd said, standing over Richie kneeling on the floor. He pushed a black Colt under Richie's chin.

"He went to the Four Seasons hotel, then he's coming back here," Richie said, seeing no reason to lie about anything anymore.

"Why?"

"To get heroin."

The gun left Richie's neck but the sensation of cold steel on his skin lingered. Floyd looked Richie over, then at Alabama on her knees beside him. He grimaced. "Fuckin' junkies. Guess we're waiting for the porn star then. You better hope he shows."

Floyd sat on the couch and leaned back into it, his hand gripping the pistol lying sideways on his knee, pointed at Richie. "What's your name?"

"Richie."

"Richie? Like Richie Rich? Well shit, ain't that ironic. What about you, bitch?"

Alabama said nothing.

"Hey, I asked you a question. Don't make me slap it out of you."

"Ala-Alabama," she said.

Floyd frowned. "Richie and Alabama? God damn. Y'all never had a chance. Don't seem like the kind of folks my boy Jeff would have nothin' to do with. How you know him?"

Facing the carpet, Richie said, "We don't know him really, we—"

"Speak up, motherfucker!"

Richie flinched. "We don't know him. We just met the other day and we got along. I don't know."

"Plan was your idea, huh? I know Jeff didn't come up with it. He just don't think that way. You put him up to this shit."

Richie said nothing and Floyd took that as confirmation, nodding now. "You picked the wrong partner in Jeff. Man ain't all there, know what I'm saying? Fool thought he could put a mask on and I wouldn't know right away it was him? Gotta be one of the most distinctive motherfuckers in LA. Didn't even cover up his hair. Stinkin' of weed, eyes red as the Devil's dick, not saying a goddamn word the whole time." Floyd shook his head, having fun. "Jeff probably thinks I don't know where he lives, neither. But me, I'm not just some nigga off the street, you feel me? I'm smart. I make it my business to know where my best customers sleep at night 'case I need to pay them a visit."

Floyd stood up and came toward Alabama. "So this the bitch following me in that nice car outside. I don't touch junkies. Otherwise we mighta had a good time. Maybe I'll take a look at those titties, though. How 'bout it, bitch?"

Richie gritted his teeth.

Floyd reached a hand toward Alabama and Richie couldn't stop himself: "Touch her and I'll kill you."

Floyd's hand paused, inches from Alabama's chest. He grinned at Richie, something sadistic in his eyes, then curled the hand into a fist and swung it hard into Alabama's jaw. The dull thump of it sounded awful. Alabama cried out and hit the floor on her back.

The black Colt was under Richie's chin before he could react. "You disrespected me enough already," Floyd said. "You try that shit again, I'll fuck this bitch's skull in front of you."

Floyd held his gaze on Richie, so much venom in it. "All right, I'm getting bored. More important than Jeff, where's the money you stole from me?"

"What money?"

"Don't wanna make this easy, do you?" Floyd pulled Alabama onto her knees by her hair, her screaming and writhing beneath him. He forced the Colt into her mouth and she went still, choking on the weapon.

"Wait!" Richie said. "I don't know what money you mean, we didn't take any money."

Floyd said, "The backpack, motherfucker! The backpack you stole from *me*. The backpack that had *my* money inside, my money that fat fuck was supposed to put straight into the safe. Yeah, you got lucky picking today of all days, the one day the money don't go into the safe right away. But your luck ran out. Where's my money? I'll shoot this bitch."

Alabama screamed or spoke or cried; whatever it was, it sounded mangled with the gun in her mouth.

"There!" Richie pointed to the backpack on the carpet, hidden from Floyd's perspective. "Other side of the couch."

Floyd released Alabama. She flopped onto the floor in child's pose, shuddering.

Floyd moved toward the couch as Richie said, "But I don't know what money you're talking about. I swear. It was just weed in there."

Floyd picked up the backpack, the zipper already open, and gazed into it. "How dumb do you think I am?" He launched the backpack across the room. It smashed the glass of Jeff's awards display.

He lunged toward Richie and pressed the thirsty pistol into Richie's forehead. "You're dead 'less the next words outta your mouth tell me *exactly* where my money is."

Richie's breaths were coming faster now, he couldn't seem to control them. Half-baked ideas to delay his execution zoomed around his mind but he couldn't grasp onto any of them. Tears stung his eyes.

"I swear I don't know! Jeff said it was just weed in there. Jeff told me, man. Jeff told me!" He stared into Floyd's face, pleading with the man to believe him.

Eyes narrowed, Floyd held his gaze on Richie for a short stretch of infinity. At last he took the gun away. "You're lucky I know when a man tellin' the truth. Jeff said there was just weed in there, huh?"

Richie nodded eagerly. "Yeah yeah, Jeff said, he said that, that the backpack just had weed in it, not worth much, and the whole fuckin' job was a bust." Richie was breathless getting it out.

"Then Jeff went to go get your dope. Just like that."

Richie nodded.

"Outta the kindness of his heart, huh?"

Richie wasn't sure what Floyd meant.

Floyd shook his head. "Jeff, Jeff, Jeff . . . didn't think you had it in you." He glimpsed the confusion on Richie's face. "What? You don't see what happened here? Jeff fucked you, that's what happened. There was one hundred Gs in that backpack, delivered direct from some of my dealers not ten minutes before we went in that house. When y'all snatched it, no way Jeff knew what was in there. But then he gets home with it, sees what's inside. So what does he do? Swaps that shit with that bag of weed I sold him couple weeks ago, tells you that's all he found in there. Then Jeff leaves this dump with all that money but tells you he's coming back with your dope so you don't go after him. Clever motherfucker used your addiction against you. You got played."

Richie felt the world coming apart at the seams. One hundred thousand dollars. Jeff wouldn't do that to him. Would he? Jeff was his friend. Wasn't he?

Floyd said, "Shit, I didn't think he had it in him. He tricked the both of us. Cool as a cucumber. Like Paul Newman in *The Sting*. Probably halfway to Vegas by now."

The truth of it settled in Richie's gut like poison. Jeff *had* done it to him. Jeff had played him like a violin. Jeff had tossed him to the wolves. Jeff had signed his death warrant. Alabama's, too.

Alabama spoke then for the first time since Floyd had arrived: "So, are you . . . are you gon' let us go?"

Silence like the lull before opening shift at a slaughterhouse. The weight of inevitability filled the room. Richie reached for Alabama's hand and felt it tremble.

"Stand up," Floyd said, no amusement in his voice now.

Alabama's fingers tightened around Richie's and, much too late, Richie realized that he did in fact want to live.

XXX

RICHIE LAY ON HIS BACK in the almost pitch-black trunk of the Audi he had stolen from someone who had once been his best friend. Bad decisions and worse consequences. Before Floyd had forced them into the trunk, Floyd had slipped zip ties around Richie's hands and ankles, and Alabama's, too—so they could not punch or kick the inside of the trunk, Richie assumed. The fact Floyd had zip ties with him spoke to his intentions in coming to Jeff's apartment.

So here they were: lying next to each other in the darkness of this coffin-like space. Alabama was shuddering and it hurt his heart but his own sadness for himself, his fear, had left him when he'd got into the trunk, resigned to the end now. Maybe he should have charged at Floyd, tried to take the gun from him, but he'd been afraid that he would fail and Alabama would be murdered for his actions. Now she would be murdered for his inaction. Like their lives these past few years, every way Richie looked at it they lost.

He could feel the car moving, its engine vibrating through the machine. Bumps on the road jerked their bodies around.

"Bama," he said.

She sniffled. "Yeah?"

"I love you."

Alabama's crying reached a new peak, her almost choking with it. "I love you too."

"You made my life worth living," he said. "Showed me a whole new way of looking at the world. I should have done better. You deserved better."

More crying, Richie's heart aching hearing it.

Alabama sniffled. "I know things didn't always work out the way we'd hoped, but for most of it I felt happier than I ever have, because we were together."

"Me too." He stretched out his neck to kiss her cheek and tasted salty tears, her skin soaked with them.

"Maybe we shouldn't have robbed all those diners," Alabama said.

"Lotta things we shouldn't have done."

"But it was pretty fun sometimes," Alabama said. "I mean, after we got away with the money and no one got hurt."

"It was a rush all right."

"I'm glad we got married." She laughed the sweet innocent laugh of a child and Richie soared to the heavens with it.

"Shit, I almost forgot. Husband and wife, you and me. How about that?"

"People always trash-talk Vegas weddings but I thought it was pretty. My mama would have a fit if she knew I got hitched in Vegas."

"I thought it was pretty too," Richie said. "I liked that it was just you and me and the open road, the future like a blank page we could write on."

"Don't forget the guy dressed up like Elvis."

"I always wanted to get married by Elvis."

"So you got all you ever wanted then, huh?"

Richie thought about all their time together, the highs and the lows and the thrills and the fears and the sweeping, majestic romance of it all.

"Yeah. I did."

"I got all I ever wanted too," Alabama said.

Grief surged up then and tears came with it and Richie let them because it was love, and he realized now, at this, the end of his time on Earth, one of life's great truths: to grieve is to love and to love is to grieve.

Alabama's lips were on his chin. He turned his face toward her and kissed her passionately, again and again, savoring the taste of his wife, the scent of her skin, the sensation of her wet lips against his and her tongue against his own. He wanted to grab Alabama's face in his hands and kiss her the way he should have kissed her every day since meeting that fateful night in a dive bar in Santa Monica but his hands were tied behind his back and he had only his lips and his words and he would make good use of them for however much time they had left, which, if he looked at it just the right way, was eternity.

Chapter Twenty-Four

TWO JUNKIES ON THEIR KNEES, one male, the other female. Lovers. Richie and Alabama were their names, according to Floyd. Sounded like white trash to her.

Jemeka stared at them as they gazed at the floor, hands tied behind their backs and feet tied together. They had not said a word since Jemeka had arrived, as if they had accepted their fate as inevitable, and this unsettled her.

She'd closed the salon early and driven straight here to Floyd's storage unit. Looking at the sorry souls before her, a pang of compassion seized Jemeka's thoughts and she forced it away, aware of Floyd and Ray-Ray watching her.

"Please let us go."

The woman was gazing up at Jemeka. Though she had said it quietly, her words were loud in this small space. The dirty yellow light of the bulb in the low ceiling accentuated the woman's gaunt, sickly visage where it shone and created bottomless pools of shadow beneath the woman's eyes and mouth where it did not. She looked like she'd died already.

"We made a mistake is all," the woman said. "Ain't everyone allowed to make a mistake in their life? We're really sorry for what we did. We just wanna go home." In her eyes swam a sadness so deep it was impossible to look at.

That twinge of compassion crept into Jemeka's mind again. But Floyd's eyes burned holes into the back of her skull. She had not forgotten what Marsellus had done on his yacht out in the silent wilderness of that black ocean. She had not forgotten his threat. If she let these people go, Floyd would inform Marsellus. Or he would see it as a sign of weakness, set in motion a plan to take over. He was hungry. He wanted Marsellus out of the picture so they could have the market to themselves, but if she proved herself too weak for the job . . .

"Please," said the other one now, the man.

"You couldn't have taped their mouths?" Jemeka said, not wanting either of them to convince Jemeka to do something stupid.

"I forget the tape," Floyd said. "Even when I was grabbing zip ties, I forgot it. Not like I do this shit every day."

"Please—" the woman began but Floyd waved the pistol at her and said, "Shut the fuck up."

"Jemeka," came Ray-Ray's voice behind.

She looked at him.

"Don't do this." His eyes pleading with her.

She glanced at Floyd. His hard expression stated clearly his thoughts on the matter.

"You need to stop talking, Ray-Ray," she said.

"Just let them go, Jemeka. This ain't right."

The junkies were staring at her now, hope coming alive in their eyes. Ray-Ray was making this worse than it needed to be.

"Get out of here, Ray-Ray."

He stepped toward her. "Jemeka, listen to me. Nothing is worth this. These people are on their knees begging for their life. Let them go. Just let them go."

Jemeka glanced at Floyd. He would not let this slide. "Ray-Ray, you have to stop talking right now and get out of here."

Ray-Ray stepped closer, inches from her now. "You've changed, Jemeka.

This ain't you. I know we never had no money, I know it makes you feel safe having lots of money, but money's changed you, Jemeka. Who are you right now? Look at them—" he pointed at the junkies but Jemeka refused to look, the awful sadness in their eyes too painful to gaze upon. "How could you do something like this?"

Behind Ray-Ray, Floyd looked furious.

"I don't have a choice," Jemeka said. "You saw what Marsellus did."

Ray-Ray shook his head, quiet righteousness simmering inside him. "We always have a choice. We could take the money we have now and leave all this behind. We could live a good life somewhere, Jemeka. You know we could."

Jemeka thought of losing everything she'd worked so hard to achieve: the salon, the potential for a franchise, the mountains of cash she would make in future and the yacht she would buy with it, the control over her own destiny, the power she could have. She imagined her and Ray-Ray living in another state or nation with new identities—nobodies living a nothing life—and knew beyond doubt that she could never return to that existence.

"I'm sorry, Ray-Ray."

"Please!" cried the woman. "Please let us go!"

"We won't say anything," said the man. "I swear."

Horror contorted Ray-Ray's face as he stared at her. She had become a monster in his eyes. If that was the price of their safety, so be it.

"I'll tell the police," Ray-Ray said.

Jemeka winced. Of all the things he could have said, that was exactly the worst.

The grating sound of metal on metal as Floyd racked the slide of his pistol and came at Ray-Ray from behind. He pushed the gun into the back of Ray-Ray's neck.

"Don't you dare!" Jemeka screamed at Floyd. "You put that away right now! You hear me?" She snarled it at him like something feral.

Looking a little surprised, Floyd lowered the gun.

Adrenaline surged through Jemeka's veins as her heart galloped. She pushed Ray-Ray toward the shutter. "Get out!" she yelled. "Get out of here!"

At last aware of the danger he faced, Ray-Ray didn't resist. He pulled up the shutter.

"Please!" cried the woman.

Ray-Ray gazed back at her. "I'm sorry." He walked out of view.

The woman hung her head and sobbed. Beside her, the man's face showed grim resolve. Jemeka expected them to scream and beg for their lives, but they did nothing, hope squashed out of them.

"Get it over with," Jemeka told Floyd. She went after Ray-Ray, pulling the shutter down behind her with one firm tug. The shutter door slammed shut with finality as she walked away, echoing through the empty corridor.

She didn't look back.

RAY-RAY DIDN'T SAY A WORD on the drive home, so neither did she. She drove the car up their street and parked outside their home. Then she killed the engine and sat with Ray-Ray until the silence grew louder than thunder. He looked dazed; she couldn't be sure he even realized they were parked outside the house.

She said, "You have to leave California."

He slowly turned his head. "What?"

"Tonight."

"What do you—"

"What you said in there, they'll kill you for that. You know that, don't you?"

A pause.

"Yeah," he said.

"Okay."

He spoke without looking at her: "I don't wanna be here no more anyways. Can't watch what you're becoming any longer."

This remark irritated her. "What, a strong independent woman?"

"No, Jemeka. You were already a strong independent woman. You somethin' else now."

"You weren't complaining when you were reaping the rewards, Ray-Ray."

"I never wanted any of this. Just wanted to pay the bills, keep the lights on and food on the table. But you . . . Jemeka, you want the whole goddamn world. Worse, you wanna take it from everybody else. Anybody gets in your way, you'll cut 'em down, I see that now, you'll cut 'em down. But when you get the world, and the world ain't be enough, what will you do then?" He held his gaze on her as if challenging her to solve this dilemma, searing the question into her mind.

Jemeka breathed slowly, withholding her retorts. Ray-Ray's judgmental tone infuriated her, but she didn't want to end this with an argument.

"You should leave before it gets dark," she said. "Don't tell me where you're going, it's better I don't know. Don't pack nothing, just take your motorcycle and go. You can buy clothes and everything else later. You got money?"

"I got too much goddamn money."

"First you had too little, now you got too much?" She shook her head. "Can't have too much money, Ray-Ray. Not in this world."

"You sure about that?" He opened the door and made for the bungalow.

Jemeka remained in the silence of the car, processing it all. The man she had loved all these years had just entered their shared home for the last time. Soon he would hop on his Kawasaki and drive out of her life forever—a relationship reduced to memories just like that.

She felt nothing.

XXX

JUST ALABAMA, RICHIE AND FLOYD IN THE STORAGE UNIT NOW. Floyd on his hunkers, refusing to look at them. Taking items out of a plastic bag and laying them on the floor. At one point during the drive from Jeff's apartment to this place, the car had stopped moving and, lying in the darkness of the trunk, Alabama had heard one of the doors open and shut. She had started yelling for help then and Richie had joined in. Unable to move their arms or legs they could only yell and hope someone would hear them. But no one had heard, or if someone had, they hadn't cared. Looking at the items spread out on the floor now, Alabama understand why Floyd had stopped the car: He had bought heroin.

They watched in silence as he dumped the contents of every one of the capsules he'd laid on the floor—at least twenty of them—into what looked like a tiny dog bowl made of metal. He twisted the lid off a bottle of distilled water and poured a little liquid into the bowl. Now he was holding one of those long candle lighters to the side of the bowl, flame licking steel.

"It was me," Richie said beside her. "Take me and let her go. She doesn't deserve this."

Floyd finally gazed at them. He didn't look like he was having fun anymore. "I can't."

"You can," Richie said. "No one will know, she'll disappear—"

"I can't. Maybe if I could . . ." He grimaced. "But I can't, so stop asking." He focused on heating the heroin mixture.

"But it was all me," Richie said. "Please let her go."

Floyd looked at Richie, his brow so furrowed it almost had a mouth, anger on his face. "I *can't*. I'm doing y'all a favor doing it like this. Isn't this how you were gonna go out anyway? That last shot that would shoot you to the stars never to return. I'm not doing this to you. You're doing it to yourself."

Richie felt silent, head hung. Perhaps, like Alabama, he saw the inevitability of this moment. Floyd might have said that to make himself feel better, to justify murder in his own twisted mind, but that didn't mean what he'd said had been incorrect. Alabama wanted to tell Richie that it would all be okay, that they would be together again soon in a world without the pain of this one, without the addiction that had led them to this moment, without her father and what he had done to her, but she wasn't sure she believed it.

What if the next world was just like this one?

What if it was worse?

Floyd stopped heating the bowl. He tore the packaging off both a disposable syringe and a needle and assembled the objects together. Without using cotton—no filter required for his purpose—Floyd sucked some of the mixture into the syringe and stood up.

He came toward Alabama, the syringe in his hand.

"No!" Richie yelled. "Not her! It was all me! Just take me and let her go! Please!" His voice raw.

Floyd grabbed Alabama's head and pushed it to the side to expose her neck. He gazed into her eyes. "I'm sorry. But you did this to yourself." He almost looked like he meant it.

"No!" Richie roared.

The needle plunged into her neck. Alabama gasped, the icy sensation instantaneous. Almost as soon as she had registered this sensation she was drowning in that same darkness she had been lost inside once before. Again memories came to her, so vivid she was reliving them: the surprise on her sister's face one Christmas as Alabama gifted her the bicycle she had so desperately wanted; that bicycle crushed beneath the wheel of the eighteen-wheeler along with her mangled sister; her father laughing at a rare family picnic in the park during those early years when he'd still been employed at the coal mine before black lung disease had surfaced, that laughter brightening his face into someone else's; her father looking at her strangely not long after her thirteenth birthday, which she had known in her gut like only a woman can symbolized the end of something and the beginning of something else; her father's large hand on her skinny thigh and the hunger in his eyes; a lingering glance on her mother's face after her father had been in her room, her mother who had, deep down, sensed something wrong but had chosen to look the other way; Heimdall lunging at her in the motel room with her father's hungry eyes; Richie's handsome face when they first met in a dive bar in Santa Monica where Alabama had snagged a waitressing job after two weeks in Los Angeles; Richie's soft hand in hers as they sat on the pier and watched the ocean glitter; Richie saying *I do* at their impulse wedding in Vegas, the look in his eyes saying he meant it, then he kissed her and Alabama's heart felt so filled with love it could burst; Richie poking the needle into her skin the first time she tried heroin, the cold rush of it in her blood, her neck dropping forward as every negative feeling she held inside her body left through her breath and the pores of her skin; Richie's mouth against hers in the trunk of the Audi, Richie telling her he loved her and her saying it back, knowing it to be perhaps the only true thing in this world.

The thought of Richie compelled her to find the light again, if just for a moment. She struggled against the darkness, swimming up through it like a sailor lost in the raging sea.

The sound of Richie screaming with fury. She was close. She fought harder.

Her eyes opened. Through a blurry haze she saw the shape of the man she loved on the floor beside her. The other man stood over him.

"I love you, Richie." She hoped she'd said it loud enough for him to hear.

Richie's strangled screams ceased.

"I love you too."

Alabama exhaled, letting the darkness wash over her now, no more struggling.

"I'll be right behind you," Richie said.

"See you soon," Alabama whispered.

She closed her eyes and waited for the end of this life and the beginning of the next.

XXX

RAY-RAY LEFT WITHOUT A WORD. Barely looked at her.

Although they could never have predicted the circumstances under which it occurred, they had both always known, deep down, that their relationship would not survive indefinitely. They had nothing to offer each other, totally different people. But Ray-Ray was a good man who had been good to her. And she had literally killed for him. Jemeka wished him well.

She hadn't told Ray-Ray that she was three months pregnant with his child.

After the Kawasaki growled out the driveway for the final time, the silence felt like something alive in the house with her. She dug out her father's old record collection, placed The Brothers Johnson's 1977 album *Right on Time* onto the dust-covered platter of her father's record player, side B facing up, and placed the needle onto the groove. A twinkling xylophone-like instrument opened "Strawberry Letter 23," followed by a synthesizer and a bass guitar dripping in funk. The song had been one of her father's favorites. When Jemeka had been little, he would show her their surname written on the cover and tell her that he was one of the brothers along with her uncle. The two men on the cover had looked nothing like her father and uncle but Jemeka's young mind had ignored that; the band had shared her surname and been based in LA, more than enough to captivate her.

Her father. What would he think of her now? She couldn't pretend he'd be proud. He'd only be proud of her if she worked in Magic Curls her whole life, never escaping poverty. But he should be proud. She'd had the guts to make something of herself, unlike her father who'd always been poor, always struggling, the reason why she'd never had anything growing up, always hungry for a better life. Her father had no right to judge her, gave that up when he went to the grave in debt, leaving Jemeka to pay it off. Damn near killed her. She was doing what he should have done for her, and she wouldn't fail her child in the same way—she would give her child the world.

The only thing to do now: climb to the top of the ladder where nobody could touch Jemeka or her child, where the world would be theirs for the taking.

She killed the music and called Floyd on her cell.

"Yeah?"

"Is it done?" she said.

"Two junkies overdosed in Skid Row. Happens every day." He sounded a little dour, not his usual jovial self.

"What about the other one?"

"Probably in Mexico by now. Not worth it."

"I don't like loose ends, Floyd."

"He ain't ever coming back, believe me."

Jemeka thought about it, didn't like the man getting away but if he went far enough Marsellus would never have to find out, nor would anyone else.

"Okay."

"That all, Boss?"

Boss . . . that was new. "You remember what you said about Marsellus?"

A pause.

"I remember," Floyd said.

"What's the word on the street now?"

"People want Marsellus gone. Man got a boot on everybody's neck, just like the police."

"Can you make that happen?"

"Maybe. Marsellus is like a king round here, but that's his weakness. He been comfortable for too long, won't see it coming. We gotta take out some heavies loyal to him, too. Do 'em all at once, then we step in before anybody got time to react. Some cops and politicians doing business with Marsellus won't like it, but that's easy to fix. Just make 'em see it like Christmas came early and otherwise it's business as usual."

"You've given it some thought."

"I'm not the only one."

Jemeka gazed at the Brothers Johnson record resting on the turntable.

The past was dead. She had her child's future to protect now.

"Start putting a plan together," she said. She hung up.

Jemeka slid her hands beneath her shirt and pressed her fingers onto the small bump of her belly.

Yes, her baby would have the world.

Chapter Twenty-Five

AUGUST, 2000

It took Mickey two days to reach the tiny town of Blaine in Washington State, which, aside from Alaska, was the northwestern tip of the United States, situated right on the US-Canada border. It had been many years since he'd driven up the West Coast; he and Martha had driven up to Canada regularly, vacationing in Vancouver and beautiful Vancouver Island, and once they had driven right on up to Alaska—all in this same Pontiac Catalina. Probably the happiest times of his life. This time, after over ten hours driving, rather than in a nice hotel, Mickey had stayed in a cheap motel at the very tip of Northern California where the toilet didn't flush properly and the walls were so thin they may as well have been sheets hanging from the ceiling. He'd watched some nonsensical TV show and ate cold fast food (his doctor would implode if she ever found out) and not since Martha had died had he yearned so deeply for her to be among the living. He'd awoken prematurely at 5 a.m. the following morning and driven on quiet I-5 through gargantuan forest a million shades of green and had sensed within the endless realm of trees an abundance of life in this last great frontier of the contiguous United States of America. Eleven hours later he had reached Blaine at 6:10 and, ravenous, he had wolfed down more fast food.

Now, Mickey parked the Catalina outside a tiny bungalow in a little cul-de-sac of similarly small homes beside a forest area which signs named Lincoln Park. He eyed the bungalow, looking for signs of life, and exited the car. A warm breeze wrapped its arm around him. So quiet out here he could hear himself breathe.

Mickey approached the bungalow. No car in the driveway. It emitted the aura of a building empty of people. He pressed the doorbell. Nothing stirred. He pressed it again. Nothing.

Mickey sighed and turned around. Behind the Catalina, trees at the perimeter of the forest waved their branches at him. The sky was so blue you could poke a brush into it and paint the sidewalk. The ecstasy of birds all around.

It was difficult to be frustrated around such beauty but Mickey gave it his best shot. What if Harvey's information had been incorrect? Or this was no longer Raymond's address?

"Hey there." A female voice.

Mickey turned his head. A plump middle-aged woman stood outside the front door of the neighboring bungalow.

"You looking for Ray?" she said.

"Yes." His eagerness spilled out with it. "Does Raymond still live here?"

"Sure does." She was pretty, looking a little like a slightly rotund version of that terrific actress from the splendid film *Fargo* that had come out a few years ago.

"Do you know where he is now?" Mickey said.

"I reckon so. Ray and my husband have been catching a beer together more and more recently. That's where they are now, I reckon, since it's Friday night and all. Louie's bar in the town. Course it's never just *a beer*. I can call my husband and find out?"

Mickey almost accepted the offer, but figured it best not to spook

Raymond. “Oh, that’s quite all right. I’m in town anyway. I’ll come back another time.”

“Oh, well, okay then.”

“Does it tend to be a late affair, these beers, or would you expect your husband home soon?”

“I’d never make the mistake of expecting him home. But him and Ray aren’t heavy drinkers the way a lot of men are. Unless there’s a big game on, they probably won’t be out too late.” She had her hands on her hips, frowning now. “Is there a big game on, do you know?”

“I have no idea.”

“Hmmm. I don’t think there is, he would have told me. My husband. I hope not. He’ll spend less money in that place if there isn’t.”

“Well, thank you for your help,” Mickey said. “You have a nice evening.”

“You have a nice evening yourself.”

Mickey returned to the Catalina and drove into town in search of a place to stay tonight. He found a cheap little hotel that looked really quite quaint where he booked a room and showered and waited for nightfall.

SITTING ON THE BED IN A FRESH SET OF CLOTHES—gray suit trousers with suspenders, white shirt tucked in, and wine-colored tie—Mickey grabbed his Moleskin from the bedside table and opened it to the pages on which he’d written Bethany’s contact information and that of various people of interest. Using the telephone on the bedside table, he dialed Bethany’s cell.

She answered after seven rings. “Hello?”

“Hello Bethany. It’s Mickey. How are you doing this evening?”

“Oh, hey Mickey. I’m all right, just trying to figure out whether to cook dinner or order takeout. You know, first-world problems.”

“Well, I might have some good news for you so perhaps you should celebrate with takeout.”

A sharp intake of breath. “Did you find him?”

“Not quite, but I have tracked down someone who I believe will be able to point me in the right direction. I’m in Washington State, a small town right on the Canadian border. I should have let you know where I was going before I left but I figured you'd be as eager for me to get up here as I was."

"Absolutely, this is great news. Who is this person who might know where Jeff is?" *Where Jeff is* . . . always so sure Jeffrey was alive somewhere.

"Well, it's quite complicated, Bethany, but the gist of it is, I think Jeffrey might have got into some trouble with his drug dealer."

The sound of Bethany's breathing ceased.

Mickey said, "The drug dealer, his name is Floyd. He seems to be in a partnership with a woman who owns a hair salon in Lakewood. Now, this woman was once in a relationship with a fellow named Raymond, and Raymond, as it happens, vanished from LA at pretty much exactly—"

". . . the same time as Jeff," Bethany finished.

"Correct."

"And you're thinking maybe Jeff left LA for the same reason as this other guy?"

"Well, I don't want to draw any conclusions just yet, but I will say that in my profession there is no such thing as coincidence."

"Yes, yes, I understand. This is very promising, Mickey. Thank you."

"Don't get too hopeful now, Bethany. It's entirely possible this might not lead to anything conclusive."

"Have you spoken to him yet?"

"No, but I've been to his home. He wasn't there but I received confirmation from a neighbor that it was indeed his home. I'll be returning later tonight. With some luck he'll be there and I'll be on the road back to LA tomorrow morning."

"Thank you, Mickey. I know I shouldn't get too excited but I can't help it. I feel hopeful for the first time in a long time. I know Jeff is out there somewhere. I can't explain how, I just do."

Mickey chewed on his lip. It would break Bethany's heart if he confirmed Jeffrey's death. He hoped he wouldn't have to.

"You must be hungry," Bethany said. "Treat yourself to a nice restaurant tonight, Mickey. On me."

"That's very kind. You treat yourself to that takeout."

"I will do, Mickey. Good luck tonight. Call me in the morning?"

"Sure thing, Bethany. Enjoy your night."

"You too."

Mickey placed the phone down and sighed. He felt restless. Whenever he came close to cracking a case, a kind of excited agitation would come over him, an anxiousness to slot in the final piece of the puzzle. Sitting on the bed watching the parking lot outside the hotel, butterflies fluttered in his belly and he knew with conviction that tonight he would learn at last what had happened to Jeffrey Strokes.

MICKEY OPENED HIS EYES and saw a cream-colored ceiling tainted by stains and years of aging. He had fallen asleep somehow, no memory of it occurring. One moment he'd been sitting on the bed and, sudden as a cut in a film, now he was on his back staring at the ceiling.

Mickey sat up slowly. Outside the hotel room day had become night. Street lamps spilled an orange glow across the parking lot. The world appeared shrunken, claustrophobic.

Raymond. What time was it? His watch told him it was 10:27. Crap, he'd let the night get away from him. It was late to be knocking on someone's door. Then again, Raymond might not have even arrived home from the bar yet, and Mickey felt no desire to delay this whole thing until morning.

Mickey sighed. Falling asleep like that . . . he was getting old. He chuckled—*getting old.* He'd been getting old for thirty years. But falling asleep suddenly . . . that was new. He'd exerted himself driving up here in two days. He should have done it over three, but he'd been eager to get here. Too eager. He'd have to reign it in with Raymond, keep his wits about him.

LIGHTS ON INSIDE RAYMOND'S BUNGALOW. Mickey parked as far away from it as the tiny cul-de-sac would allow and exited the Catalina. The surrounding forest rustled in the warm breeze, submerged in darkness. At night it became an entirely different forest than the welcoming sight during the day. Hostility emitted from the forest now, something to get lost in and devoured by. A sharp moon dangled above it, surrounded by stars like exit wounds in the black sky.

Mickey walked up the driveway, hoping only Raymond was inside. He pressed the doorbell.

The sound of heavy footsteps and the door opened. A tall, rather stretched-looking man frowned at Mickey.

"Mr. Raymond Jones?"

The man nodded, perplexed.

"My name is Mickey O'Rourke. I'm a detective based in Los Angeles. I was hoping you might be able to answer a few questions for me."

The expression on Raymond's face told Mickey that Raymond did indeed have something to hide. He'd have to be careful here.

Raymond hadn't said anything yet, gaping at him.

"Mr. Jones?"

"I don't know, Mr.—what you say your name was?"

"O'Rourke. But, please, call me Mickey."

"I'm a little busy, Mickey. Another time would be better."

"Oh it won't take long, Mr. Jones. I just have a few questions. I drove all the way up from LA and, to be frank with you, I was hoping we could wrap this up quickly so I could start the drive back home at the crack of dawn."

Raymond hesitated and Mickey stuck his foot in the door. "Please Mr. Jones, you'd really be helping me out."

Raymond cracked: "Okay, I guess." He stepped aside.

Before Raymond could change his mind, Mickey stepped into a narrow hallway, beige carpet on the floor. A striking lack of photographs on bare walls. The place smelled of stale cigarette smoke and spicy food.

"How long have you lived here, Mr. Jones?"

Raymond shut the door. "Uhh . . . about nine months, I guess."

"Nice place."

"It's all right."

Mickey followed Raymond inside a sparsely decorated living room. Two old couches waited for people to sit on them. Empty beer bottles sat on top of a cheap-looking wooden coffee table. The stench of smoke stronger in here.

"Do you miss California?" Mickey said.

Raymond looked surprised by the question.

Mickey smiled. "I know all about you, Raymond. Don't worry, I come in peace."

Raymond dropped into one of the couches like a man giving up.

Mickey sat on the other. "I used to drive up this way every couple years back when my wife was alive. I've always found it really beautiful up here. California's too damn hot."

Raymond nodded. "I like to go for walks round here, enjoy the nature."

"Do you work here in Blaine, Mr. Jones?"

"I'm between jobs right now."

"You renting this place?"

"I own it."

"How can you afford that without a job, if you don't mind my asking?"

"I've been good with savings."

"Ah."

Silence descended.

Mickey observed Raymond. "Don't you want to know why I'm here?"

"I know why you're here," Raymond said.

"Why's that?"

"Same reason I am."

"Is that right . . ."

"I've been waiting for this day ever since I left LA. Oh man, have I been waiting. It takes a toll on a man waiting for a day he knows is coming. Relief just to have it here."

Mickey nodded, considering how to play this. Raymond clearly thought Mickey knew much more than he did. Clearly there was much to know.

"It sounds like you're ready to tell your side of the story," Mickey said.

Raymond gazed at the carpet, concentrating.

"I don't know, man. How do I know I'll be safe?"

Mickey chewed his lip, wondering how to respond. "This information stays with my client and I. Nobody else. I'm not going to record you or anything like that. I just want to know what happened."

Raymond appeared confused. "Your client . . . hold up. You said you was a detective."

"A private detective, yes."

"You left out the private part."

Had he? "Oh, my apologies. It's been a long day."

"So you're not a cop?"

"No, no. I'm investigating a case for a client, privately. Nothing to do with law enforcement."

A weight seemed to lift from Raymond's shoulders. "Well, shit. You nearly gave me a heart attack."

"Sorry."

"Who's your client?"

The jig was up. "I was hired by a young woman in LA. Her boyfriend went missing a year ago and she tasked me with finding him, or finding out what happened to him."

"Who's the boyfriend?"

Mickey watched Raymond's face closely as he responded: "A porn star named Jeffrey Strokes."

A flash of alarm in Raymond's eyes before he looked away, a crease on his forehead. "Yeah, and why you think I know something about that?"

"Do you?"

"No."

"Ever heard the name Jeffrey Strokes?"

"Don't ring no bells."

"What was all that about not feeling safe?"

"I was just messing with you 'cause I thought you were a cop."

"Why did you leave California?"

"Wanted some peace and quiet."

"Have you spoken to Jemeka Johnson since you left?"

Surprise darkened Raymond's face. "I think you better leave."

"Mr. Jones—"

Raymond stood up, towering over Mickey sitting down.

"I'm not asking. I only let you in 'cause you said you were a cop. You know it's a crime to impersonate a police officer?"

Mickey leaned on the arm of the couch and struggled to his feet. He stood straight and met Raymond's gaze. "I can help you."

A shadow of something passed over Raymond's face and Mickey glimpsed the immense weight the man carried around with him. He knew something and it was eating him up.

But he said nothing.

Disappointed, Mickey said, "Well, thank you for your time."

He shuffled toward the door.

With his fingers on the handle, Mickey remembered the hope in Bethany's voice earlier this evening. He imagined telling her that the man he'd pinned both of their hopes on wouldn't talk, so Mickey had simply driven all the way back to California, leaving the man alone with the knowledge of what had happened to Jeffrey. Alone—and free to vanish forever.

Mickey gritted his teeth. No. Bethany deserved better than that.

He squeezed his hands into fists and faced Raymond. "I'm sorry, Mr. Jones, but I can't leave here until you tell me what I need to know. I know you know what happened to Jeffrey and if you don't tell me right now, I'll call Floyd and tell him where you are."

In mentioning Floyd, Mickey had gone with his gut and played a hunch. It worked: Raymond looked like he'd been slapped with a wet fish.

"Should I sit down?" Mickey said, putting a little roughness into it, hands still balled into fists.

Raymond nodded, looking suddenly exhausted.

Mickey relaxed his fists and heard his heart thumping in his ears. He returned to the couch and sat down.

Raymond had not moved, head hung in the middle of the room.

"Now, Mr. Jones. Tell me what happened to Jeffrey Strokes."

XXX

MICKEY SAT ON THE BED IN THE HOTEL ROOM, just the bedside lamp on, attempting to process all Raymond had told him. He had figured the story wouldn't be pretty, but he hadn't quite been prepared for what Raymond had told him. He had remained there, at Raymond's, for a long time while Raymond spilled his guts, becoming quite emotional as he told his tale. It had quickly become clear how much the events had traumatized the man who seemed to Mickey sensitive and soft, not the kind of person who ever should have become mixed up in violence and murder. Such events either harden a person or break them and Raymond had not experienced the former.

Mickey glanced at his watch: 12:37. Bethany was probably asleep by now. Certainly it was too late to call her. Yet something compelled him and he picked up the telephone.

She answered almost immediately. "How did it go?"

"Well, I spoke with him."

"Good, good. And?"

"It's complicated. Much too complicated for over the phone. I would like to meet with you as soon as possible. I'll be back in California Sunday night . . . are you free Monday morning?"

"Monday . . . no, I'm working, but I have a few hours free in the afternoon. You could come to the studio? Say, twelve?"

"That sounds good. Listen, Bethany, can you do something for me? I need you to make sure Riccardo is at the meeting with us on Monday. But don't tell him why. Make something up."

A pause. "Why?"

"I'm playing a hunch. Is he free then, do you know?"

"Yes, I think so."

"Okay. Good."

"Mickey . . . did you find out where Jeff is?"

Where Jeff is . . . her faith in Jeffrey's heart still beating astonished him.

Mickey bit his lip, fingers squeezing the hard plastic of the receiver. "I'll see you on Monday, Bethany." He put the phone down.

Mickey gazed at the parking lot outside, glowing amber under the streetlights. Nothing moved. More often than not, the world was a quiet, empty place full of questions without answers.

He switched off the lamp and lay in darkness.

Chapter Twenty-Six

DRIVING THE PONTIAC INTO THE PARKING LOT outside MidnightPussy Productions, Mickey was body-slammed by déjà vu. The sun burned above this parched landscape as hot as it had when he'd driven here to meet with Bethany for the first time and again he found himself believing Al Gore's warnings of an Earth roasting under that great fireball. The mountains in the distance wobbled with heat in the same way, and also unchanged was the light glinting off the yellow sign above the building. And Mickey himself—was he not the same man who'd driven here then?

Not quite. He was an hour from retirement now.

He parked the car and glanced at his watch: 11:55. Close enough.

A young, heavily tattooed woman behind the reception desk greeted him as he entered the studio. He said he was waiting for someone and, thankfully, she left him alone.

Some minutes later a woman passing by the doorway into the studio proper glanced at him as she whizzed past. She reappeared in the doorway and entered into the reception area. Mickey recognized her as the middle-aged, scarlet-haired woman who'd spoken with Bethany in the lunch room during his first visit here. Her rotund artificial breasts pointed at him like weapons as she came toward him, a smile at the edge of her blown-up lips.

"I remember you," she said, pointing at him despite the fact there was no one else she possibly could be referring to. "So you want to be a star after all?"

"I'm afraid my days of stardom are over."

She raised an eyebrow, looking him over with renewed interest. "You *were* a star?"

"I had my five minutes."

"It's never too late to get back on the horse."

"Sometimes you have to put the horse in the stable and let it grow old."

"It's a good thing we're not talking about horses then." A sly smile on her giant lips.

Bethany appeared in the doorway, wearing tiny denim shorts and a sun-yellow crop top. Her waist was narrow as a child's.

"Mickey," she said happily. She drifted over and wrapped her arms around him.

It caught Mickey by surprise. He placed a hand onto her lower back. Though her body was tiny, he could feel the impressive strength of her muscles.

"Is Rach trying to get you on camera again?" Bethany said, breaking away.

"I was, but Mickey's putting the horse into the stable," Rach said, winking at Mickey like a burlesque performer. Only a few people could pull off a wink like that outside of the theater and she was one of them.

Bethany scrunched up her face. "Okay? We're off to lunch, Rach. See you soon."

"All right, Beth. Eat a decent meal. You're gonna need it." Rach spun on her heels and power-walked through the doorway into the main area of the studio, off to organize the day's pornography.

"She's a lot of fun," Bethany said.

Mickey couldn't disagree with that.

"Let's go," Bethany said. She hooked her arm with Mickey's and moved them toward the doors. They exited the studio into dazzling white sunlight. The light bounced off the dusty dirt into Mickey's eyes. He squinted, shielding his face with his hand, and dizziness overcame him for a moment. He needed fluids.

"Can we take your car?" Bethany said. "I've been hoping I could get a ride in it since I first saw it."

"Of course."

"She's beautiful. They just don't make 'em like that anymore, huh?"

"No, modern cars have no style at all. She drives as well as the day I bought her."

Arm-in-arm, they walked toward the Catalina. Mickey unlocked the doors and Bethany hopped into the passenger seat. Immediately she was opening the glove compartment and poring through the cassette tapes he kept in there.

"Oh my god, I love this album," she said, holding Pink Floyd's *Wish You Were Here*. "Can I play it while we drive?"

Sitting in the driver's seat now, Mickey shut the door. "Go ahead." He turned the keys in the ignition and the Catalina growled.

He drove out of the parking lot. "Where to?"

"That diner we went to last time. Riccardo's meeting us there. Well, he's meeting *me* there. He's gonna be real surprised to see you."

"Has he . . ." Mickey began.

She looked at him.

". . . hit you again?"

Bethany returned her attention to the cassette case, opening it now. "No." She placed the tape into the player and fast-forwarded to the title track. As it always had, the haunting acoustic guitar intro summoned thoughts of Martha. He had played this song often in the months following her death, didn't know what he would have done without it. Thank God for music.

Mickey took the Pontiac onto the highway. He glanced at Bethany. She listened to the song closely, her expression betraying the grief that had been eating away at her since Jeffrey's disappearance.

Noticing his gaze, she said, "I'm too scared to ask you, so I'm waiting for you to tell me."

Mickey nodded. He didn't say that he was too scared to tell her, so he'd been waiting for her to ask.

They listened to the song without speaking while Mickey drove, both dreaming of better days with the ones they loved.

SITTING IN A BOOTH OPPOSITE BETHANY inside the Sunset Diner, Mickey ordered coffee only. The bad news he would soon have to deliver had stolen his appetite. Bethany had ordered a stack of pancakes, which the waitress delivered now to the table with the coffee. A cube of butter melted on top of the pancakes, mixing with golden syrup and spilling down the sides of the stack. Looking at them, Mickey felt his appetite returning. They smelled divine.

Bethany dove right in. "I crave pancakes when I'm nervous," she said between mouthfuls.

Mickey waited for his coffee to cool. "You could certainly use the calories."

"You sound like Rach. Believe me, I eat a *lot*. More than both of you put together, probably."

"Rach seems nice. You two get along well?"

"Oh yeah—" Bethany swallowed pancake, picked up her coffee mug and chugged. If the heat of it had burned her, she showed no sign of it. "Rach is the best. She's sort of like a mom to all of us. She looked out for me when I started out. I was so naive then, I didn't know anything. If it wasn't for Rach, I could have really been exploited, you know?"

"Well, that's good. Do you like the work you do?"

"I love it, I really do. And I'm lucky, I earn a lot. I know it won't last forever, but for now it's pretty great. And what lasts forever anyways?"

"Enjoying your work is all that matters." Mickey picked up his coffee and blew on it, went for a sip. It almost seared the lips off his face. He set it down as Bethany chugged from her own.

"Oh yeah, one hundred percent," Bethany said. "Too many people work jobs they hate just because they think they have to, you know? Screw that. Life's too short to sign your life away. Contrary to what most people think, though, porn's not the easiest thing in the world. It's pretty tough sometimes. You need a lot of confidence. And you need to be fit, healthy. Too many girls party too hard and burn out early on." She gobbled some pancake. "A high pain tolerance helps, too."

"I can imagine," Mickey said, immediately regretting this choice of verb.

"It's a lot harder at the beginning," Bethany said, mouth full of food. "I used to get so nervous before a shoot. I mean, I was only eighteen. You should have seen me before my first gangbang. A nervous wreck." She laughed like it was the funniest thing in the world.

Mickey worked hard at keeping his face blank.

"I still get nervous sometimes before a big shoot. Like the one later today."

Mickey knew he was expected to say something but really did not want any more details. "You have a big shoot today?"

Bethany nodded, sipping coffee. "Yep. It's my first scene with Johnny Hard-On. He's a huge star. I'm a little nervous."

"Because he's a star?"

"Oh, no, I'm used to that. I'm kind of a star myself, you know." She shot him a mock self-obsessed-diva look and laughed and it looked lovely on her face. "No, I'm nervous because Johnny's packing some serious equipment down there. Like *really*. Guy has a penis like a—"

"I get it," Mickey said, palm raised as if to block the impact of her words.

Bethany giggled, hand over her mouth. "Sorry, Mickey, I'm so used to hanging out with porn stars I forget not everyone feels the same as we do about all that stuff."

"It's not a problem." Although she was correct that Mickey felt differently about her work than she did, his reaction had less to do with the work itself and more with the fact he could not help but see in Bethany the daughter or granddaughter he'd never had. She reminded him so much of Martha at Bethany's age. Even had her eyes.

"I respect what you do," he said. "So long as you're happy, healthy and safe, that's all that matters."

This sentence appeared to affect her. She rubbed a finger under her eye.

"Oh my god, am I tearing up right now?" She wiped her eyes, but she was laughing. "I'm so emotional, it's so dumb. I'm sorry."

"That's one thing you don't ever need to apologize for."

"You're really nice, Mickey. I wish that . . . I wish that I had someone nice like you in my life when I was growing up." Suddenly embarrassed, she laughed. "It's so silly."

"It's not silly. I understand." Her reaction had tugged on his heartstrings. He reached out a wrinkled hand and laid it on top of Bethany's. Her skin was soft as a baby's.

She smiled, absorbing this affection from him like someone starved of it. It surprised him to realize that he was absorbing affection right back from her.

Tentatively, she said, "Maybe, when this is all over, I mean, only if you want to . . . maybe we could have lunch together again sometime? It would probably do me some good to talk to someone who's not in porn once in a while." She laughed, then quickly added, "But only if you want to."

"You know, I think that's a really great idea. I'd love to."

She beamed. "Okay."

"Okay."

They sat smiling a little shyly at each other. For the first time since accepting imminent retirement, a bubble of optimism floated up inside Mickey.

"What the fuck is this?"

Riccardo stood beside the table, scowling. He glanced at Mickey's hand on top of Bethany's.

Mickey withdrew his hand. "It's nice to see you again, Riccardo. We've been waiting for you. Have a seat."

"Waiting for me?" He frowned, his gaze hopping between both of them. An exceptionally suspicious man.

"That's right," Mickey said. "Have a seat."

Riccardo didn't move. "Beth, what is this?"

"Honestly, Riccardo, I don't know."

He narrowed his eyes, staring hatefully at Mickey.

"Why don't you sit down and find out, Riccardo?" Mickey said.

Riccardo sighed and slid into the booth beside Bethany.

"Some coffee?" Mickey said. Without waiting for a response, he smiled at the passing waitress and pointed at his mug. She nodded her understanding.

"Working today, Riccardo?" Mickey said.

"No, old man, I'm not. What's this all about?"

The waitress approached with a fresh pot of coffee. Mickey waited for her. He was playing a hunch here with Riccardo, one that could backfire spectacularly unless he played it just so.

The waitress poured three coffees, ignoring or oblivious to the tense silence of the booth.

"Thank you," Mickey said as she finished. She left them to their conflict.

Riccardo stared at Mickey. "I don't wanna ask again, old man."

Mickey sat back into the seat and crossed his arms. "Okay, Riccardo. We're here to talk about Jeffrey Strokes."

"No shit. Did you find him or what?"

Mickey held his gaze. "Is there anything you want to tell us?"

Riccardo's face gave nothing away. "What you mean?"

Mickey leaned over the table and stared into Riccardo's hostile eyes. "Let me lay this all out for you, Riccardo. You have two options here. The first—you tell Bethany what you did, right here and now, in your own words, explaining your side of things."

"Mickey, what are you talking about?" Bethany said.

"The second way," Mickey continued, ignoring her, "I tell Bethany what you did, then I drive over to the LAPD Hollywood and tell my friends there, too."

Fear blossomed in Riccardo's eyes. He gazed at the table, eyeballs moving rapidly in his head.

Bethany looked wounded watching it unfold. "Wh-what? What are you talking about, Mickey?"

No one said anything.

"Riccardo, what did you do?" Bethany said, a tremble in her voice.

Riccardo said nothing, still staring at the table. Panic setting in.

"Tell her, Riccardo. Or I will."

Riccardo looked at him, fear giving way to resignation.

Bethany gripped his forearm. "Riccardo, what did you do? Tell me." She was pleading with him to answer, her eyes wet.

Riccardo wouldn't look at her. "I didn't mean . . ." He shook his head as the words trailed off.

"Didn't mean what?" Bethany said. "What?"

"I didn't mean for Jeff to get hurt," he said, voice cracking on the last word.

A choked silence seized hold of the table.

Bethany gulped at the air as if she had just remembered to breathe. "What the hell did you do?" Rage behind her words. "What did you do? Tell me! What did you do?" She was yelling, whacking Riccardo with her palms. Every head in the place pointed their way. "What did you do, Riccardo? Answer me!"

Mickey lunged forward and grabbed hold of her wrists. "Shush Bethany, it's okay, it's okay. Give the man a chance to respond. It's okay." He held onto her until she stopped struggling. She burst into tears. Mickey's heart ached watching her.

"Mind your own business, folks," Mickey called out to their audience, waving them away. Most of them respected the request.

"You'd better tell her what you did, son," he said.

Riccardo shook his head, dazed and defeated. "You have to understand," he said, not looking at either of them, "I never wanted Jeff to get hurt. I just wanted him to go away."

"Riccardo, please tell me what you did," Bethany said in the tone of someone holding in immense rage. She was no longer crying but her face was soaked with tears, eyes pink.

Riccardo sighed and his muscular body, so full of tension, appeared to deflate before Mickey's eyes. Clearly he had been holding this secret inside himself like a message stuffed into a bottle. Perhaps part of him was even relieved at this opportunity to be rid of it.

Riccardo looked at Bethany for the first time since sitting down. "About a year ago, I was in a convenience store when some guy came in and held up the place. When he left the store, I don't know why I did it, just this crazy fucking idea came into my head and I didn't even question it . . . I . . . I followed the guy outside, and I told him . . ." Riccardo closed his eyes and exhaled.

"What did you tell him, Riccardo?" Fear dripped from Bethany's words.

Riccardo opened his eyes. "I told him I'd pay him ten thousand dollars to get rid of Jeff."

Bethany's mouth fell open. She looked like God had descended from Heaven and urinated on her. Mickey could hardly believe it himself; he'd figured Riccardo had been hiding something, but this . . .

"You *what*?" Bethany said.

"It's not as bad as it sounds," Riccardo said. "I told the guy not to hurt Jeff, that I only wanted him out of LA. I said it a million times—don't hurt him, don't hurt him. The guy, I think he was a junkie, he looked desperate, like he would have done anything for some cash, so I just . . . I just got this crazy idea. I don't know why I did it, I wish I didn't. If I knew what he was gonna do, I never would have . . ." Riccardo shook his head, looking traumatized.

Bethany's breaths were coming faster. "What did he do to Jeff?" She appeared close to hyperventilating and Mickey felt a desperate urge to comfort her but held back, not wanting to interrupt before Riccardo had finished.

Riccardo said, "He . . ."

"What did he do to Jeff?" Bethany yelled at him.

"He killed him."

Silence.

"He fucking killed him," Riccardo repeated quietly, as if he couldn't believe it himself. He stared at the table, every ounce of strength sapped out of him.

Mickey had expected Bethany to scream or collapse or gouge Riccardo's eyes out with her fork but she simply sat there, face blank as death, eyes glazed over.

Mickey let the silence settle. Riccardo's words resounded in his mind: *The guy, I think he was a junkie, he looked desperate . . .*

"How do you know?" Mickey said.

"What?" Riccardo said.

"How do you know he killed Jeffrey?"

"He . . . showed me."

"You saw Jeffrey's body?"

"Yes—no, not exactly—"

"Did you see Jeffrey's body or not?"

"He showed me a photo."

"He showed you a photo of Jeffrey's body?"

Riccardo nodded.

"Do you happen to know what date it was when you saw the photo?"

"It was a few days before my birthday. July twenty-first, maybe."

Mickey thought about it. "How did you know Jeffrey was dead in the photo?"

Riccardo didn't seem to understand the question.

"Riccardo, how did you know Jeffrey was dead?"

"Well, his eyes were closed, and—"

"His eyes were closed," Mickey said, unimpressed.

"Yeah, his eyes were closed!" Riccardo getting irritated now. "And he was lying in a hole in the fucking dirt, man. And he had a hole in his fucking forehead. Jesus!"

"Let me get this straight, Riccardo. You asked a man, a total stranger, to get rid of Jeffrey for ten thousand dollars, and when this man returned to you with a photo of Jeffrey lying in some dirt, you immediately accepted this as confirmation of Jeffrey's death and never told a soul about it?"

"Well Jeff disappeared, didn't he? He's gone! Of course the guy killed him."

Mickey paused before dropping the bomb. "This guy. Was his name Richie?"

Riccardo's mouth fell open.

Mickey nodded. "I figured as much. Well, I have news for you, you damn fool. Jeffrey's not dead."

Bethany had been staring into space like a zombie but now her gaze snapped onto Mickey. "Jeff's alive?"

"Well, I can't say it with any degree of certainty, but I know that Jeffrey was alive after this Richie fellow gave Riccardo that photograph."

Relief washed over Bethany's features like a tonic. She sat with it for a moment, looking scooped out and exhausted. Then rage began to congeal on her and she spun to face Riccardo. "Why did you do it?"

"Beth—"

"Why! Tell me!"

"I wanted you to myself."

She scowled. "You're pathetic."

Riccardo nodded as if in agreement. "I knew that, as long as Jeff was around, I'd never have you. Not really. Not out in the open. I love you, Beth."

"Oh shut the fuck up." Bethany's scowl had not lifted; if anything it had deepened, twisting her features beyond recognition. She appeared possessed. "You're a pathetic loser. And a liar. You don't love me. You don't love anyone but yourself."

"No Beth, I love you—"

"No you don't! You didn't want Jeff gone because of me, you wanted him gone because of *him*. You *hated* that Jeff was number one and not you. Admit it. You were jealous he was the big star. Admit it!"

"Beth—"

"Admit it you fucking creep!"

Riccardo looked like a kid caught with his hand in the cookie jar. He choked out some garbled response, something about not needing this bullshit in his life, and without another word slid out of the booth and marched out of the diner, throwing open the doors aggressively so that they smacked into the sides of the entrance. Everyone in the place watched as he hopped onto his Harley-Davidson, kicked up the stand and sped onto the highway, the powerful engine of the motorcycle roaring like a beast.

"Coward," Bethany muttered.

"I'm sorry you had to sit through that," Mickey said. "It was the only way of making him admit it."

Mickey brought a hand out from under the table. On his palm lay a tape recorder. "I recorded the entire conversation. The tape is yours, to do with whatever you wish."

Bethany hesitated, then took the machine.

"Do you know where Jeff is?" she said, but her eyes told Mickey she knew the answer.

"I'm afraid I don't. And there's really no way of finding him. He could be anywhere. Anywhere. I can keep searching if you really want me to but my gut feeling is it would be a lost cause. An expensive lost cause."

Bethany nodded, crushed.

"If it's any consolation, this is the way Jeffrey wants it to be," Mickey said.

"I'm just glad he's okay."

Mickey nodded. "Yes, he's okay."

"What happened to him? Did he just get up and leave one morning, just like that? Who's this guy with the photo? I don't understand any of it." She sniffled and wiped her eyes.

Mickey touched her hand. "Would you like to use the restroom before I tell you the whole story?"

She thought about it, nodded.

"Take your time."

Bethany left the table.

Mickey sat back into the cushioned seat and watched cars zooming by on the highway. Each driver with a life as vivid and complex as the last. Each one of them with secrets long buried.

Bethany had taken the news well. She must have known, in her heart, that Jeffrey did not want to be found. A puzzling situation. Why hadn't he said goodbye to her, his girlfriend? Not even a note, or a call, or an email . . . puzzling.

But maybe not so puzzling if Mickey accounted for one possibility: Jeffrey had known about Bethany's affair with Riccardo. Mickey imagined Jeffrey finding out about the affair, deciding to say nothing but forming in his mind a vague plan to simply disappear one day without a word when the opportunity presented itself, like a whisper in the wind. Like a shooting star.

Yes, Jeffrey had known.

Lies and deceit, infidelity and murder: just another day in LA.

Bethany returned to the table.

"Are you all right, my dear?" Mickey said.

She nodded. "I'm ready."

So Mickey told her everything, from his conversation with Riccardo in the biker bar on the first day of the investigation to everything Raymond had told him in Washington. Bethany was shocked to learn that Jeffrey had stolen $100,000 from his drug dealer with a couple of heroin addicts named Richie and Alabama. She was horrified when Mickey described how Richie and Alabama—husband and wife, incidentally—had been murdered by this drug dealer, and that Jeffrey would have been murdered along with them had he not skipped town with the cash just in time.

When Mickey had finished, they sat in silence.

"My god," Bethany said. "What an awful series of events. So those people got away with murder?"

"Yes, they did."

"We have to do something. They can't just get away with something like this."

"You certainly shouldn't do anything. I've got some friends in the LAPD. I'll be informing them of what I've learned and I'll present them with what little evidence I've gathered. I'll also try once again to convince Raymond to testify. He's pretty set on keeping his mouth shut. It wouldn't surprise me if he's left Washington already. If he has, I'll probably never find him."

Bethany shook her head. "It's an evil world, isn't it?"

"Yes. But it's also a beautiful world filled with love."

"The evil sort of stamps out the love."

"Only if you let it, Bethany. Only if you let it."

"You don't let it, do you?"

"If I did, I couldn't do my job."

"How do you do your job? I mean, I know how you do it, sort of. But *how* do you do it?"

Mickey exhaled and sat back into the seat, thinking about all the cases he'd completed over the decades. How had he managed it all?

"I do this job by following the clues, one after another, until the case is done. It's not like the movies. There are rarely gunshots or explosions, bad guys hunting you down. You follow a lead to where it takes you. Most times it takes you to a dead end and you have to return to the beginning and follow another. Usually, you have to follow dozens of leads before you get anywhere. But, sometimes, you get lucky, and every door you open leads you to another until, finally, you stumble upon the truth. It's not about justice, you see, or money—God knows it's not about money. It's about bringing the truth to light. It's not glamorous, but it makes the world a little more truthful a place. That's enough for me."

Bethany was observing him with admiration. "Thanks for everything you did, Mickey. Just knowing Jeff's okay has lifted ten tons off my back. I thought . . . I don't know what I thought." She shook her head. "I thought for the rest of my life I'd never know what happened to him. You've given me my life back."

"Well, it's time to put this whole affair behind you. Move on. You've got your whole life ahead of you."

Bethany smiled a sad little smile but there was hope in it. "Yeah . . . You can send me the bill tomorrow and I'll settle up with you."

"You don't owe me anything."

"How do you mean?"

"Consider your advance payment, payment enough."

"I don't—"

"A gift, Bethany. I have more than enough to keep me going now that I am, as of this very moment, officially retired. Which means I am now officially old. You're young, you must be saving for a house or something. In this city the way things are going you'll be older than me before you could ever buy one. Consider it a little help with the deposit."

"Mickey, I can't possibly—"

"I insist, Bethany, I really do, and I won't take no for an answer, not this time."

She looked at him with real affection, bottom lip trembling. "I don't know what to say."

"Sometimes saying nothing says it all."

"Thank you, Mickey. Really."

"You're very welcome."

"Listen, I hate to say this now but I really have to get back to work, I'm already late."

"Oh." He glanced at his watch. "Yes, the time has flown."

"Is it okay if you drive me back? My car's at the studio."

"Yes, yes, of course."

"At least let me pay for the meal?" Bethany said.

Mickey made a show of thinking about it. "Okay, I'll give you that much."

PARKED OUTSIDE MIDNIGHTPUSSY PRODUCTIONS, Bethany thanked Mickey again for the ride and for the gift and for everything and he waved away her gratitude, told her to think nothing of it.

She got out of the car and through the opened driver-side window, Mickey said, "I'm sorry I couldn't find Jeffrey."

Bethany shrugged. "Don't worry about it. You found something even better. You found the truth."

"If you had to guess where Jeffrey is now, where would you choose?"

She thought about it, looking up at the big blue sky. "I don't know. And, honestly? I don't care." She waved. "Bye, Mickey."

"Goodbye, Bethany."

In her denim shorts and little yellow crop top, Bethany breezed across the parched dirt toward the studio and Mickey watched her leave, proud of her immense inner strength. She looked lighter on her feet, almost floating across the parking lot. It surprised him how gutted he felt seeing her go. He wanted to call out to her, to keep her talking with him for just a minute more, to keep alive that feeling she made him feel a little longer—a feeling like he had a family, someone to care, and care for. But he let her go.

Halfway to the studio, Bethany stopped walking. She turned around.

"Lunch next week?" she yelled across the parking lot.

Mickey's heart skipped a beat. "Yes! Yes, I'd love to!"

Bethany beamed and waved and continued on into the studio.

Mickey almost felt embarrassed by how eagerly he'd responded, but he didn't care, not really; he was simply glad to be excited about something other than work now that there would be no more work to excite him, and, if he was being honest with himself, he simply adored that young woman and how she made him feel.

Like he mattered.

Chapter Twenty-Seven

"HOLD UP, HOLD UP," Reggie said, one hand around his cappuccino. "You're pranking me is all."

"I wish I was, Reggie."

They were sitting inside Marco's café. Out of the speakers swooned Thelonious Monk's jazzy piano. It was a beautiful morning and the café buzzed with chatter.

"So you're saying Jemeka Johnson's behind all this? The same Jemeka Johnson who cut my wife's hair?"

"That's right."

Reggie shook his head. "Well I'll be damned."

Mickey sipped his espresso, slightly sweet and velvety smooth. "So what do we do?"

"What can we do? Without your witness testifying, it's just rumors. I can't bring it to a judge based on rumors, Mick."

"No, I suppose not."

"You can't get him to testify?"

"I called him last night and he told me to never call him again. He won't do it."

"Maybe we can drive out to him together and try again?"

Mickey shook his head firmly. "No, that would only push him away."

"Where's he hiding out?"

"I'd rather keep that one close to my chest for now, Reggie, if that's all right with you."

"What for? You think I'm gonna tell somebody?"

"Because I promised my witness I would."

"It's just me, Mick."

"A promise is a promise, Reggie."

Reggie sighed, irritated. "Without that testimony my hands are tied."

Mickey nodded, a little puzzled by Reggie's relentlessness. "I know."

Reggie downed the remains of his cappuccino, wiped foam from his lips, and rose from the table. "I gotta get gone. See you for dinner soon, though. Yeah?"

"I'll see you then, Reggie."

Reggie nodded a goodbye, still a little miffed. He waded through the café and out the door.

XXX

MICKEY LABORED ON HIS KNEES IN THE BACK YARD, finally combating the chaos that had reigned supreme out here since Martha had died. This attempt to return his wife's precious garden to a state resembling how it had looked in its glory days when she had maintained it so beautifully was proving difficult but not impossible, and this offered a ray of hope. Frankly, retirement was proving to be as dull as Mickey had feared and this mission out here in the back yard gave him something to do. But it wasn't so bad spending the days in the garden. Right now the birds were chirping all around and a refreshing cool breeze tickled his skin and it beat staking out a motel for six hours straight hoping for a glimpse of infidelity.

The sound of a telephone ringing. It took Mickey a couple seconds to realize that it was *his* telephone doing the ringing.

He dug the hoe into the earth and leaned on the handle as he got to his feet, groaning at the aches in his knees and shoulder. They were getting worse with each passing day.

"I'm coming, I'm coming," he muttered as he shuffled toward the bungalow as quickly as his little legs would allow, which was not quickly at all.

Amazingly, the phone was still ringing when he reached it.

"Hello?"

Silence.

"Hello?" he repeated.

"Mr. O'Rourke, it's . . . it's me."

A jolt of excitement surged through Mickey's veins. "You've had a change of heart."

"How'd you know?"

"Because you're a good man, Raymond."

Silence. Mickey chewed on his bottom lip and waited, the telephone cord curled tightly around his finger, his entire heart beating inside of it.

Raymond said, "I don't think I could live with myself much longer if I didn't do something. Shit, I don't think I could. This past year's been rough. Can't get it outta my head. Can't sleep, can't eat. Maybe if I come clean, I'll feel better."

"I think you will."

"You want me to come to LA?"

"No. You stay there. I'll get my friend, the police officer, to talk to a judge. We'll get you in witness protection as soon as possible."

"All right."

"Thank you for doing this, Raymond. It's the right thing to do."

"Shit, I hope so."

"Nobody else knows where you are. Right?"

"Nah, nobody knows shit."

"Just me? You're sure?"

"Just you."

"Good. Keep it that way. I'll get the ball moving right away and I'll talk to you soon."

"All right, Mickey."

Mickey ended the call and stood a moment beside the telephone.

"Yes!" He fist-pumped the air. There was a chance yet to dish out justice and lock up the murderers of that young couple.

Mickey hurried into the bedroom and changed into one of his casual suits. This was too important to wait, he had to tell Reggie immediately.

On his way out of the bungalow, Mickey glanced at a framed photo of him and Martha on their wedding day. It stopped him in his tracks. They stood arm in arm on the steps of the cathedral, beaming, both of them looking a little shy about being husband and wife, but both so handsome, so full of hope, their whole life together spread out ahead of them.

How many times had he passed this wonderful photograph and never stopped to look, never spared a moment to *remember*?

"I love you, Martha," Mickey said. He touched the glass frame gently. "And I'll see you soon."

He continued toward the front door.

"But not yet."

XXX

JEMEKA WAS SWEEPING THE SALON ALONE after a long and busy day when a knock on the glass startled her. A dark face surrounded by the blackness of night stared in at her. It took her a moment to recognize who it belonged to.

She unlocked the door and the uniformed police officer stepped into the salon and shut the door behind him. Jemeka stood holding the broom, watching him.

"He's gonna testify," the cop said.

"You're sure?"

He nodded.

Jemeka squeezed the broom handle. "Fool never could keep his mouth shut."

"We're presenting the case to a judge tomorrow. They'll move quickly to put him in witness protection."

"You gotta find out where he is before they do."

The cop grimaced. "I can't, I tried. If I press any further, Mick will know something's up."

"Make him tell you."

"What if I can't?"

Jemeka looked him in the eyes. "You know what happens then."

The cop looked like he was in pain. He exhaled sharply, hands on his hips. "If I do this, if I find out where he is, then I'm done after that, you hear me? I'm not doing another goddamn thing for you after that."

The man was near breaking point. Jemeka felt a sting of pity for him but it vanished so fast she might have imagined it. "Okay, Reggie. After that, you're done."

A ray of light broke across the cop's features. "All right. You give me your word that after I do this, my nephew is safe?"

"I give you my word. Now if you'll excuse me, I got to finish sweeping this place so I can get home to my child."

Expression one of grim determination, Reggie moved toward the doors. He hesitated. "With Marsellus gone, it's just a matter of time until everybody knows it's you running the show. You can't stay hidden in the shadows forever."

"I know."

The cop nodded. He pushed open the doors and vanished into the night.

Jemeka sighed, her back getting sore. She resumed sweeping and didn't finish until she'd swept every last hair off the floor.

She returned the broom to the closet and grabbed her purse from the reception desk. Another day over.

By the doors, ready to lock up for the night, she thought about Ray-Ray, about what had to be done. She felt torn up about it. He was a good man.

But no one would rob her child of a mother—of a future. Not even the child's father.

Jemeka switched off the lights and the salon fell into darkness.

Epilogue

THEY SAY THAT IN PARADISE the ocean is blue as a dream and the sand is golder than Fort Knox and the women are gorgeous goddesses wearing clothing so scant they're barely clothed at all and there is more bud than you could smoke in ten lifetimes and a big yellow sun shines over it all for twelve hours per day, not too hot, not too cold—*perfect.*

This is how Jeff knew he'd found Paradise.

He lay on his back on the warm sand and listened to the waves crash against the shore. Clamped between his lips was a fat blunt of the world's finest weed and he puffed at it with ecstasy.

Well, maybe that wasn't what they say about Paradise, now that he thought about it. It was what *he* says about Paradise.

Jeff laughed at this realization, and the laughter turned into a fit of giggles. He closed his eyes and let it happen to him.

"What the hell are you laughing at?" said a distinctly American-woman's voice.

Jeff opened his eyes. Sitting up beside him, Melanie stared at him. He'd completely forgotten she was there, and this set off another wave of giggles.

"Ummm, hello?" Melanie said. Or was it Melody? "What the hell are you laughing at?"

"Honestly, I don't remember. This bud is incredible. Do you want some?"

"No thanks. My husband will know if I'm stoned and then he'll have a *lot* of questions."

"Suit yourself." Jeff took another deep drag of the blunt.

"We've got a surf lesson with you in two hours. Are you gonna be okay to teach like this?"

"Baby, there isn't a thing on this earth I couldn't do like this."

Melanie or Melody or whatever the hell her name was had a lustful look about her all of a sudden. Maybe it was because he'd called her baby.

"Oh yeah?" she said, inching her perfect little ass closer to him on the sand. Her manicured hand found Jeff's thigh, which had become so golden from all his time spent under this glorious sun it had virtually camouflaged with the sand.

Melanie said, "He'd go crazy if he knew I was here with you." Putting a little sexy into it.

"You probably shouldn't tell him then."

"I wish we'd met sooner, Jeff. I have to go back to New York in a few days."

Jeff stared at a tiny boat far out on the ocean and puffed on the blunt. "Yeah. Bummer."

"What if I stayed here with you? I could start a new life, be a whole new person." She bit her lip, hand still on his thigh. "I'd have to be crazy to leave a place like this."

Although Jeff agreed that, yes, she would have to be as crazy as every other vacationing fool who actually left this place at the end of their sad little departure from the grind of their daily existence to return to such misery, he didn't say anything. He had developed an aversion to attachments.

"No, I gotta go back to New York with Steve," Melanie said. "But it's fun to pretend."

Her hand crawled beneath Jeff's pink swim shorts and kept on going. Jeff marveled at this woman's forwardness—he'd only met her yesterday at her and her husband's first private surf lesson and here she was fondling him.

Her hand closed around his dick.

"Oh my god," she said.

Jeff didn't need to ask what had caused this exclamation.

The hand rummaged under his shorts some more, blood surging toward Jeff's groin.

"Oh my *god.*"

Jeff nodded vaguely, no stranger to this reaction.

She glanced around, making sure they were alone. In a low voice barely exceeding a whisper, she said, "Can I see it?"

Jeff sucked on the blunt, savoring the subtle watermelon beneath the initial chlorophyll-like flavor. "Knock yourself out."

Greedily, like someone starved of food, Melanie licked her lips and tugged at his shorts until his semi-erect penis flopped onto his chest. At the kiss of the pleasant breeze blood flow to the region increased.

Melanie's jaw hadn't shut much since they'd met but it was swinging off her head like a necklace now, her gaze flicking from Jeff's genitals to his face and back again.

"Are you *serious*?" she said.

Jeff didn't figure it a question worth responding to.

She said, "You should be in porn. You could make a *fortune.*"

"You think?" Jeff puffed at the blunt, head getting light from the combination of marijuana, heat and horniness.

"Oh yeah. You could be a porn *mega*star. Has no one ever told you that?" She was staring at it again.

"No, nobody's ever told me that."

Her fingers wrapped around him. Now she was sweeping her hair behind an ear and moving her head toward it.

Jeff lay back on the warm sand and closed his eyes.

Yeah, he'd found Paradise.

Photo: Alexandra Rose Scott

Philip Elliott is an award-winning novelist and screenwriter. *Nobody Move* won Best First Novel in the Arthur Ellis Awards. Feature-film screenplay *The Bad Informant* is currently in development with Passage Pictures. Born in Dublin, Ireland, Philip lives in Vancouver, Canada, with his wife and spoiled pug where he is never not listening to rock 'n' roll.

philipelliott01 philipelliott__ philipelliott__

AngelCityNovels.com

www.ingramcontent.com/pod-product-compliance
Lightning Source LLC
LaVergne TN
LVHW100036181026
850499LV00001B/22
* 9 7 8 1 9 9 9 0 8 6 8 3 1 *